HIJACKED

A CHAMPION SECURITY NOVEL

LUCY LENNOX

MAY ARCHER

HIJACKED

Renowned cardiologist Carter Rogers is used to having things under control. His life, his prestigious reputation, his career, his future.

Things he can't control this time around:
• His meddling grandfather
• His annoying gamer cousin
• Buggy South American jungles
• Being the meat in a feuding cartel sandwich
• Getting kidnapped by a monologuing drug lord
• Falling for his very hot, very mouthy ex-Special Forces bodyguard

In short, Carter's peaceful, well-planned life has been… *hijacked*.

1

RIGGS

If I'd known I was going to walk into a reaming, I would have downed a few shots of whiskey first.

"Who in the fucking fuck takes a private client call in front of their Grindr hookup?" Champ raged.

I knew he didn't really want me to answer, but I did anyway. I was no shrinking violet. "He was in the bathroom, ah, taking care of some... things. I didn't think he was listening."

My boss's broad shoulders made his wingspan look even bigger than it was as he waved his long arms around our office reception area. *You didn't think.* That's what I hear when you flap your fucking jaws. You didn't think. No shit, Sherlock. What would have happened back in Ghazni if you'd simply 'assumed' Azim was preoccupied with his douche routine while we were trying to break in and disarm the bomb?"

I tapped my lips with a finger. "I don't think Azim was gay. And if he was... the dude was putting off major toppy vibes. At least before the, ah... bomb thing happened."

"Riggs, damn it, shut the fuck up." The vein on Champ's

temple that sometimes bulged enough to worry me was making an appearance, so I shut the fuck up.

I respected Percival Champion more than anyone else in my life. (Which was why I'd never call him by his first name.) He'd been my commanding officer through some seriously sketchy moments, and he'd always gotten us out of the shit. Sometimes it seemed like magic. Where Champ led, I would always, always follow. And I hated that I'd let him down. So if he wanted to ream me over one relatively insignificant mistake—which, yeah, okay, had led to the loss of a pretty significant client—then I was gonna take it and be quiet.

Mostly quiet.

"If you'd underestimated Azim, we'd be dead," Champ said, continuing his tirade. "But yet you had a whole convo with the guy from HOG Corporate about their massive upcoming personnel reallocation—"

"Layoffs," I corrected under my breath. I didn't think the dozens of graphic designers and programmers that the HOG CEO had wanted me to escort out of the building the morning after that fateful call felt "reallocated." They felt unemployed.

"—where your Grindr hookup could hear every damn word and then *relay* those words back to the lead developer, who, upon hearing that *he* was one of the people about to be reallocated—"

"Fired," I interjected, ignoring Champ's glare.

Champ ground his teeth together so hard they squeaked, which could not have been good for his oral health. "—then took off with a mission-critical software access code, a code he could use to disrupt gameplay for *Horn of Glory*, the world's largest and most popular video game, and potentially put HOG out of business. And now it seems like the man has been trying to sell that code to the highest bidder, and no one can get in touch with him because he's left town. And HOG understandably fired our asses and *only* chose not to prosecute us for violating the nondisclosure agreements we'd signed because they didn't want the publicity. Sound about right?"

"Buck Nutter and his Magic Seed," I said helpfully.

Champ blinked at me. "I… what? *What?*"

"The lead developer is Buck Nutter. And the code he took is known as his Magic Seed. Apparently they call it that because—"

Before I had a chance to explain further, a woman came blasting through the front doors. She had on slim-fit hot pink pants, a flowy white blouse that didn't do much to hide a zebra-print push-up bra, and at least four-inch stiletto heels that *click-click-clicked* across the marble floor. I expected her to bite the dust at any moment.

"I need to speak with Percival Champion," she wailed. It was only then I noticed the smeared makeup, tear tracks, and bird's-nest hairdo.

Champ's jaw tightened. "There's no one here by that name."

When I say Champ hated his name, I mean he really hated it.

The young woman wailed even louder. "I'll talk to anyone at Champion Security, it doesn't matter who. I need any strong man! Won't somebody please help me?"

Champ and I looked at each other before looking back at the hot mess in front of us. I took a chance. "Are you here for the receptionist position? Because I'm afraid it's been filled."

It hadn't been filled. We'd had a string of horrible people using the position as a high-speed revolving door. But I wasn't taking any chances with this one. I could tell she was nothing but a soap opera in high heels.

"No, I've lost my brother. Not *lost* so much as… oh my heart!" she said, pressing her cleavage. "I can't stand it. The forces of evil have *taken* my brother. They have him in their clutches." She collapsed into sobs.

The theatrics echoed off the walls of the nearly empty reception area.

Champ and I had a silent conversation where he communicated with a series of increasingly violent head nods that he expected me to take care of this situation, and I blinked back at him innocently like I had no idea what he was talking about.

I'd take a bullet for the man, but weeping women gave me hives.

Finally, Champ stepped forward. "Who's your brother, Miss…?"

"Nutter. Kandi Nutter. Buck's my big brother. And they *took him!*" She wailed again, this time throwing herself against Champ's chest as she did so.

Champ turned to glare at me, like just by saying Buck Nutter's name, I'd conjured his sister and that somehow this whole situation, including the mascara stains on his shirt, was *my* fault, which it wasn't.

"What makes you think someone took him, ma'am?" Champ asked, guiding her to the lone chair in the lobby and handing her a tissue from the box on the desk.

"Well, he's *gone*, isn't he? Just up and left town without telling me or anyone in the family." She sniffled. "And he wouldn't do that. Not Buck. He's the kind who doesn't go so far as the front porch without tellin' everyone he knows." She blew her nose, not very delicately. "Never been one for keeping secrets, our Buck."

I gave Champ a look that said, *Are you gonna explain to her that her totes-not-secretive brother's probably on the run in a secret location with his secret stolen intellectual property, or am I?*

Champ rolled his eyes.

"And what possible motive could someone have for kidnapping him?" he asked with a perfect poker face. "Who'd want to do such a thing?"

The waterworks stopped on a dime, and her expression turned hard. "If I knew their names, I'd have already taken care of the situation. I'm a Nutter. I have *resources*. All I know is, Buck was trying to sell... er, *something*," she said cagily. "Something on the internet. He changed his mind in the end, but it was too late."

"Something?" I repeated. "Like... collectible figurines?"

"Well, no. They wanted to get their greedy hands on his Horn, obviously." She blinked up at us. "Like from the game *Horn of Glory*?"

I'd been afraid of that. Except it probably wasn't his Horn they wanted; it was his Magic Seed.

I didn't say that out loud, though, because Champ had already started making wheezy, pained sorts of noises at the mention of *Horns*, and it was all I could do to fake a cough to cover my laugh.

I'd had no idea that the man was so incredibly pun-averse until he'd set up our offices in Licking Thicket, Tennessee, and the jokes had started writing themselves. For the record, I absolutely *never* made those puns on purpose just to watch his eyebrow twitch because that would have been *wrong*. Ahem.

He shot me another angry look, like he'd heard my laughter... or like he thought it was *my* fault that the disgruntled programmer had had advance knowledge of his impending layoff and had taken off with a back door to the HOG system, which he was apparently trying to sell to a dangerous criminal and which might or might not have gotten him kidnapped for reasons I couldn't fathom.

And… okay, yeah, come to think of it, that one was probably on me.

"We know what *Horn of Glory* is," Champ admitted reluctantly. "The video game HOG Corporate produces—"

"*Horn of Glory* ain't just *a video game*," Kandi said passionately. "It's a whole lifestyle. It's literally the most popular video game system on earth *ever*, even though it's only been out for a few months. I think half the people in the world must have a Horn! The first-generation Horn devices sold out in a day and a half. And my brother was the one who came up with the whole idea for the game while he was driving a tractor on our great-uncle Amos's farm. He made the original Horn prototype. He did all the coding for the game too, even though it took him years. It was his life's work. And now he's *gone*. And I'm, like, ninety-nine percent sure he didn't go voluntarily." She sniffled again. "Or, like, maybe eighty-two percent. Something big like that."

"Something big like that." Champ nodded sagely. "Uh-huh. And have you taken your concerns to HOG Corporate?"

"No way." Kandi's eyes flashed. "I wouldn't warn Jacob Horn if a tornado was heading for the Thicket. Not after the way he treated Buck. Besides, y'all are HOG's security folks, and there wouldn't *be* any HOG without Buck Nutter, so I figure all y'all should, you know, secure him."

"Secure him," I repeated, scratching my head. "From an unknown location. Where he may or may not have gone voluntarily."

Let's face it; it was almost definitely voluntarily.

Champ shot me a look. "What Mr. Riggs is trying to say is that there isn't a lot of information to go on, Ms. Nutter. Was Buck's passport taken? Were any of his clothes or suitcases gone? Can anyone access his accounts to see if he'd made any large purchases or withdrawals?"

"Weeeellll…" Kandi licked her lips, then admitted, "His girlfriend said Buck's passport's gone. And *technically* he'd bought tickets for them to go to Mexico the day after he disappeared. And if you want to get specific about things, he maybe had both their suitcases packed and in the trunk of his car when he went out to the Dairy Queen to get Kellie some soft-serve, but his case is gone now…"

Ah, the old going-out-for-soft-serve-and-never-coming-back schtick. I felt almost bad for Kandi. And Kellie.

"But you don't understand," Kandi implored, seeing the truth on both Champ's face and my own. "The man who was greedy for Buck's Horn… Buck said he was a big-time criminal from another country. And Buck was scared."

I would be, too, if I were selling stolen information to a criminal, but I didn't say that.

"In that case, is it possible that your brother was planning to complete the sale after all, maybe *because* he was scared?" Champ asked gently. "That he flew out to Mexico alone but didn't take Kellie because it was too dangerous?"

Kandi blinked.

"It's hard to think someone you love might not have been totally honest," Champ went on. "But you need to understand, Ms. Nutter, that this isn't a matter for Champion Security. We no longer work for HOG, so we don't have client security needs to maintain, and what you're talking about is a serious matter. You should contact the authorities. You can start with the police right here in Licking Thicket, or I have a, uh… a contact or two at the DEA," he admitted.

Kandi only just then seemed to notice Champ was a fine specimen of man, the kind the US military put on recruitment posters and public relations ads. He was a real-live superhero with a square jaw, a dimpled chin, and biceps that strained the sleeves of his T-shirt. What she didn't see was the fact he was gay.

"Oh. Oh my. Why, aren't you *sweet*. And it's Kandi, please. I... I would like to speak to you in private if you don't mind, sugar. See if we can't come to an... *understanding*. One where you could start working for me, and I could... compensate you." She blinked her black eyelashes rapidly, pretty clearly spelling out S-E-X in Morse code.

I wasn't sure why, but Champ always seemed shocked when women hit on him. How he wasn't used to it by now was beyond me. He took a step back and crossed his arms in front of his chest, not realizing he could also get top billing as a forearm porn model.

"I'm afraid that's not possible. It would be unprofessional of us to step on the toes of our former client. I'd advise you to go to the authorities for help or, barring that, to contact HOG Corporate and see which security firm they've selected to replace us."

She reached out a lacquered fingernail and ran it along one of his forearms. I enjoyed the resulting look of maidenly shock on his face, but I bit back the laugh because I valued my life. "But... I have *needs*," she said with a pout. "*Client security* needs."

Champ met my eyes over the woman's head and communicated everything with one simple glance. *Get rid of her.*

Because Champ seemed to be nearing the end of his patience—which was concerning since I figured I still had a good bit of reaming left to endure—I didn't pretend to misunderstand him this time.

I cleared my throat. "Ma'am... ah... Kandi, Champ's *husband* is on his way here with a load of new weapons he picked up from the gun show."

Damn it, the woman looked even more impressed. I'd forgotten we were in rural Tennessee where guns weren't very intimidating.

"Also, he's bringing his…" I glanced at Champ with an apologetic wince. "His drag queen friends along. It's… ah, Drag Queen Firearm Friday. But I'm sure you already know that."

Champ literally face-palmed.

Fine, I wasn't known for my ability to think up lies on the spot. Sue me.

But it apparently did the job because the woman threw up her hands. "Christ on a Christmas cracker! Is everyone in the Thicket gay now?" Then she pivoted on one heel and stormed out.

As soon as the half-red, half-gray Honda Civic peeled out of the lot, I turned back to Champ with a puffed-up sense of pride at my success. "Am I forgiven?"

"I don't know. Maybe I'll ask my *husband*. The gun-toting drag queen."

I pointed at him. "May you be so lucky. If you weren't a workaholic, you could totally land a nice buxom queen instead of that big, callused hand you're married to now."

Maybe it was a good thing he ignored my comment about his masturbatory habits.

"As for whether or not you're forgiven for losing our largest client, the answer is no. In fact, as punishment, you're going to represent Champion Security at the Licking Nuthatch Gala."

I tilted my head and peered at him. "I'm sorry. You want me to lick your what?" Licking Thicket jokes never got old.

Champ ignored me, except for that telltale twitchy eyebrow, and continued.

"It's a fundraiser for a cardiac wing at our regional hospital. It's being put on by the Rogers family. They're an old-money family from Nashville. One of the men in the family moved to Nuthatch and took over a cardiology practice, and the family is celebrating his move to the area with a charity fundraiser. They want to endow the new wing in his honor."

"Jesus," I muttered. Must be nice to have that kind of money. The kind that said, "Oh? You're moving to nowhere, Tennessee? Here's a hospital wing to give you something to do with yourself." When I'd moved to the Thicket a few months ago, my family had given me every single novelty mug they could find with the words "licking" or "thick" on it. I now owned enough mugs to open a very inappropriate cafe. "Must be nice."

"You're going to find out tonight at the gala. And no hooking up while you're there. I know it'll be rough for you, but try to stay off Grindr for at least a few hours."

Those were fighting words. "Do you have any idea how rare it is for me to hook up with someone these days? All I do is work. Last weekend was the first weekend I've had off in months, so I swiped right just *one time*—"

He held up a hand to shut me up. "Save it, Riggsy. I don't want to hear about your lonely dick. I'm still pissed. I'll get over it eventually..." He smiled in a way that was not at all comforting. "But today is not that day, my friend."

I sighed. "I'm just trying to reassure you, there's no way my dick's getting any less lonely while I'm at the party. You know how I feel about high-maintenance guys."

Or really, any-maintenance guys. But I was especially not into the rich, privileged, gala-throwing type.

"Yes, that's very reassuring. And speaking of high-maintenance guys, I neglected to mention you're also going to babysit the cardiologist as your next assignment."

"No! What? *No!* I hate personal protection."

"I know," Champ said gleefully. "The doctor's your new

principal, and he's headed out on some kind of charity stint in South America. It's all in the file I just sent to your email. Make sure he doesn't get hurt."

Okay, this was going down a road I wasn't interested in traveling.

He continued. "And, given that you'll be busy in a jungle outside of Caracas working off the consequences of your poor Grindr hookup choices, you're officially out of the auricle implant program. Until further notice, you're our resident rich-guy babysitter. Congratulations."

"What?" I breathed, feeling a slight head rush as my brain dried to wrap itself around his words. There was no way he meant what he was saying. I'd busted my ass researching implant comms tech in order to qualify for that elite training program in Arizona. "Are you fucking kidding me? You're taking me off AIP to send me to the fucking jungle to babysit a rich do-gooder? All because I made one little mistake?"

"You lost us the Horn of Glory!"

"It sounds so dirty when you say it like that," I lamented.

"They're the biggest client we've ever had, Riggs. And you heard Kandi! *Horn of Glory* is the hottest handheld video game in the world right now. They're expanding globally at light speed. Do you have any idea what that contract would have done for Champion Security? Do you? We were *this close* to expanding from personnel background checks, on-site guarding, and security monitoring to doing the big shit—location assessment, security systems consulting, and executive personal security. And then *you* decided to fuck it all up with a quick chat in front of some horny stranger. If *you* can't be professional, *I* can't justify the expense."

Okay, maybe I couldn't just take this reaming quietly.

"I took a call from Jacob Horn, the CEO!" I retorted angrily. "That's all! I answered the phone when *the important client* called. Was I supposed to not answer while I took the time to find pants and exit the room? And I can't help it if the man screams every word he says on the phone loud enough for the Grindr dude in the bathroom to overhear."

Champ crossed his arms in front of his broad chest. I tried not to look at them because they truly were porn-worthy.

He sighed in exasperation. "Riggs, you need to learn that not everyone is your friend. Not everyone is trustworthy. Learn to keep your fucking mouth shut in general, and especially about client information. Have a hookup, fine. But don't fucking tell him your life story while you're at it. You share too much. Just fuck the guy and be done with it. No emotions necessary unless you're looking for a spouse. You looking for a spouse, Riggs? Because I gotta tell you, that wouldn't exactly gel well with your job. I'm not sure your Grindr husband would want you flying off to parts unknown the next time you're lucky enough to get nominated for something like AIP."

This wasn't the first time he'd cautioned me against my big mouth. I had a tendency to overshare, and it had gotten me into plenty of trouble in the past, like the time I'd told a guy I was dating where I worked and he'd marched into Champion Security to declare his undying love for me in the middle of the lobby right in front of a client—like there would *ever* be a time when I would be cool with PDA in my workplace.

But that was in the past, and it had *no* bearing on this current mess. I hadn't spilled any fucking beans, and my boss needed to know that.

"No, I am *not* looking for a spouse." I valued my freedom way too much. "And just so we're clear, Jacob

Horn was the one who said he was laying off thirty percent of the local development team. I didn't say a word. My only crime was taking a call at the wrong time."

Champ lifted that fucking eyebrow again. The Eyebrow of Accusation. "Maybe you shouldn't have been fucking a HOG employee in the first place. Maybe then Mr.... what was his name again? The missing developer?"

"Buck Nutter. And I don't know why you keep making me say his name when it gives you that constipated look every time you hear it. Just so we're clear, Buck wasn't my hookup. The Grindr guy's name was Dim. Ding. Dino. I can't remember. And working a food truck in the HOG parking lot doesn't make him an employee. Besides, we didn't fuck. I kicked him out as soon as he came out of the bathroom. But by then it was too late."

He ignored me. "Maybe then Buck Nutter wouldn't have taken off with this mystical porthole code thing and put the cybersecurity of millions of gamers at risk."

"Seed," I corrected. "Buck Nutter's Magic Seed. It's an asset inside the game. When you have the magic seed, you get backdoor access—"

"Every word you say just makes this worse," Champ said before turning away and heading to his office. "I'm living in a nightmare," he muttered under his breath.

"You're the one from a town called Licking Thicket," I called after him. "I only work here."

He waved his hand as if to dismiss me. "For now," he replied archly before disappearing down the hall. "Focus on the job, Riggsy. Don't let me down."

I wanted to scream. He knew how much I sacrificed for this job. How devoted to it I was. How much sleep and sweat and blood I'd happily given up for it.

A slow clap came from the chair behind the receptionist's desk. I turned to see our resident hacker, Jasper Huxley, sitting there.

"Where did you come from?" I asked.

"Been sitting here the whole time. I even thought about DoorDashing some popcorn at one point. The tension was A plus. You two should fuck."

I gagged. "No, thanks. It would be like fucking one of my brothers."

Hux stared after our boss and former commanding officer. "Agreed. He's hot as hell, though. Shame."

I pictured Champ's perfect looks. I had to admit the blond-hair, blue-eyes combo really did it for me. What a waste. "Anyway, the man doesn't date or even hook up. I don't think he's had sex since 1942."

"He's only thirty-seven years old. I think he hooks up, he probably just keeps it on the down low."

I shook my head, repeating Champ's own words from earlier. "Don't care. Right now, all I care about is getting reinstated on the AIP. Got any ideas? Surely he's not going to punish me as severely as he made it sound."

Hux went back to clicking away on his laptop. "You fucked up pretty good. He's mad."

Thanks for stating the obvious.

"Any ideas for me to unfuck it?" I asked again.

Hux looked up and me and pursed his lips as if considering it.

"Yeah," he said finally. "Go to that gala. Be *professional.* And then go to the jungle and bodyguard the shit out of that doctor dude."

I pressed my fingers into my forehead and took a deep, cleansing breath. Hux was right.

I needed to bodyguard the shit out of that doctor dude. And I was sure as hell not going to get close to the guy.

2

___

CARTER

I leaned an elbow on the makeshift bar and stared across the grand ballroom of the stately old mansion my grandfather and his party-planning minions had managed to find on the outskirts of Licking Thicket. Finding a place like this was a miracle in and of itself since the town of Licking Thicket was more about milking parlors and ridiculous-but-unavoidable double entendres than ballrooms, but I wasn't focused on the house right now. I stared at the seriously hot couple in the center of the dance floor.

The taller of the two guys wore a dark suit and a big, besotted smile — the kind of smile you'd expect to find on an earnest farmer who kept a pet pig and let her sleep in his dining room yet had somehow managed to land himself a highly intelligent, highly adorable doctor for a husband, which was another kind of miracle.

The smaller man wrapped his arms tightly around his husband's waist and grinned a mischievous, loving little grin in return — a grin that said he knew the man he'd chosen was never going to help him solve a crossword clue, but that it didn't matter in the slightest because his sweet hubby's enormous heart more than made up for his lack of vocabulary.

It was fucking *gross*.

"Hit me again, barkeep." I tapped my glass on the bar top.

Alana Jackson raised an eyebrow but dutifully poured me another drink. "Everything okay there, Doc Rogers?"

"Oh, dandy." But I couldn't help looking back at the dance floor and pursing my lips. "Just look at those two, would you? Don't they realize this is a public place? I don't have a problem if they choose to live their lives that way, but do they have to shove it in our faces?"

"You mean… Dunn and Tucker?" She blinked in shock. "But… I thought Tuck was your friend. Y'all went to medical school together."

"He *is* my friend. Closest one I've got."

"And your ex-boyfriend."

"That too," I agreed, slamming back my drink.

We'd actually dated for quite some time a few years back, and our relationship had gone *swimmingly*. We'd never fought. We'd had the same friends and interests. We'd enjoyed the same wine and worked at the same hospital. We'd been two peas in a pod, and being with him had been as instinctive and effortless as breathing… right up to the day Tucker informed me that I wasn't really in love with him and, in fact, he didn't think I'd ever be the settling-down type.

I'd then gone and proven him right about the settling down by leaving on a medical aid trip to Eswatini. Or had that been the trip to Burundi? The fact that I couldn't remember exactly when we'd broken up suggested Tuck had been right about the not-really-in-love part, too.

"And I thought you and Dunn were friends now, also."

I twirled the ice in my glass. "Eh. More or less." Today it was less.

"So… how can you have a problem with them being gay?"

"Good grief, Alana." I scowled. "I don't care that they're *gay*, I care that they're all lovey-dovey while some of us are excessively single."

"Ohhhh, gotcha!"

Not that I wanted a boyfriend or a commitment at *all*. Just that after months spent dating nearly every available man in the neighborhood and not finding any that suited me, it was starting to feel less like I was single by choice and more like I was single by necessity. This felt exponentially less fun.

It also felt like maybe Tucker had been right about the not-the-settling-down-type business too, damn it.

A guy two stools down from me made a noise that sounded like a choking cough, and I darted a sharp glance in his direction, but he twisted his body away from me, so all I got was a view of his shoulder.

It was a really nice shoulder. Muscular and well-proportioned. Encased in a dark gray suit jacket that fit like a second skin. Attached to a man with a tall, muscly frame and overlong dark hair and—

Jesus Christ. I really needed to make more effort at the whole dating thing if I was about to write a fucking sonnet to a stranger's scapula. Maybe expand my search radius.

I forced myself to face forward again.

"One more time, please, Alana." I tapped the rim of my glass expectantly.

"Three? You sure?"

Alana bartended at the Thicket Tavern, and as such, she knew what her patrons could tolerate. But this wasn't just any night; this was a celebration.

My grandfather had just endowed a new Rogers family wing at Licking-Nuthatch Hospital, which was going to help the people of this community for generations to come. He'd also set up a fundraising gala for it, which was lovely, even if he *had* chosen to hold it in this over-the-top redbrick monstrosity. Having grown up in Grandfather's Belle Meade mansion, I was no stranger to big houses, but who needed a house so big it had wings shooting off the central building like spokes on a bicycle tire, and a butler who greeted you at the door to direct you to the Northwest Wing so you didn't get lost?

Still, I couldn't get upset about it because this was my last night in the country for a whole month. In twenty-four short hours, I'd be far from Tennessee and the small cardiology practice I'd taken on here. I'd be in the jungles of Venezuela working for Doctors Across Continents again for the first time in a couple of years. It was exactly the change I needed to get my life back on track.

Nothing had gone according to plan since I'd come home from my last volunteer stint. Tucker, who I'd sort of expected I'd end up marrying one day, if only to please my grandfather and his parents, had married a *dairy farmer*, for heaven's sake.

And then somehow I'd found myself leaving my job in Nashville so I could follow Tucker to the boondocks—not precisely to Licking Thicket, where he lived, but to Great Nuthatch next door—where I'd settled way too quickly into the role of small-town cardiologist. I prescribed beta blockers and cholesterol medication by day, then curled up with a cozy mystery in my little two-bedroom rental or grabbed a drink with Rainbows Over Tennessee, the local LGBT group where I volunteered, by night. I'd made a ton of friends, I'd attended way too many bovine-centric festivities (which was Licking Thicket's claim to fame), I'd eaten more barbecue than a cardiologist ought, and I was on track to get the mayor's wife's coveted secret family recipe for sweet tea since she'd unofficially adopted me. And all of that would have been *fine*, it would have been *excellent*, except… I'd been born and raised a Rogers, with every privilege known to man and a bone-deep knowledge that it was my job to help make the world a better place. I had a legacy to protect.

What I was doing with my life did not map to what I knew I *should* be doing, which meant I'd taken a wrong turn somewhere.

But when you discovered you were lost, the best thing to do was retrace your steps, right? So tomorrow I'd start retracing. And once I got back out in the world and started saving lives, I was confident everything was going to click back into focus, and I'd know what I should do with the rest of my life.

I for sure would not be partying after I landed in Caracas. Tonight was my chance to live a little, let off some steam.

"I'm positive," I told Alana. "I'm a doctor. A cardiologist. I have a degree from Vanderbilt. I think I know my limits."

"Alright." Alana grabbed her soda hose reluctantly. "But if you can't sleep tonight 'cause you've had three full-sugar, full-caffeine Cokes, I don't wanna hear about it."

"Hmph." Opinionated small-town neighbors were incredibly annoying.

And more often than not, correct.

Señor Shoulders made another choking noise from down the bar, and my eyes shifted his way… in concern, obviously. Medical concern. "You okay?" I called. "I'm a doctor, and if you need help, I could—"

I had no idea how to end that sentence. *Take your temper-*

ature. Kiss your boo-boos. Explore your tonsils. Check you for ticks. Whatever you need.

"Evenin', Doc Rogers!" Red Johnson clapped me on the back, interrupting my drooling over the random guy's shoulder. His ruddy face was creased in a smile. "You sure know how to throw a party, son. Cindy Ann's taking all sorts of pictures to show the rest of the folks on the Thicket Beautification Corps. She's gonna give you that sweet tea recipe yet."

I glanced around the ballroom, which was festooned with fairy lights, floral arrangements, and crystal stemware. At the rear of the space was a giant representation of the Rogers family crest done in white and blue flowers. On an easel near the front entrance sat an enormous oil portrait of a blue-eyed woman from the eighteenth century, who reclined on an embroidered divan and managed to look both friendly and bored out of her mind.

It was over-the-top for this neck of the woods, but for reasons I'd never understood, you had to show you already *had* money if you wanted to *raise* money, which probably explained why Grandfather had rented this place.

"I wish I could take credit, Red, but I didn't have a thing to do with it," I said honestly. "My grandfather was in charge of everything... along with his party planners, of course."

"Ah. And the lady in the painting by the door. That your grandma?"

"What? Oh, no. No, it's an ancestor of ours." One who'd probably been dead two hundred years before my grandparents were born. I explained, "We're descended from Her Grace the Duchess of MacArtar, which is a Scottish title that transfers through the female line. I was named for her, actually. Carter, like MacArtar? Anyway, the duchess was a renowned philanthropist, so my grandfather likes to display her portrait at all official Rogers Family Foundation events. It's sort of a lucky charm."

"Well, it doesn't surprise me to hear you're descended from selfless, generous folks. Not after what you've done for me and my heart condition. And what you did for my friend Kirt."

"Oh." I squirmed on my stool. "No, that wasn't anything, really. I'm just glad he's okay."

"He's more than okay—he's over there waltzing with his wife"—Red gestured across the room—"thanks to *you*. If you hadn't caught his stroke the day of the Fisherman's Float out at the lake, it all coulda ended differently. We all figured he was slurring his words that morning 'cause he'd been hittin' the sauce to ward off the morning chill."

"It's common for laypeople to miss the signs of stroke," I assured him. "Pretty easy to spot when you're trained, though. No big deal."

"It was an awful big deal for Kirt's family," Alana chimed in. "Like when you convinced Gramma Sophie that her headaches weren't about needing a new prescription for her eyeglasses but because she had high blood pressure. She got to spend another Lickin' with her family this past summer, thanks to you."

The woman had only needed a prescription for her high blood pressure. It wasn't like I was some kind of medical trailblazer over here. Not like my father, or even my grandfather.

"Well, I'm glad I could help in some small way." I smiled tightly. "So, Red, how are Ava and Paul's twins?"

Ava was technically Red's son's former childhood sweetheart and not related to their family in the slightest. That didn't matter in a town like Licking Thicket, though. Red was their honorary grandpa.

"Cricket and James!" Red's grin widened. "Hang on, I've got pictures on my phone here—"

"Excuse me, Doctor." A tuxedoed waiter appeared at my shoulder. "Your grandfather would like a word with you. He's waiting for you in the Turquoise Salon." She nodded toward a paneled door on the far side of the room.

I nodded. I'd been waiting for this summons all evening. Grandfather and I had barely had a chance to greet each other since we arrived, but I knew he was not best pleased with my decision to go "running off, looking for trouble" in South America.

I'd bet money he was going to ask me for the thousandth time in three months if I was *really, really sure* I wanted to go. He'd already tried threatening, guilting, and cajoling me about it. In fact, I was low-key certain this whole hospital endowment had been an attempt at distracting me from leaving town, which was hilarious because he'd initially been horrified when I'd moved from Nashville to Great Nuthatch, but apparently even Great Nuthatch was better than the jungles of Venezuela.

I was curious what his last-ditch attempt at keeping me in Tennessee would be.

I excused myself from my friends, straightened my tuxedo jacket, and followed the waiter toward the door. But before we got there, a hand reached out from the shadows, grabbed my elbow, and pulled me behind an enormous potted tree.

"Hey!" I yelled. "What the—?"

"Carter!" my cousin Kev whispered happily. He threw his arms around me and held on so tight his lean arms nearly cracked my ribs. "Shit, I've been waiting for you to walk by my tree! I thought for a second there I was gonna have to go out there where all the people are to find you. I'm so glad you came by!"

"Kev." I shook my head, stunned. "What are you doing here?"

My cousin Kev was incredibly brilliant. He was also incredibly socially awkward and introverted, to the point where he rarely left the house in Belle Meade if he could help it... and certainly not for an event like this.

"Ugh!" Kev shoved his black-framed glasses up his nose, folded his arms over his tuxedo-printed T-shirt, and shuffled his Converse-clad feet. His brown-and-purple hair stood up like he'd suffered a mild electrocution. "Long story. Grandfather made me come. Blah, blah Rogers family. Blah, blah responsibility. Blah, blah too much gaming and not enough fresh air and sunlight." He waved a hand. "It's like the man doesn't understand how my UV lights and tricked-out ventilation system even work. All I can say is when the zombies attack and we're all forced into bunkers, some of us will have adapted, and some of us will not."

I opened my mouth, then shut it again. I wasn't sure which of these groups Kev thought I was in.

I wasn't sure which one I *wanted* to be in.

"It's fine, though," Kev went on, "'cause I wanted to see you anyway. You haven't been on your HOG at all this week, even on Tuesday when the parsnips were delivered! I had to defend our settlement from a Horde all by myself, and I got worried. It's not like you to miss Parsnip Tuesday, man."

"Oh, shoot. About that." I bit my lip to cover a wince. "It's been a long week, and I, uh—" *Forgot.*

But there was no way I'd admit that to Kev, even under pain of death.

See, like me, Kev had been raised by our grandfather during his formative years. Unlike me, who'd lost my parents early to a car accident, Kev had lost his parents in middle school due to general parental dysfunction. Essentially, they'd dropped him off at Grandfather's mansion for a couple of weeks one summer, and thirteen years later, he was still there. He even worked from home.

With no idea how to handle a brilliant but awkward teen, our normally strict grandfather had gotten him a video game setup, and we'd figured out a way for Kev and me to play together even while I was at college. Since then, it had become kind of our casual cousin-bonding thing.

At least, it had been casual until a few months ago when *Horn of Glory* had appeared on the market. Kev had preordered one of the first cow-horn-shaped gaming devices to come off the assembly line, and he'd ordered *me* one a week later so we could play together. Suddenly "casual" had become "fanatical" in an instant, at least where Kev was concerned.

"You packed your Horn away already, didn't you?" Kev rolled his eyes good-naturedly. "You put it with your stuff to take to Venezuela so we could keep playing while you were gone, and you didn't wanna unpack the suitcase to get it out."

I found myself nodding along to this lie. "Yup. Yes. Yeah. That's… what happened, alright. I totally spaced on Parsnip Tuesday, though, dang it. I could have really cashed in. I've been out of pips ever since I let my draft hippo die of dysentery, and I had to get a new one to till my fields."

"Dude! You can buy more pips with your credit card, you know. They're reasonably priced, like all the in-game purchases."

"Sure, but aren't you the guy who told me anyone can *buy* a win, but the truly honorable player wins with nothing but hard work and the might of his horn?"

Kev's face broke out into a glorious smile. "You remember me saying that?"

I pushed his shoulder lightly. "Obviously. You're my go-to HOG guru. The man who showed me the Way of the Horn."

"Oh my God, and I have so much more to teach you!" he said excitedly. "The chat rooms are freakin' blowing *up* right now. Unicorns are coming in January! Stampeding unicorns. That's technically just a rumor, but I'm almost positive it's real, and I'm building a fence of iron to protect our homestead."

"Oh. Ah… Good."

"Also? There's a magic seed, which is like a skeleton key that unlocks any level of the game, plus does a bunch of other stuff, no one's really sure what. And there's only one, and it's not for sale any longer, so probably you have to earn it through some combination of quests and maybe cheat codes? Not sure about that either. Information is thin, but I'm on the case."

"I bet you are," I agreed. "Kev, I—"

"Also-also? The apple and pear markets are *corrupt*. I can't prove it, but I'm pretty sure 'Big HOG' is involved somehow. When I give you all the details, you're gonna just…" He mimed an exploding motion near his temple. "But don't stress, because I'm keeping our apples in the root cellar, and when the shit hits the fan, we'll be ready."

I forced a bright smile, like my sweet cousin hadn't just confessed to being a *Horn of Glory* doomsday prepper. "Yeah? Wow. Okay, then. That's… gonna be amazing," I agreed. "Can't wait. But Grandfather's looking for me right now, so…" I motioned toward the door.

Kev rolled his eyes. "You'd better go. But first?" He reached into the cargo pocket of his baggy pants and pulled out a lurid purple sparkly Horn of Glory. "I got you this. For your trip."

"Oh." I stared at the device for a beat in wonder. *Wow*. I had definitely not known they came in that color. "That's so sweet, Kev, but—"

"I know, I know! You already have one! But this one is tricked-out. Anti-slip grip, anti-fatigue thumb buttons for improved gameplay, better graphics. Plus, it has satellite capabilities! You can't get that commercially, you know. I added that feature myself."

"Yeah?"

"Yeah." He smiled shyly. "You know the beauty and the curse of the Horn is that it's Wi-Fi only, right? But I figured you might not have great Wi-Fi, or *any* internet connection at *all*—" He shuddered lightly. "—when you're out in the jungle. So, I've been working on this one for a couple weeks, trying to fit a satellite transceiver inside a traditional Horn shell, and I finally got it to work. Long-life battery will last you *weeks* under normal conditions. And I even loaded seventy thousand pips on this account for you, just in case of emergencies, which *isn't* cheating because I gifted you those pips from my own account, I didn't buy a single one of 'em." He shrugged and averted his gaze. "I thought this way, even when you're far away, you and I can keep in touch. And if you message me through the game any time of the day or night, I promise I'll jump right on so we can play."

I shut my eyes for a brief second, then grabbed Kev in a hug nearly as tight as the one he'd given me. "Best cousin ever," I murmured.

"I know, right?" Kev pulled away with a little sniffle. "I'm gonna miss you, loser. So, like, don't forget me, okay?"

"I couldn't possibly."

I squeezed the Horn in my hand and hesitated. I loved

my cousin, which meant I worried sometimes about him being lonely. "Kev, have you thought about maybe —"

"Hoooo, boy! Nothin' I love more'n seein' a man grippin' his Horn! And that's a mighty impressive specimen you got, Doc Rogers! Ain't it, Emmaline?" A stooped figure with thinning hair jabbed his cane in my direction.

"Sure is," the elderly woman clutching his elbow agreed. I didn't know whether she was meant to be supporting him or if he was supporting her. I wasn't sure they knew either. "Nearly as nice as yours, Amos. Doc's is maybe a little bigger. Not quite as purple, though."

I shut my eyes briefly, thinking fondly of the thirty-five years I'd spent having conversations that *weren't* laden with double entendres only I seemed to hear. In retrospect, it had been such a happy, innocent time. "Good evening, Mr. Nutter."

"I'm a *Proud* Nutter now," the man corrected. "Since me and Emmie, here, got hitched. Besides, I thought I told you to call me Amos?"

"Amos," I agreed. "Right. Well. I —"

"Ah, Doc, watchin' you holdin' that Horn makes me think of my Buck." Amos sighed. "D'you know, when my Buck started experimentin' with Horns, I was the first man who volunteered to help him?"

His wife clucked sympathetically.

"Uh." I was 99 percent sure we were still talking about the game, but beyond that, I was incredibly confused. "Were you?"

"Sure thing! A man's not supposed to play favorites, but I don't mind telling you, Buck's got a little more Nutter in him than the average." His chest puffed up with pride.

I nodded. "Uh-huh. Uh-huh. And Buck is your...?" I trailed off expectantly.

Amos blinked at me like *I* was the one being deliberately

obtuse. "Great-nephew, obviously. The one what created that there Horn."

"Ohhhh," I said in relief. "Right, no, obviously he's your great-nephew! Ha ha. I mean, what else could you have meant?"

"Oh my God," Kev squeak-breathed, clutching his chest. "You mean, you know *the* Buck Nutter? The Buck Nutter who's the creator of *Horn of Glory*?"

Amos grinned. "Know him? I helped raise the boy! Like to think I'm the one who passed on a bit of the ol' Nutter entrepreneurial spirit. Taught himself all about electronics and computer programming, didn't he, Emmaline? Added in what he knew about farmin' and *wahlah*. Instant success."

"Wait," I said, finally catching on. "You're saying *Horn of Glory* was created by someone from the Thicket?"

Kev gave me a pitying look. "I explained all this to you, Carter! Remember? I begged Grandfather to let me move here so I could be closer to HOG's corporate office? And to you, of course," he added quickly.

Uh-huh. I didn't remember any part of this. I must have blocked it out.

"So is Buck here?" Kev glanced around the ballroom. "Do you think he'd sign my Horn?"

Amos shook his head. "'Fraid not. Boy's on vacation down in… Mexico, ain't that what Kandi said, Emmie? Snorkeling, I expect. Or maybe diving? Nutters are real fond of water sports, you know. I just hope he's having a good time. Poor boy's been miserable ever since he sold the game rights to those investors. I told him, Buck, there's no way I'd trust a stranger to lay so much as a finger on my Horn, but did he listen?" He sighed.

Emmie patted his arm again. "Let's go dance, honey-bunch. You know flossin' always makes you feel better." She shot me a wink as she led him away.

Good Lord. The people of this town baffled and challenged me on a daily basis, but I was pretty sure I was gonna miss them.

"Well, *that* was exciting, huh? Like two degrees of separation from a real-life celebrity." Kev rocked back and forth on the balls of his feet happily, eyes wide at the thrill of meeting Amos Nutter, an octogenarian best known locally for his flatulent herd of cattle and his pasture out by the Licking Thicket town sign. "You should go see Grandfather now, but do *not* tell him where you found me. And I'll warn you, he's been crankier than usual this past week. Told Martine not to sprinkle sugar on his grapefruit anymore because if his damn fool grandson insists on running off to the damn fool jungle, he's gonna have to stay alive long enough to keep the Rogers Foundation afloat until the damn fool gets back." He raised an eyebrow. "The damn fool is *you*, FYI."

"Yeah. Caught that." I rolled my eyes, dismissing Amos Nutter from my thoughts. "But Grandfather's immortal. And he doesn't even *like* sugar on his grapefruit."

"True story," Kev agreed. "But he's old. And he loves you. And he worries. He wants you to carry on the Rogers family legacy. Five generations of doctors and all that."

I sighed. That's exactly what I was *trying* to do. In my own way.

When I finally found my grandfather a few minutes later, he was sitting at a linen-covered table drinking a cup of tea with Martine, his personal assistant, in the relative quiet. His white hair was immaculately groomed, and his tuxedo and bow tie were flawless, but in the second I saw him before he noticed me, I noticed that his hair was a little thinner than it used to be, and the lines around his eyes were a bit more pronounced.

It made my stomach jolt unpleasantly. He wasn't *actually* immortal, after all.

"Grandfather? They said you wanted to see me?"

"Carter! Yes, indeed." Grandfather pushed himself to his feet and smirked a little as I shook his hand, and Martine and I exchanged smiling nods. "Hell of a party, isn't it?"

"Yes, sir. Everyone seems to be having a wonderful time. Your party planners outdid themselves."

"A fundraising gala in *Licking Thicket*." He shook his head in amusement. "I never thought I'd see the day you'd attend one, let alone ask me to host one. You've changed since you moved to the country, my boy."

Not so much. Not really. I liked to think I was just shedding a little of the polished veneer I'd put on years ago like a suit of armor. I liked to think I didn't need it anymore. And I liked to think I was closer to being my authentic self now than I'd been when I was working in Nashville. I just wished I was having an impact on the world while working here in rural Tennessee.

"Nearly four million raised so far, did you see?" Grandfather went on.

"I did. It's wonderful," I agreed.

"And it's not going to spend itself. The Rogers Family Cardiac Wing won't do much good without direction from someone we can trust to know what the people of the area need. Someone like *you*." His blue eyes twinkled cannily. "You know, I've been thinking about your little trip—"

I stifled a sigh. "Grandfather, we've been over this a dozen times. I've already committed to the Venezuela trip. I'm not backing out."

"No, no, I understand. I do. Your good name is at stake. I'm reconciled to that. But you do agree that no one could take on the leadership role for this branch of the foundation the way you could, don't you? I mean, eventually?"

"I…" I frowned. There was for sure a catch in there. "I suppose. I'm not sure this will be my last trip abroad."

I wasn't sure *what* I wanted to do.

"Exactly." Grandfather nodded like I'd agreed with him. "And to assist you in that endeavor—in really building a foundation in the community you're serving—I bought you a house." He spread his arms wide. "Congratulations."

"A house? What house?" I literally looked around, like a game show host might come through one of the doors carrying a picture of a small cottage, or a midsized colonial, or *anything* that didn't have five wings and a ballroom.

"This house."

"*This* house?" I looked around again, and only then did I understand. "Wait, this giant estate? Grandfather, it's way too big—" *Not to mention gaudy, too big, and in every conceivable way, over-the-top.*

"But that's the best part! Plenty of room for me and your cousin to visit!"

"To v-visit?"

"Extensive visits!" He beamed. "You can thank me later, once you're home safely."

I mentally revised that to *I would cancel this transaction once I was home* safely, because I was way too shocked to deal with it just then. "And speaking of you coming home safely… a prospective future leader of the foundation, I think it's wise to take some precautions to ensure your safety while you're gone." He paused. "And it would help me sleep a lot better at night too."

He's old. And he worries.

I pursed my lips. "What sort of precautions?"

"Nothing unreasonable," he assured me. "For one thing,

I'd like you to make sure you notify the American embassy of your location, in case of natural disaster for example."

"Oh." I blinked. That *was* reasonable. Unlike the house. "Yes, sure. I already planned on that."

"And for another thing, I'd like you to contact us by satellite phone once a week so we know you're alright."

"I will," I said fondly.

"I'd like you to make sure you wear sunscreen and bug spray *daily*. Malaria in Venezuela is no joke."

My heart squeezed. "I promise."

"And I'd like you to take along something else for your protection too. Martine, if you could?" He nodded at his assistant, who hurried away.

"Alright, I'll take whatever you'd like me to take." I grinned and impulsively clasped his hand. "I really appreciate you trying to understand my point of view here. Compromise is so imp—"

"You wanted to see me, sir?" a voice behind me rumbled, so deep it set off small earthquakes in my gut.

"Ah, Riggs!" Grandfather smiled widely. "Meet my grandson Carter."

I turned to look at the man and quickly realized I had to adjust my gaze up… and then up again.

Holy shit, it was Señor Shoulders from the bar.

And, even holier shit, how flipping tall was this guy? He had to be some kind of genetic anomaly.

The man lifted a hand to push his dark hair back from his chiseled jaw, and his flexing bicep seemed to push against the seam of his jacket much the way his enormous quadriceps pulled against the legs of his pants.

Oh. Okay, then. So… less a genetic anomaly and more like a preview of human evolution.

Well.

I, for one, welcomed the future of humanity. Couldn't get here fast enough.

Do not swallow your tongue, Carter. Don't do it.

"Carter, meet William Riggs. Your new bodyguard."

"My..." Shock broke through the lust haze like being thrown into cold water. "My who now?"

"Your bodyguard." Grandfather grinned slyly, like a hunter about to spring a trap. "The one you agreed to take to Venezuela for your protection."

"I... what? No. I agreed to take a *thing* to protect me. A four-leaf clover. A can of mace. I did *not* agree to take an entire... tree-sized human being with me—"

"He's fully vaccinated, trained in first aid, and I'm paying his expenses." Grandfather drew a deep breath and sighed in satisfaction at a job well done. "I appreciate you trying to understand *my* point of view, Carter. Compromise really *is* important."

"I... but..."

"Remember, now! Satellite calls once a week. Sunscreen daily."

"I'll make sure of it, sir," Shoulders said, respect dripping from his voice. "I promise you, no one will touch a hair on his head."

"Excellent. I'll be reporting great things to your boss, Riggs! Now, I'll just leave you boys to sort out the details." Grandfather patted my arm as he departed, leaning on Martine's arm for support.

I set my jaw.

Okay. Alright. This was fine. This was an old man's overreaction, and I understood it, even if I didn't like it. But that didn't mean that Shoulders and I couldn't come to an agreement that satisfied *all* parties.

"Mr. Riggs," I began with a friendly smile. "I need you to understand a few things—"

"Riggs."

I frowned. "Uh, yeah. That's what I said."

"Nope. You said *Mr.* Riggs. I go by Riggs with everyone but my friends." He folded his arms over his chest. "And you and I are not friends, Carter. You're a principal. A body I'm protecting. A *job*. Remember that."

My head went back, and my shoulders followed. Of course we weren't friends. I had no interest in being his friend. But who the hell talked like that, to a client especially?

"Well, I go by *Dr. Rogers* with everyone who's not a friend," I lied. And when he rolled his eyes, I added in a nasty voice, "Especially people who work for me, *like yourself*. So, as I was saying, I need you to understand—"

Riggs shook his head firmly. "No, I need *you* to understand. You and I are getting on a plane for Caracas tomorrow because you've chosen to put yourself in harm's way—"

Was he for real?

"So I can do important, life-saving work," I reminded him.

He rolled his eyes again. "Sure. Okay. Whatever. In any case, we're getting on a plane for Caracas—"

"Don't you *whatever* me. Admit I'm right! Say 'Yes, you're doing important, life-changing work, Dr. Rogers.'"

I had no idea why I was pushing this issue. I didn't know this man from Adam. I sincerely hoped I'd never see him again. Why did I care what he thought? But after dealing with Grandfather's worry, and my own worry over Kev, and this palatial but un-asked-for house, I felt like my life was spinning wildly out of control. And Riggs's smirk was the final straw.

His smirk grated on me, but that would have been fine until he opened his mouth. "Listen, you're probably a nice enough guy, but clearly you haven't spent much time outside of Tennessee if you think passing out Band-Aids to people who are living in abject poverty is actually changing lives." He shrugged. "Not that it's any of my business, just that I'll have to take your need to play hero into account while I'm protecting you, that's all. Which is why I'm sticking to you like white on rice the whole time, and you're gonna do every single thing I say."

I literally gasped. Nice enough guy? And I hadn't spent much time outside Tennessee? He thought I was going to *obey him*? I laughed out loud.

"Oh-ho-ho, that's where you're wrong, Mr. Riggs. Because you're fired." I nodded firmly. "Fired, effective this very instant. Your delusions of grandeur end here. And you'd better believe your boss will be getting an earful from *me* about your attitude with clients."

Mr. Riggs smiled—a silky, sexy, smug thing that should *not* have hit me like a blow to the solar plexus. "That's where *you're* wrong, Duchess."

"Duchess?" I demanded, hands on my hips. "What?"

"Descended from royalty, huh?" He tilted his head back toward the bar, where he must have overheard my conversation with Red Johnson. *Fuck.* "I bet you're real used to getting your way. One of those guys who can't *stand* not being in charge of alllll the pieces on the chessboard, every minute of the day. Well, get used to it, Dr. Rogers, because you are my one shot at redemption. Your safety is my mission." He leaned in toward me, so close I could feel the heat of his body coming off him in waves and smell the tangy woodsmoke of his cologne. "You don't have to like me, but you *are* going to let me protect you. And—" He lowered his voice to a whisper that crawled into my brain. "—you can't fire me, because *you* are not my client—your grandfather is. *You* are just the job."

3

———

RIGGS

After two days as his bodyguard, I was ready to throttle my principal my own damn self.

I was also covered in more sweat and filth than I'd been on my worst day ever in Afghanistan.

The duchess, meanwhile, seemed as pristine as the moment we'd landed, of course—and unfairly fucking gorgeous, not that that mattered. But then again, he hadn't been the one schlepping all of the supplies on and off buses, up and down half-broken stairs, and into a stifling storage room at the back of the small medical building where we'd be spending the next month of our lives.

No, that privilege had been all mine ever since he'd brilliantly pulled the "grandfather card" on me. It was a card he'd been slapping down at least once an hour since we'd left Tennessee.

"Grandfather would be upset if I got a hernia."

"Pretty sure my grandfather wouldn't want me coming home after only a day because I strained my back hauling boxes around."

"I would hate for you to get in trouble with your boss if I slipped and fell into that rocky ditch."

"I wonder what my grandfather would think about a former Marine who was afraid of a little physical labor."

That had been the straw that had broken the camel's back, as I'm sure he'd intended. You didn't throw down a challenge to someone's service branch like that. It just wasn't done.

Besides, hauling his shit kept my hands too busy to throttle the fucker… or to kiss him. And that was becoming more and more necessary as this interminable day wore on. I had thought being a jerk to him at his grandfather's house would have helped me keep my distance from him. It would be easier not to be tempted by the beautiful, successful man if he hated me.

But instead of being an asshole back to me, he was an enticing kind of passive-aggressive. He acted like he was sweet as pie while he pursed his lips in false disappointment for having to force me to do all the grunt work.

The doctor was diabolical. And it only made me want him more. I'd watched him at the gala. The adorable way he joked with the bartender and the kind manner he had with the locals were enough to attract my notice even before I'd discovered he was my principal on this job.

But he was off-limits, so I needed to shut my attraction to him down and shove it away if I wanted to stay on my boss's good side.

As I re-entered the main room of the clinic, I heard Carter's cultured voice speaking to Eriko, the man who'd welcomed us to the Doctors Across Continents facility in the rural town of Gelada. "No, no, getting here on our own was no problem! Mr. Riggs—oh, and please make sure you call him *Mr.* Riggs, because he really enjoys that—that man is never happier than when he's useful. Carrying things is literally his favorite activity! Many a time I've tried to encourage him, 'Mr. Riggs, please put down the box! That's too heavy!' but he simply refuses. 'I'm enjoying myself too much, Dr. Rogers!' he'll say, and then he'll pick up more boxes. So by all means, if you have heavy things to be moved, please don't hesitate to ask."

Eriko murmured a reply I couldn't hear over the gritting of my teeth, and Carter laughed lightly.

"Oh, no. He's not really my *manservant*, per se. More like a *man* who *serves* as… my assistant. And of course he'll be happy to help transport any patients who can't get here on their own! I daresay he'd enjoy the challenge. A few more notches on his heavy-things-I've-carried belt! He's good for the physical tasks, not so much the…" He glanced up at me innocently when my boots made a sound on the floor. "Oh, speaking of the *devil*. Mr. Riggs, I was just telling Eriko that you'd *love* to help retrieve any invalid patients who need help getting to the center. Isn't that right?"

The look on his face begged for a solid love tap from my fist. But at the same time, the look in his eyes—teasing, intensely intelligent, just like he'd been at the bar that night at the Licking-Nuthatch Gala—made me want to tap… other parts of him. Parts that would land me in serious trouble with Champ or possibly on the unemployment line, if my distraction didn't land us in danger first.

I could not afford to like this guy.

"I think it makes more sense to stay here and assist you, Doctor. Remember the problems you've been having with your…" I glanced at Eriko with a grimace. "Digestion? I'd hate to leave you alone in case it comes *roaring* back."

Carter's eyes narrowed the slightest bit. I'd made up the part about the digestion problems.

Or, okay, I hadn't *made them up* so much as transferred them from me to him.

"Yes, right," he said, rather than correcting me. "You do like to clean the toilets as soon as I'm finished. Thank you for the reminder." He turned back to Eriko. "Such a helpful boy. Don't know what I'd do if he *fell off the side of a cliff*. Or whatever. Anyway, we should be ready to begin receiving patients at seven tomorrow morning. Hopefully we can prioritize the people who need to get to work."

As he coordinated the clinic details with the local man, who at this point looked like a deer caught in confused headlights, I got the lay of the land. We were in a fairly large room, maybe twenty by thirty feet. The building was made out of cement blocks, which actually provided a little break from the heat of the day. Large industrial fans that looked like they were several generations older than Eriko blew from two corners of the room, creating some much-needed ventilation. Two windows on either end of the room were covered with thick iron bars for security, and there was a similar metal security door on the front and back of the building. They were currently propped open to keep the air moving. Several locals had already poked their heads in and asked if the clinic was open yet.

"*Mañana*," Carter had said with a patient smile. "*Regresa mañana, por favor.*"

I'd gotten excited at the airport in Caracas for a minute thinking Carter was fluent in Spanish, but when he'd wanted the bus driver to help us undo the *ropes* so we could get our luggage off the roof and had instead asked the guy for help removing his *ropas* —which meant clothing—I'd realized while Carter might be able to find us a *baño*, he was never going to get us through a small-town Venezuelan police corruption scheme if we ran into one.

I'd immediately downloaded an extra translation app on my phone just in case. I spoke passable Spanish—maybe slightly better than passable—but I preferred to keep all language fluency quiet until and unless I desperately needed it. The practice had come in handy more times than I'd expected while stationed in Afghanistan.

"And the bedroom is just here," Eriko said, gesturing to the other door at the back of the building. I glanced over at the small room, replaying his sentence in my mind until the word "bedroom" turned plural from wishful thinking. "There is a pallet on the floor for your helper."

I tilted my head at him. Was he trolling me?

Carter's sparkling eyes suggested Eriko was being sincere. "Excellent! I'm sure Mr. Riggs will appreciate your kindness."

Eriko looked very pleased. He informed Carter that someone from the community would be stopping by with our dinner and we were welcome to spend the rest of the evening setting up for tomorrow's clinic.

"We are very grateful you are here. The people of Gelada have to travel very far to see a doctor. Many of them do not have money for the bus. When you come with your supplies and medicines… well, we are truly blessed."

Carter's face softened. Suddenly, I could see the doctor behind the snarky duchess. "It's my pleasure. Thank you for having us."

As soon as the local man was gone, closing the outer door and making sure Carter locked it from the inside, Carter's smile disappeared.

"You're in charge of making sure the med cabinet stays secure. It's one of the biggest security challenges on a project like—"

I cut him off. "I know. Next." This wasn't my first professional mission. I knew better than to show up in a remote town in any foreign country without doing my research and determining the risk factors involved in operation security.

Carter tightened his jaw and nodded. "I need to show you how to give a shot. We need to get as many vaccines in arms as we can, especially for yellow fever. The program sent us with mosquito nets too. Give one out to every person who gets a vaccine and anyone else who wants one. It helps prevent malaria."

"I know how to give a shot, and I served in Afghanistan which has the third-largest malaria burden in the world," I told him. "What else?"

Carter moved over to a stack of folding chairs and began unfolding them. "Let's set these up as a kind of waiting area, then we'll see what we can do for an exam table and some patient privacy."

We worked for the next hour and a half cleaning the dirty tables and chairs with a generic Pine-Sol solution and rags made from old clothes. Eriko had left a few boxes of donated supplies from the village, but it looked like we would be on our own for anything even remotely sterile.

There was no way to create a private exam area in the main room, so I suggested moving our supply boxes into the bedroom and converting the storage closet into a makeshift exam room.

Carter pursed his lips in thought. "Okay, but someone needs to be in there with me if I'm with a patient."

I stared at him. "I don't think they're going to sue you for inappropriate touching, Duchess."

"It's not about a lawsuit, Mr. Riggs. It's about making patients, especially female patients, feel comfortable when they're at their most vulnerable. Maybe we can get a female volunteer to help. Eriko said he's sending someone."

I schlepped all the boxes back out of the storage room

and into the bedroom, leaving only enough room on the floor for the "pallet," which turned out to be literally two wooden pallets covered by the kind of long cushion my grandma used to put on her screened-in porch chaise lounge. I eyed it with distaste.

"Aw. Someone looks like he's having a grumpy day," Carter remarked with fake sympathy as he passed me. "What's wrong, Mr. Riggs? Not enough box carrying for you?"

"Just thinking that this pallet looks like it's going to hurt your back." I folded my arms over my chest. "Might consider hitting up the med cabinet before hitting the hay, Duchess."

Carter didn't even turn around and look at me. He simply said, "Duchesses don't sleep on pallets, Mr. Riggs. This is well-known. In fact, I'm pretty sure there would be something in my grandfather's contract about that. *If* he knew you were implying otherwise, that is."

I glanced at the double bed in the room. Honestly, it didn't look much better. It had a very obvious crater in the middle of it, which was going to wreak havoc on the doctor's spine tonight. The bottom line was both of us were going to be in hell.

You've slept in worse conditions.

I tried not remembering some of the worst. Instead, I buckled down and finished organizing supplies so we were ready for tomorrow.

"You have an awful lot of bandages here," I noticed. It reminded me of the med kit I'd had as a medic in the Marines.

He looked at me like I'd said something odd. "What do you think people come to medical clinics for?"

"Sickness. Pills," I said. *Shrapnel wounds.*

"Sprains, strains, cuts, scrapes, rashes. Sometimes

broken bones. Sometimes upper-respiratory infections or gastro complaints. Definitely the mosquito-borne illnesses. Dengue, malaria, chikungunya. And the vaccine-preventable ones like measles, yellow fever, and even diphtheria. Hopefully we can make a dent in the local population's risk with some of the vaccine supply we brought, but we'll really have to work hard to convince them to let us vaccinate as many people as we can."

For some reason, hearing him speak like a doctor settled the agitation in my gut. He sounded intelligent and capable.

However, I *really* didn't want to like Dr. Carter Rogers, so I quickly changed the subject. "I didn't figure you for a gamer," I said, after noticing him playing a handheld game on the flight to Caracas.

He glanced up from the stack of papers he was organizing at the old metal desk that would double as the reception desk and the "office." When Eriko had apologized for the inconsistent Wi-Fi and the spotty cell reception, Carter had assured him we'd brought everything in paper anyway. "I learned that lesson the hard way in Eritrea," he'd said with a wide smile as if anything was easy in a place like Eritrea. Just picturing the clean-cut doctor there made me low-key nervous. He was lucky to have gotten out of there safely, especially if he'd been in the more dangerous areas where programs like this operated.

"I wouldn't call myself a gamer," Carter said. "Why do you ask?"

I picked up the bucket of cleaning solution and began wiping down a folding table. "I saw your sparkly purple game thing on the plane. Looked like you were into it."

He barked out a laugh. "Game thing? That's a Horn. As in, *Horn of Glory*? The game everyone in the world is into right now?"

I bit back a sigh. Of course it was. It figured that stupid

game had followed me all the way to South America. "I've definitely heard of it, but I wouldn't know what it looks like. I'm not a gamer."

He snorted. "You don't have to be a gamer to be into *Horn of Glory*. Even grandmas play that game. It was created by someone from Licking Thicket. Did you know that? The company runs out of that big tech building on the edge of town, and it's brought in executives and developers from all over the southeast. The company has had a huge economic impact on the Thicket. I would have thought Champion Security would have heard of them."

I wasn't about to explain my company's history with HOG Corporate, especially after Champ had reminded me never to speak about clients to anyone. I shifted the conversation. "I thought it was like some kind of silly game where you pick apples off a tree and put them in a basket or something."

Carter opened his mouth to respond but thought better of it. He took a minute to consider his words before replying. "Well, sort of. I mean, that's definitely in there. The game is a bit like FarmVille. Do you know it?"

I shook my head, so he continued.

"But it's also a little bit of a shooting game and has fantastical quest elements to it. The developers basically found a way to appeal to all kinds of gamers with one product. So each player starts with a farm where they grow crops from seeds. They sell their crops for silver pips, which is the coin of the realm, or they can trade for other things like more seeds, household items, or weapons."

"Weapons? For what? Defending your apple trees?"

Carter nodded, his paperwork all but forgotten now. I tried not to notice the flush of excitement on his cheeks or the way his eyes flashed as he described the game. "Weapons are necessary to defend your farm from marauding orc hordes, obviously, or you can use them to attack other farms to steal their stuff, if you're that kind of player. It's a multiplayer online game—I mean, you *can* play it solo, but it's epically boring—and the world is filled with other players' farms. There are also daily, weekly, monthly, and seasonal challenges like scavenger hunts, and specific crops to harvest for bonuses, and—" His expression turned suspicious. "You sure you don't already know all this? How is it possible you haven't played *Horn of Glory* yet?"

"Because I have more important things to do. Like maybe retrieving a kidnapped CEO from a Russian terrorist organization or infiltrating a *real* weapons-smuggling operation to determine how they're stealing from our client."

Both of those things were true, even if they were the highlighted parts of my job rather than the usual. The usual was oftentimes arranging on-location security for the day a global corporation decided to let 30 percent of its workforce go.

Carter sniffed and went back to his paperwork. "Yes, well, obviously I'm busy saving lives most days. I only play *Horn of Glory* to keep in touch with my cousin Kevin. It's important to him."

I cursed myself for shutting him down. Even though the blue-blooded Dr. Rogers pushed all of my buttons—in bad ways and in good ways, which were even more difficult to ignore—I still preferred talking to him over listening to the echoes in this run-down building.

"That's nice that you play a game with your little cousin," I said, trying to make amends. "I'm sure he appreciates you taking time out of your schedule for him."

Carter surprised me by laughing, and fuck if he wasn't the prettiest damned thing ever when he laughed. I wanted to make him laugh more, see that smile as often as possible.

"He's twenty-five and has a degree in Systems and Network Administration. But yeah. He lives with our grandfather and doesn't get out much. He's incredible with games and tech, though. And he's a *HOG* fanatic. The kind who's in the chat rooms and fan forums where they spout all kinds of conspiracy theories and share links to videos of hours-long gameplay. Needless to say, Grandfather would like Kev to find a 'real job' sometime soon."

"Maybe he should join the service," I suggested, knowing full well a family like the Rogers would never sacrifice their children to the US military.

Then again, maybe I needed to stop being such a presumptuous ass.

A rapping sound came from the security door. Carter glanced at it before turning to me. "That's probably our dinner. You can fetch it and set it up on that table you just cleaned."

I stared at him. *Fetch* it? Was I a dog? Was this one of the things I supposedly enjoyed carrying? Or just another duty as his *manservant*?

Instead of punching the fucker in the face, I decided to get some distance by answering the door. I was here to protect the asshole, after all, so it was my job to get between him and potential risk.

The risk came in the form of a gap-toothed boy who looked all of ten years old. He carried a canvas bag filled with mismatched food storage containers and two big bottles of water. "*Aquí está su cena, señor*," he said with a proud grin.

"*Muchas gracias*," I replied with my own smile of thanks. Whatever was inside the containers smelled amazing. "*¿Que hay para cenar?*" I wasn't picky at all, but I still liked to know what I was eating in unfamiliar places.

He giggled a little, presumably at my American accent

butchering his native language, but quickly answered politely, "*Asado Negro.*"

I put my free hand to my chest and mimed inhaling happily. "*Bueno, tengo hambre.*"

After returning the kid's wave of goodbye and watching him run down the dusty street, I returned inside and locked the door again before bringing the food to the folding table I'd cleaned. "This smells amazing. I'm going to dig in."

Carter didn't even look up from the papers he was sorting. "Actually, you're going to wash your hands first."

I froze with one hand already deep in the food bag. "You're not the boss of me," came out of my mouth before I could stop myself.

Carter simply raised one imperious eyebrow. *Aren't I, though? And do you really want to be spending* more *time in the bathroom?*

I growled and turned around, walking casually to the bathroom in the back of the building as if I didn't give a damn one way or the other.

Which was bullshit. I cared. I cared a lot. I didn't want to be here in this stupid place. I wanted to be anywhere else but here with the generic Pine-Sol scent permeating the sparse cinder-block building, the entitled Dr. Rogers finding every opportunity to make me feel unwelcome and disrespected, and the knowledge the auricle implant training program was slipping through my fingers with every day I spent here.

I washed my hands with the hospital-grade pump soap we'd brought in the supply boxes, dried them on my dirty pants just to spite the germaphobe, and then returned to dish out the food.

Instead of the awkward silence I'd expected to fall between us during our meal, conversation came easy. We talked about how quirky the town of Licking Thicket was, how oddly endearing it was, and how we'd never in a million years expected to wind up in a place most known for its milk pail race.

The evening hours passed quickly with more cleaning and organization, but shortly after nine, I noticed Carter flagging.

"You've been at it for sixteen hours," I said, reaching for the mop in his hands. "It's time to sleep now."

I could tell he wanted to argue with me, but he was too tired. By unspoken agreement, he used the small bathroom first. I heard the shower spray, followed by the sounds of him brushing his teeth. I tried not to imagine his slender muscles wet and dripping under the water. When he emerged, his blond hair was damp but tidy, he was dressed in thin cotton pajama shorts and a color-coordinated tank top, and he smelled clean and fruity.

My nose wanted to follow him straight to the bedroom and then sniff him for a solid three hours.

Instead, I followed the same scent to the bathroom, where I noticed he'd left a full-size bottle of bodywash in the tiny shower stall. It looked expensive, and the only word I recognized on the French label was "pample-mousse," which meant the sweet smell was grapefruit.

I brazenly scrubbed my own body with the stuff since I hadn't thought to bring my own bar of utilitarian soap. When I finished up, I brushed my teeth, slipped into a clean pair of boxer briefs, and padded back to the single bedroom that was mostly full of our supply boxes at this point.

Dr. Duchess was already laid out in the bed with some heretofore unseen bed pillow, an ivory satin eye mask, earplugs, and the finest fucking ass on this planet.

He lay on his stomach on top of the sheets with his arms under the pillow and his head turned toward the side. I stared at the curve of his back, the way it dipped down and then rose again. My eyes devoured the man's muscular butt the way my mouth wanted to.

His skin was clean, and he smelled amazing. Something about his body chemistry made the bodywash smell a thousand times better on him than me. A peek of armpit hair made me itch to run my nose and tongue up the inside of his arm and see if there was any remaining scent there from the day of hard work and travel.

He'd barely done any work.

The reminder wasn't really true. He'd worked plenty. For a man probably used to lifting nothing much more than a stethoscope and iPad, he'd done an impressive amount of heavy lifting. We wouldn't have made it from the airport in Caracas onto several different buses if he hadn't done his share of the work.

As I smoothed out the thin sleeping bag I'd brought, my eyes kept straying to his long, sexy form. There was no denying he was a gorgeous specimen. He obviously kept fit and healthy like many doctors I'd met over the years, even though it was a different kind of fit than my military friends. He was sleek rather than bulky, and I imagined exploring his long lines with my hands and mouth. I imagined him grinning up at me with those blue eyes of his, my rough fingers combing through the silky blond of his hair as I let him tease me. I imagined how it would feel to know his smile was because of me, and I wondered how his laughter would taste—

Inappropriate, Marine. Hands off.

This was going to be a problem. A serious problem.

I unzipped my bag and folded it open before lying down. We'd temporarily moved one of the fans into the tiny room, but it was still warm as hell.

Noises from the small town made their way through the bars on the open window as I reached up to click off the small bedside lamp on the stand between us. As the semi-darkness fell over the room, I became very aware of his nearness.

"You smell like my Blague bodywash," he muttered without moving. "You're welcome."

"It was either that or bathe in the Acute-Kare shit in our supply boxes," I said. "I'm saving that for your precious handwashing instead."

"Mpfh."

A floodlight from the corner of a nearby building was perfectly positioned to shine right in my left eyeball. "Fucking streetlight."

"If only you'd thought to bring the eye mask from the airplane like I suggested," he replied. His voice sounded deliciously sleepy, like if I were to roll him over and nuzzle into his neck, he'd be warm and pliable.

I gritted my teeth and squeezed my hands into fists. "Don't need a face mask, Duchess. Marines can sleep anytime, anywhere."

An hour later, Carter was deep in sleep, and I was still staring at the ceiling. I turned onto my side to face away from the window but came face-to-leg with one of Carter's long shins.

His leg had fallen over the side of the bed, and my eyes followed the slender limb up the tight muscles of his calf, around the bend of his knee, along his toned quad, and… into the gap of his sleep shorts.

My heart thundered as I caught a peek of shadowy sac.
Holy fuck.

I was a creep. But I couldn't stop looking.

My mouth pooled with saliva. He wasn't wearing anything under those snooty pajama shorts. He was free-balling it only two feet away from me.

I squeezed my eyes closed, but the visual memory was

seared on my brain. I imagined running my fingertips up his inner thigh and teasing the crease at the top. Great. Now I was panting.

There was no way I was going to rub one out with my principal only two feet away. Moreover, I wouldn't give Carter Snob-face Rogers the satisfaction of knowing he'd turned me on this much.

Go to fucking sleep, Marine.

I finally gave up and tried the military method of falling asleep, which must have worked because three minutes later, the sunrise was lighting up the room with a golden glow and Carter was fully dressed in khaki cargo pants, a Doctors Across Continents polo shirt, and his doctor's coat. "Wake up, slacker," he said, nudging me with a sneakered foot. "There are breakfast sandwiches in a basket on the check-in table and a line of patients already waiting outside."

I sat up so fast, I almost tumbled off the ridiculous chaise cushion. "You opened the door without me?" My heart thundered with worry before my brain reminded me he was safely standing here. No harm had come to him.

He lifted an eyebrow. "I didn't open the outer door until I saw it was a woman who was eighty if she was a day. Pretty sure I could have taken her in hand-to-hand combat. The only way she's going to kill us is with the carbs and fat in that sandwich, but it was worth it."

I grunted and moved around him to find my own clothes. The feel of Carter's eyes on my body was almost a physical thing. I might have taken my time sliding my pants on and leaned over a little more than was absolutely necessary, but when I finally turned around and saw his cheeks pinker than they'd been before, I realized it was well worth it.

"What are we waiting for?" I asked.

Carter looked everywhere but at me. "Yes, well. Right. Ah…"

"Patients," I said, trying not to smirk.

Carter shot me a glare. "Of course. Patients."

This was going to be fun.

4

CARTER

"Could you be quiet, Duchess?" The deep rumble of Riggs's disembodied voice floated up from his floor pallet. "I can hear you sighing from down here."

I lay on my back on the right side of the double bed, which was marginally closer to the fan, and stared up at the ceiling in the muggy darkness. "I'm not *sighing*, Mr. Riggs. I'm *breathing*," I informed him. "And I'm not planning to stop, so MacGyver yourself some damn earplugs."

After two weeks of eighteen-hour days seeing patients, some of whom hadn't seen a doctor in years, I was tired to the core in the best possible way. But despite all that physical drain, I was also on my second week of really shitty sleep, thanks to the man on the floor and his systematic campaign to drive me insane.

Suffice it to say, my patience with him was thin.

Thinner than thin.

Basically nonexistent.

William Riggs was the most annoying human in the universe, with his stupid nicknames and dismissive attitude. But he was also sexily competent at things like speaking foreign languages, and giving vaccinations, and eating *reina pepiada* without getting avocado on his clothing, and—ironically—carrying heavy boxes, so I couldn't help but watch him surreptitiously whenever he walked into a room.

He was bossier than Attila the Hun despite calling *me* Duchess, and he did not understand how friendly chitchat was supposed to work, which enraged me... but then he also got incredibly protective in a way that was not part of his job description, like the night he'd forced me to shut down clinic hours at 11:00 p.m. because I was dead on my feet, and that made my chest go gooey.

He had biceps so enormous I'd started fantasizing about being bench-pressed... but he was prone to doing diabolical things with those muscles, like forcing the bathroom door open while I was in the middle of a stress-relieving shower jerk session right before bed (the only kind of masturbation I could manage, since the man wouldn't leave me alone). He'd claimed he was worried for my safety because he'd heard "sounds of a struggle," but his smirky smirk had given that lie away... and now I was engaged in a *real* struggle as I attempted not to poke a hole through my thin cotton sleep shorts with the raging erection I couldn't get rid of.

I couldn't figure him out. More to the point, I couldn't figure out how I felt about him, even after spending days and days together in close quarters.

"No can do on the earplugs, Duchess," Riggs said with mock regret. "What would your grandfather say if I let you get hurt because I wasn't actively listening for threats?"

"In fourteen days, the biggest nonmedical excitement around here was when that five-foot capybara trotted through town," I scoffed.

"First of all, not true. There were those guys standing

across from the clinic the other day watching you. The bearded one and the tall guy with the curly hair—"

"Oooh, *watching* me." I rolled my eyes. "Couldn't be because I'm the blondest, palest person for miles, could it?" If I had a nickel for every little kid who stared at me, I'd be able to buy the people of Gelada a whole new clinic.

"Possibly," he allowed.

"So you're saying the capybara *was* the most exciting thing," I said triumphantly.

I could practically hear Riggs's amusement. "A capybara's still a wild animal. Have you seen the teeth on that thing? It could murder you while you sleep." He yawned.

"But it *wouldn't* hurt me because capybaras are vegetarians."

Riggs sighed sadly. "That's what they said about Genghis Khan."

I rolled my lips together, amused against my will. "People keep them as pets," I reminded him.

"That's a terrible argument! People keep all kinds of animals as pets even when they shouldn't. Tigers, bears… or that story you told me about Bernadette, the sow who sleeps under your ex-boyfriend's dining room table."

I huffed. I regretted telling him that story about Dunn and Tucker and their pig, just like I regretted telling him stories about Kev as a teenager, or about my frat bro neighbor who'd used me as his big gay experiment, or about the way I failed my driver's license test three times because I couldn't parallel park to save my damn life.

But two weeks was a long time to be with someone twenty-four seven and keep up the silent treatment, at least for me. And when it was too hot to sleep sometimes and the walls closed in, the words started spilling out of my mouth. Sometimes I felt like if I couldn't talk about something besides sickness and patients and the criminal lack of medical supplies in Gelada, I might break down.

The only, *only* thing that made my oversharing remotely okay was that every once in a while, Riggs would comment something funny or silly or tell me about how his brother Zeb had only passed *his* driving test because the road test guy was tired of seeing Zeb every other week. It was really hilarious when Riggs put on the instructor's high-pitched voice and said, "I do *not* earn enough to take my life in my hands this often!"

But even so, I realized I shared ten times more than Riggs did. After every story he told me, he'd retreat back into his shell again, and it bugged me a little more each time. I didn't get why he was so determined not to be friends with me or trust me at all, but it made me feel like I was back in high school, trying desperately to get the hot basketball player to notice me... and failing utterly.

"We can't get complacent about capybaras, or before you know it, we'll be complacent about security altogether," Riggs drawled. "My job is to stay vigilant."

Great. Lovely.

"You should take this as a compliment, Rogers. There are a limited number of people in the world I'd save from a rampaging capybara. In fact..." He yawned again. "It's just you."

How ridiculous was it that I found this charming? Clearly my standards were slipping.

I leaned up and flipped my pillow over, hoping to find a coolish spot, and then I lay back down with a huff.

Riggs's pallet creaked as he shifted. "Go to sleep, for fuck's sake."

"Oh my *gosh*, Mr. Riggs, what a great idea!" I shot back. "Why don't I just get rid of my insomnia by sleeping? Later, I'll rid myself of allergies by not sneezing and cure patients of diarrhea by suggesting they not use the restroom. What would I do without you and your advice?"

"Without me, you'd have fallen into a ravine earlier today while following some random dude down the side of a jungle mountain like a Bear Grylls wannabe," my own personal demon reminded me. "Repeat after me, Duchess: we do not leave the village for any reason. That's not just *my* rule, that's a Doctors Across Continents rule for safety and liability purposes."

"Hey! I'll have you know, I was milliseconds away from grabbing a tree branch, *and* I was nowhere near the edge of the ravine! I didn't need your help at all," I mostly lied. "And don't make it sound like I was out on some kind of wilderness adventure. That 'random dude' was a man whose wife was having a complicated labor all alone. I did what I had to do so I could get to her."

It was hard to care about things like liability and personal safety when someone's life was on the line.

Riggs was silent for a full second. "You did good work," he grunted finally. "If you hadn't controlled her bleeding with oxytocin, she would have died. Instead, you kept her calm and made sure she and her son were healthy."

Perversely, I was nearly as annoyed by his praise as I was by his insults. How the heck was I supposed to know how to take him?

"Yeah, well, it's a good thing I keep oxytocin tucked in my bag right next to the Band-Aids I hand out while *pretending to save lives*." I flung his words from the gala back at him.

He ignored this, because of course he did.

A thought occurred to me, and I frowned down at him in the darkness. "Wait, how do you know the name of the drug I gave Lourdes?"

Not that it was a secret, of course. It was standard

protocol for treating postpartum hemorrhage. But Riggs had mostly stayed outside the one-room home to give her privacy, so I wasn't sure how he'd even had a chance to notice... unless he already knew the treatment protocol somehow.

Riggs said nothing, and he said it loudly.

"Have you had some kind of medical training? I know you know how to do vaccinations and first aid, but I figured that was some kind of Army basic training program—"

"Marines," he corrected like I'd known he would. "And we don't learn to give vaccines in basic training, no."

"Okayyyy." I pulled the word out into three full syllables. "So you *have* had medical training, then?"

Riggs clammed up once more.

"For God's sake, Riggs. I'm not asking for your credit card number and sexual history here. I'm just trying to make small talk. I told you all about my family, didn't I? About Kev and his *Horn of Glory* obsession? About my grandfather? And you can't even... Ugh!" I blew out a breath. "Never mind."

"I'm not here to be your BFF," Riggs gritted out. "I'm here to protect you."

"You can be friendly and still protect me!" I curled my abs and sat up straight in the bed. "And Jesus, protect me from what? There's nothing here to protect me from!"

At that exact moment, as if on cue, a loud banging noise rent the still night air—the sound of the metal security door at the front of the clinic being shaken nearly off its hinges.

"What in the—?" Before I could finish the sentence, Riggs had grabbed my wrist with unerring accuracy despite the darkness, pulled me off the bed onto his pallet, and rolled himself on top of me, all in one smooth movement.

"Shhh," he whispered, bracing himself over me on his hands and knees.

"Is it the guys from the other day? Are they robbers?" I demanded, not at all shushing. "Are they trying to get at the medical safe? Are they—?"

Riggs put his hand over my mouth. "Shhhh, Duchess. Trying to assess the threat. Be still while I listen," he breathed in my ear.

He held himself perfectly still for one beat, then another, and I could make out just enough of his face in the shadowed light to see how fiercely he was concentrating.

In that moment, I realized for the first time on a visceral level that he was really, *really* here to protect me. That if an intruder came through the door, Riggs would step in front of me. That if I'd slid down that ravine, Riggs would have rappelled down and rescued me.

And yeah, he was motivated by his devotion to his job and his desire to please my grandfather, but it didn't matter. It was a heady notion and a fucking hot one, and despite the danger in the air, I felt myself getting hard… or, more accurately, hard*er*.

I felt around on the floor for anything I could use as a weapon and came up with a little round tin of antibiotic salve that I pressed against Riggs's hand. "Here, take this. Your aim is probably better than mine. If they storm the room, you can hit them. I trust you, Riggs."

Riggs exhaled a warm breath of air. I wanted to think he was overcome by my compliment but knew he was more likely stifling laughter because I was an idiot who thought we'd take down robbers by throwing something at them, a la David and Goliath, when he had a gun somewhere around here. His hand closed around the tin anyway.

Thirty seconds later, the metal door clanged again, but this time it was followed by a disembodied female voice singing Selena Gomez's "Baila Conmigo" at the top of her lungs.

"*¡Te quiero*, Dr. Carter! *Ven aquí! Eres tan* sexy!" another woman's voice slurred, followed by lots of high-pitched laughter that moved off down the street along with the drunken singing.

I did not require a translation app to know what that last word meant or to understand that the "intruder" was a group of village women who'd probably had too much *aguardiente*.

I stared up at Riggs for half a beat through the shadows, and he stared back, and then I started laughing—a deep belly laugh that felt like it had been trapped inside me for days.

"Hush," Riggs said softly, his palm still against my lips. "We don't know if they might—"

I grabbed his wrist in both of mine and yanked it away. "But we do, though!" I crowed. "They're not here for medicine—they're here for *me*. Because the only threat in this village is my *sexiness*!"

Riggs snorted. "You're such an idiot."

"All this time, you've only had to protect me from myself!" I said giddily.

Riggs laughed too, a deep rumble that came out of his chest, and I got the feeling that he was mostly laughing at my laughter, but I felt so free, so *relieved* I didn't care.

And then he moved, just the slightest bit, and it rubbed his hard, naked chest against my tank top–covered chest in a way that made my nipples go hard. I stopped laughing altogether and sucked in a gasp instead.

We both went quiet, staring at each other in the almost-darkness, eyes wide, and the tension between us spun out and crystallized.

I was painfully hard, and the heat and strength of Riggs was mere inches away, tantalizing me. I tried to compel him with the power of my mind to *move*, to want this, to make it happen.

And miracle of miracles… it worked.

Slow as a glacier, telegraphing every micro movement of his body like I was a rabbit who might get scared off, he dipped his pelvis to rub against mine.

It was the lightest of touches. The barest friction. But I'd been storing up arousal like gunpowder for days, and that tiny movement was like a lit match.

"Fuck, yes," I breathed. "More."

Riggs blinked down at me helplessly. "Carter," he began —not Duchess, not Dr. Rogers—"I don't want to hurt you."

Hurt me? How the hell could he hurt me except by leaving me wanting again? I lifted my hips off the floor to rub my aching shaft against his. "This hurts, Riggs. *This* hurts."

"Fuck," Riggs groaned, and I realized a second later that was the sound of a very controlled man slipping his leash.

In the next moment, his lips were on mine and we were kissing—hard, sucking, biting kisses, like he'd been ravenous for this as long as I had. When his tongue delved into my mouth, I could taste the tangy mint of his toothpaste, which seemed almost unbearably intimate. The grapefruit scent of my own bodywash rising off his sweat-damp skin amped my arousal so high, I could feel the precum soaking my shorts.

He rutted on top of me, the hard ridge of his cock perfectly aligned with mine, and it was *glorious*.

"You're… fuck, you're so hot. Get these off," he whispered, tugging at the waistband of my shorts. "I want skin."

"Oh yeah." I twisted my body to help him yank them down, then stripped off my tank top and threw it somewhere on the bed while he got rid of his own boxers.

"Come back, come back, come back," I hurried him, beyond caring how desperate that sounded. I *felt* desperate, because nothing else in the world would satisfy me except having his body laid out over mine.

"This what you want?" he teased, coming back over me again and lining our bare cocks up just right, sinking his weight against me. "Just like this?"

God, that deep voice got to me *always*, but especially now, especially like that. And I didn't think I'd be able to hear him say any damn thing ever again without thinking of that moment.

Jesus fuck. I could not believe how hard I was. How close to the edge I was with hardly any contact at all.

The last few months aside, I'd hardly been a monk. I'd had more than my share of sexual partners, and I knew exactly what I wanted from each of them. I'd have told you, had you asked, that I'd lost my taste for quick-and-dirty frotting around the time I got over my fondness for luke-warm keg beer, which was to say sometime before high school graduation.

But this, with Riggs, was something next-level, something primal and raw. I had no technique to impress him with in this, and no artifice to hide behind either. I was one hundred percent pure need.

I felt cracked open, like some part of my soul was on display, and I couldn't fight that any more than I could fight my attraction to him. Maybe it was because of the setting, far away from reality. Or maybe it was because of the hot, hushed night that made it feel like we were the only two people in the world. Or maybe because it was *him*. This guy I didn't even know if I *liked*, but who I wanted more than my next breath.

I dug my fingertips into the firm muscles of his ass cheeks, molding and spreading them, urging him on. Our breath mingled as we panted open-mouthed in the still air. A bead of sweat ran down Riggs's forehead onto my face, and I didn't care. Riggs was fire, and I wanted him to consume me.

"You," he gritted out, almost accusingly. He nipped the edge of my chin, then licked the bite. *"Fuck."*

I threw my head back and groaned. He was so much, this man. Overwhelming my senses, short-circuiting my brain.

"Come for me, Duchess. I want to know what you sound like when you fall apart."

Oh, shit.

"Riggs!" My legs stiffened, and my toes curled into the sleeping bag beneath me. I realized dimly how damn wrong it was that my body obeyed his command, bypassing my executive function entirely, but I couldn't care because just like that, a tremor shook me from head to toe.

I came and came all over my stomach, with Riggs following behind me just a second later. He collapsed against me, like maybe his arms had given out, and for a moment I held him there, all his weight grounding me to the earth as we both caught our breath.

"Holy fuck," I whispered.

Riggs snorted. "Yes it was," he said, and I giggled—*giggled!*—helplessly.

But as my toes stopped tingling and my body cooled, I swear I felt the air pressure in the room change. It was like we both came back to our senses at the same moment and realized exactly what—and *who*—we'd done.

Riggs cleared his throat and got himself back into push-up position. He stared down at me, opened his mouth like he was going to speak, then hesitated. He rolled smoothly to his feet and headed to the bathroom without a word.

Mother. Fucker.

I squeezed my eyes shut and thunked my forehead with my palm. What the hell had I been thinking? If I'd been actively brainstorming ways to make the situation between us even more tense, I couldn't have come up with a better option than this.

"Hey." Riggs came back a second later carrying a wet cloth. In the light from the bathroom, I saw that he was still completely naked, but his face was firmly arranged into his default expression of Impatient, Impersonal Bodyguard, so he might as well have been wearing armor.

He stood over me uncertainly, like he wasn't sure if he was supposed to offer to clean me off.

I snatched the cloth from his hand and quickly mopped myself up before tossing it aside. "Thanks."

"Yeah," he said gruffly. He rubbed at the back of his neck while I stared up at him. Belatedly, I realized he was probably staring down at me because I was lying on his fucking Cinderella pallet and he had no place to sit unless he chose to sit next to me, which he clearly didn't want to do.

Face burning, I clambered up onto the bed and turned away from him. I heard a rustling noise that meant Riggs had laid back down on his sleeping bag.

I took a breath. "So, that was… nice. But I feel like we should set some—"

"Sleep, Duchess."

"Yes, okay. But first, let's just agree that—"

Riggs yawned. "Jesus Christ, Duchess. I just gave you the best orgasm of your life. If you don't pass out in the next five minutes, it's because you're *trying* to stay awake."

I opened my mouth to protest, then shut it again on a yawn. I mean, he wasn't *wrong*, precisely. About the orgasm part, at least. Not that he knew that, the egotistical jerk.

But he made it sound like he'd been doing *me* a favor!

And if he thought I was just going to be able to fall asleep after he said something so rude and insulting, well, he didn't know *shit* about physiological reactions to psychological stressors. Furthermore, never in the history of falling asleep had anyone fallen asleep because they were told to fall asleep... except maybe if you were a Marine, which I needed to remind him I... was... not...

I woke up in the morning to bright sunshine in my face. I was lying on my back with my mouth open, which meant I'd been snoring, and I was also horribly sure I'd been drooling.

The good news was Riggs was already up and gone, probably looking for breakfast, so I didn't have to deal with him and all our awkwardness. The bad news was *since* Riggs was already awake and gone, it meant he'd seen me in all my postorgasmic hard-sleeping glory.

I groaned. The law of orgasms said the harder you came, the more humiliation you had to suffer the next morning, and apparently there were no exceptions for accidental midnight frots with your domineering bodyguard.

I got up and got ready, pulling on another variation of my cargo-pants-and-polo shirt look, and I grabbed my Horn, promising myself I'd check in with Kev again that morning. I'd been too busy the last few days to keep my promise of staying in touch, but I was pretty sure Saturdays were Kumquat Saturdays, and I didn't want to let Kev down.

What I was *not* going to do that morning was obsess over Riggs or what I'd decided to call the Unfortunate Insomnia Frottage Incident. Riggs couldn't answer a damn question about whether he'd had medical training, so there was no way he'd be capable of a mature discussion about the parameters of our nonrelationship. Therefore, we were just gonna carry on as we had done. Hate-rousal for the win.

"'Take a bodyguard,' they said. 'It'll be great,' they said," I muttered as I went out to the main room of the clinic. Great if you wanted emotional whiplash, maybe.

Riggs opened the door to the clinic as soon as I got out there, and for the first couple of hours of the day, he managed to find things to occupy him in the back room or out in front taking patient information.

Trust *him* to find a way to hover protectively while still clearly avoiding me.

Later that morning, though, when the crowds thinned out as the village prepared to celebrate the Feast of Santo Roque, Riggs finally stopped reorganizing supplies that clearly hadn't needed reorganizing and appeared at the door of the makeshift examination room.

I was already seeing my third patient of the morning, but when I heard the distinctive clomp of Riggs's boots, I glanced up to give him a once-over because I couldn't *not*. Out of concern for his health, obviously.

He looked… *Ugh*. He looked perfect, which was yet another fucking annoying thing about the man. He appeared perfectly cool and comfortable in his khaki pants and boots, despite the drenching humidity, and he didn't appear even the tiniest bit tired, damn him. If there were any justice in the world, he would have been drooling. Like, epic levels of drool.

"Gonna close up in twenty minutes or so, and we can take the afternoon off," he said, bracing a hand above his head and not quite meeting my eyes. "Gonna try to check in with my team."

"Yeah," I agreed. "Fine."

He nodded once, then walked his sexy self away.

My patient, a tiny four-year-old, giggled up at me from her mother's lap and said something in soft, rapid Spanish.

"She thinks you funny," her mother said in halting English. She made a circular motion around her own face, then pointed at mine. "You are… angry?"

I grinned down at the little girl, whose recurrent fevers and fatigue suggested malaria, but who managed to be so cheerful despite it.

"Not angry. Just silly." I stuck out my tongue to make her laugh again. "Silly Dr. Carter, thinking silly thoughts when he should be putting other silly people out of his head."

I gave the girl's mother some medicine and a mosquito net and let my translation app tell her when to come back to follow up.

Thankfully, that was the final patient of the day. I fantasized about spending the afternoon in bed with my sexy but grumpy bodyguard, even though I knew that was about as likely to happen as seeing him perform a violin solo in the streets of Gelada.

Just before I closed the clinic doors, a woman rushed into the clinic, first addressing Riggs, who was inventorying supplies closer to the door. "Doctor? Excuse me, are you the doctor?"

Riggs frowned, but I piped up, "I'm Dr. Rogers."

The woman turned to me, and I saw that she was young —maybe only fifteen or sixteen. She was also sweating and almost shaking with exertion like she'd run some great distance.

"Are you okay?" I demanded. "Is there an emergency?"

"No." She shook her head. "*¿O tal vez sí?* Not emergency for me —for my grandmother. Her heart." The girl thumped a hand over her own chest. "*Es muy rápido.*"

Rapido. I was positive that meant *fast*, but a fast heart-beat could mean her grandmother was suffering from any one of a hundred things, from a heart attack to dehydration.

Riggs inserted himself into the conversation. "*¿Donde estas tu abuela?* Is she here with you?" He looked over her head at the makeshift waiting area expectantly.

The girl shook her head. "*En la casa.* She is too sick to come."

Oh. I immediately began assembling a list of things I might need for a heart patient.

But Riggs gave the girl a single firm head shake. "*Debes traerla aqui.* We don't make house calls. She has to come to us."

"Is too far," the girl argued. "She said, 'Marisol, I cannot walk there. If it's my time, *mi preciosa*, it's my time.'" Her big, brown eyes filled with tears. "Please," she begged. "Please come help her."

"I'm sorry, Marisol," Riggs began. "We can't—"

And that's when I got pissed.

Truly, the man's bossiness knew no bounds.

He didn't want to talk, so we didn't talk. He wanted to sleep, so we slept. *Fine.* But I was not going to let him dictate the way I doctored my patients. I was in control of this situation.

"*Vamonos,*" I told Marisol. "The clinic's closing down anyway. Let's go."

"Uh, fuck no. There'll be absolutely no *vamonos*-ing," Riggs shot back, hands on his hips. "It's not safe to leave the compound. Remember what I told you the night of the gala? No heroics."

He was right. He was. And under ideal circumstances, I'd like to think I might have given his idea due consideration.

But today was not that sort of day.

"I don't remember us *talking* about very much last night at all, Mr. Riggs. So you can stay behind if you'd like, but I'm going. And there's nothing you can do to stop me."

5

———

RIGGS

I wanted to throttle him. It wasn't a new feeling, but it was a strong one. I was still kicking myself for crossing a line with a principal last night, and he'd provided me with an easy excuse to take my frustrations out on him.

"I absolutely *can* stop you," I bit out. "Pretty sure I can incapacitate you right here, right now."

Carter met my eyes. I'd expected a continuation of his defiance, but his deep blue gaze held serious concern. "Please, Riggs. We have the afternoon free anyway, and I can't let someone die on my watch if there's any way I can help them. Surely, you understand that feeling. You're a soldier."

His sincerity stopped me in my tracks, just long enough for him to take advantage and bolt out the door with the go-bag I'd put together with the necessary items we'd need in a fast evacuation situation as well as the portable AED machine. "Grab the EKG," he called over his shoulder.

Had I tried arguing, I would have been arguing with a Carter-shaped dust cloud. He was already out the door, and I was going to lose him if I didn't hustle to catch up. I grabbed the portable EKG and the big trauma backpack, patting myself down to make sure I had everything I needed. Knife, gun…

I snorted when I found the tin of salve Carter had handed me the night before during the "attack" from one of his fangirls — the tin I'd picked up that morning and stuck in my pocket for reasons I didn't want to think about too much.

I trust you, Riggs.

I tossed the tin in the backpack with the supplies and raced after him.

And came skidding to a halt when I saw Carter and Marisol approaching a footpath that led directly up the mountain.

"Nope," I said, already pouring sweat. "Not carrying all this stuff up that hill." Not only would it suck, but my hands wouldn't be free in case I needed to react to a security situation.

"There is a truck at my friend's house here in town," Marisol said hesitantly. "Maybe he will drive us."

Her friend turned out to be perfectly willing to drive us. For a large fee. And only if we sat in the back like cargo.

We loaded up in the bed of a small, battered pickup truck that looked about as reliable as Champion Security's last three receptionists had been. I shot Carter a disgruntled look and shoved in next to him. "This is a bad idea."

"Maybe so. But we're doing it."

We were on the edge of town in three seconds and bumping up a narrow, unpaved mountain road five minutes later. It seemed like we drove through the trees forever, but I knew from experience distance wasn't as great as it seemed when you were traveling slowly on an unpaved road.

"Did you ask how far this place was before you jumped in a stranger's vehicle?" I asked Carter under my breath.

"Does it matter?"

"Of course it matters. They could be taking us across the border into Colombia."

"I'm not," Marisol said. "I am taking you to Las Grutas. It is only five kilometers."

I leaned forward so I could see around Carter. "Doesn't *grutas* mean *caves*?" I didn't wait for a response before I elbowed the stupid doctor. "She's taking us to the caves. That doesn't sound sketchy at all."

"Not sketchy. At least, not the part where my *abuela* lives." Her wobbly smile wasn't reassuring.

"I'm beginning to think Marisol speaks English," Carter muttered.

I ignored the Carternapping woman and focused on the doc himself. "Could you not at least have asked a few simple questions first? Like, 'Hey, stranger, what town are we headed to, and is your sketchy friend going to return us after?' Or, 'Can you wait a sec while I message HQ and let them know we're traveling deep into uncharted territory?'"

He shrugged.

I glared at Marisol again. "You're taking us back to Gelada after we see your *abuela*. Do you understand? No setting up a clinic in your village or whatever. The doctor's program doesn't allow —"

"How did you learn English?" Carter asked Marisol in the same friendly tone he used to put nervous patients at ease. "You're far away from a city out here."

"*La antena parabólica,*" she said with a laugh. "American television channels."

"Satellite dish," I said to Carter. The truck bounced hard enough to bruise my spleen.

They talked happily for what seemed like ten hours. I

spent that time trying desperately not to think about the feel of Carter's hot naked body beneath mine and the sharp gasp he made while coming against me. That simple frot had been hot as fuck, and I couldn't help but replay it in my mind on a dirty, mesmerizing loop.

Stop thinking of fucking your principal.

According to my watch, it was actually closer to forty-five minutes by the time the pickup pulled into a cluster of small buildings. We'd gained a little altitude, and the trees had opened up to reveal earthen buildings with clay tile roofs. The area in front of the buildings was paved in stones, which didn't make the ride any smoother.

The few people out and about craned their necks to see who Marisol had brought back with her. Before pulling up outside of a small house that had been painted pink once upon a time, Marisol repeated her thanks to Carter in both Spanish and English until he'd finally said, *"No mas, por favor,"* with a kind smile on his face.

She led Carter into the building while I grabbed our supplies and followed. Just before stepping into the dim light of the building, I took another look around the hillside village. Several pairs of eyes were watching us, which was no surprise, but I noticed a teenage boy turn and begin to run up a mountain path as if going to tell others of our arrival.

As soon as he turned his back to me, I saw the familiar outline of a handgun under his T-shirt. He clearly had a holster on the waistband of his ratty cargo shorts. Why was he armed?

I'd done plenty of research about this part of Venezuela before leaving on the trip. As much as I hated being on a babysitting job, I still took my job seriously. That included mission prep which necessitated location intel, multiple evacuation plans, background checks of the principal people Dr. Rogers would come in contact with, and keeping critical information and communication devices close at hand.

Doctors Across Continents had assigned Carter to Gelada, which was located on the edge of the Andes mountains. It was a good two hundred kilometers east from the border of Columbia, where 80 percent of the world's cocaine supply was produced. Venezuela had its fair share of drug trafficking, but I'd made sure there was no cartel activity anywhere around here before I'd approved the Gelada assignment. Champ had even reached out to a contact at the DEA for the latest intel on the area and verified that all the known cartel members with ties to the region were currently operating out of Caracas or elsewhere.

But that didn't explain why a kid in a rural village was open carrying... unless the intel was seriously wrong.

I stayed extra close to Carter once we entered the small home. My eyes were constantly on the move, and I immediately looked for alternate exits and sketched out escape plans. I was almost positive it was an overreaction, but my gut didn't usually ping unless there was trouble.

It was a low-key ping, but it was there.

I pulled out my cell phone and wasn't surprised to find no service. The satellite phone was in my emergency kit. I rummaged through the bag until I found it and slid it into a pocket in my pants just in case. I also checked the knife I always had strapped to my calf as well as the Glock 19 I'd smuggled into the country and carried at my lower back. I went ahead and slipped an extra mag of ammunition in another pants pocket while Carter was busy making nice with the old lady on a bed in the corner of the one-room house.

After bringing the medical supplies closer to Carter, I

took another peek outside from one of the front windows. Marisol watched me pace between windows. When I turned to ask her to make sure her friend wasn't leaving with the truck, I noticed her biting her lip nervously.

"*¿Que pasando?*" I asked in a low voice.

"You're making me nervous," she said. "You're a soldier?"

I shook my head. "No. Only the doctor's helper."

She didn't believe me, but she nodded anyway before wandering back over to help translate for Carter and the *abuela*. It was obvious the older woman was very sick. Carter gave her some oxygen from the small portable bottle we'd brought and connected the EKG leads while reassuring her in a measured voice with simple words like "*Está bien*" and "*Càlmate.*"

I couldn't deny the man had a stellar bedside manner. He was kind and gentle, patient and considerate. I could see why he'd become a doctor and why he'd done so well at Vanderbilt in Nashville. It was less obvious to me why he'd moved to Great Nuthatch in the middle of nowhere, Tennessee. I couldn't imagine what about the place appealed to a blue-blooded guy like him. But listening to his stories about his friends—and their pig—and seeing how hard he worked to make a difference... maybe it wasn't such a stretch to see why he fit there.

After a few minutes, I heard Carter laugh. I turned away from the window and watched his face flush with mirth. "No," he said. "No..." He looked up at Marisol as if searching for the right word. The young woman rolled her eyes and blushed.

"*No casado*," she said, looking away.

Not married.

I glanced back out the window and noticed everyone had gone back to not paying us much attention. Yul, the guy who'd driven us up the mountain from Gelada, had come into the house and helped himself to a pitcher of *chicha*, a sweet, refreshing rice drink. I heaved a sigh of relief knowing our ride hadn't taken off without us.

Carter spoke to Marisol. "Tell her she's not *my* mother so she doesn't get to tease me about getting married."

I watched him continue to work. He was paying closer attention to the old woman on the bed than he appeared to be. Tiny wrinkles of concern bracketed his mouth the way they'd done when he'd diagnosed a small child with pneumonia a few days ago.

After he consulted the portable EKG, he met my eyes across the tiny room. I knew without him needing to say it the news wasn't good.

I stood and walked over to him. "What do you need?" I asked softly.

The sadness in his eyes was a punch to the gut. "She needs a cath lab, but..."

I already knew what he was going to say. Even in the large city of Caracas, the wait list for a procedure like that was incredibly long, and the patients often had to source their own supplies and medicine. There was no way this woman, who probably hadn't ever been further than twenty kilometers from home, was going to make it hundreds of kilometers to a city big enough to have a cardiac facility.

I squeezed his shoulder. "Baby aspirin?" I murmured. We'd brought a large supply since it was a simple and cheap method to help prevent stroke and heart attack. It certainly wouldn't cure her heart disease, but it might give her a little more time.

Carter nodded. I turned toward the trauma backpack and pulled out one of the large bottles of generic low-dose aspirin while Carter explained the treatment. We had labeled the bottles with preprinted stickers in Spanish, but

Carter liked to make sure patients understood the danger of the medicine to children especially.

When he was done, Marisol expressed more gratitude, even though I was sure she could tell the news wasn't promising. "Won't you please have a glass of chicha or a soda before you go? I have some cookies too."

Carter nodded and accepted the offer of hospitality while I squatted down to pack up our supplies. Just as I stood up, Marisol reached out to take the pitcher from her friend Yul, and the entire contents of the pitcher poured over my head and clothes.

Poor Marisol was horrified. Yul was overcome with laughter, and Carter simply pinched his lips together between his teeth and snorted.

"Please, please," Marisol said, flapping her hands helplessly. "We have water outside for you and soap and towels. Oh! Your clothes are ruined."

She was so upset, I tried reassuring her. "It's okay."

Carter reached into the supply bag and pulled out an extra pair of scrubs. "I always carry spares just in case things get messy."

I followed Marisol out the back door, where a corrugated tin cubicle held a large tank of water on a pedestal overhead. A handheld shower nozzle hung from it.

After pointing to a bar of soap and handing me a towel and a plastic sack for my wet clothes, Marisol left me to it. Thankfully, the water was somewhat sun-warmed from the tank. I stripped down and began rinsing the sticky drink off. The water was cool, but the sun was hot. It felt good to clean off the dust and sweat of the day.

I thought back to last night, to the hard press of Carter's body against mine. To the breathy gasps that came from him with every stroke of his dick against mine. To the aggressive way he returned my kisses and clutched at my ass with his strong fingers.

God, that one stupid slip in control had resulted in the hottest frot of my life. The reserved country club doctor had slipped off his mask just long enough for me to catch a glimpse of the hot, desperate need underneath.

I wanted more. So much fucking more.

Messing around with a client was the height of stupidity, especially when I was on this assignment in the first place as a result of other unprofessional actions involving my sex life.

But, fuck. The man was irresistible. I wanted to strip his mask away again and take him apart, hear him beg and whimper for release.

Suddenly, I realized if I hadn't fucked up with the HOG phone call, Champ would have most likely assigned Byrd to escort Carter to Venezuela. Byrd—aka Baby Byrd due to his youth and inexperience—would have been the one in charge of keeping Carter safe.

The kid had plenty of potential, of course, and he'd been trained by the best. But imagining him here with Carter instead of me... what if something happened? What if Carter was hurt or lost? Upset, even.

No. I had to admit to being glad I was the one here with Carter. Even though the chances of him being in danger on this assignment were slim to none, I was relieved Champ had assigned someone with as much experience in personal protection as I had.

Liar. You just want in his pants again.

It was true. There was no denying my dick's desire to fuck the beautiful doctor. But I also had to admit to enjoying his company. He was smart and well-read, but he was also pretty funny. He enjoyed observing quirky characters and making up stories about them. When he was able to forget the animosity between us and relax, he even slipped into quasi-impersonations which had caused me to almost piss myself the other night when he'd told me the story of his grandfather's attempt to learn to bowl at the Nuthatch Bowl-a-Rama when Carter's clinic workers had invited Carter to their regular bowling night.

"Carter, why ever would I want to insert my freshly washed digits into such mysterious and germ-ridden orifices?"

Through the laughter, I'd asked him why his grandfather had even gone to a place like that in the first place. Carter's smile had softened, and his cheeks had turned a little pink.

"Because I asked him to," he'd said. "And he loves me."

There'd been glimpses of *that* Carter Rogers this week, the one with a tender heart and a desire to please the nurses and office staff who worked for him. I didn't want to like the man. I definitely didn't want to be his friend. But he was making it more and more difficult to remember how much I had to lose if Champ found out about my unprofessional relationship with a principal I was supposed to be guarding.

Thankfully, the shower water was just cool enough to keep me from getting hard at the memory of Carter's handsome face and sexy body.

I cleaned myself off quickly before dressing in the scrubs and shoving everything else in the grocery sack.

I let myself back into the house and was just getting ready to thank Marisol again when I realized there wasn't any noise in the room.

I looked up and froze. Three men with assault rifles had come into the house at some point. One held Carter at gunpoint, one stood over Marisol and her grandmother by the bed, and one kept watch over the street from the front door.

My eyes flashed to Carter as my training kicked in. I tried not to notice the worry and silent apology in his eyes.

"What's going on?" I asked in English, holding my arms a little out from my sides to reassure them I was no threat. The bag with my clothes, sat phone, and weapon hung uselessly from my grip.

"*El doctor viene con nosotros,*" the man holding Carter's biceps barked. *The doctor is coming with us.* "*No sigas.*"

Don't follow? Was he crazy?

If he thought I was going to let him take Carter without following them, he was mistaken.

6

CARTER

"No, no, for real," I told the frail woman in the bed. *"No es mi novio."*

Riggs was *so* not my boyfriend. Half the time, the man couldn't stand me. And thank God he was outside showering where he couldn't hear what she was saying.

I wasn't sure whether the translation app was failing me or if Luz was feeling well enough to tease me, but either way, her face creased with a tired smile that said she didn't believe it.

"El estará pronto, entonces," Luz said as Marisol walked back into the room. *"Veo en la forma que él te miró."*

The third woman—Marisol's mother, I assumed—nodded her agreement, then murmured something to Marisol and left.

I felt my face turn pink, and I busied myself reorganizing my backpack of trauma supplies by laying everything out at the end of the bed before repacking them. I was pretty sure she'd said something about the way I looked at Riggs, and the idea that my mooning over the man was so obvious that even an elderly woman having a cardiac incident and her worried relatives would notice it was mortifying.

"She says he will be soon," Marisol translated helpfully. "She says she can see it in the way he looks at you."

"Yes, well. I—" I looked up at her quickly. "Wait, the way *he* looks at *me*?"

"*Si.* It's very like…" She widened her eyes and blinked her lashes rapidly. "He never takes his eyes from you."

"No," I said firmly. I moved around the bed so I could check Luz's pulse and listen to her heart. "No, something is definitely getting lost in translation."

Marisol chuckled softly and said something to her grandmother that I couldn't catch. She took a seat on the end of the bed and pointed at my *Horn of Glory*, which was sitting on top of my open backpack.

"You play this?" she asked.

I nodded. "With my cousin from back home." In fact, I'd managed a very brief conversation with Kev that morning on my way up the mountain, in which he'd recounted his adventures defeating a marauding group of pirates and also deplored the way inflation had driven up rutabaga shares.

"20 pips for a single seed is OutRaGeOuS!!!!!" he'd written, like a perfect hybrid of a teenager and our grandfather when he went on one of his tirades about what things were like back in his day. "Doesn't even pay to try farming anymore. I'd better find the magic seed soon so I'll be able to skip levels and earn my pips doing ADVENTURES! Hey, don't forget to harvest our kumquats!"

I had almost no idea what he was talking about, but the fact that he was safe, healthy, and relatively happy was what counted. So I'd taken the time to harvest kumquats, even though I couldn't have cared less about them.

Horn of Glory was Kev's love language, and I was about as fluent in that as I was in Spanish, but I kept trying.

Marisol turned the device over in her hand. "I didn't know they came in this color."

"They don't." I grinned. "My cousin fixed it up so he and I could send text messages to each other even when I'm in the jungle."

"*¡Qué bueno!* Remember, tomorrow is the, uh… *¿como se dice?* The *piña* day."

"*Piña?* Oh! No, we don't grow pineapples on our homestead… wait, do you have a Horn?" There was almost definitely no internet connection around here, but there *was* an option to play in solo mode. It was just that the solo option was, as Kev would say, "utterly lame."

Marisol shook her head. "Not me, but Yul does. His friends got him a brand-new orange one a few weeks ago, and he showed me how to play."

"Wow. Nice friends." The Horns weren't prohibitively expensive back home—a basic model was only around $60, which was why it sometimes seemed like everyone and their brother (or socially anxious cousin) was playing it—but that seemed somehow exorbitant in a rural hillside village like this one.

"Not all of them are nice." Marisol pursed her lips like she was tempted to say more.

"Well, if you give me an address, I'll send you one when I get home so you can play with me and Kev." I figured Kev wouldn't mind tricking out another one with satellite capability. "And you can use mine now if you want. Pretty sure some trolls are heading toward the homestead, so you can fight them off." I showed her which buttons to click while her grandmother looked on.

Luz's heart rate was within normal range, but she was still in very critical condition. Back in Tennessee, I would have access to a lab that could do bloodwork, a cath lab, and a whole host of surgical options, and I found myself enraged yet again that none of those things were possible for her. With so much crime and corruption around, even the best hospitals weren't able to help the people who needed it most. But there had to be something the Rogers Family Foundation could do.

I got out my blood pressure cuff and showed it to Luz with a smile, hoping she could follow my English if I used props. "Let's check this one more time, okay?"

"*Okay*," she answered tiredly.

When I heard Riggs's boots clomping through the front entrance, I told him without looking up, "When we get back, I'm talking to my grandfather. There has to be something we can do about—"

"*Manos arriba*," a rough voice—definitely *not* Riggs's voice—said behind me. Marisol jumped off the bed with a gasp, dropping the Horn on the coverlet, and lifted both hands in the air.

"*Eep!*" I whirled around to find a painfully skinny man holding a big, giant machine gun pointed right at me, so I raised both my hands too. My stethoscope dangled uselessly from my ears. "I don't have my wallet!" I stammered out, like this was some kind of generic Nashville mugging situation.

"*Eres el doctor?*" Skinny demanded.

A guy with a beard holding a second giant gun filed in behind him and trained his gun on Marisol, while a third guy stood in the door with his big weapon trained on the street.

Really, one gun would have been plenty. *Plenty.*

Marisol cleared her throat. "*El doctor?*" she repeated, looking at me significantly, like she wasn't sure why I wasn't speaking.

Oh. For the briefest of seconds, I thought, "What would Riggs do?" and concluded that he would not want me to volunteer any information whatsoever. But considering the stethoscope dangling off me, it would be kinda hard to pretend I was just a lost tourist, right?

"*Sí*, um… *Y-yo estoy el doctor.*" I paused and licked my lips nervously. "I mean, *yo* soy *el doctor*. Whichever. Please don't shoot me."

"*Soy*," Marisol whispered. "*Soy* for things that don't change. *Estoy* for things that change, like weather."

"Hunh." This was distracting enough that I turned my head away from the gun to look at her across the bed. "That's so interesting. I didn't realize Spanish verbs were—"

"*Cállate!*" Beardy barked out, and I jumped.

On the bed, Luz began breathing rapidly, her eyes filled with fear.

"You guys, can we cool it with the guns, please? This woman is very ill. Her heart. Her *corazón*." I took a chance and lowered one hand to place over my own heart in demonstration.

Beardy and Skinny exchanged a look. Skinny raised his eyebrows significantly, and Beardy grunted and called to Silent, over by the window, who nodded in agreement.

"*¿Eres cardiólogo?*" Beardy demanded.

Did that mean cardiologist? Uh…"Yes. I mean… *sí?*" Riggs was not gonna be happy with me.

Beardy and Skinny had an extended conversation in Spanish too rapid for me to begin to follow, but included the words *"enfermo" and "corazón"* and, inexplicably, *"estupido mierda,"* which I thought meant some stupid piece of shit had a sick heart, but I couldn't be sure.

Then Silent spoke up and said, *"Secuestralo,"* which,

judging by the way Marisol's eyes widened, was not a good thing.

"Kidnap," she whispered to me from the corner of her mouth, which was really helpful since then *both* of us started to panic.

"*¿Cómo se llama?*" Skinny asked me.

"Dr., um…." I had a mental image of them sending a ransom demand to my elderly grandfather. "Carter?"

Skinny nodded. "*Vamonos, Dr. Carter.*" He grabbed me by the arm.

Ah, fuck. Riggs had been ready to kill me for *vamonos*-ing with sweet Marisol on a mission of mercy. He wouldn't hesitate to murder me if I *vamonos*-ed with armed men. But also, what else was I supposed to do when they were holding a gun on Marisol? At least I knew he'd find me and rescue me.

I nodded like a bobblehead. "Okay, yeah, we—"

The sound of happy whistling drifted in the door before Riggs did, and I saw him stop dead the second he realized we weren't alone, his entire body going on high alert. He glanced at me, trying to convey some kind of message, which I sincerely doubted was "Hey! I've been trained for exactly this type of situation! I will disarm these hostiles and have us on the road to Gelada in no time!" Even a guy like Riggs could not handle *three* gunmen at once.

"What's going on?" he asked in English.

"*El doctor viene con nosotros,*" Skinny explained. "*No sigas.*"

Riggs frowned like he was gonna argue about not following, but did the man not understand the benefit of him staying behind so he could alert the cavalry and rescue me later?

"That's right, Nurse Riggs!" I said a little desperately. "I am going with these fine gentlemen for… reasons! And you should stay here! Also for reasons!"

"Carter," Riggs began in that warning voice of his where the "you're a fucking idiot" was implied but not stated.

"Yes, I am!" I said brightly, two seconds away from peeing myself. "*Dr. Carter*, at your service. And now… I must go! To save a piece of shit! Who is sick! With his heart!" I sounded a little like I was calling out a murderer in Clue. "I'm sure I'll be back very soon."

"*Diles que el no puede hacer nada sin mi,*" Riggs told Marisol in a flat voice.

Huh?

Marisol looked back and forth from me to Riggs. She nodded vigorously at Beardy. "*Es la verdad. El guapo odia ensuciarse sus manos.*"

Wait, what? I freakin' hated that I didn't know what was going on.

Skinny snorted at Beardy. "*¿Siempre con jefes, eh?*"

Beardy rolled his eyes. "*Muévete.*" Move. That one, I knew.

"But I need to put my outdoor clothes on first." Riggs jiggled the bag in his hand. "*Mis ropas.*"

"Now's not the time to talk about *ropes*, Nurse Riggs!" I said urgently. We didn't need to give the guys any ideas.

Riggs looked at me, and his eyes softened, but he shook his head in exasperation anyway.

Beardy looked Riggs up and down in his medical scrubs, then shook his head. "*No ropas.*" He gestured for Riggs to put the bag down, so Riggs did… gently and with clear reluctance. I could almost hear his teeth grinding in frustration from across the room.

"We need supplies too," Riggs tried again. "*Equipos.*"

We? Was he still planning on coming? I thought we'd settled that.

"*We* don't need supplies. *I* do," I said loudly. "Only *yo* is a, um, *doctor*, so you need to stay here and *patiently await my safe return!*"

Riggs shot me a look that said "shut the fuck up" in every possible language.

Beardy pointed at the portable EKG machine and the defibrillator, then gestured at Riggs to take them outside while Silent guarded him.

Dang it.

Then Beardy nodded at Marisol. *"Chama, traerlas."* He pointed at our bags of supplies.

Marisol swallowed hard but nodded. She hefted the heavy trauma backpack, but Beardy stopped her and gestured for Skinny to go through it first.

Skinny upended the contents on the end of the bed—moment of silence for my careful organization—and sorted through it like he was looking for possible weapons. In the end, he scooped everything on the bed back into the bag.

Marisol made a move toward Riggs's go-bag on the floor, which contained maps, emergency food, and our IDs, but Beardy stopped her with a string of Spanish.

"He asks what's in the bag," Marisol told me in a whisper.

"I… uh… important things? More clothes. Blankets. Food," I answered semi-honestly.

Beardy shook his head and barked out another order, and Marisol dropped the bag with an apologetic look at me.

Fuck.

"Let me just check Luz one more time," I told Beardy, glancing down at her. He nodded once but eyed me closely.

I laid my hand on her wrist to check her fluttering pulse.

"Remember to give her the aspirin exactly as discussed," I told Marisol.

She nodded.

I grabbed the medicine bottle off the table by the bed and pretended to point to something on the label.

"And if you could get a message out for me. Let them know we're in trouble—" I began in the same instructive tone.

Marisol's eyes widened. "I can't," she whispered. "I'm so sorry. Yul works for them sometimes. If I leave to deliver a message, he'll know."

Oh, so *those* were the friends who gave him the Horn? Great.

I nodded. "No, I get it. I would never want you to put yourself at risk. Take care of your grandmother—"

"*¡Andale!*" Beardy grabbed my arm and towed me out the door.

Outside was a Jeep with the most enormous wheels I'd ever seen and a freakin' gun turret perched on the back like we were in one of those *Mad Max* movies. Skinny was already at the wheel, Riggs was in the back seat with a sack over his head and his hands tied together, surrounded by our equipment, and Silent manned the rear gun. Beardy pushed me roughly into the back seat and bound my hands in front of me before taking the front passenger's seat for himself.

"You okay?" Riggs demanded in a low voice, turning toward me slightly.

"Yeah. I'm fine," I said a little dazedly. "Mostly," I corrected as I realized exactly how serious this predicament was.

I was *zip-tied*, for heaven's sake. And that was *so* not one of my kinks. There was no silver lining to this situation.

"Shit. I wish I could *see* you," Riggs said, and I remembered Marisol saying, "He never takes his eyes from you."

I blinked that away.

"This is all my fault," I whispered, moving closer to

Riggs on the cramped seat. "You were right. The capybaras weren't the worst thing. We should have stayed in Gelada. Instead, I made us come up the mountain, and I *still* couldn't really help Luz, and now we're being taken to a ranch by men in a *Mad Max* mobile, and if Marisol says anything, they'll hurt her — !"

"Breathe, Carter," Riggs said firmly.

I nodded obediently, though he couldn't see me, and sucked in a shaky breath.

"Marisol knows better than to say anything to anyone. She's going to be fine. Luz is as well as you could possibly help her to be. And you and I are going to be fine too. What I need you to do for me is to calm down as much as you can. Hear me? Panicking helps nothing. You know this." His voice was dry and devoid of sympathy, which was exactly what I needed in that moment. Clear thinking. Logic.

"Right. No, you're right. Okay." I took another breath, more naturally this time. "I still wish you'd stayed behind — "

"Fuck, no. I am *exactly* where I need to be."

"Tied up in the back of a Jeep, careening down a mountain road, *perilously* close to the edge?"

"No, with *you*," he said, which was really sweet. Then he added, "Because it's my job to keep you safe."

Right. His job. Obviously that.

"You need to not do anything stupid," Riggs said.

"I won't!" I promised.

"That includes things like telling the bad guys that you can go off without me."

"It was a solid plan," I argued.

"Solidly stupid," Riggs shot back. "If Marisol hadn't gone along with it when I said you were useless without me, they might have left me there."

I smacked Riggs in the arm. "*That's* what you told them?"

"Yep. Marisol said you don't like to get your hands dirty."

I gasped. "That's *so* untrue."

"I know," he said quietly, deflating all my outrage in two simple words. "You're extremely good at your job, Carter. Now it's time for you to let me be good at mine."

7

RIGGS

Champ was going to kill me, and rightfully so.

I was a shitty personal security agent if I'd allowed my asset to get captured so easily. After seeing the kid with the handgun, I should have trusted my gut about us being close to some drug activity and not relied on the intel. I should have never gone out back without Carter.

Carter's voice was too low for the men up front to hear him over the rumble of the tires on the rocky trail. "Can we please take a moment for my bodyguard to throw himself a pity party? I'm sure it won't take but a min."

I hated that he could read my mind. "Shut up, I'm thinking."

"Please do. We could use some thinking right about now."

"Can you breathe okay?"

"Uh… yeah?"

I realized his voice didn't sound muffled at all. "Do you have a hood on?"

"Negative."

I rolled my eyes. Why me? Why did I get one and not

Carter? Maybe they'd shown up only expecting to rudely steal one person instead of two. "Pay attention to where we're going. Note landmarks. Try to remember."

"Landmarks," Carter muttered. "Sure. I see… a big leafy tree? It's directly next to an even leafier tree in a darker shade of green? It's all rainforest, Riggs. But we're going uphill, if that helps."

It helped just enough to make me nervous. Especially when I tuned into the conversation the two men up front were having. I couldn't hear much, but at one point I heard the name Gustavo a couple of times. That wasn't good.

Gustavo Santiago was a high-level member of the Cartel de la Luna. His name had come up on a list of about ten active cartel members who had ties to this region. Even though he'd been born in nearby Socopó, my intel from Champ's DEA friend had placed Santiago in Caracas.

If we were being taken to Gustavo Santiago's mountain compound, we were in some serious shit.

No one knew very much about the man, but rumor suggested he was incredibly intelligent, as well as wildly unpredictable and temperamental. Suspected associates of his went missing with troubling frequency, but no charges ever stuck thanks to the liberal bribes he allegedly gave local and federal law enforcement agencies.

"Improvise, adapt, and overcome," I muttered, mentally scanning the contents of the trauma backpack to figure out what resources we'd have access to once we arrived at our destination. The portable AED was a decent option, but it wasn't exactly ready to shock the minute you turned the thing on.

"Don't you have a gun?" Carter whispered.

I wanted to laugh. Even if I'd been able to attach my holster to the flimsy waistband of the scrubs, my little

Glock wouldn't have been very effective against three men with AR-15s.

"It's back at your friend Marisol's house along with my dirty clothes." I didn't tell him I still had the knife strapped to my calf because I honestly didn't expect to hang on to it for long. I had to assume Santiago's men would take it off me as soon as we arrived.

The ride seemed to take forever, much longer than the ride from Gelada to Marisol's small village. It most likely meant we'd gone deeper into the mountains and further away from anyone who could help us even on the off chance I could figure out a way for us to escape.

Carter's body moved closer to mine with each bump of the Jeep until his thigh was pressed up against mine. I leaned over until our shoulders touched. "It's going to be okay."

"Don't be nice to me right now, damn it." Carter's voice held a shaky tone that worried me. "I don't want to be handled. I want to be trusted. Is this one of the executive kidnap-and-ransom situations? I have K&R insurance. It was why I was trying to get you to stay behind."

"I don't think that's what this is."

"What else would it be? I mean, unless they were looking for a doctor? They seemed to know I was a cardiologist. Maybe someone needs medical help?"

I took a minute to determine the best course of action. He was right. He deserved the truth. At least some of it.

"I believe we've been picked up by men who work for a cartel," I said as softly as I could, not daring to mention the man's name in case I was overheard. "One that's connected high up in the Venezuelan military and government."

Carter made a noise that sounded suspiciously like a laugh. "Oh, is that all? We've been snatched by a cartel. No problem."

"We have no chance at getting out of this if we don't stay calm," I reminded him. "And a very good chance of getting out if we do."

"Easy for you to say," he hissed. "Mr. Super Soldier Special Force—"

"Jesus," I hissed back, cutting him off. "Shut the fuck up. Are you trying to get me killed?" I didn't mention how annoying it was for a Marine to be referred to as a soldier even when there weren't armed combatants present.

The sound of his silence lay heavy between us for a few beats. "Riggs… fuck. I'm sorry."

I pressed my arm against his again. "Just keep quiet as much as possible and let me think."

Thinking wasn't easy while I was pouring sweat inside of a stifling, stinky hood. It brought back memories of my time in Afghanistan, which was both good and bad. Bad, because I didn't like remembering those dangerous times. But good, because it was the same mindset I needed to get back into now.

The survival mindset.

"I can get out of the zip ties, but there's no way we can make a run for it with that gun in the back and whatever firepower the two in the front have," I said. "Our best bet is to go along with them until we find a better moment to escape. We might be able to make a deal with them."

"I have…" He hesitated. "You know my grandfather. I have resources if we need them. I told them my name was Dr. Carter, but we can tell them the truth if you think it'd help."

He meant money, and that was a good thing. Drug lords in general tended to be opportunistic. They liked money. If Carter's family could pay a ransom, even if that wasn't the motive for the kidnapping, it could possibly get him out of here. I knew Champ would do the same for me if needed.

But my gut was telling me this wasn't that kind of situation—too many things just didn't add up—and I wasn't going to ignore my gut again.

"Let's hope it doesn't come to that. Keep that information in our back pockets while we assess, yeah?"

Carter didn't say anything, which was frustrating when I couldn't see him to assess how he was doing.

"Duchess?" I asked softly.

"Yeah, I'm here. Just thinking."

"Don't volunteer the grandpa thing, okay? Let's wait and get a lay of the land first."

"Yeah."

We bumped along in silence for a while. The periodic chatter from the men up front seemed to be mostly about irrelevant topics like movies and music, someone's brother who'd gotten the wrong girl pregnant, and even a petty argument about the best rum to use in guarapita.

After what seemed like an entire day, I finally felt the Jeep rumble to a stop. Shouts of greetings came from around us, and the warm press of Carter's body against mine was suddenly gone. Someone yanked my hood off, and I took a deep, grateful breath of clean air while I blinked against the blinding sunlight.

Belatedly, I realized one of the guards was asking why one of us didn't have a hood. The other one barked out, "*Se suponía que solo había uno de ellos.*" *There was only supposed to be one of them.*

The guard snipped off the zip ties on my wrist. I guessed they knew we were screwed even if we managed to run off. Being this deep in an unknown terrain could be just as dangerous as being kept by the cartel.

They made a cursory attempt to pat me down but didn't go low enough to find the knife before someone beckoned to us from the entrance.

It was as I expected, a jungle compound full of men with guns and various armed vehicles that could handle the rough terrain. We were led through a metal gate set in stucco walls to the main building within a large courtyard. Some curious eyes peered at us, but several people kept their eyes averted instead.

Carter slowed down enough for me to catch up. "I feel like I'm on the set of a shitty movie," he murmured. "I keep expecting Jack Black to jump out with a Zorro mask."

My eyes scanned the area, trying to pick up as much data as I could. I counted men, took stock of what kind of weapons they had, and noted the position of the sun overhead. Carter continued babbling nervously, mentioning the time his cousin Kevin forced him to watch the entire *Breaking Bad* series and then tried to get him to stick around for *Dexter* too.

"Maybe I shouldn't mention shows about serial killers," he said with a huff of laughter. "Carter, read the room," he added to himself.

"It's going to be okay," I said again. "Been there, done that. You get me?"

I hadn't told him about the time Champ, Elvo, and I had been snatched by a Taliban group and held for three days in a frozen shack in the mountains near Kajran. It had been a harrowing experience, and I'd been scared out of my mind —though I was for *sure* not telling Carter that part—but we'd managed to escape with a combination of patience and some smooth-talking by Elvo.

Carter turned to me. "Really?"

I nodded, still squinting against the overbright sunlight. When we passed through the open double doors and into the main house, the air dropped several degrees, and my eyes had the reverse problem of trying to adjust to the new dimness.

Guards flanked us on both sides, gripping our arms to make sure we didn't veer off into unauthorized parts of the house. Someone trailed behind us with our supplies, and Carter kept looking back over his shoulder to make sure they were taking appropriate care of the electronics.

We finally entered a dark upstairs room with curtains drawn over the windows and a few lamps covered in colorful cloth to dim the light. A huge bedstead stood in the center of the left side of the room, and clusters of small sofas and chairs filled the right side. Women in black congregated here and there, weeping into handkerchiefs.

Whoever was in that bed must have been in bad shape.

We were stopped at the entrance while the head guard approached the bed and spoke in rapid Spanish too low for me to follow. I finally heard a different voice call in English, "Bring him to me."

After shoving us into the room and closer to the bed, the guards held me back a little and nudged Carter the rest of the way to the side of the giant bed. A beefy man who looked to be fifty or sixty lay in the center of the bed. He had a head of thick dark hair and a bushy black mustache.

Why did all South American drug lords look the same? Was there some kind of bro code the way middle school girls tended to dress like each other? Or did they all secretly wish they were Maduro himself?

One of the guards said, "Gianlu—" Someone nearby hissed, and the guard froze before starting again. "*Gustavo. Señor Santiago. Este es el doctor. El cardiólogo.*"

"You are the doctor?" the man on the bed—who we now knew was Gustavo Santiago, considering the giant bed looked like a bedroom throne—asked with a suspicious, squinty look. "Heart doctor?"

Carter nodded. "Yes. I'm a cardiologist. Dr., ah... Dr. Carter." The tips of his ears turned pink the way they did when he told a lie. I'd learned his tell on one of the first nights in Gelada when we'd been bored enough to play poker. "Are you sick?"

As if suddenly recalling some ailment, Santiago clutched at his chest and winced. "Yes. The pain. I am dying. You must save me."

Carter blinked, shocked by the sudden onset of symptoms, but I frowned. Nothing about our intel suggested Santiago was unhealthy, but maybe that explained why he hadn't been known to be active in the area.

Carter turned to gesture to the man with our medical gear. Within moments, he was listening to Santiago's heart with a stethoscope.

Except... Santiago wouldn't shut up.

"It has been this way for weeks and months! It came on suddenly, you see. The pain. The heart pain. I would valiantly battle it back by day through the enormous strength of my will, only for it to steal my breath again at night. I knew right away it was not good, for everyone said, 'Gustavo, this is not good!' They said, 'Gustavo, you need a doctor! Even the bravest of men — which is you, you're the bravest, Gustavo — cannot fight this demon on his own.'" He coughed weakly.

Carter opened his mouth to say something, but Santiago kept talking over him.

"So I asked our local doctor. A man named... what was his name, Javier?" He snapped his fingers but didn't wait for any Javier to respond. *"Pendejo estúpido.* His name was *pendejo estúpido.* Because that doctor said I was fine when I am clearly *not fine,* and we dealt with him the way we always deal with liars." He paused to tell Carter as an aside, "We threw him off the mountain."

"Oh." Carter nodded as if this were utterly reasonable. "I see."

"If I were fine, I would have defeated this heart pain the way I have defeated all of my enemies, would I not, Dr. Carter?"

"Er. Yes?" Carter guessed.

Santiago nodded slowly. "Yes. *Exactamente*. Perhaps you are smarter than the last doctor." He sucked in a breath through his nose and let out a long, lusty sigh that had Carter taking a half step back. "It has been a long time since I have felt the energy of youth. But once… once I was a very strong young man. Full of vitality, like a… like a…" He snapped his fingers once again. "What's a strong animal?"

"A… a bull?" Carter suggested.

"*Yes*. There is much bull about me still, is there not? You see it don't you?" Santiago smirked and quirked one dark eyebrow. "But once, Dr. Carter, I was full of bull."

"I believe that," Carter said solemnly, not a single eyelash twitching.

"Everyone saw me this way, did they not, Raoul?"

Once again, no one named Raoul responded, and once again, Santiago continued his speech, unbothered.

I wondered if calling out names at random was just a thing he did.

"But then, *boom*!" he shouted, scaring poor Carter and half the ladies in the room into jumping at the loud noise. "I was struck down in my prime. I have lived a long and satisfactory life, have I not, Eliana?"

The women looked at each other helplessly, but Santiago kept monologuing.

"And yet, here I am at the nightfall of my glorious day on earth. My dusk, if you will, of a day that has seen much." He waved his arm through the air, almost taking out Carter's head in the process. "I have seen the Bolivarian Republic of—"

Carter finally broke in. "*Sir*, I must ask you to give me a moment of silence so I can listen to your heart. Please."

Santiago looked startled, but he eventually gave a gracious wave of his hand and allowed Carter to step forward again. But as soon as Carter pressed the stethoscope to his heart, Santiago opened his big mouth.

"Moment of silence… yes, that is right. I believe I *need* a moment of silence. A moment of silence for the beauty of my life, which has been threatened by the devastating disease whose horrific nature Dr. Carter will now diagnose." He sighed dramatically, "Let us all take a moment of silence to think about the long and varied life I, *Gustavo Santiago*, has led while he prepares for us his diagnosis."

Carter nodded, and his jaw finally started to relax… but then the drama queen started up again. Something about this wasn't right. There was no way the man on the bed could be a diabolical leader in one of the most dangerous drug cartels in South America.

"Be sure to commemorate the high moments in this moment of silence, for there have been many. The day I stood on the hilltop and claimed this land for my own. The very first shipment of… ah… goods to successfully reach… er… foreign shores. And, of course… the many additional successes I've had over the years of my time in this life. I was once honored as a dinner guest at the home of the minister of land transportation. Alas, he was humbled by my very presence in his home. He certainly was. His lovely wife… I forget her name now as it was not important to me then or now… presented a fine table, but nothing like the table of Major General Mamani. No, that dinner was one that will remain top in my memory for the finest—*oof*!"

Carter shot him an apologetic smile after thumping his chest with the drum of the stethoscope. "Sorry, it seems you're right. There is something going on here, but it is difficult to hear it while your… chest is vibrating from the talking."

"Mpfh." The monologuing drug lord finally shut up.

After a minute, Carter turned to me. "Nurse Riggs, please prepare the EKG."

I turned to the man with our supplies and grabbed the portable EKG before stepping up next to Carter and handing him a fresh pack of electrodes to place on the man's chest while I untangled the wires of the machine.

When he was all hooked up, Santiago threw himself deeper into his stack of pillows and sighed dramatically. "This is it. This is the moment we shall all look back on. Mark the time, Eduardo!" he called to no one in particular. "For this is the hour when Rome fell! When the great *Gustavo Santiago* was no more. I can feel it here. Right here in the center of myself."

He tapped his sternum harder than a man with a fatal heart condition should have been able to. In fact, after working for a while with Carter in Gelada, I'd picked up a thing or two about cardiac patients. This man wasn't one of them.

Not only was he not a heart patient, he also didn't seem much like an evil mastermind. If this was the same Gustavo Santiago that helped run the cartel, US intelligence needed serious help determining true threats. Surely, this man wasn't one of them.

Unsurprisingly, a few minutes later, Carter nodded at the EKG results with a relieved expression and opened his mouth to give Santiago the good news.

Before he could, I grabbed his elbow. "Shouldn't we confer first?" I asked with a fake smile. "Second opinion and all that."

His brows furrowed. "Who's giving the second opinion? *You?*"

I tried my hardest to send him psychic messages. It must have worked because his eyes suddenly widened, and he nodded again. "Yes, yes, of course. Let us confer. We can't be too careful." He turned back to Santiago. "One moment, please, sir."

Santiago inclined his head regally.

Carter took a step back with me and leaned in to whisper in my ear. "The man needs an antacid. And possibly a therapist."

"Babe, if you tell him that, he's going to get rid of us the way he did that other doctor who tried telling him he was fine."

I hadn't meant to let the endearment slip, but when Carter's cheeks turned pink to match his ears, I realized it was worth it.

"But... you don't mean you want me to..." He lowered his voice to a whisper. *"Lie to a patient?"*

Lord save me from doctors with integrity.

"He's not a patient, Carter," I reasoned. "He kidnapped us, remember? And when he says the doctor was tossed off the side of the mountain, that's not a euphemism. If this is the Santiago connected to the cartel, he means literally tossed. With complementary bullet holes, I bet. Listen to me. You have to stall for time. This test was inconclusive, and you need twenty-four hours to run some bloodwork. Understand?"

I could see the proposal of medical deception didn't sit well with him, so I tried another tack. "You're not misdiagnosing him. You're only taking extra time to be sure of the diagnosis. Anyone would understand that in a serious cardiac case."

"But this isn't a ser—"

"I must know of what you discuss!" Santiago boomed, scaring Carter into making an *eep* sound. "It is as I feared, is it not? How much time do I have to get my affairs in order? Wait. No! You are an American heart specialist. Surely you can fix it. Surely you have the skills to make this better, buy me more time with my beloved Yelitza."

A gasp came from a woman in the room—he'd gotten a name right, it seemed—and another began fluttering over her in reassurance.

"And my beloved Evalin! Of course." He cleared his throat and looked back at Carter. "I have too many mistresses to always keep straight. But they each and every one of them mean the most to me of all of them."

Carter opened his mouth, presumably to lecture the man on the definition of superlatives, but he thought better of it.

Good man. The best.

Santiago continued. This time he waved his arm around again, nearly ripping off some of the EKG leads. "I cannot leave them all alone. I must get better. You must heal me from this devastating condition." He side-eyed Carter. "What is this devastating condition, exactly?"

Carter clenched his jaw, and his ears pinked again. "I need more time. The test wasn't exactly conclusive. I'd like to draw some blood and perform some lab tests overnight if possible. I would... I wouldn't want to get the diagnosis wrong with someone of your... important... standing."

Santiago's narrowed eyes widened. "Yes. Yes, of course. Of course you would not. I *am* very important. You see this right away. It is necessary to get it right."

He looked at me and the others in the room. "I like this Dr. Carter. He and his manservant—" Jesus, I was demoted to manservant again. "—are to be given the finest suite in the compound. Make sure he has all the necessary supplies for his medical lab. Also..." He seemed to be searching for a particular person and finally settled his eyes on the tallest, beefiest, and most good-looking of all his guards. He snapped his fingers at him. "Deo. Give the man your blood. He needs it for a test."

The guard closed his eyes and sighed.

Carter looked back and forth between Beefcake and Santiago. "Um, no. That's not... no. I need *your* blood, sir. His blood will not show me what's going on inside *your* body."

As Carter spoke, Santiago realized how stupid his order had been. His face turned florid with embarrassed anger. I stepped forward to be ready to protect Carter, but Carter himself seemed to realize the danger that was brewing.

"Although," he said nervously. "Actually, I misunderstood you. You mean this man could give me a baseline from which to compare yours to. Excellent idea! I will take blood from both of you. You are so thoughtful, sir. Thank you. I should have been the one to think of it. I apologize."

Santiago's tension deflated somewhat, but he still looked peeved. "Yes, exactly. That is what I meant. Of course."

He nodded at the guards who'd brought us in. "Go. Get rid of them."

Carter made another sound of despair at Santiago's poor choice of words, and Santiago seemed to realize his mistake. "Not like that," he said imperiously. "Like... like show them to their rooms. You may return this evening for the blood after I have had time to eat my dinner properly. I will need my strength, you see. Red meat for iron. Fried yucca for potassium. Bacon for sodium. I know my minerals."

I could tell Carter was having to hold himself back from lecturing the man about eating all that with a suspected heart problem, but then he must have remembered Santiago didn't, in fact, have a heart problem.

"Yes, sir," he said instead.

We followed the men out of Santiago's room and down

several hallways until entering what appeared to be a two-room suite. "*Quédate aquí,*" one of the guards said. *Stay here.*

We both nodded and waited until they left and locked us in before we took a deep breath.

Three seconds later, I lost all the air in my lungs again when Carter lunged at me for a panicked embrace.

I closed my eyes and held him tight.

How the hell was I going to keep this sweet man safe?

8

CARTER

I pulled back from Riggs long before I was ready. Leaning on him was too easy and felt way too good. Scary-good. I hated feeling needy, and I *especially* hated feeling needy with someone who blew hot and cold like Riggs did. It also didn't escape my notice that I seemed to always be the one to initiate contact between us.

Maybe humoring me was part of his job description.

I turned away to get my bearings and saw that we were in a little suite with two bedrooms and a living area. The living room was outfitted in modern jungle lodge, complete with a velvet leopard-print couch. I peeked into the doorway on the left side of the room and saw that it contained a king-sized bed in heavy wood, covered with velvet hangings, like we were in a medieval castle and not the middle of a South American jungle. I couldn't imagine how they managed to keep fabric like that from moldering in the heat and humidity, but I guessed being a crime boss meant you didn't have to worry about stuff like fabric... or coordinating.

Through the door on the right, there was another bedroom that seemed to be outfitted the same way.

"So… this is fancy, huh? I mean, as prisoner accommodations go?" I thumped the back of a sofa and swallowed like my heart wasn't pounding hard enough to shake the mountain. "Could be worse. No chains in the wall. No torture rack. You want the room on the right or the left?"

"I want the one on the right."

"Easy peasy! Then I'll just…"

"Also take the one on the right."

I turned to face him and blinked. "What?"

Did this mean he wanted a repeat of the previous night? And if so, how did I feel about it? My dick was a hundred percent on board, despite the danger we were in, but the rest of me had concerns. Like, there would have to be ground rules so feelings didn't get hurt, and—

"We're sharing a room, Carter. What if they come for one of us in the night?" Riggs kept his voice low and eyed the suite door cautiously. "I can't protect you if I can't see you. We need to stick together. Safety in numbers."

"Oh." I ran a hand over my throat as unreasonable disappointment and very reasonable fear warred inside me.

The fear won, though I tried not to let Riggs see it.

"So what do we do?" I whispered, unsure whether Gustavo's men were standing right outside.

Riggs dragged me through the bedroom on the right to a tiny en suite bathroom. Then he locked the door and turned on the shower. "They might have listening devices out there," he explained in a low voice.

Holy shit. "Do you really think so?"

"Honestly? No. See this?"

Riggs lifted his leg and set his booted foot on the vanity before lifting the hem of his scrubs and removing a knife he had strapped to his muscular, hairy calf. Just the sight of his naked leg made my pulse accelerate, and suddenly I was horny again, despite the danger… or maybe partly because of it, just like I'd been last night.

This inappropriate fear-lust stress response was a real problem.

"They didn't search me for weapons when we got here, and I'm almost positive they didn't put a guard on the door either." He shook his head in disgust as he hoisted himself up to sit on the counter. "These guys are either poorly trained or really don't give a shit about protecting the guy in the bed."

I snickered, then clapped a hand over my mouth. Add *inappropriate humor* to my list of stress behaviors right under *inappropriate lusting*. "Sorry, it's not funny! I know it's not funny. You just sound so put out about it. Like you're offended that these were the best henchmen the cartel could come up with. You want to give them a course in remedial badassery, don't you?"

"No," he said shortly. "In fact—" He hesitated for a moment while the water drummed against the tile floor of the shower.

"Tell me," I demanded when it seemed like he wouldn't speak. "Remember, you're supposed to be honest with me?"

Riggs blew out a breath. "Something's going on here that I'm not understanding. A guy as connected as Santiago…" He broke off. "He's just not what I expected, that's all. And his operation isn't as efficient."

"But that's a good thing, right? Maybe he's distracted because he thinks he's gonna die. Maybe he had a bunch of guys quit. Maybe good evil henchmen are hard to find. Maybe that means they're not as dangerous and we can get away."

Riggs shook his head. "Poorly trained men can sometimes be more dangerous than trained ones, Carter. They didn't blindfold you on the way up the mountain, and they're not worried about us seeing their faces. I don't think it's a simple K&R. You need to stay on your guard, okay?"

"Oh." *They're gonna kill us.* "Right. Of course." My heart rate quickened again, for a much less pleasant reason this time, and my knees wobbled embarrassingly before I caught myself on the counter. "S-so we need to think up a plan to get ourselves out of here before we end up like the last doctor, huh?" I blew out a breath. "Jesus, my grandfather would have a fit if he knew what was happening. He begged me to stay in Tennessee."

"Why didn't you?"

Unlike at the gala, Riggs didn't sound judgmental so much as curious. Like I was a puzzle he was trying to figure out.

But it really wasn't that complicated.

I shrugged. "My parents were big believers in providing medical care to the most vulnerable populations. I want to carry on their legacy. That's why our family is so big on raising money for programs in underserved communities, volunteering in rural areas—"

"*That's* why you moved to Great Nuthatch," he surmised.

"Partly," I agreed. "That and Tucker living nearby. But wanting to help people is the reason I've gone on a bunch of medical aid trips in the past." I forced a smile. "None of which involved getting kidnapped, so that's a new wrinkle, huh?"

Riggs ignored all of this and picked up on something I'd hoped he'd miss. "They *were* big believers?" he repeated.

"Yeah. Yup. They died when I was young. Car accident while they were setting up a hospital in what used to be Zaire."

"Ah." He gave me a look that said he saw more than I wanted him to.

"Anyway. Enough about that." I cleared my throat. "You were about to share the plan for not dying?"

"There's no need to be scared." Riggs's voice turned soothing. "Just vigilant."

I scowled. "I didn't say I was scared."

Riggs ignored this, probably because I was still clinging to the vanity for support. "I've already thought through the situation. For right now, there's only one possible plan that keeps you safe, and that's waiting for reinforcements. If we're not back by nightfall, the Doctors Across Continents people will report us missing. Someone will come for us." Riggs laid one huge paw on the back of my neck in a comforting sort of way. "As long as you don't try to be a hero, it'll be fine."

But when I glanced up at him, I could tell by the look on his face that he wasn't giving me the whole truth. I knew because I wore that exact expression when trying to soften bad news for a patient.

"What are you not telling me?"

"Carter," he said in a placating tone. "I promise—"

"No. Don't do that." I shook my head and straightened up. "Don't make empty promises. You've got to be up-front with me. We already talked about this. I know you don't necessarily like me. I know you think I'm silly, and you think the work I'm doing is the equivalent of peeing on a forest fire—"

"That's not true," he argued. When I shot him a disbelieving look, he added, "Okay, I maybe suggested something to that effect before we left the States, but I know better now. The work you do might not fix the problems in Venezuela, but you're changing the lives of individuals. It's inspiring—"

I held up a hand to stop him and tried to pretend his words didn't matter, that they didn't burrow under my skin and chase away the chill of fear. "My point is, we only have each other right now. You're the *one* person in this whole country I can count on. And I can't count on you if you're keeping things from me, even if you're doing it to protect me."

Riggs ran both hands through his hair in frustration and relented. "Look, I wasn't *lying* about anything I said, but…"

"But?" I prompted.

"But with the political climate being what it is, it won't mean much for Doctors Across Continents to report us missing," he admitted. "The US can't just mount an armed rescue in a foreign country, and if these guys *are* connected to the cartel, the local police are probably on the payroll."

Well. I'd asked for honesty, right?

"Champion Security will be the ones to get us out of this mess," Riggs continued confidently. "And they will. One hundred percent. But it's gonna take time for them to get the word that we're missing and then to formulate a rescue."

I clung to this measure of hope and nodded like a bobblehead. "How long?"

"Maybe a day or two before they hear, unless we can speed that up? Another day or two to figure out where we are. Another day or two to get here and get us out."

"That's…" I cleared my throat. "A lot of days."

He nodded. "It is. And frankly, that's best-case scenario. We need to be prepared to be here for as long as a week."

"A week!"

"Or more, potentially."

"Wow. Okay." I leaned over again, hyperventilating just a little. "So we're screwed."

"No," Riggs said firmly. He yanked me upright and put

his hand under my chin, compelling me to look at him. "You don't think like that, you hear me? Because if you *think* you're gonna fail, you're gonna *act* like you're gonna fail, and I need you to be at the top of your game for both our sakes. You've got to believe it's going to be okay, Carter. Really believe it. Can you do that for me?"

His fingers were rough on my face, grounding me in reality, and I nodded… then I shook my head. "I want to believe it, Riggs, but how am I going to keep drawing out his heartburn for a week without him getting impatient? It's cruel to let the man think he's dying when all he needs is an antacid, and it's cruel to not give him an antacid when I could. And even if I were okay with all that, I suck at acting, especially under pressure. When my kindergarten class performed *The Rabbit Who Wanted Red Wings*, I played a *rock*, and I still screwed it up. There's no way I can pretend for that long."

"But you won't be acting." His thumb stroked my chin. "The truth is, you don't know for sure he's *not* dying, do you? You think he's not, you're almost positive he's not, but that isn't the same thing as being sure. Is it?"

I blinked. "I suppose not."

"You are just being a super-diligent medical professional by triple-checking everything. Urine sample, a few days of EKGs, loads of bloodwork. It's not acting," he repeated. "It's just not sharing all the information you know. It's *discretion*."

I made a face. It was a stretch, but he wasn't wrong.

"You like to be in control of things, right?" he asked softly. "I get that. Same here. So control what you *can* control, Carter."

I nodded. I could do that.

And Riggs had been right earlier too. I hadn't consented to be our captor's doctor. I had no obligation there.

"Okay, I can try. Is there anything we can do to speed this process up, though? Maybe bribe a guard, or—"

"No. Definitely not. We don't know who we're dealing with here."

I frowned. "You mean, we don't know the guards?"

He nodded robotically. "Yes. The guards. That's... that's what I meant." Before I could call him on his hesitation again, he continued. "What we need is to gain access to the internet somehow so we can get a message out. All I need is ten unsupervised seconds, and I can open a search portal that will ping our computer guy, Hux, to track my search. It's a back-end thing he set up after an assignment went wonky in Jakarta and we almost lost— er. Never mind." Riggs cracked his neck from side to side.

Riggs was right. There were some things I *didn't* want to know. "Okay, so maybe I ask Señor Santiago if I can consult with a colleague back in the States about his very delicate condition? Or say I need to check which pharmacies in Caracas carry the meds he needs."

"Exactly." Riggs chafed my arms. "You're a natural."

The steam from the shower billowed around us as I looked up into his face. "And what if it doesn't work? What if I can't convince him?"

"Then I sneak out and poke around on my own and find one. I'm a trained operator, Carter," he added when I made a disapproving *eep* sort of noise. "This is my job."

No, *I* was his job, as he kept reminding me. And I was very afraid my poor choices were going to get us both killed.

"Kinda makes you wish we'd stayed back in Gelada and let the rampaging capybaras have their way with us, huh?" I said, not even joking.

"Doesn't matter if it's rampaging capybaras or mono-loguing drug lords with indigestion—"

I snorted. "God, he really does monologue, doesn't he? I'm glad I'm not the only one who noticed it."

Riggs shook my shoulders gently. "*Listen*. My point is, it doesn't matter what the danger is, I'm gonna keep you safe. We've got this."

Awww.

The sound of something slamming against the bathroom door stopped me from getting too sappy. Someone yelled something in angry Spanish from the bedroom.

"*Adelante,*" Riggs yelled to them. "Shit," he muttered to me. "Santiago's asking for us. Here, you take this. Just in case." He bent down, hiked up my pant leg, and affixed his knife in its sheath. He looked up at me with solemn dark eyes. "I have every faith in you, Carter."

The banging escalated.

"*¡Esperate un segundo! Está atascado,*" Riggs called. To me, he added, "I told them to wait a second 'cause the door is stuck. FYI, we're in here together because the shower is broken and we're trying to fix it."

"It is?" I whispered, glancing dubiously at the perfectly functional shower.

Riggs turned the temperature control to cool and whacked the side of the showerhead with his hand, causing water to spray everywhere. "It is," he confirmed.

He threw the door open, and two guys jumped in brandishing handguns. One was Beardy, from earlier, but the other guy was new and wore thick black glasses.

"Hey, hey, hey!" Riggs scowled. "We're just trying to fix the shower so my boss here can clean off."

"Why you locked the door?" Glasses asked me in accented English.

"We didn't," I lied unconvincingly. "It must've gotten stuck. You know, what with the steam warping the wood and the, um, the door-locking mechanism? Kind of a common problem with older homes. The seals get corroded and things get loose and before you know it, things are oxidizing left, right, and center!" I laughed nervously and tried to stop talking, but it didn't work. "Chemistry, am I right? Can't fight it! Why, one time, back at my grandfather's house in Tennes—"

"Dr. Carter?" Riggs interrupted.

"Erm. Yes, Nurse Riggs?"

"I'm guessing these men don't need a lecture on oxidation. Not at this juncture."

"No. Right." I swallowed hard. "Thank you."

Add overtalking to the top of my list of terrible, terrible stress responses, damn it.

I prided myself on staying calm and collected in a crisis—I'd be a pretty terrible doctor if I couldn't—but apparently that calm only extended to situations I could *control.* Throw me in a tiny, steam-filled Venezuelan bathroom inside a drug lord's jungle compound with a couple of armed men and a sexy-as-fuck bodyguard, and apparently I panicked as much as anybody. *How lowering.*

Glasses looked back and forth between us like he was confident that we were up to something, but he wasn't sure what... which was fair, because I wasn't entirely sure either.

"Señor Santiago needs *el doctor,*" he said finally. "His heart is getting worse."

"Okay. We'll come now." I motioned toward the bathroom door.

"Not you." Glasses caught Riggs in the chest with his palm and halted him in his tracks. "You stay here."

"Hell, no," Riggs shot back. "Dr. Carter needs me. He's useless without me, remember?"

"Yes," I agreed. "Nurse Riggs is correct, I need my nurse. He assists me with all, um, tests and diagnoses, so—"

"Not him," Glasses insisted, brandishing his gun. "Señor Santiago says *sólo el doctor.*"

I eyed the gun nervously and gave Riggs a helpless shrug. "Fine. Certainly. Well. I'll be back, then, Nurse Riggs."

Riggs's nostrils flared. "What happened to safety in numbers, Doctor?"

"You have your job, and I have mine," I reminded him. We had to stay the course for a week, right? This was still only the first day.

So I nodded at Glasses and let them lead me away.

When Glasses and Beardy let me in Santiago's bedchamber, it was much darker than it had been earlier. The cadre of weeping women was gone, the shades were drawn, and the room was in almost total darkness, save for the dim yellow glow of a bedside lamp. Santiago lay flat on the bed with his hands resting on his chest, perfectly motionless, and for a second I wondered if I'd been wrong earlier—if maybe the man *had* taken a turn for the worse somehow.

But as I hurried over to the bed to check, his voice rang through the room loud and clear, and I jumped.

"I'm sure you're wondering why I have called you here for a second time, Dr. Carter."

"Uh." I slowed my steps. "I need to take your blood. But also, your men said you'd gotten worse?"

"Eh." Santiago waved a hand in the air. "When one is on the brink of death as I am—" He coughed weakly. "—there is no *better,* there is no *worse,* there is only suffering. When the heart spasms come, my body suffers. When the physical pain subsides, my soul is in agony—"

My gut clenched in sympathy. I really did hate to see anyone in pain, even drug lords with heartburn who threw other doctors off—

"—for I pity the many women in the world who have not met me yet and now will never get the chance."

I blinked. *The what now?*

Santiago wiped aside a single tear. "My poor ladies! My darling Evalin. My sweet Lucrecia! They are faithful to me and only me, for no one can satisfy them like I can! But at least they can cling to their memories to comfort them. My heart breaks for the ones who've never been loved by me." He looked at me with shining eyes. "For I am a fabulous lover, Doctor. As you will no doubt verify from the blood samples you will take."

Was he serious?

"Actually, there's no way…" I began. Then I heard Riggs's voice in my head, reminding me of all that was at stake, and I lied my ass off. "Erm. There's no way they won't show exactly that, I'm sure. Once I've had a chance to analyze them." I cleared my throat. "That could take… many days."

Santiago narrowed his eyes. "But it has been nearly an entire day already!"

More like an hour. Maybe ninety minutes.

Lie, Carter, lie.

"I assure you, sir, I'm as impatient as you are. I've been waiting for your men to show me to your lab equipment. I'll need a blood gas analyzer, a chemistry analyzer, an immunoassay analyzer, a computer with access to the National Institutes of Health's databases, an electron microscope, an autoclave, and a sterile work environment. I'll take *no* chances with your health, for you're clearly an extremely important person, as you mentioned before. Several times. And the situation is… complex."

That was for damn sure.

Santiago grunted in satisfaction. "You are a man of great intelligence, clearly."

"Thank you, sir."

"That is why I called you here again this evening. I wished to know your thoughts on what my fatal illness might be. I saw how you conferred with your manservant earlier, so I know you have *some* idea."

"Oh. Um. It's far too early in the diagnostic process to even speculate—" I began.

"But you must," he said firmly. "Tell me which diseases you think might take me from my beloved Irma and my darling Gracia!"

Just how many girlfriends did the man have? Or I wondered if, like earlier, he was just listing off random names that didn't correspond to anyone in particular.

"Uh. W-well." I licked my lips. "It could be... pyrosis?"

Gustavo gasped and clutched at his chest, his fingers digging into his silk pajamas. "Never say so! Porry-po-po-sis was the very disease that claimed my father! Now I am to be another Santiago struck down in his prime!"

I tried to dredge up an appropriately concerned expression and nodded solemnly. *Pyrosis* was a clinical term for heartburn, which never killed anyone on its own.

"What else?" Gustavo demanded avidly. "What other conditions might be stalking me like a beast in the night?"

"Er. Well... we'll certainly want to rule out cardialgia?" I went ahead and started the process to take blood from his arm.

Gustavo moaned enthusiastically and addressed the ceiling. "Cardio-la-la-logiala! And now he names the very condition that stole my mother! *Ay, Dios.* Truly, this is a disease that claims only the most beautiful and vibrant."

I bit my tongue against a smile. Cardialgia was *also* a name for heartburn. His relatives clearly had terrible digestive issues.

"I can't even imagine," I murmured, focusing on finding a vein with as little fuss as possible.

"When death has stolen me, who will protect my brother?" he demanded. "He will be all alone in the world. Weak and friendless."

Glasses made a noise from the corner that sounded like a cough. Or maybe he was crying? I couldn't see him well enough to say.

"Wow. I didn't know you had a brother," I said sympathetically. "Are you close?"

"So close. So very close. I am his confidant. I am his best and most trusted friend. I provide him wisdom and moral counsel. He says to me sometimes, 'Gian—er, *Gustavo*, I do not know what I would do without you! I love you more than the mountains of our homeland. I love you more than any amount of money. If only I, too, could be strong and handsome like you!'"

Glasses cough-sniffled from the corner again, and Gustavo himself seemed quite moved by his brother's words, judging by the tears in his dark eyes.

"That's... lovely," I agreed. Then, I began conversationally, "You know, I have a cousin, but he's like a little brother. I worry about him too. He can be lonely sometimes. He's a little shy, but he's really loyal and kind."

Gustavo blinked up at me. "He sounds very... admirable."

Admirable? I'd never thought of Kev that way, but he kinda was. I smiled. "He used to try to be like me when we were younger. It was sweet."

"You... spent time with him. As a brother."

I frowned. "Well, yeah. Of course. I love Kev." I cursed myself the second Kev's name was out of my mouth. I shouldn't have volunteered anything.

Gustavo nodded thoughtfully.

I cleared my throat. "So, you're not married, then? To any of your... women?" I prayed for him to fill the vials faster. Small talk of any kind was not my forte, but apparently I really sucked at small talk with dangerous criminals.

Gustavo chuckled. "I could hardly confine myself to one. That wouldn't be fair."

Glasses coughed.

"And, uh... no children?" I pulled the needle out, pressing a gauze pad over the site.

"No, alas. My brother is my only living relative. You see, I have been cursed with exceptionally powerful seed."

"Ah, gotcha. That's too—" Glasses stepped forward instantly to whisk the used supplies and the vials of blood away, murmuring something about storing them in the lab, and only then did I finally process Gustavo's comment. "Wait, what?"

"My seed," he repeated. "It is so formidable that when I unleash it into a womb, the womb cowers in terror." He sighed sadly. "There may be a woman who can handle the power, but I have not met her yet, though I continue to search."

I was torn between horror and laughter. "That is... fascinating. And how did you come to, ah... understand this very true fact about yourself?"

"After the stupid local doctor falsely diagnosed me—" Gustavo's eyes flashed angrily. "—Gustavo brought in a fertility specialist from Hungary to assess the situation. He seemed a man of great intelligence, much like yourself, and he proved very useful." He paused, pursed his lips, and shrugged. "Until he didn't."

I swallowed hard. Gustavo had started talking about Gustavo's self in the third person.

Yeah, I was officially afraid.

And I could only imagine the fertility doctor must've

been equally terrified if he'd actually suggested "ultra-powerful semen" as a fertility issue. I really didn't want to share that fate.

"So, ah… how many doctors would you say you've had to… throw off the mountain?" I asked conversationally.

"Oh, one or two. Five. Eight?" He shrugged. "You know, I don't *actually* throw them off the mountain, of course."

"You… you don't?"

"Of course not! What kind of man do you take me for, Dr. Carter?"

"Oh! Oh, gosh. Really?" I laughed weakly. "Because I thought you meant you actually—"

"I considered it, obviously. It would have been convenient." Gustavo examined his nails in the weak light. "But then we would have a pile of bodies right outside our door. The ladies would be upset. And what would Gustavo's friend Don Pablo—the chief of police in this region, you understand—say when he came to visit? So I have Pedro and, ah… Miguel and…" He snapped his fingers like he was trying to think up a name. "Erm… *Ricardo*… take them further up into the mountains, *then* drop them." He flicked his fingers toward the window.

Oh. Well, then.

This guy was legit insane, and it probably wasn't a good sign that he was telling me all about this.

"Right. Okay. So. I should probably go and let you rest—"

"*Argh*," Gustavo cried, squeezing his eyes shut and clutching his stomach in true agony. Beads of sweat popped out on his forehead, and I wondered if he'd had untreated reflux for so long that he'd developed an ulcer. "The end, it nears!"

"Sir, perhaps if you sit upright a bit more?" I suggested before I could stop myself.

He cracked one eye open. "*¿Perdón?* What would that do for my heart?"

Fuck. What *would* that do? Good going, Carter. "Um. Now that you tell me of your powerful seed condition, I wonder if maybe your heart wants to be elevated like a, you know… king? On a throne?"

Gustavo stared at me with narrowed eyes for one beat, then another, until I thought the end really *might* be near.

"Like a king on a throne," he repeated, sitting upright. "Yes. *Yes!*"

"This won't cure you, of course," I added quickly, settling some pillows behind his back. "Not long-term. But it might help temporarily. Until I can do the testing on your blood, that is. But of course I'll need the equipment first."

"I have the heart of a king," Gustavo said, like he was testing out the words, and then he nodded to himself happily. "Rodrigo!" he called.

Glasses opened the door. "*Si, Gian—uh… señor?*"

"Chalo, get Dr. Carter whatever equipment he needs immediately."

"*Si, señor.*"

I struggled to restrain my smile. *Computer access, here we come.* Riggs would be so impressed that I—

Gustavo pursed his lips. "And if he needs information from the internet, you will get it for him."

Rodrigo-Chalo-Glasses nodded again.

Shit.

As Glasses led me down the carpeted hallway, my mind churned over all the possible outcomes of this situation, and for the first time ever, I found myself a little homesick for the Thicket, and for my grandfather and Kev too. Heck, I even missed—

"Hot butter on a biscuit!" someone yelled. "You can't just keep a Nutter confined like this! Nutters need to be free!"

I stopped, right there in the middle of the hall.

Holy shit. I was hallucinating old Amos Nutter in the jungles of Venezuela.

This was the most troubling stress response yet.

But just before Glasses hurried me along, I caught sight of an open door just a little further down the hall. The guard on the door said something in angry Spanish that sounded like a warning, and inside the room… Holy shit. Inside the room was the *motherlode* of technology, including maybe a dozen monitors showing video game screens and a rack of computers with flashing lights. There was a single chair inside the room, and on it sat a middle-aged man with the world's most epic blond mullet and a Hank Williams T-shirt.

I blinked my eyes, pretty sure *that* was a hallucination too, and sure enough, when I looked back, the door was closed.

Still, I made sure to count my steps as we went down the hall so I could tell Riggs where the computer room might possibly be. Four doorways, take a right, six more doorways.

Glasses paused outside a door on the left where Beardy stood guard, and at his nod, Beardy opened the door, tossed me inside, and locked it behind me.

"*Hasta mañana,*" one of the guards called in a nasty voice.

Riggs was already crossing the living room toward me when I got to my feet.

"Hurry up and let's go to the bathroom!" I whispered. "I have so many things to tell you—*mmpfh*!"

Riggs hauled me against the vast continent of his chest,

cradled my jaw in both of his big hands, and pressed his lips to mine, bruising, hard, and demanding.

I was so shocked that he'd initiated this contact, so entirely overwhelmed by the heat and scent and *passion* of him, that I floundered at first, my hands flailing in midair before finally coming to rest on his thick shoulders. Then I sank into it because I couldn't *not*. Because it felt more like home than home did, even though it shouldn't.

"You scared the shit out of me, Carter Rogers," Riggs said hoarsely when he finally pulled back enough to let me breathe.

"Because I'm a *principal*," I said breathlessly, my fingers stroking up and down his neck. "And your job and your reputation are on the line if you don't protect me. I know."

"Fuck the job, Carter," he growled. Then he tugged on my hair, tilted my head back, and captured my mouth again.

9

RIGGS

I couldn't believe Carter Rogers could kiss me the way he did, make me hard the way he did, and still think he was simply a job to me.

He wasn't. When they'd taken him to Santiago without me, I'd gone out of my mind with worry. Worry he'd say the wrong thing in his earnest effort to be a stand-up physician or that he'd say the wrong thing accidentally out of sheer terror.

There was every chance an unpredictable and dangerous man like Gustavo Santiago could get triggered by something minuscule and demand Carter suffer for some perceived slight. And if this wasn't the same Gustavo Santiago related to the cartel, then why were there many armed guards? And who was the man in the bed?

I hadn't told Carter of my suspicions. It was better for him to assume the worst. Fearing Santiago and his gunmen would keep Carter compliant, keep him safe. Hopefully long enough for me to figure out what the hell was going on here. Regardless of who was in that bed, he didn't seem nearly as dangerous as I'd first feared. But the moment they'd taken Carter away without me, it hadn't mattered. I'd felt every bit of danger as if the entire cartel had taken him away from me.

The wait for Carter's return had been interminable, and the minute he'd returned intact and brimming with healthy energy, I'd been unable to keep my hands... and lips... off him.

He tasted so fucking good. And when I held him in my arms, I finally felt like I could maybe, just possibly, keep him safe.

"You're making me dizzy," he slurred against my lips. We'd been kissing for a long time, and it hadn't been enough.

"Take a breath," I said without letting him go long enough to do it.

He pulled back but then quickly put his lips back on mine for one, two, three more quick kisses before pulling back again. "What are we doing?"

"No talking, Duchess," I said, pulling him back to me with a hand against the back of his head. He made a noise of weak agreement and melted back into me.

A few moments later, our hard cocks brushed against each other, and Carter sucked in a breath. "Arousal is a..." He kissed me again. "Is a... um. Arousal is a stress response." His words drifted off as he leaned in for more kisses.

I moved down to nip at his chin, his throat, his collarbone.

Then I dropped to my knees.

Carter's eyes widened comically. "And, ah, adrenaline is a vasodilator, so..."

I kept my eyes locked on his as I began to peel open his cargo pants. "Or you can keep talking," I muttered to myself with a small smile. He was fucking adorable when he was nervous.

I wasn't sure when I'd started to find his overtalking endearing. A huge liability, obviously, but still… kinda cute. It was a huge departure from his calm confidence in a crisis, and I wondered how many people got to see this side of him.

Thanks to the crazy, zebra-patterned rug covering the floor tiles, my knees weren't in too much pain. I settled in for a while. After nosing the front of his briefs, I made eye contact with him again and began to pull them down. "Tell me to stop," I said, hoping like hell he wouldn't.

"I'm not stupid," he said through a hiss as I ran the stubble of my chin across the top of his thigh. His legs were toned from regular running, and his leg hair was a darker blond than the hair on his head. I dragged my tongue through it to the crease where his thigh met his groin.

"Want to make you scream," I said softly. "But you can't. You have to be silent, Duchess. You got me? Not a sound while I suck on your cock."

He squeezed his eyes closed and fisted his hands by his sides before nodding.

I ran my hand up under his Doctors Across Continents polo shirt, feeling his warm skin and fit body. His nipples crinkled under my fingertips, and he opened his eyes again to look at me.

His eyes said a thousand different things. He was hungry for touch, scared to ask for it, unsure of me, and worried in general.

I wanted to fuck the fear right out of him.

My tongue found the crown of his dick and swirled around it, making his breath catch. I moved one hand around to squeeze his ass. If only he would let me take him away from this dangerous situation for a few minutes, give up to pure pleasure and let go.

"Look at me, Duchess," I said softly. "Don't take your eyes off me."

His lips were moist and full, and his face was flushed pink with desire. His blond hair was so messy, I must have put my hands in it while we were kissing earlier.

I ran my tongue around his dick before swallowing his shaft and squeezing his ass.

I loved sucking cock, but I especially loved it with a man as expressive as Carter Rogers. He was so sure of himself at work. While in his role as a competent cardiologist, he was decisive and forthright. But when he was alone with me, half-naked and wanting… he was vulnerable and needy.

And I wanted to consume him.

Carter's fingers moved through my hair. "Just like that," he breathed. "Oh God, I'm gonna come."

I moved a hand around to his balls, running a finger behind them to press into the warm skin there. He brought his forearm up to his mouth and grunted against it as if he was *just* on the verge of his orgasm. I grasped his balls and gently pulled them down, away from his body.

His eyes flashed open wide in shock. "Wha?"

"Take a deep breath," I said, pulling off his wet dick and jacking him with my hand. "Not going to finish you off that easily."

I didn't want it to be over. I wanted to give him pleasure all night, take him away from this crazy compound in the foothills of the Andes and make him unable to remember his own name.

"I can't… what? Why? Why?" He was dazed with lust. It made my dick hard as iron.

I stood and yanked at my clothes, wanting to be free of them so I could jack myself off while I sucked him.

Carter stared at me. "What are you doing?"

Instead of answering him, I stripped his top off and threw his pants, his underwear, and the knife sheath in a pile.

When both of us were completely bare, I got back down on my knees. Carter stared down at me. Our eyes met and stayed locked together for one beat. Two.

"I want you," he said so softly, I almost didn't hear him. "I want you so badly, I ache."

My stomach and chest tightened. "I'm yours."

Carter tackled me onto the ground, shoving me onto my back on the thick rug. As soon as his naked body landed on top of me, I devoured him with my hands and mouth. We grappled with each other, hungry for as much skin and touch as we could get, until we found ourselves in a dirty sixty-nine on the floor, sucking each other off breathlessly.

My dick was in heaven. Carter's hot, wet mouth licked and sucked on it hungrily. His hands jacked the length he couldn't fit in his mouth. His hips pulsed his own cock deeper into my throat, even though I wasn't sure he was aware of it. I quickly sucked a finger into my mouth and slid it inside him to make it as good as I could before my own orgasm hit and my brain went offline.

"*Gnfh*!" He almost choked on my dick as he came, and the sound, together with the thought of him gagging on my cock, made my own orgasm slam through me. I quickly pulled off him, gritting my teeth against the scream and clutching Carter's full ass cheeks with my fingers.

We were a mess. There was sweat, cum, and spit seemingly everywhere, but I didn't give a shit. It was hot as fuck.

The sounds of our ragged breathing filled the room around us for a while. I finally swung around to lie face-to-face with him. His hair was messy, and a hank of it was plastered to his forehead. I moved to the side and then ran my hand down the side of his face.

"You okay?"

His eyes were still glassy when they met mine. "We probably shouldn't have done that."

I bit back a sigh and pierced him with a look. "Don't."

Carter sat up. "Okay, but like… we're hostages."

He was right, of course. I needed to get him out of here and back to safety. But I could probably do it with a much clearer head now that I'd finally gotten rid of my doctor boner. I needed to get us cleaned up and put Carter to bed before sitting down to think through our options and make a plan.

"I know," I said, standing up and reaching my hand down to help him up. "But we're also humans."

He followed me into the bathroom and stood there while I started the shower. "What's the plan?" he asked when his brain began functioning again. "I mean… you implied you've been in this kind of situation before?"

I nodded. "The key is to stay calm and be ready. We need to find our moment and take advantage of it, but we need some intel first." I was grateful for the shower noise in case the walls were thin. "I need to figure out how well guarded this place is and get some kind of idea of where to go if we can get out of here. Can you tell me what you saw on the way here from Marisol's place?"

After I nudged him under the clean spray, he told me he mostly saw mountainous jungle. There was an area with a large outcropping of rocks, but nothing helpful like a sign or village.

"When we pulled up to the compound, I saw what looked like a small airstrip, though," he mentioned.

My ears perked up. "Did you see a plane?"

Carter shook his head. "No, but the grass was worn down like it gets plenty of use."

"That's good," I said, thinking about options.

Carter's hands moved across my body, slick with soap. I closed my eyes and focused on his touch. What had started out as a utilitarian wash turned sensual quickly.

"Fuck," I murmured. "Don't stop touching me." I wrapped an arm around his waist and pulled him closer. Our soft cocks moved against each other, but I was too worn-out to get hard again this fast. That didn't mean I wasn't turned the hell on simply by holding his body against mine.

He pressed a kiss to my shoulder and neck. "Bad idea," he murmured again, moving his lips under my chin to the edge of my jaw.

"Mm-hm. Terrible." I used my hands to tilt his face up until I could kiss his lips. We kissed for a long time. The water beat down on us as we moved through the spray in a languid make-out session. When we finally felt the water cool, I knew it was time to call it a night. "Come on. You're half-asleep."

Carter didn't argue with me. He simply followed me through the tooth-brushing routine until I led him to bed. The crisp, white sheets were cool and fresh, and the mountain air coming in through open windows felt perfect for sleeping.

If only there hadn't been decorative iron scrollwork across the windows too.

I slid into the bed behind Carter and grabbed him up in a spoon position.

"Feels good," he murmured, relaxing against me.

"Mm-hm. Glad you're safe."

"Me too. I was… I was trying to see if I could get some intel, but… I couldn't really find anything useful."

I appreciated his effort to try and be helpful, but I also didn't want him getting himself into trouble in case someone noticed him looking too closely near Gustavo. "We'll figure something out."

"Riggs?" he asked after a few more minutes.

"Yeah?" I pressed a kiss behind his ear. He smelled clean and sleepy. I wanted to kiss him all over just to smell and taste more of him.

"I can't get my brain to slow down."

"Think about something else. Something good."

"I tried that," he said. "It didn't work. I need you to distract me. Tell me a story."

I thought about what I could possibly tell him that would help him relax. Most of my stories were scary and dangerous.

"Where are you from?" he asked. "Do you have a family? What are they like?"

I chuckled and shifted him a little closer, moving my legs between his until they pretzeled together. "You won't believe this, but I'm from Yee Hah, Oregon."

"You're right. I don't believe you."

"Says the man who lives in Licking Thicket," I teased.

"I work in Great Nuthatch," he corrected with a sniff.

"I stand corrected. Anyway, it's a tiny town most famous for our high school mascot, the Fighting Dragons. And before you make fun of them, you need to know that my brother Will once led the Yee Hah Dragons to the state semifinals in wrestling."

The sound of Carter's laughter in the quiet bedroom made my muscles ease. "You're a good storyteller."

"I'm not making this up, I swear." And, honestly, I was surprised by that. I hadn't thought of my job or of Champ's disapproval even once since the moment Carter had walked through the door. I couldn't believe I was sharing shit about my family and my past with a client this way. Yes, I was known for being a big talker, but not usually about stuff that was important to me. Besides, I was having a hard time continuing to think of Carter Rogers as a client.

"Fine. Continue your dragon story."

I kissed his shoulder and thought of what other stories I had from home like it was the most natural thing in the world. "Well, I'm from a long line of Marines. My great-grandfather fought in Iwo Jima in World War II. My grandfather was in the amphibious force in Vietnam. And my dad is still active duty as a recruiter."

"You're kidding?"

"No. And I have three brothers and a sister. Two of my brothers are still active duty Marines, and my sister is an army nurse."

"That snake in the grass," Carter hissed dramatically. He'd heard me gripe about branch competition enough times to know the betrayal my sister had put us through when she'd chosen the army.

I couldn't hold back the laugh. "Exactly. But she said it was her peaceful protest against the Marines' sexism. I can't blame her."

"She sounds tough."

"She is. She can kick any one of our asses and she's only five feet two and like a hundred ten pounds dripping wet."

"Poor thing growing up with four tough guys."

I leaned back on my pillow and pictured Lizzy as a little girl. "Nah. She loved bossing us around and then using us as muscle with her high school boyfriends. She used to threaten to send her goon squad after them if they didn't treat her right."

Carter turned over and propped his head on his hand. "And did she ever follow through?"

I grinned at him. "No, but we took initiative a few times without her knowledge."

Carter laughed and fell back on the bed, covering his face with his hands. "I can't imagine four Marine-types showing up to scare me away from their sister. I would have pissed myself."

"That's about what they did. One guy was absolutely not good enough for her. We convinced him to hit the road. The other two just needed a gentle reminder of how to treat a lady."

Carter turned back to me and put his hand on my chest. "How did they handle you coming out? I can't imagine that would have been easy in a family with such a... traditional history."

I covered his hand in mine. "It probably wouldn't have been, except my grandfather's best friend in Vietnam was gay. Grandpa didn't find out until later, after they were back stateside and got jobs at the same metal machining factory outside of Portland. It was actually my grandma who figured it out and told Grandpa. Grandpa was pissed. Apparently he lit into Dwight, like really tore a strip off the guy."

"He was that angry that his friend was gay?" Carter's forehead crinkled in concern.

I smiled at him and reached out a finger to smooth the crinkles. "No, he was that angry Dwight had never trusted him with the truth. I mostly know the story because I heard Grandma tell my mom about denying Grandpa marital rights for two weeks because of it. I had to ask my mom what marital rights were. I thought it was something like maritime law."

Carter's bark of laughter filled the room before he slapped a palm over his mouth. "Oh my God. Leave it to a little wannabe Marine to think that."

"Needless to say," I muttered, "I didn't appreciate being corrected. I was horrified."

"And so you chose to be gay to get out of having to participate in those pesky rights," he teased, running a hand down my chest to my stomach.

I grabbed his wrist before he got any further. It wasn't because I didn't want more action with him. I definitely did. My need for him only seemed to grow. But he was exhausted. And I wanted him to fall asleep while he was happy and relaxed.

"Exactly," I said. "I vowed right then and there to do whatever it took to avoid marital rights. And that's how I became gay."

We shared another laugh over it until I realized his finger was drawing a lazy loop on my chest. I ran my hand up his arm to the back of his head and leaned in for a soft kiss of his lips. "Go to sleep," I said, planning on holding him only for a few more minutes until I knew he was out.

But his body felt so good in mine as it relaxed into sleep. And the air was cool and fresh. And the day had been long and stressful.

I finally allowed myself to drift off with the promise I'd wake myself in a few hours to strategize.

Being in bed with Carter Rogers was too tempting. So I slept.

10

CARTER

You know that part of the animated *Snow White* where she wakes up and slowly stretches, smiling happily at the thought of another beautiful day?

Yeah, waking up with William "Badass" Riggs was nothing like that.

"Holy fuck!" the man said, sitting bolt upright in bed.

Since I'd been curled up on his pec, half on top of him, this meant I sat up too.

"Wassit?" I demanded, rubbing the sleep from my eyes with one hand while reaching for my phone with the other, ready to respond to the callout from the hospital.

Except there wasn't a callout. And there wasn't any phone.

"What the fuck fucking time is it?" Riggs demanded eloquently, throwing open the door to the empty living room. He grabbed his underwear and pants and dragged both on. "Have they been in here? Have they seen us together?"

"They" I assumed meant Skinny, Glasses, Beardy, or any of Gustavo's other dwarves.

"Um." I scrubbed a hand through my hair, which I was pretty sure had dried in a super-stylish chicken-comb style. "I'm a light sleeper, so I don't believe so. Fairly sure I'd have heard them."

Riggs gave me a withering look. "I'm *usually* a light sleeper. And I'm *always* up by dawn."

He said this accusingly, like he held me personally responsible for having a magic tongue that made him orgasm so hard he'd slept past dawn and missed his sunrise calisthenics.

I guessed this meant there'd be no morning-after repeaty action. Moment of silence for my morning wood's hopes and dreams.

"This is why people don't fuck around on missions," Riggs continued. "It leads to distraction, and we cannot afford distraction." I could have sworn he mumbled something about regretting telling me things, but I chose to ignore him.

I bristled. "Which is what *I* said last night, and you were all, 'Oh, but we're *humans*, Carter. Let's fuck around some more in the shower!'"

Riggs's nostrils flared. "So we agree that this won't happen again. Back to business."

"Obviously it won't happen again," I scoffed. Then ego demanded that I tack on, "Even if you maul me like you did yesterday."

Riggs snorted. "Maul? *Please.*"

"Even if you sink to your knees in front of me and tear off my pants again."

"God." He folded his beefy arms over his extra-beefy chest. "You make it sound like—"

"Even if you're all, 'I vow to you, Carter, that you're not just a job to me! I so ardently wish to touch your penis with my tonsils!' I'm gonna say, 'Thanks, but no thanks, Riggs, 'cause I'm on a *mission*. And I'm all about the fucking *job*.'"

I tossed off the blanket, stalked past Riggs to the living room to get my clothes, then stalked past him again on my way to the bathroom to shower because my hair was seriously out of control.

Riggs, because he was Riggs, interpreted the closed bathroom door as an invitation to follow me.

"I didn't mean to suggest that I was blaming you," he began. "I'm not. I'm blaming myself."

"I'm showering. Go away."

"I seriously never sleep in. *Ever*. It's like my brain has a built-in clock."

"The body's circadian rhythms are a wondrous thing," I agreed. "Go *away*."

"I'm just saying, I was feeling wrong-footed and—"

"And you took it out on me." I pushed the knob to shut off the water after barely wetting my hair, and I reached out a hand to grab a fluffy towel from the rack. "What a charmer you are."

Riggs sighed. "I want to protect you, Carter," he said as I wrapped the towel around my waist and stepped out of the tub. "Not because you're a job, a principal I have to protect, but because you're… you. And I keep *not* doing that. Or not doing it well, anyway. And I'm frustrated with myself. The fact that you're so fucking hot is no excuse."

I pursed my lips. *So fucking hot*, huh? I didn't consider myself a particularly shallow person, but it was hard to stay angry when he put it that way. And more than that, he seemed sincere. His dark eyes were haunted.

"Have you ever had things go wrong with a client?" I asked, forgetting for a second that sharing time was over and we were back to client/bodyguard mode.

His face closed off immediately, whatever doubt I'd imagined I saw immediately hidden behind a blank facade.

I sighed. "Well, for whatever it's worth, I feel very safe with you." I laid a hand on one of his crossed arms. "You're good at your job."

Riggs grunted noncommittally like he believed I was just trying to make him feel better.

"I'm serious. That's part of why *I* slept so hard. I mean, the other part was sheer exhaustion from being on edge all day—I was so tired on my way back from Gustavo's room that I hallucinated someone from Licking Thicket was speaking to me—but I'm being serious when I say the fact that I fell asleep and stayed asleep under *these* circumstances?" I waved a hand around the well-appointed bathroom, which was not nearly so nice when you remembered it was our prison for the time being. "That means you're doing a good job."

Riggs's eyes lightened a little, but he snorted deprecatingly. "Voices, huh? Were they talking about the Thicket's annual milk pail race event thing?"

"I believe you mean the *Lickin' Lope*." I may have sounded a trifle smug since I considered myself something of an expert on all Thicket-related trivia these days. "And no, not that, but close. I could have sworn I heard one of my patients, old Amos Nutter, talking about how Nutters need to be free. Except the only person around besides me and the guards was a middle-aged dude with a mullet who was definitely not old Amos. Have you met Amos?" I grinned at Riggs, who frowned at me in the bathroom mirror. "If you're driving out of Licking Thicket towards the highway, Amos owns the pasture on the right side, near the town sign. He's the one who puts letters on the sides of his cows, and they end up spelling out interesting shit."

I grabbed a toothbrush from the vanity and turned on the faucet.

"Wait, say that part again?"

"Cahws," I garbled around the toothbrush. I spat into the sink. "Er, *cows*. With letters. Like, one time Amos wanted them to spell out 'Field use denied' because kids had been playing ball in his pasture, right? But they rearranged themselves as they grazed, and they spent hours spelling out 'Defile us indeed.' Some people took pictures."

It was possible that I'd been one of those people.

"Not that." Riggs shook his head. "I don't give a shit about the cows. I meant, repeat the part about a Nutter being here in Venezuela."

I snorted. "He's *not*, that's what I'm saying. Amos is eighty-something with a trick hip, and unless you're thinking Santiago's grand plan for world domination involves getting capybaras to spell out rude Spanish words, there's no reason he'd be staying at *el Fortress de Scary Dudes*. I'm saying I was so stressed that I hallucinated Amos's voice as I was walking down the hall near the— Oh! Oh, shit! I forgot to tell you!" I whirled to face Riggs and shook his elbows excitedly. "There was a computer room!"

"What?"

"Yeah, yeah! That's where the-Amos-who-isn't-Amos was. I looked up because I thought I heard Amos Nutter, and I saw this blond guy with a mullet inside a whole room filled with computers and monitors playing *Horn of Glory*— which, okay, now that I think about it, the whole thing might have been a hallucination because everyone knows you can only play it on a handheld Horn." I frowned. "Anyway, it's worth checking out because the room I saw was full of computers and probably internet access, but damn. What had my brain been trying to tell me with that hallucination? Or was the universe trying to send me a message?

If so, I really wish it wouldn't deliver it in Amos Nutter's voice."

Riggs put his hands on my shoulders firmly. "Carter. *Chill.* You're doing that nervous babbling again."

Fuck. "Am I?"

"You are," he confirmed in a low voice that rumbled through my stomach and made me feel unaccountably good. He chafed my upper arms much like he'd done the day before, and I found myself melting into him, wanting to bury my face in his bare chest. I forced myself to stand up straight.

"Okay. Let's try this again." I took a deep breath and recounted all I'd heard and seen in the same detached way that I ran down a patient's health information for another physician. When I was done, Riggs looked more troubled than he had when he'd woken up.

"It was a guy who sounded like Amos Nutter? And it was definitely *Horn of Glory* he was playing?"

"Yeah. Why? Do you think I'm losing it?" I shrugged. "The good news is, I know exactly how to get there from here — six doors down, left turn, four more doors. Bad news is, there's a guard on the door."

"We need to get in that room," Riggs said.

"Yes, obviously. So should we —"

Before I could suggest causing a distraction so Riggs could sneak out, a key jangled in the lock out in the living room.

Riggs pointed at the pile of clothing he'd torn off me the night before, and I gathered it all up while he snapped up his shirt and threw it over his head. It wasn't until I felt the hard outline of the knife I'd scooped up with my clothing that I understood why he was so upset. We'd almost given away our weapon.

Beardy stepped in the door first, brandishing his gun

per usual, and he looked even less pleased to see us than I was to see him. "*¡Ven ahora!*" he commanded without preamble. "*Señor Santiago está muy molesto.*"

I frowned. Santiago was… in pain? Shit. I didn't know what *molesto* meant. When we got back to the States, I was *so* taking Spanish.

Riggs glanced at me. "The boss is angry," he translated. His voice was carefully even, but his eyes flashed a warning. To Beardy, he added, "*¿Molesto? Porque?*"

But if Beardy knew why, he wasn't saying.

"Let me just get dressed." I lifted the ball of clothes and headed back to the bedroom.

"*No.*" Beardy shook his head emphatically. "*Aquí.*"

There? He wanted me to change in front of him? I shot Riggs a panicked look. I wasn't particularly modest, but if I put down the clothes, Beardy would see our knife.

Riggs set his jaw. "*El doctor necesita privacidad,*" he insisted in his You Will Obey Me voice. He stepped between me and Beardy. "Carter, hurry."

I didn't need to be told twice. I scrambled to the bedroom and threw my clothes on, then hesitated over the knife before taking the extra two seconds to attach it to my leg. I seriously doubted I'd ever use it, but it was nice to know it was there. Like a security blanket or something. Plus, if they searched our room while we were gone, I didn't want it found.

When I got back to the living room, Riggs and Beardy were still trying to out-badass each other (Riggs was super winning, though Beardy had the gun), and Glasses had joined them, holding the bag of medical supplies I hadn't seen since I'd run my initial tests on Santiago.

He tossed the bag at my feet for me to pick up.

"Knife's secure," I murmured as I passed Riggs. "Thanks for the distraction."

Riggs blinked, and then his eyes widened, like maybe he hadn't been talking about the knife at all. Like maybe he just hadn't wanted Beardy to see me naked.

Sure. And maybe Gustavo had a parachute he could sell me too.

"Come," Glasses commanded, ushering us out the door with Beardy bringing up the rear. "The boss is extremely angry."

My heart rate picked up as I hurried to follow after him. "Is he worse? I mean, sicker?" I demanded. Maybe sitting up hadn't helped. Maybe he had an ulcer, and maybe the ulcer was—

"No," Glasses said angrily, breaking into my thoughts. "He is better!"

Better? I had to be misunderstanding something.

The answer became clear when we arrived at Santiago's bedchamber. The group of wailing women was there, wailing even more loudly this morning. One was on her knees with her hands clenched in front of her as she sobbed. Two others clung together, hunched over and weeping into each other's embrace. A fourth woman clutched her stomach as she murmured something unintelligible to the ceiling.

And Señor Santiago? He sat—like a king, as instructed—in the center of his enormous bed, looking...

Perfectly healthy, actually. Rosy-cheeked. Pain-free.

"Sir. I'm so glad to see you looking so much better!" I exclaimed, striding toward the bed.

"Silence!" he roared, stopping me in my tracks. "Dr. Carter, my Lucrecia here has reminded me that this 'sitting like a king' that you have suggested is the very same thing that the *first* stupid doctor suggested. *¿Verdad, Lucrecia?*"

The standing woman clutched her stomach harder and pressed the other fist to her mouth like she might vomit.

Her eyes were wild. She babbled an apologetic denial and shot me an imploring look.

"How can it be that the idiot doctor who misdiagnosed me has prescribed me the same treatment as you, Dr. Carter? I am surrounded by incompetence!" Santiago's face was an apoplectic red, and veins protruded from his forehead. Had he had an actual heart condition, this situation would have been very dangerous for him.

Since he didn't, it was very dangerous for me. And for Riggs.

And possibly Lucrecia, who'd pointed out the correlation.

I swallowed hard. "Señor!" I shot back angrily. "You must calm yourself! You have one of the worst cases of pyrosis I have ever encountered, and this excitement will not help! I'm glad you're feeling better this morning, but you simply cannot risk your important self with all this stress."

Santiago narrowed his eyes and lifted his chin. "One of the worst cases, you say?"

"If not the *very* worst," I confirmed. "A lesser man would not be experiencing such a remarkable—but no doubt temporary—recovery. Should you actually go into cardiac arrest, there would be very few things I could do to help you," I went on, as though pyrosis and a heart attack were in any way related. "Just yesterday, I nearly lost a patient with a serious heart condition who needs to be seen at a cath lab in Caracas, but the facilities are so crowded, I couldn't get her seen even if I could get her to the city. I would not want to explain to your beautiful, er… *ladies* that I could not save you."

Santiago darted a glance at his women and huffed out a breath. "Explain, then, why this trick of yours worked on my debilitating heart condition."

Because you don't have a debilitating heart condition, you fucking—

Riggs cleared his throat, probably reminding me to keep my temper, and I glanced behind me. He was standing way closer than I'd thought, almost looming over me.

Though he looked none too pleased with me and was probably cursing me for telling Santiago to sit up straight—even though I had no way of knowing Santiago would associate it with his first doctor—his hovering felt protective and sort of lovely. Far more comforting than it should have been.

There are a limited number of people in the world I'd save from a rampaging capybara…

"It's because your blood didn't have to pump as hard while you were sitting up," Riggs lied smoothly. "This is well-known."

I wasn't sure how much English Lucrecia knew, but she nodded like a bobblehead, corroborating his lie, and that's when I noticed that although she *did* look nauseous, she wasn't clutching her stomach like it hurt. In fact, she was actually rubbing the protruding bump of it. Almost… almost protectively. In fact, very extremely protectively.

Realization struck. "And!" I exclaimed. "You must be even more cautious if you are about to have *un bebé*! *Muchas felicidades* to you and Lucrecia."

The assembled ladies gasped in surprise and stared at one another.

Santiago blinked at me for one beat, and then his face turned purple again. "You mock me, Dr. Carter? I have explained to you the facts of my condition, the curse of my all-powerful seed, and you would use this information to—"

"No, no!" I glanced at Lucrecia, whose eyes were wide, and I realized I'd either been totally wrong or I'd totally spoiled the surprise. *Damn it.* "I mean. I mean, I may have misunderstood—"

The man gasped, and his gaze swung toward Lucrecia.

"Is this true, Lucrecia? Has Gustavo's seed rooted itself within you? Is it even now ripening into a youthful virile man like myself who will one day be the heir to all the Santiago holdings?" He cast an arm wide, encompassing the house and the mountain, possibly all of Venezuela.

For the sake of his dependents, I *really* hoped Gustavo was better at crime than he was at metaphors. And I noted that he was talking about himself in the third person again, damn it.

Lucrecia nodded slowly and forced a smile. "*¡Sorpresa!*"

"*Oh my God! Felicidades!*" Gustavo breathed. He tossed aside his heavy covers and stood—all five feet of him—before hurrying to Lucrecia and hugging her tightly.

It was very, *very* moving. Or it would have been. If not for, you know, the whole imminent death thing.

"Sir, if you'd like, I could speak to Lucrecia after your men show me to the lab so I can begin testing your blood samples," I offered. "Prenatal care is so important. Especially, um, in a case involving… this."

I tried to make myself say "the miracle spawn of your ultra-powerful seed," but I could not get there.

Gustavo waved me away. "Yes, of course. Only the best for precious Lucrecia and Gustavo's heir."

We followed Beardy out of the room with me still hauling our backpack of supplies. When we reached the same corridor where I'd heard Amos the night before, I paused and jerked my head toward his door.

Riggs nodded once, and we kept walking.

Then a voice said, "Ah, goldurnit! Now you've gone and made this whole thing higgledy-piggledy! I told you fools, the magic ain't in the seed, it's in the Nutter!"

"*Oh my God.* Do you hear that?" I breathed. If not, the universe was talking to me about Gustavo's miracle child, and I wasn't sure how I felt about that.

"Holy shit," Riggs whispered. He squeezed his eyes shut. "It can't be. It was supposed to be *Mexico.*"

But whatever was supposed to be in Mexico, the look on his face suggested, was right here.

"What's in Mexico?" I demanded. "Do you know who that is? Do you think he can get us out of here?"

"What? No. Nothing." Riggs shook his head slowly. "Not a clue. But you're right. He definitely sounds American."

"*¡Mueve!*" Beardy shouted. "*¡Callate!*"

I frowned. "But—"

"You heard the man," Riggs said, pushing me forward gently. "Move it along and keep quiet."

11

———————

RIGGS

When the guards led us to some kind of small employee break room with a muttered comment about using it as a lab space for the doctor, my mind was reeling with what I'd just found.

Buck Nutter was *here*. Here in Venezuela. Here at Gustavo Santiago's hidden compound.

Well, I'll be damned. Kandi was right.

A drug lord really had stolen her brother. But what would a guy like Santiago want with a video game access code? Was he hoping to hold the game hostage? Make HOG Corporate pay?

And what were the chances we'd stumbled onto the same drug lord? Especially considering the idiot in the bed did not have the intelligence to be a major player in the cartel. Was Gustavo playing us? Or was someone else pretending to be him? The way he kept referring to himself in the third person sure made it seem like that. Did it matter?

If I could find a way to get both Buck and Carter out of

here, I might be able to redeem myself in Champ's eyes, earn back the right to take my place in the auricle implant program, and maybe even smooth things over with Jacob Horn and the Horn of Glory folks.

But that meant I had to think. I opened my mouth to explain before shutting it again with a snap. Champ had warned me time and time again not to talk about clients to others. Did this count?

In the end, I decided it didn't really matter. Carter was a nervous babbler. I couldn't risk telling him about Buck in case he said something in front of the guards. Besides, it appeared one of the guards had made himself at home on a chair in the corner of the room. He glared at me like he expected me to eat his lunch out of the employee fridge.

I looked around at the small break room. It was half-kitchenette, half-lounge space, with old, battered sofas, a hand-me-down table and chairs, and three different coffee makers on the counter. Santiago clearly didn't lavish his guards in luxury the way he did his guests, even the prisoner guests.

"What am I supposed to do now?" Carter whispered. "They took the blood samples from me last night to store them. I don't have them."

I glanced at the guard again. "*¿Donde estan las muestras de sangre?*" *Where are the blood samples?*

He nodded in the direction of the fridge. Great. They'd been stored next to someone's ham sandwich.

I stepped toward the fridge and opened the door. Thankfully, the only thing in there was the plastic baggie with two vials of blood in it. I pulled it out and set it on the counter. "Now what?"

Carter shot me a nervous look. "The simple stuff takes ten seconds which is too... ah... quick. As for a more complex assay, I don't usually do those myself." He dropped the medical backpack on the table and began to sort through it. "Even in Gelada, we sent them out to a lab in Socopó, remember?"

I did. Carter had a handheld bloodwork analyzer to do some simple tests, but the more complex bloodwork orders had been sent to a lab.

"Do the best you can," I said softly. "It doesn't really, uh…" I glanced at the guard again and was surprised to find him holding a *Horn of Glory* console. His attention was clearly on the game. "It doesn't really matter," I continued, "if he has what you think he has, right?"

"True."

"Just make it look good," I said in an even softer tone.

He busied himself pulling out vials and pipettes, a little stand to hold the vials, bandages and alcohol wipes, blood-draw kits, and anything else that could make his little lab operation look legit. He finally grabbed his handheld analyzer and began working. I stepped up close to him at the counter and tried to look like I was assisting him so I could talk to him without the guard overhearing.

Carter's hands stayed busy, but his eyes flicked up at me through his lashes. "So… Gustavo was angry."

I wanted to comfort him, hold him tightly and reassure him everything was going to be okay, but I couldn't. At least, not in front of the guard while we were supposed to be working.

"Why the hell did you treat him like he had heartburn?" I hissed, remembering my reaction when I realized he'd had Santiago propped up on pillows. "I told you to buy us some time. He's going to kill you if he thinks you're the same as that other doctor."

Honestly, I wasn't nearly as worried about the man himself as I was about the guards with the giant guns. But either way, Carter needed to stop being such a damned do-gooder.

His hands shook, and I could have kicked myself for griping at him. His voice was breathy. "I couldn't stand seeing him in pain when I knew a way to help alleviate it. I'm… I'm sorry, okay? You called me a control freak the first time we met, and you're right. I'm usually more level-headed, but it drives me crazy when I can't fix things. I don't know why I can't keep it together better."

I let out a breath. I needed to remember Carter wasn't used to dangerous situations like I was. He wasn't trained for this. I stepped closer until our arms touched. "No, I'm the one who's sorry. I just don't want you hurt. I'm trying to protect you, but you have to help me out here." I tried to think of a way to distract him. "How did you know that lady was pregnant? That was some quick thinking."

He allowed himself a small smile. "She did that stomach-rubbing thing pregnant women do, and when we first came into the room, it looked like she was on the verge of hurling." He shrugged. "Lucky guess."

"Lucky is right. One time I gave up my seat on the tube in London to a woman I thought was pregnant. She kicked me in the nuts and told me to fuck off."

Carter snorted and glanced at me with dancing eyes. "You're kidding?"

"No. I learned a valuable lesson that day."

"Never assume a woman is pregnant, even if they're a day away from delivering the baby?" Carter suggested.

"That, and always wear a cup on public transport."

Hearing his soft chuckle made my shoulders relax like they were under the hard, pounding spray of a hot shower. I wanted to hear more, so I kept talking. "Then there was the time I accidentally proposed to a man during a military operation."

Carter's head whipped around. "You're kidding? How do you accidentally propose?"

"Believe it or not, I was asking for someone nicknamed the Butcher. Apparently 'butcher' and 'marry' are very close in Romanian. The man and his friends were not happy with me."

Carter went back to what he was doing, but I could feel his body relaxing against mine. After a few minutes, he told his own story.

"Speaking of proposals, you know how my ex got married recently?"

Oh, I knew. Carter talked about Dr. Tucker Wright—now Tucker Johnson—a lot. A *lot* a lot.

Tucker was sweet. Tucker was handsome. Tucker was hilarious. Tucker was so smart he could probably solve crossword puzzles without even reading the clues. Tucker was one of the reasons Carter had moved from his fancy life in Nashville to the backwoods of nowhere.

Not that I was *jealous* of the guy! Obviously. For one thing, Tucker was happily married. For another, Carter and I weren't like that. I just thought it was interesting that a person could have such positive, friendly feelings for their ex-boyfriend. I was worried about Carter's well-being, that was all.

"Yeah, married to the dairy farmer with the pet hog. I remember."

"Well, I believe the proposal involved reference to corn rotting on the cob." He smiled in a fond little way. "Remind me not to marry anyone from the Thicket, I guess."

I watched his forehead crinkle in concentration as he maneuvered a pipette onto a slide. As if we had a microscope. "Hey, are Dunn and Tucker the couple you were watching at the gala?"

He glanced over at me. "You saw me watching them dance?"

I nodded. "And I overheard you talking to the bartender."

"Mpfh. Well… it…" He stopped and sighed, pretending to focus on the slide he was preparing.

"You, ah… you still have feelings for him? The ex?" I asked, feeling uneasy. When I'd seen him watching the couple on the dance floor, I could tell he was envious of something.

"No. Not really. I mean, I love Tucker. He's a good man. But he needed Dunn to spice up his life and keep him on his toes. Sometimes being a doctor can get… overwhelming. No, that's not the right word." He paused and stared at the wall for a second. "*Dark.* Sometimes it gets dark. And Dunn doesn't do dark. He's the life of the party, always making Tucker laugh and pushing him out of his comfort zone. It's a nice escape from practicing medicine."

I tried to figure out what he meant by that. "But you don't think you'd like someone like Dunn? A Thicket-living corncob-proposing farmer-type?" I was teasing, but I kind of wanted to know what it was about those two that had put the envy in his eyes.

"God, no. Jesus. Dunn is a little too much Tennessee for me. Not that I don't like Tennesseans. He's just… he's…"

"A country boy," I suggested.

"No. He's like an eager puppy. He'll do anything for Tucker."

His hands were still shaking, and he spilled a little alcohol from the bottle he'd opened. I reached for the paper towels to clean it up.

"You don't want someone who'd do anything for you," I said.

"Stop trying to interpret what I'm saying," Carter said, clearly frustrated. "Of course I want someone like that. I just don't want to be with someone I could walk all over. Tucker could walk all over Dunn, and Dunn would thank him for it."

"I think that's kind of sweet," I admitted. "Sounds like they're really in love."

He sighed and closed the alcohol bottle before stashing it back in the backpack. "Yeah. Crazy in love, in a way that works perfectly for them. Dunn gives Tucker what Tucker needs. I want someone who gives me what I need. Someone who'll put me first. Someone who'd save me from a rampaging capybara—"

I didn't think he'd intended to admit something like that out loud to me, but once it was out there, the air between us thickened. Carter's shoulders stiffened.

"Never mind," he muttered. "I didn't mean *you*."

Of course he hadn't meant me, but hearing it spoken was a kick in the gut anyway. "'Course not," I mumbled, busying myself packing other supplies back in the pack.

Carter glanced at me. The anxiety was clear in his expression. "Not that you wouldn't be a great boyfriend. I'm sure you would. I didn't mean it like—"

I held up a hand. "I'm fine. I promise."

"Besides, Tucker once told me I'm not the settling-down type." Carter shrugged. "Maybe he was right."

"Same. A long-term relationship in my line of work would be nearly impossible. Can you imagine someone being fine with the fact that I'm gone on assignment nearly as much as I'm around?" I shook my head. A boyfriend would expect me to make sacrifices. Especially if it were someone like him.

He kept eying me while he continued to pretend to do a blood test. A glance at the guard revealed him to be too engaged in a rousing game of *Horn of Glory* to pay much attention to us.

"Riggs..." Carter began.

"Let's just focus on this," I said, hoping like hell to put an end to this excruciating conversation.

Carter went back to his work. After a few more minutes, he couldn't leave it alone. "So... you don't want to fall in love? It's not the same thing as settling down, you know. You could always..."

I didn't want to talk about love with Carter Rogers. This entire conversation made me feel itchy and raw. "Love is fine. If it happens, it happens."

"They should put that on a greeting card," Carter teased.

The guard's voice made Carter jump. *"El equipo está en el gabinete."*

Carter glanced at me with a frown. I told him, "The equipment is in the cabinet." I began opening cabinet doors until I found a microscope and some other items. Shit. They'd actually gotten what he'd asked for.

Carter spotted the equipment and plastered on a fake smile. "Ah, *gracias.*"

I pulled out the microscope and the item he'd called an autoclave. He busied himself looking at his slide and making notes on a piece of paper. It looked like calculus problems to me. When he finished fake-microscoping, he began fake-autoclaving. He prepared several tiny vials for the machine and then set them to run before glancing back at the guard.

"Tell him we're done for several hours," he said to me. "These need time to... cure. Or whatever."

I bit my lip against a grin and turned to the guard. *"Hemos terminado por ahora. Las pruebas toman tiempo."*

He grunted and stood up, slipping his game into a cargo pocket in his pants. "Come," he barked.

The guard joined one who'd been stationed outside the break room before the two of them escorted us back to our rooms and closed the door behind us.

"Okay, now that we're alone, spill. What weren't you telling me?" Carter hissed as soon as the guards were gone.

"About what?" I asked, even though I knew what he meant. We'd heard the American on the way to the "lab," but since the guard had been with us the entire time, we hadn't been able to talk about it.

"The 'holy shit' you blurted earlier, like you'd discovered something when we passed the computer room. Was it a way in? And what were you saying about Mexico?"

"Mexico? Did I say that? Huh. I can't remember. But that guy is an American," I said stupidly. I was a horrible liar in the spur of the moment.

Carter tilted his head at me and narrowed his eyes. "Duh. Was it the 'goldurnit' that tipped you off or the 'higgledy-piggledy'?"

"No, I mean… you were right in what you said earlier. Maybe he can help us. Maybe he can give us access to those computers. Maybe he's on our side."

I could only hope. But then again, what if Buck was voluntarily working for Santiago? What if he'd sold him the seed and was working for him as part of the deal? Surely not. But we'd have to be careful regardless.

Carter threw the medical supply bag down on the velvet sofa and slumped down next to it. "And how do you propose we do that when we're guarded all the time?"

"I need to think."

"By all means. But think fast because I can't turn heartburn into parasitic myocarditis no matter how common Chagas disease is around here."

I ignored him and wandered over to the window to peer out. From here, I could see a courtyard with creeping pink trumpet flowers planted in pots and climbing on columns. There was a large, sparkling blue pool behind the house and to the left, which led me to believe we were in an east wing. Dense trees started off to my far right, but the area ahead, beyond the pool, was clear of trees. A corner of what I assumed was the landing strip was visible in the far left distance. I couldn't see enough of the area to determine whether there was a plane or not.

I didn't see any sign of a path or access road from here. The road we came in on might have been the only way in or out besides the runway. Or unless you had sturdy boots and a machete.

But if I could get word out… maybe my crew could figure out where we were and bring in a plane.

"What I would give for a sat phone right now," I muttered, beginning to pace.

Carter sat up and snapped his fingers. "You can use my Horn!"

I shot him a look. "Thanks, but I thought maybe I'd try and figure out an escape plan instead of taking a video game break. We really need to focus on this right now, Duchess."

He rolled his eyes. "No, listen," he said, grabbing the med bag and rifling through it. "My Horn is special. It has upgrades. It's tricked-out."

I winked at him. "I can't disagree with that. Bah-dum-bum."

Carter sighed in disgust. "Stop. I'm being serious." He found what he was looking for and pulled it out of the bag in triumph. His purple sparkly Horn console looked as useless as ever. "Let me show you how to use it."

I couldn't help but tease him a little more. "I'm familiar

with your fancy horn. Pretty sure I showed you last night…"

"*My HOG has a sat link,*" he snapped.

I stared at him as the words sunk in. Suddenly, I was striding across the room to grab the device. "Holy shit. *Holy shit.*"

"Yeah, that's what I mean. We can contact my cousin and ask for help."

I sat next to him and handed it back. "Get it started, and then let me talk to him."

He powered on the game and opened the messaging page to type out his first message.

KevsCuz: *I'm being held hostage by a Venezuelan drug lord.*

"Kev's Cuz?" I lifted an eyebrow.

"Two guesses who came up with my username." Carter shrugged. "Kev says being related to him gives me cred. He's a pretty well-known player, I guess."

HogDocKev: *Carter!! YAY! Hey, what level are you on? I've defeated orcs, trolls, moon kittens, zombies, fae, and clowns, but I haven't encountered any drug lords. Also, can you bring me down some chips?*

"What the fuck?" I asked.

Carter sighed. "He thinks I'm talking about the game, and he's clearly forgotten I haven't lived at our grandfather's house in half a year."

KevsCuz: *I'm in Venezuela. No, I cannot bring you chips. I need help.*

HogDocKev: *Sick!! I've been waiting for you to ask me for help for YEARS. So did you run out of pips? Remember, you can get cheat codes. Also, if there's no chips, can you see if we have popcorn? Or we could get pizza. My treat.*

KevsCuz: *Kev. Focus. I'm not talking about the game. I'm literally in a drug lord's compound in the mountains north of Socopó, Venezuela. I need your help.*

"Fuck this," I said, grabbing the Horn. I began typing my own message.

KevsCuz: *Contact Huxley at 615-555-0102. Give him this username and tell him Riggs needs him in this chat ASAP.*

HogDocKev: *Fine. If you think there's someone who can help you with this game more than I can...*

Carter grabbed the device back.

KevsCuz: *KEVIN!*

HogDocKev: *OK, I sent him a text.*

A notification popped up on the screen asking permission to add "HogMasterHux" to the chat. I rolled my eyes and clicked to accept. Carter's cousin messaged again before Hux could.

HogDocKev: *Ah, crap nuggets. No way are you getting help from HogMaster! Trust me, you do not want any part of this gourd-hoarder, Carter!*

HogMasterHux: *Well, well, well. HogDoc, we meet again.*

HogDocKev: *Up yours, you two-pip eggplant bandit. You're an insult to the game!*

I turned to Carter. "What's a two-pip eggplant bandit?"

He frowned. "I think it's someone who destabilizes the eggplant market by selling them really cheap? Or Kev just made it up. Either/or."

I took the device and began typing.

KevsCuz: *Can we focus? Hux, this is Riggs. Best guess, my client and I are being held 200 klicks north, northwest of Socopó.*

HogMasterHux: *Let me read Champ in.*

There was no way I was letting Champ know what kind of shit I'd gotten our client in until we were safely out of it.

KevsCuz: *No. Remember that op in Riga?*

HogMasterHux: *Oh, 10-4. What do you need?*

HogDocKev: *WHAT LEVEL IS THIS? Who's Champ? Because I guarantee, I can beat him.*

I sighed and typed.

KevsCuz: *Thanks for your help, Kev. We don't need you anym —*

Carter tried to grab the Horn out of my hand, but I accidentally hit Send before finishing the message. "What the hell?" I asked.

"Ah, now you've done it. You've hurt his feelings! He's very sensitive."

I could tell by the concerned look on his face, Carter was being serious. I squeezed his knee. "I'm sorry. I didn't know." Our eyes met for a beat, but then the device pinged with a new message.

HogMasterHux: *Who has you?*

KevsCuz: *Gustavo Santiago. And there's more. I found the magic seed.*

Of course Carter's cousin popped back in at that.

HogDocKev: *That's impossible! No one's gotten to that level yet. Is it in Riga? Does this Champ person know how to get there? Is he part of Big HOG?*

Carter sighed. "Kev's really into HOG conspiracy theories. He reads the message boards."

HogMasterHux: *The Magic Seed… Is there in Venezuela… With you.*

Carter leaned closer until I could smell the familiar scent of his skin. "What's he talking about? Is that the skeleton key into the game that Kev mentioned at the gala the other night?"

Shit. This meant that Buck's attempt to sell the seed had gotten him noticed by more than just Gustavo?

I made a sound implying he needed to hold on while I continued talking to Hux.

KevsCuz: *Long story bro.*

HogMasterHux: *Extraction plan?*

KevsCuz: *Yes, please.*

I told him everything I knew so far about how many

guards we'd seen, what kind of weapons they had, how incompetent Gustavo himself seemed, and the health nonissue he was dealing with.

KevsCuz: *Needless to say, there are plenty of challenges.*

HogDocKev: *Not to mention the turnip blight scheduled for tonight…*

HogMasterHux: *Dammit, HogDoc, we're not talking about the game!*

HogDocKev: *Obviously. But my point is, you'll lose comms tonight during the hard reset.*

I looked up at Carter. "Do you understand what they're talking about?"

He shook his head. "Don't think so?"

HogMasterHux: *Shit, Kev's right.*

HogDocKev: **eyeroll emoji**

Carter snorted softly. "Kev hates that they haven't integrated the emoji keyboard into the game yet."

KevsCuz: *Why a hard reset?*

I wondered if it had something to do with Buck being here. The timing was awfully coincidental. What if the hard reset gave Buck the kind of access he needed to screw something up in the game using the seed?

I still couldn't figure out what that would have to do with a Venezuelan drug lord, though. What would the cartel want with a video game? Why kidnap a developer? What could it mean?

Hux and Kev both responded with explanations about HOG doing a hard reset for a large upgrade or important patch. I kept typing.

KevsCuz: *Could that have anything to do with the Magic Seed?*

HogMasterHux: *Whoa. Whoaaaa.*

HogDocKev: *Can someone clue me in here? What does the*

Magic Seed have to do with a Venezuelan drug lord kidnapping my cousin?

Carter turned to me. "Good question. What's going on? What's the magic seed? I thought it had something to do with the game?"

I hesitated, trying to figure out where to even start. How did I explain that the originator of the game code had absconded with a critical back door to the entire inner workings of the game, and now that back door seemed to be in the hands of a very dangerous drug cartel? And how could I explain it when I had no idea the significance of Gustavo Santiago's connection to it in the first place? Or whether this truly was Gustavo Santiago?

Carter's brows furrowed at my delayed response, but before I could say anything, a piercing shriek rent the air. It sounded like someone was being slaughtered.

I raced to the door and put my ear against it to determine what was going on. Carter jumped up and began shoving things back into the med bag. Heavy boot steps came running toward our room, and the door was flung open. I barely jumped back in time to avoid being knocked on my ass.

"*¡Doctor, ven con nosotros ahora!*" *Doctor, come with us now.*

I shot a glance at Carter, whose face had morphed from confused hostage to competent, controlled doctor as he hustled over with the backpack and asked for a sitrep. "What is it? What's happening?"

"*Es el hombre de la computadora. El esta herido.*"

"The computer guy is hurt," I said in case he didn't catch it.

"Why? How? What happened? Was that him screaming?" Carter peppered the guards with questions, but they clearly didn't understand a word he was asking. Instead of answering him, they grabbed him by the arms and carried him out. I tried to grab him back from their hold, but one of the guards shoved me back.

Carter let out a cry of distress and turned back to help me, but the guards pulled him down the hall. "Riggs!" he called.

"Coming," I said, scrambling to catch up.

I raced along behind them, not daring to leave his side. There was no telling what someone like Gustavo would do when faced with a doctor who might or might not have the ability to save their important hostage.

And I needed to be prepared for anything.

12

CARTER

Glasses and Skinny drag-carried me down the carpeted stairs, across a wood-paneled hallway, through an opulent dining room, and down yet another hallway to an enormous kitchen of the sort you'd expect to find in a fancy restaurant. The floor was covered in terra-cotta tiles, but all the countertops were stainless steel, and the appliances were high-end commercial-grade stuff. On the stove, steam puffed out from beneath the lid of a gigantic pot.

No one in the kitchen noticed, however, because all of them—two women, plus Beardy, Silent, and a couple of guys I didn't recognize—were all clustered around a scarred wooden worktable in the center of the space where the blond, mulleted dude I'd seen the night before was laid out, bleeding profusely from a gash on his leg.

"Move back," I commanded Beardy, who'd decided the best way to deal with a badly injured man was to wave his gun around.

Silent had been attempting to wrap a tourniquet around Mullet Guy's upper leg while Mullet flailed against the two women restraining his shoulders and wailed in pain.

"Oh, sweet Jesus! Oh, grits 'n gravy! You best watch yourself, buddy, because without these ladies holding me down, I'd be on you like a duck on a June bug, and then you'd be sorry!"

I made a shooing motion and moved all of them away too. "Give the poor man room to breathe! *Muévete* away from the table."

"Dude," the injured man said, turning pleading eyes on me. "You're a doctor? A real one?"

"Very real," I assured him. "Riggs, ask the guys for some of the water boiling on the stove and to get me some very clean cloths." I knew without looking that he was right behind me because I could sense him there, an oasis of calm in an ocean of chaos.

Sure enough, Riggs relayed my words in rapid, some-what-halting Spanish.

"Rags and boilin' water?" Mullet demanded. "I ain't with child, son. You *sure* you're a doctor?"

"Positive. How'd you hurt your leg?" I demanded. I whipped my own polo shirt over my head, thankful I still had a T-shirt underneath, so I could wipe away the blood and make sure there was no debris in the wound.

"Weeeeell, you might say this has been coming on for years. I always knew I was destined for greatness. You see, I was born—"

Dealing with the monologuing drug lord was bad enough. The last thing I needed was for *all* my patients to start monologuing.

"More recently," I snapped.

"Well… One night a couple weeks ago, I stopped by the Dairy Queen, 'cause I love me a sundae—"

"More recently than that," I demanded. "Within the last twenty minutes."

"I fell out the upstairs window and cut my leg on a ding-dang metal spike embedded in the ground," he admitted grudgingly.

"He was trying to escape," Glasses said.

"Now I told you fellas, it was an accident!" Mullet insisted in a deep drawl. "I wasn't *escapin'!* Heck, nah. I was just… just pacing near my open window upstairs when a breeze come along and carried me —"

"So you might have other injuries besides this one?" I interrupted.

"Well, no. Or maybe yes? The right side of my butt hurts awful bad, come to think. D'you s'pose I broke my ass?"

"Doubtful," I informed him, especially given the way he was moving around. "But you might have bruised yourself pretty badly. I couldn't say whether anything's broken without an X-ray."

I rummaged through the medical bag while one of the guards set down a large bowl of water and a stack of clean rags. "Riggs, could you — ?"

"On it," Riggs said, dipping a rag in the water.

"Okay, but first make sure you —"

"Test the temperature? It's fine," he assured me. "Not too hot."

I nodded, grateful that he and I were so in sync with this. I'd worked with medical professionals who'd required more instruction.

Then again, I had no idea what Riggs's training might have been, did I? Because he hadn't told me. Just like I had no idea why he'd been so excited when we overheard Mullet Dude in the upstairs hall earlier. And no idea if I'd really hurt his feelings when we were in the lab.

I tried to push all of that aside and focus on the patient, but it was difficult. I wasn't sure hot and cold described the way William Riggs was with me anymore; it was more like boiling and frigid. There were moments when it felt like we were sharing something *real*, a connection that was about more than just sex or danger, but actual respect and appreciation. I'd found myself telling him things about my family, things about my past—stuff I didn't share with most people… or really *anyone*—and he'd responded exactly the way I hadn't known I needed someone to respond, with a commiserating look and a matter-of-fact attitude that said "I see you, but I don't pity you."

He'd shared stories about his family or about the missions he'd been on, but I wanted more than the facts and the funny anecdotes. I wanted to know how he felt about things—about his family and being in the Marines, about his job at Champion Security, about our chances of getting away from Gustavo. About *me*. But it felt like whenever I'd try to actually talk about feelings, he'd blank his expression, clutch his badass, commando pearls, and splutter about how we *weren't meant to be friends, Carter*.

Why did that bother me so damn much?

I grabbed my flashlight so I could check Mullet's pupils, but I glanced at Riggs out of the corner of my eye as I did my exam. He irrigated the man's wounds with a firm hand and a reassuring smile. He was just so freakin' competent. So *trustworthy*. I couldn't help wanting him to trust me in return.

After Riggs finished cleaning the wound, I began swabbing it down with Betadine to disinfect it, and of course Mullet kept complaining.

"Sweet Jimmie Johnson! What the hell d'you think you're doin' with that brown stuff there, friend?" Mullet Dude attempted to scramble away, even when he would have scrambled himself right off the table and onto the floor. "You're making it worse! You're injurin' my injury!"

"I'm trying to save your leg," I shot back, which was an

exaggeration, yes, but if it kept him still, I was beyond caring. "By all means, please keep moving around."

That shut Mullet Dude up. At least until I began the sutures. I hadn't known a single human could make so much noise.

"*¡Ay, Dios!*" Gustavo appeared at the doorway to the kitchen wearing a silk dressing gown, Lucrecia on his arm, just as I finished the final stitch. "*¿Que esta pasando?*" He snapped his fingers at one of the guards. "Alessandro!"

The guard cocked his head.

"Alejandro," Gustavo ventured.

The guard tilted his head in the other direction.

"Alberto?" Gustavo guessed.

"Luis, Señor Santiago," the guard corrected.

"Really? Hmm." Gustavo pursed his lips, then shrugged. "Luis!" he said, as though he'd known the name all along. "*¿Que esta pasando?*"

I shot Riggs a glance, and he responded with a wide-eyed look. Seriously, how could the man not remember *any* of his associates' names?

Luis answered back in rapid-fire Spanish, gesturing upstairs and outside angrily before finally pointing at Mullet and then at me.

"Doctor!" Gustavo said. "What is happening?"

I looked up from the bandage I was applying to Mullet's leg and shrugged. "This man fell from a second-story window and cut his—"

Riggs's enormous, booted foot pressed firmly on mine where Gustavo couldn't see it, and when I glanced up at him, he gave me a significant look.

"Señor Santiago wants the truth, Dr. Carter. You don't need to lie to stop him from worrying."

"Er. Right." I licked my lips. "The truth is, this

gentleman has a severe laceration to the posterior portion of his left lower extremity."

Santiago gasped and pressed a hand to his chest. He looked at Mullet with wide eyes. "My God. But he's so young!"

"Severe lassy-who?" Mullet demanded. "*Shiiit.* I thought it was just a bad cut!"

I pushed my lips together. "He also has probable contusions and a possible hematoma in his, uh… his gluteal area."

"You really *are* a doctor," Mullet breathed.

"Oh!" Gustavo wiped a hand over his forehead. His skin looked clammy. "I cannot… Can you save him? This man, he has a crucial job that must be performed tonight. It cannot be delayed. If he is not able to do it, Gustavo will be furious!"

Back to the third-person thing again?

Gustavo clutched Lucrecia's hand and leaned against her. "Can you heal him, Doctor?"

"I'll try my best," I said solemnly. "Er. Nurse Riggs, please assist me in putting on this bandage and turning the patient over."

Gustavo took a step closer, like he wanted an up-close view of the proceedings. "No, Señor," I said with a shake of my head. "We'll need to concentrate. And with your condition, you should be sitting down and keeping cool."

Gustavo's nostrils flared, and he clapped his hands. "Luis, Rodrigo! You heard the man! Help me into throne position, or I shall *die!* Teresa! *¡Enfriarme!*"

A woman I assumed must be Teresa—or had decided to respond to that name, anyway—grabbed a fan and began waving it at him.

Riggs leaned close as he pretended to help me apply some gauze and a Tegaderm patch to Mullet's leg. "We need to get out of this place," he whispered. "*Now,* while we're out of our rooms and Santiago's got the guards distracted. If we follow the river on the west side of the property, it'll lead us down the mountain. I saw it from my window. We can send someone back for this guy."

"Send them back?" Mullet Dude squeaked. "Aw, come on!"

I shook my head at Riggs. "We can't leave him." I nodded at Mullet Dude. "They might kill him."

Mullet Dude pointed a finger at me. "Good call, Doc. Smart choice."

"Then I'll put him over my shoulder," Riggs whispered. "I'll carry him down."

"Ohhhh," Mullet Dude said. "Even *better* choice. I'm with you, big guy."

"You're gonna carry him down the mountain and… what?" I hissed as softly as I could. "Keep carrying him for ten *hours* over hard terrain until we can get to a big city?"

Riggs ground his teeth together.

"You know what? You make a compelling point, Doc. That doesn't sound comfortable at *all*," Mullet Guy agreed. "I'm back on Team Doctor."

I rolled my eyes at him, then tilted my head to one side and stared at Riggs. "You said yesterday that the smartest thing to do was wait for reinforcements, right? That's why we haven't already busted out of here? So let's get on the Horn, make sure the reinforcements are on their way, and wait for them."

"That was the smartest plan *before*," Riggs began. He returned my stare, and I couldn't begin to guess at the thoughts flying behind his eyes. "Carter, I can't—"

"Please," I whispered. "I know you want to do this by the book, but I couldn't help Marisol's grandmother. I need to make sure he doesn't exacerbate this injury, Riggs."

Riggs made a frustrated noise. "Fine. *Fine*. But if we're staying, you'll do exactly what I say, exactly when I say it."

I nodded solemnly. "I promise."

"I don't believe you even a little," Riggs grumbled. "You know, honesty is critical on a mission like this."

"I'm being honest. I've *been* honest. Trust me, Riggs," I begged.

I wasn't sure if Riggs knew I wanted him to trust me about so much more than just staying behind.

But either way, he sighed and reluctantly nodded, which was when all hell broke loose on the *other* side of the kitchen.

"Doctor!" Teresa called. "*¡Ayúdalo!*"

I turned my head to see Santiago slumped over in his chair. *Jesus*. What now?

I grabbed my medical bag and hurried across the room just as Luis and Glasses got Santiago stretched out on the tile floor. Lucrecia took a cushion from a kitchen chair to use as a pillow for him.

"Shit. Pupils are dilated." I got out the blood pressure cuff. "Seventy-two over forty," I muttered to myself. "He's fainted," I told Glasses. "Get him up to his bed."

Glasses nodded, and I sent a quick, apologetic glance over my shoulder at Riggs. Even if he wanted to second-guess the decision not to escape, now he couldn't. But I couldn't very well leave Gustavo passed out on the floor.

Riggs nodded once, like he'd come to the same conclusion I had, and the simple gesture filled me with warmth.

I followed Glasses up the stairs to Gustavo's room, where they laid him out on the bed. Lucrecia and Teresa hurried in behind us.

While I got out the portable EKG machine, Lucrecia ran a hand over Gustavo's forehead.

"*Ay, pobre Gian*—uh… Gustavo."

I frowned. Why did people keep saying that. Was that some kind of Venezuelan respect thing? Was his name Gian-Gustavo? I wondered if Riggs knew.

By the time I got the EKG monitor hooked up, my patient was already coming around, and his blood pressure had risen slightly. I asked Glasses to get him some strong coffee and bottled water, as well as a snack.

"Doctor?" Gustavo asked weakly.

"Right here," I told him. "Your blood pressure went quite low and you fainted—"

"Ah, my heart!" he began. "I always knew—"

"No," I interrupted. "Señor, this was not from your heart. Your heart is in good condition. Your EKG results look quite normal. This was a type of low blood pressure called orthostatic hypotension, and *no*—" I held up a hand before he could get excited about this new diagnosis. "—it's not caused by a faulty heart, but by something as simple as spending too much time in bed." I gave him a reproving look. "How much time have you been spending here?"

Gustavo for once looked more guilty than angry. "Many hours? The pain in my chest, it is… it is severe. My brother, he is a slave to his heart condition, as well. He and I have this in common, you see?"

I nodded slowly. I was kind of afraid I *did* see. Sort of. Maybe? All I knew was, there was a glimmer of Kev in this guy's eyes just then… a kind of hero-worship thing for his brother, which didn't track at all to him being a violent cartel-honcho drug lord, but there it was anyway.

"I'm sure if your brother is the sort of man you think he is, he just wants you to be happy and healthy."

Gustavo looked away, and his jaw tightened. "You have saved my life, Dr. Carter. I owe you a great debt of honor."

I set my jaw and darted a look around the room to see that the guards had not come back yet, and the women sat quietly in the corner. "If that's the case," I whispered quickly, "then for heaven's sake, let us go. All of us. Me, Riggs, and the other guy—"

Gustavo shook his head. "What you ask is impossible. My brother will be coming soon, and he has need of the seed man. Gustavo will not let him go."

The seed man? Was that Mullet? I noticed he didn't say it was impossible to let me and Riggs go.

"Please," I said again. "Sir. Señor Santiago. To clear your debt to me. For the sake of my cousin, who's like a brother. I beg you…"

Gustavo swallowed hard, and as he stared up at me, I knew in my heart that he was going to say *yes*, and I would be able to tell Riggs I'd saved us.

But then he caught sight of something over my shoulder, and his face hardened.

"Leave me, Dr. Carter," he commanded.

"But—"

"Ah, Rodrigo! I'm so glad you're back. Escort Dr. Carter back to his room immediately, while Luis serves me my coffee. And please ensure that our other guests are also taken care of and that the seed man is ready to perform his job. Gustavo's plan must be executed perfectly! Let there be no mistakes."

"Sir," I protested one last time, appealing to his hypochondriac nature. "You should let me continue to monitor you, at least. Your blood pressure—"

But Gustavo merely shook his head, and before I could say another damn word in my favor, I found myself out in the hall.

Fuck.

13

―――――――

RIGGS

I couldn't stop second-guessing my decision to stick around for Buck's sake. I had to trust Carter knew what was best for Buck's health and stability, but with Santiago gone, this was our best chance at escape.

"Y'all don't happen to have, like… uh… one of them opioids they're always talking about on the TV, do ya?"

I glanced down at Buck, who was still writhing in pain. Sweat beaded his hairline and dripped down his neck.

"'Cause this hurts like a sumbitch."

I grabbed the bottle of high-dose Tylenol Carter had left instead of the opioids Buck had begged for. I asked one of the fretting women nearby to grab some water, and we managed to get the pills into Buck. As soon as Carter raced out of the kitchen to help Santiago to his room, I leaned in close to Buck so no one could hear.

"Are you Buck Nutter from Licking Thicket?"

"Great googly moogly!" The man's eyes widened enough for me to see brain matter behind them. "Are you one o' them psychics?"

How could this guy be responsible for the latest gaming

sensation taking over the world right now? It was impossible.

"If I was, would I be here?" I grumbled. "No. But I work for Champion Security, and I'd like to get you out of here."

"Champion… wait. You guys are the ones who tipped me off about the coup at HOG! I owe you my… well, maybe not my life since I'm laying here gutshot. But I at least owe you a beer, man."

"You're not gutshot. It's a gash on your leg, and you're going to be fine. But I need to know what they want with you. Why are you here?"

His eyes flitted away, and he looked embarrassed. "It was a big misunderstanding."

"Tell me."

Buck glanced back at me with a little whimper of discontent. "But you'll think I'm two rounds shy of a full clip."

I stared at him, wondering if it was possible the man had *any* ammo in his clip at all. "Naw," I lied. "It takes a smart man to come up with something as popular as HOG. You can't be stupid. I'll bet you were simply taking advantage of a business opportunity."

His eyes brightened. "Yeah. Yeah, exactly so. You hit the nail on the hammer, my friend. It was taking advantage of a business opportunity. Ya see, I invented *Horn of Glory*. It was my baby. And when I heard Jacob Horn was gonna get rid of me, gonna force me away from my life's work, I done lost my mind over the injustice of it. I left HOG Corporate before they could make me leave. Ain't no big-brother corporation going to pull the cotton over this guy's eyes, you know? Not again. So I did what any self-respecting man like myself would do. I listed my seed for sale on the internet. The dark web. Where the bad guys are.

Which… in hindsight… maybe weren't such a great idea. So happens they don't like taking no for an answer."

The man had to be smarter than he appeared, but the way he kept stressing *"his seed"* unironically made me wonder just how naive he was. I imagined him typing "dark web dot com" in his browser, like he expected to get to some kind of alternative eBay with verified sellers who followed the rules, took credit cards, and posted thoughtful reviews. *"Zero out of five stars. This buyer would not take no for an answer."*

I closed my eyes long enough to pray for patience and a straight face. "And then what happened?"

"I got hoodwinked. Literally. Buncha guys came at me outside of Dairy Queen one night and put a hood on me. Next thing you know, boom. I'm in this place. I think maybe they gave me something because I don't remember much in between."

"Because they want backdoor access to the system?"

Buck's eyes got shifty again. I followed them and noticed most people weren't paying much attention to us. Two guards were watching us, but I was pretty sure they didn't speak English. I continued to act like I was helping him stay calm through his injury.

"Kinda. They, uh… they want my seed."

For the love of God, if this man didn't stop saying things like that, I was going to turn into a thirteen-year-old boy. "Explain. What does Gustavo Santiago want with your video game?"

"So, like, I wrote some code into the game so I could have a way of getting into it from anywhere. Little tricks within the game that open portals to the back end. It wasn't exactly authorized, but it was dead useful for testing later levels of the game directly from my Horn, and…" He hesitated. "When the money guys came along, I got scared, you know? Like, I always heard about them business types wanting to take from the little guy. I'm not a little guy, but I'm a little guy if you catch my drift. I had to protect my game." He seemed defensive, like he knew how many laws he'd broken when he'd tried to retain control of a game that wasn't legally his.

"Go on."

He sighed and winced, reaching down as if to touch the leg wound. I batted his hand away from the bandage. "Crap, okay. Gawd this hurts like a mofo. Anyways, there's a little seed icon I've hidden deep in the game so it'd be damned near impossible to find unless you knew where it was at. It only appears when you complete Level 13 by declaring a truce with the Dragon King of Thumlor and doing the Epic Dance of Peace—which *no one does*, because that dragon is such a jerk, he'd make even my Grandma Loving curse a blue streak, and Essie Loving-Nutter was never one to take the Lord's name in vain, rest her soul. You with me?"

"Not entirely," I admitted.

"Point is, there's a hidden seed, and the seed is the access point. Got me?"

"Got you."

"But here's the thing. If you can get into the game, you can get into the, uh… the money stuff. Like, if you're playing in online mode, you tie your game account to your bank account so you can buy and sell silver pips." He glanced around to make sure no one had gotten closer. "Which I guess is a really convenient way to launder money… or it would be, if the game were set up so that those transactions bypassed the HOG Corporate server and weren't recorded. So that's what they want me to do. They want me to hide their drug shit in the game."

"Drug shit. Just the transactions? Or their deals and sales? Contact information? What?"

He nodded and winced again. "All that. I have all the bank account information for Santiago's associates. Turnip blight is scheduled for tonight—they happen from time to time so HOG Corporate can upload bug fixes and whatnot—and that's when they want me to make the changes. Once it goes into the system… they'll be able to do all their business through the game. The transactions will be hidden, and anyone with a Horn will be able to make drug deals with the cartel. It's all tied to usernames instead of real names. If the feds come sniffing around, destroy the Horn. Once they're gone, buy another one and log in with your username again. Easy peasy."

"But the Horn purchase itself would lead back to you."

"Naw, man. Buy it in an airport with cash. Grab it at Walmart. Get your little cousin to pick one up for you. They're not tracked that closely."

I thought it through. "And they're available all over the world."

Buck nodded. "And when you're playing one, no one thinks anything of it."

"But couldn't the *chats* be monitored by corporate HOG? The feds could subpoena that information from HOG's servers."

"And they'd find a bunch of anonymous chats between randos. And the chats are about eggplant trades or carrot prices." He lifted an eyebrow at me. "Got me?"

"So this update is supposed to happen tonight," I said.

"Yeah, man. And once it's done, it can't be undone. And they're gonna kill me so hard, dude. Gustavo's going to order me killed as soon as he gets back home."

I opened my mouth to ask another question when his words hit me. "Wait. What? When he gets back home?"

"Yeah. He went somewhere for treatment. For his heart."

I glanced at the doorway Carter and Santiago had left through a couple of minutes ago. "His bedroom?"

Buck's face crinkled in confusion. "His bedroom in Texas, maybe. Does he have a place there?"

"What the hell are you saying? Gustavo just went back to his room with Dr. Carter. Didn't he?"

Buck glanced at the door and back to me. "Oh, naw. Naw, that's his brother. Gianluigi's just… he's a pussy cat. A little bit hypocondriatical maybe, but it's the guards you have to worry about. They work for Gustavo, and those boys don't play."

I stared at him. It made sense. But Gianluigi had claimed to be Gustavo. "Are you sure that's the brother?"

He nodded. "I heard them talking about Gustavo needing medical treatment in Houston, but he didn't want some rival cartel to find out about it. He got his brother to come stay and pretend to be him."

"You picked all that up from the guards?" I asked suspiciously.

"Well, I'll tell ya a little something. I speak Spanish," he whispered, clearly not wanting the guards to find out. "Thanks to years of watching *Caso Cerrado* at my buddy Tajo's house. His mamacita lived with them and didn't speak English. It was Telemundo all day, every day. I'd like to have clapped on noise-canceling headphones, but we didn't have nothing like that back then."

My brain scrambled to put this new information into what I already knew. It made so much sense, but what did that mean for our chances of escape?

The guards were still cartel muscle.

"When is Gustavo expected back here?"

Buck was clearly uncomfortable, but I needed information. "Dunno, but not yet, I don't think. When we talked about the upload tonight, it definitely sounded like he wasn't going to be here to supervise me. He put the fear of God in me instead."

I remembered the computer room and his access to the internet. "Can you get me GPS coordinates of where we are right now?"

"I can try," he said, glancing down at his leg. "If, ah… if I can walk."

"Shit. Okay. Be ready for anything. Stay alert and pay attention. We need to get out of here. Don't load that stuff online. Stall for time. Unplug a device. I don't know. Just make sure that information doesn't get uploaded."

Before he could answer, the guards began shouting. I jumped up and saw Carter walking back in with his hands up. "*El doctor*," he reminded them. As soon as they relaxed, Carter hurried over to help Buck.

"Ya gotta gimme some the good stuff, Doc," Buck wailed. "It's killin' me!"

Carter stayed calm. "You're going to be fine. It's not as bad as it looked. You're lucky it wasn't any deeper."

"I'm not feelin' all that lucky right about now, Doc," he whined.

Carter checked the wound and murmured some soothing words assuring his patient he would make a full recovery. He dug out a packet of antibiotics for Buck.

"You have to take this entire pack for it to work," he said. "Keep them in a pocket in case…" Carter looked around. "In case you get *moved*. Okay?"

Buck swallowed nervously. "Yessir, Doc. Whatever you say. And can I just say I'm right glad I didn't have a heart problem because it seems like you're not all that great with those. But you're sure good at impalements!"

Carter exhaled and shot me a look. He was exhausted

and pale, stressed and scared. I wanted desperately to get him out of here. I leaned my shoulder into him. "Just a few more minutes, Duchess," I said softly. "Then you can rest."

"What about you?"

"No rest for the wicked, I'm afraid." I gave him my most reassuring smile before standing and pulling him up next to me. I turned toward the guards. *"Necesitamos ayuda para trasladarlo a su habitación." We need help getting him to his room.*

They grumbled amongst themselves until finally coming to help. Buck wailed like a dying piglet as they lifted him and carried him out of the large kitchen. Carter and I followed closely behind until realizing he was being held in the room right next to ours. That was a lucky break if we could figure out how to get rid of the guards. Maybe we could find a way to slip them a sedative now that we had the med bag in our possession.

Once Buck was settled on his bed and Carter had made sure he had a glass of water and more pain pills for later, the guards forced us back into our own suite. While I waited for the familiar snick of the door lock, I noticed Carter's hands were shaking.

"C'mere," I said, pulling him into a hug. "You did a good job."

He struggled against my hold for a few seconds before giving up and letting himself slump in my arms. "Santiago was unstable to begin with, and now he's having low blood pressure."

Fuck. I could tell he was stressed and scared, and I wanted to do whatever I could to put him at ease.

"You did good, Duchess," I said. "You got him settled. But, listen. I need to tell you something."

I led him over to the velvet sofa and pulled him down next to me. He looked completely wiped out. I knew he was more scared than he wanted to admit to me, and having the pressure of everyone's healthcare was clearly weighing on him.

Before I could say anything to try and ease his mind, the door opened again and a woman came in carrying a tray of food. I was starving, and whatever the tray held smelled amazing.

Carter wasn't interested in the food, but I forced it on him. "You have to eat. If we can find a way out of here tonight, you'll need the calories."

"How can you eat food from that kitchen after everything that happened?" He eyed the chicken soup with suspicion.

"Because Marines learn to compartmentalize, or they faint while on a mission and get dead. Eat your damned food, Carter. Don't think about it, just get it down."

He reluctantly tucked into his food and alternated between bites of it and the fried flatbreads that accompanied the soup. "I guess this is better than whatever you had to eat in Afghanistan."

"You don't even know," I said, appreciating the soup even more.

"Who's the guy who got hurt? And why does he sound like he's from Tennessee?"

I thought about what to tell him. "He's from Tennessee," I admitted. "He was kidnapped by the cartel to do some computer work for them." All of that was true. I felt uneasy about the parts I left out, but the more information Carter had about the connection to *Horn of Glory*, the dark web sale, and the cartel's financial transactions, the more danger he could possibly be in, not to mention we were now somewhat dealing with a Champion Security client, albeit an ex-one. And Champ had made his stance clear on talking about client business.

Especially to people I was sleeping with.

Especially to men who were chronic overtalkers when they got stressed-out.

"What kind of computer work? No offense to Mullet Dude, but he doesn't seem like my first choice for a computer genius."

"His name is Buck," I said, deliberately not telling Carter his last name, if only to keep from laughing. "And he tried selling his services to the wrong people. They decided to take what he was offering without giving him money in exchange."

"Oh." Carter's forehead crinkled in concern. "Are they planning on keeping him forever?"

"Either that or they're planning on killing him after he finishes the job. And it's due to be finished tonight. Pretty much when Gustavo gets back, we're all in trouble."

Carter dropped his spoon in his empty bowl. "What do you mean 'when Gustavo gets back'? Where's he going? He's not stable enough to travel right now. Did you see him faint?"

I took a breath and reached for his hand. "Apparently, the man we know as Gustavo is actually his brother. His name is Gianluigi, and he's impersonating his brother, who actually does have a heart condition. He's getting treatment in Houston. Gustavo doesn't want a rival cartel to find out he's gone."

Carter blinked at me in shock. "Well... what do we know about Gianluigi? Is he bad? Dangerous? What?"

"I don't know. He's not a known player in the cartel as far as I know, but he has to be in charge of Gustavo's guards while Gustavo is gone. And those guys have real guns. I think... I think he's not as much danger to us as the real Gustavo would be, but we still need to get the hell out of here as soon as possible. Especially before Gustavo returns and realizes his brother kidnapped two Americans."

Carter leaned against me. "Riggs… this is too much. What do we do? Are you going to ask your friend Hux to try and find us?"

He looked pale and tired. Inky smudges lined his eyes, and his hair was a mess. The usually put-together cardiologist was scared, and it was literally my job to make sure he wasn't.

I swallowed my pride. "Yes. I'm going to contact Champ, my boss, and tell him what's going on. He'll find a way to get us out of here."

Carter let out a breath and sank into the chair. "Good. Okay. I think that's a good idea. We need to save this guy Buck before Gustavo gets back and takes his anger out on all of us."

I stood up and piled our dishes back on the tray before reaching for Carter's hand. "Come on. I'm going to draw you a bath. You need to relax. I know it's not easy, but I think a bath will help."

He nodded and followed me into the bathroom, where the large tub on clawed feet stood waiting. I filled it and helped him strip down before watching him sink into the hot water. The cool air from the mountains had dropped the temperature in our rooms significantly, so Carter let out a sigh of pleasure as he sank into the hot water.

"You're going to contact your team?" he asked, closing his eyes and inhaling the steam.

I reached over and brushed his hair back before leaning over to kiss his cheek. "I'm going to do it right now. Just relax."

"Mm-hm."

I left him there while I went back out to the main room of our suite and found the game device. The Horn booted right up on the message page.

KevsCuz: *Hux, you there?*

HogMasterHux: *Yeah, man. Been waiting for you. Still ok?*

KevsCuz: *No. It's gone to shit. We need extraction. Time to read Champ in and come up with a plan. Working on getting you GPS coordinates.*

HogMasterHux: *On our way. Sitrep?*

KevsCuz: *I've got the magic seed man. He's been injured. Flesh wound in thigh. Will make escape a challenge.*

HogMasterHux: *What happened?*

KevsCuz: *TL;DR: man we thought was Gustavo is actually brother Gianluigi. When Gustavo returns, shit will hit fan. I have to get him out of here.*

HogMasterHux: *The seed man?*

Buck Nutter wasn't my priority right then, even though I hoped to save him too.

KevsCuz: *I meant the doc. I'm worried about him. Of course, Carter's all worried about everyone else, cause that's the kinda guy he is. Hanging on by his fingernails so he can take care of people. He's exhausted.*

HogMasterHux: *Who are you and what have you done with my man Riggs?*

KevsCuz: *Explain.*

HogMasterHux: *The doc is a grown-ass man with a high-stakes job. I'm sure he can handle it. Since when do you worry over the guy you literally called a "spoiled silver spoon" when Champ gave you this job?*

I winced and wondered how to erase the message history on this thing. It was Carter's Horn, after all.

KevsCuz: *I was wrong. Carter's a good man. Generous and kind. Funny as hell. Smart as fuck. And when he smiles… he makes people feel like they can do anything. I like him, Hux. He didn't deserve to get caught up in this.*

HogMasterHux: *Dammit, if this thing had emojis, there'd be pink hearts flying at your face right now. Someone's in lurve.*

I frantically searched for the erase function, but I couldn't find any way of deleting the messages.

HogMasterHux: *Don't get pissed at me for giving you hell. But maybe distract the doc for a while. We can leave Tennessee for Venezuela w/in the hour, and I'll try to trace private flight plans filed at the airport in Caracas to see if I can figure out your general neighborhood. Stay cool.*

"Riggs?"

I spun around and saw Carter standing in the doorway to the bathroom with nothing but a towel wrapped low on his hips.

"Yeah?" I squeaked in my least masculine voice. I cleared my throat. "Yeah? Ah, you good?"

The edge of his mouth came up in a teasing smile. "I could be better."

He pulled the corner of the towel out from where it had been tucked. It fell to the ground in a heap, revealing the doctor's perfect fucking body. I stared at him.

"I... I, uh... I could help you with that," I stammered, tossing the Horn down on the velvet sofa.

Hux had suggested distracting the doc.

And I aimed to serve.

14

CARTER

I hated feeling out of control.

I'd hated it as a child, when my parents had died and left me behind, and I hated it as an adult, which was why I tried to take charge of things whenever possible. But I had *never* felt as out of control as I had the past couple of days, and I could feel the strain of it catching up to me.

I'd kept my fear at bay fairly well while I'd focused on treating Buck and then Santiago. I'd tried to knock it down when the guards had led us upstairs. I liked to think I'd only lost my composure a little bit when Riggs had spun me a half-assed tale about how *another* Tennessean had become a prisoner here in Venezuela and how Gustavo wasn't Gustavo —which explained a whole lot, the more I thought about it, like the whole third-person talking thing, and how Lucrecia had "miraculously" gotten pregnant with Gustavo's baby, and how an egotistical, possibly infertile hypochondriac with big-brother issues and chronic indigestion could also be a highly placed leader of a notorious drug cartel. (Answer: he wasn't.)

But the second Riggs had left me soaking in the bathtub, all of that overwhelm had come roaring back, stealing the breath from my lungs and making me feel like I was drowning with my head above water.

When we'd first been taken prisoner, I'd honestly been more concerned about how much time we were wasting, how many patients I could have been seeing while I fake-doctored Gustavo, but now the truth of our situation was crystal clear. Riggs didn't admit defeat out loud, and I was trying hard to play along and stay positive, but we both knew that when the real Gustavo came back, our lives were probably forfeit, and despite my best efforts, I hadn't been able to convince Gianluigi to let us go.

I knew Riggs had promised to contact Hux on my Horn while I bathed, but when we were first captured, he'd said Champion Security would need a week or more to find us and mount a rescue. We had no idea how long we had until Gustavo came back, but somehow I doubted it would be that long.

This knowledge made everything sharper, *realer*. It brought things into focus in a way I'd never experienced before. All the big, important things I'd worried about—carrying on my parents' legacy, making the right choices to take the one right path toward a happy future—seemed so silly with this new perspective.

This soak in the bathtub with Gustavo's fancy soap would probably be the last time I ever experienced that luxury. The food I'd just eaten might be the last thing I'd ever consume. The words of annoyance I'd spoken to my grandfather before I left would probably be the last things I ever said to him, which broke my heart, and my text convo with Kev would be the last one we ever had... but at least I'd harvested the kumquats.

I missed the Thicket and the people there. I missed the

simple life, helping people who needed and truly appreciated me.

And then there was Riggs.

Riggs, who was a bossy asshole but who'd put my safety before his own. Riggs, who'd called me Duchess but had listened to me without judgment when I told him about my family. Riggs, who never answered a question about his job or his clients but told me stories about his Romanian gaffes when he knew I needed a laugh. Riggs, who drove me out of my mind with his high-handedness and out of my mind with lust.

Riggs, who I was realizing was exactly the person I wanted to spend the last days or hours of my life with, even if I hadn't known it until now.

The two times he and I had touched each other had been explosive. The most incredible sexual encounters of my fairly experienced life. And they'd both been the closest thing to accidental — one insomnia frottage and a fear-fueled blow job. It was enough to make a guy wonder what deliberate, on-purpose sex with Riggs would be like.

Enough to make me want to find out before Gustavo came home and threw us out of a plane.

I hauled myself out of the tub, dried off hastily, and padded to the doorway.

The sight of Riggs sitting on the velvet sofa, Horn in his hand and a little pucker of concentration on his forehead, was enough to make me stop right there just so I could watch him for a moment.

"Riggs?"

"Yeah?" He whirled around to look at me, and his eyes consumed me from my very naked chest to the towel around my waist. "Yeah. Ah, you good?"

He was so damn cute. "I could be better." I loosened the towel and let it fall to the floor.

Riggs's eyes grew more intense. "I... I, uh... I could help you with that." He threw the Horn on the couch and stalked toward me like a prowling animal, and for once in my life, I was happy to be the prey.

"I was hoping you would," I purred.

But just when I was thinking he was gonna put his mouth and hands on me and *make* me stop overthinking... he paused directly in front of me, lowered his forehead to mine, and just... breathed me in.

"You smell really good, Dr. Rogers." He ran his big hands down my arms, and I swallowed convulsively.

"Do you think? I'm not sure what kind of soap Gustavo has here, but it's nice, huh? Maybe I should get some when I get home." I licked my lips. "I mean, unless whatever post-abduction therapist Doctors Across Continents hooks me up with tells me that's really Stockholmy and I should —"

"Carter."

"Yes?"

"It's not the soap that smells good, baby." Riggs rubbed his nose against mine. "It's you."

"Oh. Well. That's..." I coughed slightly. "Good." I nodded crisply, as if this were no big deal, and I had men calling me baby and *sniffing me* all the time, though I did *not*. In every hookup I'd ever had, whether I'd topped or bottomed, I'd always been the baby-er, not the baby-ee. Men looked at me and saw the degree, the polished facade, the air of control, and they made assumptions I'd never cared to challenge.

Riggs, though... he saw. This total jerk with a heart of gold understood me better than men I'd dated for months. How fucked-up was that?

"Carter?"

"Yeah?"

"*Breathe*." Riggs demonstrated, drawing a deep breath of

his own and letting it out slowly. "The bath was supposed to help calm you down, but I swear you're tenser now than you were when you went in." He squeezed the muscles in my shoulders. "It's gonna be okay, okay? I messaged with Hux. He said Champ and the team are on their way."

"Good." I nodded. "That's good. When my parents died, we had a hell of a time getting the bodies back. I don't want my grandfather to have to go through that again."

Riggs shook my shoulders firmly. "Stop it. We're not dying, Carter."

I rolled my eyes. "I appreciate you trying to be protective or whatever. You're a five-star bodyguard. But I told you from the beginning to level with me. We have no idea when the real Gustavo is coming back. They're not getting here in time, Riggs."

"*Yes*. They *will*."

I stared into Riggs's eyes, which were blazing with something between worry and anger. "Riggs—" I began impatiently.

"Do you remember what I told you when we were first captured, Doc? You've got to believe it's going to be okay. Because if you think you're gonna fail, you will."

"Yes, yes, that's very inspiring." I took a step away from him and waved a hand. "Put that saying on a picture of a cute kitten, and you'll sell a million posters. But you can't self-fulfilling-prophecy your way out of this. I can think positive thoughts all day, and Gustavo Santiago is still gonna kill us."

Riggs was silent for a moment. "It's okay to be scared—"

"I didn't *say* I was scared!" I yelled back. I squeezed my eyes shut, well aware of how ridiculous I sounded, and my shoulders slumped. "I'm terrified," I admitted. "And I hate it. I hate feeling this way. I hate that I can't control it. But it's no good telling me not to be, okay? I'll hold it together when it counts, I promise. I'm not going to be a liability." I picked up my towel from where I'd dropped it and wrapped it around me again. I wasn't doing *this*—whatever this was—naked. "I should find my clothes and go see if they'll let me check on Buck and Gianluigi."

Riggs reached out a hand and grabbed my wrist, dragging me over to the bed and forcing me to sit facing him.

"Did I ever tell you about the time I was held hostage in Afghanistan?"

I raised one eyebrow. He knew perfectly well he hadn't.

"Right, okay." He licked his lips in an uncharacteristic show of uncertainty. "This is not my favorite story to tell, 'cause I come off like an idiot, which means you'll love it."

I snorted. Might be nice for him to be the one who looked like an idiot for a change.

"So, me, Champ, Bishop—who was our comms expert at the time—and this other guy, Elvo, were working a rescue job in Afghanistan near... well. It doesn't matter where." He cleared his throat. "We didn't usually do these jobs, 'cause the military can get shit done way more efficiently than a private organization in certain parts of the world, but this client was..." Again, he hesitated. "Eh. Who he is doesn't matter either."

I frowned. "Is this stuff classified?"

"Sorta, yeah? I mean, not officially. But we're a security company, you know? It's in everyone's best interest for me to not go blabbing information." He shifted uncomfortably. "*Anyway*. Suffice it to say, that mission was a goatfuck—and that part was *not* my fault and is the reason Bishop doesn't work for Champ anymore—but it ended with our comms knocked out, Elvo running off to who-the-fuck-knows where, Champ with a head injury so bad he couldn't stay awake for more than thirty minutes at a stretch, and me sitting in a shack maybe forty klicks from our exfil location, trying to keep him alive, while prisoners in other rooms — guys who were taken at the same time we were — were crying out for help."

"Holy shit." I wanted to touch him, to comfort him, even though this had obviously happened years ago, but I wasn't sure if I should. I wasn't sure if he'd welcome it.

"For three fucking days, these armed guards stood right outside the door and mentioned us by name, trying to figure out which of the prisoners in the place was Riggs and which was Champion, and every time they said my name, my gut would cramp because I'd known guys who'd been taken prisoner before, and the kidnappers always wanted them to either give up intel on American troops, which we didn't have, or ransom money, which I also didn't have. I'd been trained for this stuff, thought I had a handle on how to be a good prisoner, but after forty-eight hours with no food or water, huddled with Champ for warmth in subzero temperatures, thinking he was gonna die, unable to feel my toes and knowing I might not be able to run even if I got the chance, my mind was…" He blew out a breath. "It was dark, baby. I knew for a fact that I was gonna end there, and I was scared to death."

Riggs's eyes went unfocused as he stared at something over my shoulder, and I was pretty sure he was mentally back in that shack.

"What did you do?" I whispered. I rested my palm on his knee, just a light touch to let him know I was there, and he set his larger hand atop mine, squeezing gently.

"I gave up. I focused on the fear and let it become bigger than me. Let it fill my head and push aside all my training, everything I *knew* to do in that situation. I started thinking all sorts of desperate shit about how these were my last hours. I figured maybe I'd lie and pretend I had intel in exchange for them getting Champ medical help. I deluded myself that once the guards were in the room, I'd jump them, get their weapons, and escape before frostbite got me." He snorted. "Calling that plan a Hail Mary would be an insult to Hail Marys."

"Oh my God," I breathed, leaning into his space further, trying to remind myself that he was alive. "Did you do it? Tell me you didn't do it."

He smiled ruefully. "No, fortunately, or I'd have been dead for real, and you'd be here with some other idiot." His eyes darkened. "And I don't even wanna contemplate that, Carter."

I swallowed hard past the lump in my throat. I didn't either.

"What happened was that Champ woke up—really woke up—for the first time since we'd been taken. When the guards came back, he actually listened carefully to what they were saying, even though he didn't speak their dialect, and heard them mention Elvo, who hadn't been taken with us. Champ realized how weird it was for them to know E's name, which is something I should have realized, myself, but my logical processes had switched off." He tapped his temple and shook his head in disgust. "So Champ yells out that he's Champion, and they dragged us out of the cell… then gave us a hot meal and some coffee." Riggs rubbed a hand over his face and groaned in embarrassment. "It turned out Elvo had gotten away, and since he couldn't exactly mount a rescue on his own, he'd been offering these guys bribes for two days to set us free, but they couldn't figure out which two prisoners they were supposed to be freeing. Two *days* I sat there, Carter. Two days when Champ could have died. And all because I'd let the fear get so big it paralyzed me."

"It's not your fault." I pulled his hand away from his

face and held it in both of mine. "You didn't know how it all would end, and being cautious is a good thing—"

"But I wasn't proceeding with caution, I was lying there thinking it was all over," he corrected. "That's the problem. Fear is very real. And it's smart, to an extent. Healthy. It's what makes you run away from wild hyenas and think twice before you run into a burning building. But when you let it consume you—when you start to believe a problem is bigger than your ability to conquer it, bigger than your *team's* ability to work through it or get around it—it can destroy your life. Literally. Back in Gelada, when the capybaras almost got us, you said you trusted me. I need you to trust me now, Carter. Because trust is—"

"Essential on a mission?" I quoted his words from earlier.

Riggs gave me a half-smile and threaded my fingers between his. "Aww, that's so cute. You hang on every word I say, don't you?"

"You wish," I scoffed, rolling my eyes. But honestly… yeah, I kinda did. Especially at that moment, when he'd shared something so important. It made me feel like we were part of a team, stronger together than we were apart.

"I was gonna say, trust is the opposite of fear. So, believe me when I tell you that Champ and Hux are on their way. And they'll find us and save us, if we don't find a way to save ourselves first. Okay?"

I nodded and sucked a deep breath into my lungs, which finally felt like they were working properly again. I believed in Riggs. I couldn't explain the logic of it, but that didn't make it any less true. Something in me recognized something in him and trusted him implicitly. Even when we'd first met, when I hadn't liked him at *all*, I'd trusted him.

But then something about his story occurred to me, and I frowned. "Um, so… What happened to the others?"

"The others?"

"The other prisoners being held in the same facility. The ones you heard."

Riggs's grin split his whole face, and he cupped my cheek in his palm. "You're one of exactly two people I know who'd think about them, Carter Rogers. Most guys in the security business would focus on saving the ones they could. The ones it was their job to save."

"Most doctors too," I agreed sadly. I glanced down. "And triage is necessary sometimes."

"Yup." His hand drifted down to my neck, and his thumb traced the line of my jaw. "Fortunately for those other prisoners, though, Champ is the other person I know who thinks the way you do."

"Wait, what?" My gaze flew to his, amazed and pleased.

"We got every single one of them out, got them medical attention, and got them repatriated, even though it cost Champ truckloads of his own money to do it. Which is another reason I'm telling you Percy Champion won't give up on us. He's fucking amazing as both a team leader and a friend." Riggs's cheek twitched up in a half-smile. "Don't tell him I said that, though."

"Well, I think *you're* pretty amazing," I said softly.

"Wow. Not sure if you realize, Dr. Carter, but you just complimented me. Is that the fear talking again?" Riggs teased—except part of me wondered if it was really all a tease or if there wasn't a part of him that was sincerely asking the question.

And because that was so, I took a second to evaluate his question so I could give him a sincere answer.

"It's not," I told him honestly. "And I know that because I'm still very much afraid, but… I do think we're going to get out of here." I said the words with conviction, believing them for the first time since that scene in the kitchen. "And thank you for telling me that story. For... for trusting me with that," I added softly. "It helped."

"Good." He brushed aside a lock of damp hair that had fallen on my forehead and pressed a chaste kiss to my lips, then leaned back against the pillows and stretched out, pulling me against his side. "Maybe we should get some sleep so we'll be rested for whatever tomorrow brings."

"Or." I scrambled to my knees and threw my leg over his waist to straddle him, not caring that the move made my towel come undone. "We could get back to what we were going to do before I 'let the fear get in my head.'"

Riggs brought his hands up to my hips in an instinctive gesture, but when I leaned down to kiss him, he pulled back, his eyes darting back and forth between mine, checking on me. Protecting me, even in this.

Whatever he saw on my face must have convinced him I was all good because his thumbs stroked the ridge of my transversus abdominus muscles, making wide circles across my lower belly that made need pool low in my gut.

"And what exactly did you think we were going to do before?"

I felt my smile grow. "*Well*. I thought about the last two times you and I were together like this... which were seriously hot."

"Mmhmm. Agreed."

"And I thought, 'What would it be like if we actually *set out* to have sex for once instead of falling into it in the heat of the moment?' And I decided I wanted to experience that, no matter what happened tomorrow. I still do." I looked him directly in the eye, letting him see how much I meant it. How much I wanted him. "I want you inside me. I want you to fuck me."

Just thinking of it, just imagining it, made my half-hard cock go fully erect against the hard slab of his abs, and I rocked a little, knowing from experience how phenomenal it would feel.

Riggs's breathing hitched, and when he looked at me, I knew he was remembering that night back on the little pallet at the clinic just like I was. He shifted me slightly so his hardening cock lined up with the crease of my ass, and I made an involuntary little *mpfhh* noise.

"Ah, shit, that's so good," I groaned as I moved again. "I knew it would be. You know, even way back on the night we first met at the Licking Nuthatch Gala, I thought—"

"Carter," Riggs interrupted. "That was a little over two weeks ago, baby. Not exactly *way back*." His fingers tightened on my hips, setting a lazy rhythm for my rocking like the bossy bastard he was. I was shockingly okay with that.

"Only two?" I frowned. Then I blinked because holy shit, he was right. I felt like I'd lived four lives since then—traveling to Gelada, meeting the people there, this whole nightmare with Gustavo... But I guessed there were some things in life that were just so huge, they changed you in an instant. My parents dying had been one. This trip to Venezuela was definitely another.

"Only two," he confirmed.

"Feels like more," I grumbled.

"It does." Riggs's circling thumbs moved in widening arcs, brushing through my trimmed hair. "Facing down hordes of capybaras together does that, I guess."

Capybaras. I snorted. Then I rotated my hips against him, making his eyes roll back in his head.

"Well, whenever the fuck it was," I said breathlessly, "I noticed you at the bar that night even before my grandfather introduced us. I had no idea who you were, and you kept your face turned away from me, but there was something about you. I was practically writing poetry to your shoulder, since that was the part of you I could see best."

Riggs snickered. "I'd like to hear that poetry sometime."

I shoved at his shoulder playfully and retaliated by rolling us over on the bed, bringing our dicks into alignment with him on top.

He fumbled for my hands, grabbing one in each of his and pressing them against the mattress by my shoulders, holding me in place. Then he dipped his head and kissed me, slowly at first and then hotter, his tongue sliding against mine in a simulated fuck that was wet, and sloppy, and ruthless, and perfect.

I couldn't help but wonder who the fuck I was, letting someone else take control like this…

Then Riggs broke the kiss, only to graze his teeth over my jaw before licking over the spot he'd bitten, and my cock literally jumped in a way I hadn't known was anatomically possible.

"Oh, *fuck*," I gasped dazedly.

Whoever I was, I was fucking loving this. I'd clearly been missing out.

He moved his mouth lower, pressing openmouthed kisses against my neck that made me writhe with pleasure, sucking a bruise right by the join of my shoulder, just because he could.

"I remember that night a little differently," he offered. His warm breath fanning out against the damp skin of my neck made me shiver head to toe. "I noticed you too, but I already knew who you were, of course —"

"Of course. The…" I gasped as he sucked at my collarbone. "The babysitting job you didn't want. That's why you were such an asshole, mocking my distinguished lineage." I grabbed at his hair with both hands, needing something to hold on to.

"Kinda." He braced both palms on the bed and lifted himself up in push-up position so he could look at me. "I'm never rude to clients, though. You were the exception."

"Lucky me."

"Not because I didn't want you, Duchess." Riggs's deep voice curled around those two syllables, taking the name from an insult to an endearment. "It was because I *did*. Because when I saw you at the bar, when I overheard you talking, I knew I'd have to put some distance between us, or else I'd want you in my bed. Champ doesn't have a lot of rules for us, but fucking around with clients is an absolute no. I hate disappointing him."

"Didn't seem to stop you," I noted. I tightened my fingers in his hair like maybe he'd have a really delayed attack of conscience and put a stop to the proceedings, and he leaned more of his weight on me so my cock pushed against his stomach.

"Barely made me hesitate," he agreed. "How could I when you're so... you? Defiant. Competent. Taking care of everyone, taking on their problems." He worried my nipple with his teeth, and I jumped, accidentally yanking his hair harder than I meant to.

He chuckled into my skin.

"What are we doing here?" I demanded, pulling at his hair on purpose this time, making him raise his head. "I said I wanted you to fuck me, and you decided it would be fun to, what? Torment me? Is this your idea of foreplay?"

"Yep," he said cheerfully. "I decided you need more than just a quick fucking, Dr. Carter. Now your job is to lie there and take it."

Any desire I had to argue—and let's be clear, I'd have been arguing just for the fun of it, because who says no when a six-foot-something solid mass of blistering hot sex tells you he wants you to lie back and take it? Not me—

faded away when he moved even lower, licking at the join of my hip.

"Just promise me you're not going to regret this tomorrow," I demanded, using the last of my brain cells that hadn't been zombified with lust.

He raised his head again, and the look in his dark eyes was... I didn't know how to describe it. It was hot as fuck, obviously, like everything Riggs did, but it was so much more than that. It was amusement, and affection, and something like *wonder*. All the things that were written on Dunn's face every time he looked at Tucker. All the things I hadn't thought I'd ever see on someone who was looking at *me*.

You could fall in love with a man who looks at you like that, Carter Rogers, a voice in my mind whispered.

Which was ridiculous. *Ree-dick-yuh-liss*. Jesus Christ, it had only been two freaking weeks! And I was not the type of guy who did the hearts-and-flowers thing even under the best, most logical circumstances, which these were not.

Shit. Was love some kind of advanced stress response? If so, I was a medical oddity.

"I promise," Riggs said solemnly. He pressed a kiss to the tip of my dick... then he sat back, pulled my hip to roll me, nudged me onto my hands and knees, and exposed my ass to his curious gaze.

Oh. My. Fuck.

"Anyone ever tell you that you're fucking gorgeous, Duchess?" Riggs growled, kneading my ass cheeks, pulling them apart.

In point of fact, many men had. But I wasn't sure I'd ever *believed* any of them the way I did with Riggs.

"You make me so fucking hard, baby. I need to get you ready. Need to open you up so I can take you hard. Make sure you remember every second of having my cock inside you. Wanna bite that ass. Wanna kiss it until it knows exactly who owns it."

I'd almost swear he was muttering to himself, a stream-of-consciousness kind of thing that just so happened to be the filthiest dirty talk I'd ever heard. My cock was so hard it was *painful*, bursting with the need to come even though he wasn't close to being inside me yet. I felt his warm breath flutter against my hole.

I looked over my shoulder. "Riggs, I *need*—"

Riggs leaned in and brushed his flat tongue over my sensitive opening, and my brain flatlined.

"Jesus fuck!" somebody yelled, and I was pretty sure it was me.

Riggs moved his hand between my spread legs to grab my cock, his big fist jacking me perfectly in time with the flicking and sucking of his mouth, and my elbows wobbled at how fucking good it felt. My hands fisted in the bedsheet, yanking it away from the corners of the mattress.

But I needed more. I needed everything.

"Riggs," I chanted. "Riggs, Riggs, Riggs, *Riggs*." And like his name was some kind of magical incantation, he redoubled his efforts, working my cock, using my precum to help his fist glide faster, and working his mouth over my ass. He speared his tongue into my hole, and I started babbling, cursing, praying to whole pantheons of gods for him to give me his dick.

"P-please," I cried. "Oh, Riggs. *Please*."

Riggs pulled back and bit my left cheek so hard I was confident it would bruise, and then he slapped the place he'd bitten—one single whack that made me whimper.

"Give me your hand," he commanded, and I brought one hand behind me while I supported myself on the opposite forearm.

He guided my hand to my ass. "Hold yourself open for

me, just like that," he demanded, his voice wrecked with lust. "Don't move a single muscle. "

I didn't. Couldn't. It was too good, and I wanted more. I was dimly aware that I'd be horrified when I remembered this—Riggs fully dressed and me completely naked, out of control and keening from the need to come. But in the moment, that just made it hotter. This Other Carter—the Carter I could only seem to be with Riggs—was shameless in his pursuit of pleasure, and I liked it.

"Fuck, Carter. *Fuck*. You're so goddamn perfect."

I heard Riggs throw off his clothes and rustle through the medical backpack. A second later, a stream of cool lube trickled over my ass. My hips bucked against the air, and I needed both arms in the mattress to keep my balance.

"Come on," I begged, pushing back against him. My leaking cock bobbed against my stomach with every movement. "Inside me. I need…"

He spread the lube over my hole, his fingertip catching on my oversensitized rim, and I cried out again. "I think we already established that I know what you need, Doctor."

Yes, he did. Yes, he really fucking did.

He fingered me open for what felt like days, until he had three fingers inside me and I was rocking back against him with every thrust. "Mother of God," he muttered, curling his fingers to brush over my prostate and make me yell. "Carter, you are…"

"Dying," I said hoarsely. "Riggs, I need you—"

"Yeah, I think you do," he said incomprehensibly.

I heard the crinkle of foil, then Riggs's hands were back on my ass, pulling my cheeks apart. The blunt head of his cock pushed at my entrance, breaching the ring of muscles there, and suddenly the entire focus of my consciousness was on that one small area and the very big invasion it was currently undergoing.

"Ohhhh," I moaned, reveling in the pleasure-pain of it, in the fullness of it, in the *rightness* of it.

I tried to fuck back against him, but Riggs wouldn't let me, because he was a bossy know-it-all that way. Instead, he held my hips and entered me slooooowly, every inch interspersed with a kiss to my back or my shoulder or a few quick strokes of my cock, no matter how often I shouted for him to go faster.

Finally, he bottomed out, and we both stilled for a moment. He was right. This *was* goddamn perfect. And we might not be dying the next morning—okay, we *categorically would not*—but that didn't mean I wasn't experiencing the best fuck of my entire life.

I lifted myself up on my hands and turned my head around. "Kiss me?" I whispered without giving myself time to think about it.

"Always." Riggs wrapped one arm under my shoulders, planted the other on the bed by my hip, and leaned over to give me another hot, wet, drugging kiss. The motion pushed him deeper inside me, and we both groaned into the kiss. "Carter, I've got to—"

"Move," I commanded at the same time. I reached up and anchored a hand in his hair again, which was apparently my new favorite thing.

And then he *did* move, and I was reduced to communicating in grunts and keening wails, not even caring if Buck or the guards or Gustavo Santiago himself could hear us, because the way Riggs fucked was as single-minded and sexily competent as the way he did most things. The way he moved inside me made me feel like I was floating, while the sensation of his hard, warm chest rubbing against my back made me feel protected and secure and grounded. And I was a goner.

"Touch yourself," he growled in my ear. "Want you to come for me, Carter."

Pfft. Like that was a thing he could control with words. Like that was a thing people did on command. I really needed to explain the physiological process of orgasming to him, which had several distinct phases that—

"Come for me," he growled again, "and when you do, I'm going to pull out and come all over your ass. All over the handprint I left there."

"Ah, *fuck*," I groaned, moving my hand down to jerk myself. It took literally three tugs before I was shouting his name, coming all over the sheets.

The next second, Riggs pulled out of me, and I craned my head to watch him jerk his gorgeous cock and come all over me, exactly as promised.

He let out a gasp, then collapsed beside me on the bed. Without a word, he pulled me against him, away from the wet spot, so my sweaty chest lay against his. Then he dragged his fingers through his cum and painted it over the skin of my ass.

I felt like that should have felt weird.

Inappropriate or cavemanish or… I dunno. Unhygienic, at the very least. But as I lay there wrapped in his arms, both of us panting in the stillness, all I felt was relaxed, and nourished, and safe…

And entirely unafraid.

15

RIGGS

After Carter fell asleep, I gently extracted myself from around his body and slid out of bed. As much as I wanted to stay wrapped up in him and relive the incredible love-making we'd shared—to hold him while we watched the sunrise, to wake him with my mouth on his cock, to say all the sweet, sappy shit I'd never even *considered* saying to another lover—I needed to get him the fuck out of Santiago's manse before the man returned. Our time was running out, and I needed to know if Hux and Champ were any closer to an extraction plan. Once Carter was safe, we'd have time to explore the feelings that had been building between us—feelings I couldn't and didn't want to ignore any longer.

I listened at the door to the hallway and didn't hear a sound, but after carefully trying the knob, I confirmed it was still locked from the outside. I made my way back over to the sofa and grabbed the Horn from where I'd dropped it earlier.

KevsCuz: *Hux, you there?*

HogMasterHux: *Yep. In flight on way to Socopó. Sitrep?*

KevsCuz: *No change. No eyes on magic seed man for six hours. As far as I know, Santiago hasn't returned. When he does, shit will go south quickly.*

HogMasterHux: *We think we have a general idea where you might be. Champ is working on satellite images to pinpoint possible locations. Can you get out of compound and hide nearby?*

KevsCuz: *Hang tight. Lemme see.*

I walked back over to the window and inspected the metal scrollwork that acted as prison bars. After checking the one in the main room, I checked the bedroom we'd never used and then checked the one where Carter still lay sleeping. None of them were even remotely loose, but I did reach out and feel the place where a drill bit or screwdriver would go to remove them.

Did we have anything that could work? I moved over to the medical backpack and dumped it out, searching for anything that could be used as a screwdriver, but there wasn't much. Bandages and monitors. Medical devices and suture kits. Burn ointments and carefully labeled packets of medication. And the tin of antibiotic salve — the stupid salve Carter had given me that last night back in Gelada, the first time he said he trusted me. I'd assumed I'd lost it along with my gun, my clothes, and everything else I'd brought to Venezuela, but of all my belongings, this *one* thing had made it. I squeezed it in my palm.

I *was* going to get us out of this. I *was* going to be worthy of his faith in me. I wouldn't let myself think anything else.

I tried both pairs of shears and the hemostats with no luck, but I realized one of the tiny zippers on the bag might work. After struggling to rip the damned zipper pull off the bag, I managed to get it working slowly but surely in the first screw hole on the window bars.

Every few minutes, I had to duck down to hide my activity from patrolling guards, but I made progress. After the first screw fell out, I took a break to update Hux before getting back to work.

It seemed to take hours, and I almost dropped the zipper pull several times. The second screw of six finally fell out. My back and fingers were cramping from doing such tiny work with my arms out the window at an odd angle, but I was determined to get Carter out of here before sunrise if possible. If I could remove our bars this way, hopefully that meant I could remove Buck's too, once I got outside.

I carefully timed the guards' rounds as I worked. The only time they didn't come regularly was when I smelled cigarette smoke on the next pass.

Finally, I got the third screw out and was halfway through when I heard footsteps behind me. I fumbled the zipper pull and dropped to the ground.

"Riggs?" Carter whispered. "You out here?"

I sighed and stood up, stretching the kinks out of my back before walking over to him and pulling him into a hug. He looked sleepy and smelled delicious. "I'm here."

"What're you doing out here?"

"I got half the screws out of the window bars. It should take me another hour or so to get the rest. Why don't you try and get a little more sleep?"

He pulled back and looked at me with confusion. "But then what? If we can get out the window, what about Buck?"

"We'll get him out too. I'll need your help with the screws on his window bars, though. It'll go faster that way."

"But he's not mobile. What are we supposed to do if he can't walk?"

I didn't want to scare Carter more than he already was, but he needed to understand the stakes. I pushed the messy hair off Carter's forehead. "Babe, remember we talked about this. At some point, the real Gustavo is going to return and be very angry his brother went off the rails. We can't be here when that happens. The plan is to get as far away as we can from the compound and then wait for my team to find us."

He thought it through and then nodded. "How can I help?"

Good. That's what I needed. Maybe if I could give him a task to focus on, it would help distract him from his fear. "Pull another one of those tiny zipper pulls off the backpack. I dropped the one I was using outside when I heard you approach."

He muttered an apology as he reached for the backpack and began fiddling with one of the little zipper pulls. I stepped back over toward the window and glanced out again. The only clock I had was the one on the Horn. I reached for the device, intending to shoot Hux an update, but when I turned on the screen, a message blinked up. It looked like a cartoon newspaper with a large headline:

Turnip Blight devastates Hornlandia!

The text in the "article" below gave a little more information.

All Hornlanders must hunker down for the duration. Godspeed and good luck. May your previous harvests carry you through the blight. We expect our crop dusters to conquer the blight in approximately...

Below that was a countdown timer that showed eight and a half hours left.

"Fuck," I snapped after it wouldn't let me open the messaging portion of the game. "Fuck, fuck."

Carter glanced at me. "Turnip blight?"

"Why didn't they leave that part online? Now we're completely out of touch with my team." I couldn't believe my mission comms were reliant on a handheld game. This was like a screwball comedy. If it hadn't been for the very real threat of death, I'd want to laugh.

Hux's suggestion of escaping and hiding nearby had to be our plan now since that's the last communication we'd had with him. I grabbed the zipper pull from Carter's outstretched hand and got back to work.

"Go get dressed, and bring me my clothes too," I said over my shoulder. "As soon as I get the last two screws out, we need to be ready to move."

Carter did as I said without question, making sure to strap the knife to his calf before pulling his pant leg down over it. I dressed quickly while he took a turn with the screws, and then I got to work detaching the remaining zipper pulls so we'd each have one when we got to Buck's window. Everything was going to plan until I heard the guard come back around. This time, he wasn't alone.

"Duck," I hissed at Carter.

"*Gustavo estará aquí hoy,*" one of them said. *Gustavo will be back today.*

The other one sounded relieved. "*Sabrá que hacer con los rehenes.*" *He will know what to do with the hostages.*

The first guard laughed as they passed the window and walked away.

"Fuck," I said. "Gustavo's on his way back." I scrambled as fast as I could to finish the last screws, but before I could get the second-to-last one out, I heard Gianluigi's voice in the hallway outside our door.

"*Obtener los americanos,*" he said, the panic clear in his voice.

Another man said, "*¿Déjalos caer en las montañas?*" *Drop them in the mountains?*

"*¡Tomarlos en el avión! No quiero verlos de nuevo,*" Gianluigi said in response. *Take them in the plane! I don't want to see them again.*

"Shit," I muttered. We needed to get the hell out of here. As soon as the guards outside the window had rounded the corner of the house, I stood back up and rammed my shoulder against the metal grate over the window in a desperate attempt to force it. The remaining screws held tight, and the only gap that opened was too small for either of us to fit through. I began working the zipper pull again, but it was tedious, slow work. Too slow.

Hard boots hit the tile outside of our rooms, and I knew we were out of time. "Do as they say," I said quickly, shoving the Horn into one of Carter's cargo pants pockets and then scrambling in the medical bag for as many small tools as I could fit in his other pockets. "They're taking us to the plane. We'll find our opportunity. Be ready to follow my lead." I didn't mention the part about one of the guards mentioning dropping us out of the plane. Carter didn't need anything else to be terrified of, and our chances of getting out of this alive weren't all that great.

"Maybe they're letting us go," Carter said excitedly. "Maybe they're flying us to Caracas."

And maybe pigs were going to fly right alongside us.

"*¡Vamos!*" The guard rushed into our room. I could hear another guard doing the same next door. At least we'd have Buck with us in case we got an opportunity to escape.

The guards grabbed Carter roughly and pulled his hands behind him, tying his wrists together with rope before doing the same for me. They weren't total idiots since they noticed my attempt to hold my hands thumb sides together instead of wrists together. The man barked an order at me and yanked the ropes tight enough to cut off my circulation.

They hustled us outside in the rosy beginnings of dawn. Gianluigi was waiting for us outside, screeching in panic.

He swung wildly between English and Spanish, but the bottom line was wanting us gone ASAP.

I walked faster past him in hopes the guards would get us onto the plane before Gianluigi simply lost his cool altogether and ordered us shot where we stood. He hadn't seemed like a dangerous man, but panicked people were unpredictable, especially panicked brothers of cartel members. There was no sign of Buck until I was shoved up the small stairs and into the plane.

"Shew, I thought it was just me on this joyride," he said. His face was pale and damp with sweat. I couldn't imagine how painful the rush out to the plane would have been for him on an injured leg. "Y'all're a sight for sore eyes."

The small red-and-white plane was old as hell, to the point I wasn't quite sure it was air-worthy. It was a single-engine bi-plane that looked like Santiago had maybe gotten it cheap at Drug Lord Planes 'R Us. Or maybe that dark-web eBay where Buck had tried to sell his seed.

The guards shoved us down on the crazy metal benches lined up against the interior walls of the cargo area. It was obvious most of the cargo area had been cleared for cargo rather than human passengers. Carter kept flicking his eyes back at me as if expecting me to *do something*. The main guard tied Carter's and my hands to a metal pole behind the benches. Clearly this wasn't their first rodeo.

Thankfully, the pilot climbed past us and threw himself into the cockpit quickly, starting up the engine while Gianluigi was still fretting.

"Goodbye, my American hostages!" he shouted. "I wish that things could have ended differently. We could have been friends! I will remember you fondly. You have made this great man an even greater man by being… great. My women will thank you for healing me, although I will remain in throne position as is decreed by my especial Dr.

Carter and, obviously, the respect that is due to one such as myself."

Someone else shouted something at him in rapid Spanish that I didn't catch, and then Gianluigi's voice came back more stressed than before. "Be off! Be gone! Godspeed and good luck. May God have mercy on—"

I didn't catch the rest. The guard who'd tied us to the rails jumped out before tying Buck to the wall of the plane. Carter and I exchanged a glance.

A second guard jumped in and slid the door closed before moving up to take the other seat next to the pilot. There was no door between the cockpit and the cargo area, so the pilot and guard could look back at any time to check on us.

As soon as the plane began moving, I leaned across the narrow aisle and asked Buck if he could turn around and grab the knife in Carter's pants with his hands. I kept my eyes on the guards to make sure we had enough warning to get back in position.

It took some work, and Buck had to brace through a ton of pain as the plane bumped down the rough runway, but he finally sliced through the ropes on my wrists. After handing me the knife, Buck returned to his seat and closed his eyes. He looked like he was going to puke.

I quickly cut through the rope on Carter's hands. The noise from the plane's engine was loud enough to cover most of my furtive instructions. Anytime the second guard turned his head to check on us, we quickly resumed the positions of compliant hostages with our hands behind our backs, but the minute he faced forward again, I got back to work with the knife.

"What about me?" Buck hissed.

I didn't trust him not to fuck things up. He didn't seem

like the smartest Nutter in the Thicket, so I was hesitant to rely on him.

After cutting his ropes, I told him to stay here on the bench and wait for instruction. "You need to stay here and keep your injury from opening back up."

The plane was just lifting over the treetops when I stopped to take a breath. I turned to Carter. "I'm going to subdue the guard first, but just in case this pilot has a death wish, I'll need to be ready to take over the controls. That means you're going to be the one tying these guys up."

"Wait. What?" He looked a little confused.

"Babe, we're hijacking this plane."

Instead of panicking, Carter let out a breath and firmed his chin. "Fuck yeah, we are. Let's do this."

I started to stand, but he grabbed my arm and handed me something. "Wait! One of the things you shoved in my pocket was a prefilled syringe of Versed." He looked nervous. "Try not to use it since we don't know if the guard will tolerate it, but if you need it… it's a fast-acting sedative."

He was worried about the thug who was potentially charged with throwing us out of this plane.

I gripped the back of his neck and pressed a hard kiss on his lips. Buck made a surprised noise behind me. "You're the kindest man I know, Duchess," I murmured. "Grab the ropes and be ready."

I slipped the syringe into the chest pocket of my scrub top and held the knife in my right hand as I crept up to the cockpit. The wall behind the guard's seat gave me enough coverage to wait until he looked back again and saw I was missing from the bench. He made a noise of surprise and crawled out of his seat to come back to the cargo area. As soon as he was within reach, I grabbed him and wrestled his arms behind his back before putting him facedown on the floor of the plane and patting him down for his weapon.

Sure enough, he had a handgun at his hip. I shoved it into my waistband and reached for the rope from Carter. I tied the guard up and then hauled him further down the cargo area before tying him quickly to a cargo bolt in the floor. When I stood back up to return to the cockpit, I felt the plane take a steep turn to the right. The pilot was yelling into his radio and trying to control the plane with a gun in his hand. Buck had smartly moved over to Carter's side of the plane, and they'd both moved forward so they sat behind the pilot's seat where he couldn't see them or aim at them.

I wasn't as lucky.

"Riggs!" Carter yelled seconds before the pilot took a shot. I dropped to the floor and banged my knee and elbow hard, but at least I hadn't been shot. The gun fell out of my pants and slid deep under the benches.

"Are you fucking crazy?" I shouted at the pilot, scrambling over to the side where Carter and Buck were. *"¡Nos vas a matar!" You're going to kill us.*

"¡No te voy a lastimar!" he shouted back. *I'm not going to hurt you!* As if I would believe that from a man who'd just shot at me.

I crouched low and shuffled closer. Christ. These men were nuts. Carter grabbed my wrist and pulled me close to them. "Give me the Versed."

I handed over the syringe without thinking. Before I even realized what he was doing, Carter had stepped up and jabbed the pilot in the arm.

"What are you doing?" I cried. "We need him to fly the plane!"

Carter looked back at me in shock. "I thought you knew how to fly the plane!"

I lunged forward and grabbed the handgun out of the pilot's hand as he began to slump forward in the pilot's seat. "Fuck, fuck," I hissed, yanking at his seat belt so I could pull him out of the chair. As soon as I got him out, I shouted for Carter to tie him up in case he regained consciousness, and then I climbed into the chair and grabbed the yoke.

"Fuck," I repeated under my breath. All of the controls were in a Cyrillic language. I recognized the brand of plane as an Antonov, which was built in Ukraine. "Fuck."

Carter appeared over my shoulder. "I… shit. I… oh my God, are we going to crash? I'm sorry! What do I do?"

I tried to stay calm. "I know the basics of how to keep us in the air, but I'm going to need help navigating us somewhere and figuring out how to land. See if they have a phone or something."

The minute I tried radioing anyone official in Venezuela, we'd be at the mercy of the corrupt government and who knows who else around here.

The guard on the ground started moaning. "*¡No íbamos a lastimarte! Gianluigi dijo que te llevara a un lugar seguro. Quería que te dejáramos ir!*"

"Uh. You guys get that?" Buck asked. "My dude says Gianluigi wanted to let us go. They was takin' us to safety."

Carter clapped a hand over his mouth, and I knew from looking at him that he was torn between feeling sentimental over Gianluigi having mercy on us in the end and even more guilt over unnecessarily drugging the pilot… and potentially causing us to crash.

"We can deal with that later," I said sharply, jolting him out of his guilt spiral. "First things first. Phone?"

"No, but I have my Horn!" Carter said. "Hang on."

"The Turnip Blight," I reminded him. "We've got another seven hours and something. We're fucked."

"Do what now?" Buck said. "You talking about the HOG Turnip Blight?"

No, jackass, we're talking about another turnip blight. Christ.

"Yes," Carter said. "I have a sat-enabled Horn, but we can't communicate while it's down for maintenance."

"Aw, well, that's easy. Just tap the strawberry in the logo, and then slide your finger between the corn husk and the grapes in the cornucopia. It'll give you access to your message page."

Carter and I both turned to stare at the man.

"Are you some kind of Horn prodigy?" Carter demanded.

"The original Horn prodigy," Buck agreed.

"Hmm." Carter frowned.

Fortunately, Carter was too preoccupied to connect the dots at the moment and realize who Buck was, but I knew he'd be annoyed later. I planned to explain the situation—a version that wouldn't get me in trouble for spilling client secrets—to him once we were on the ground.

Assuming we survived the landing.

"Focus. You can force the Horn's chat function to work even during the Blight?" I demanded.

"Sure. What's that look for?" Buck asked, blinking innocently. "The only reason HOG don't want people using the message app while we're doing maintenance is because they'll inevitably contact support, and we want all our resources on the upgrade. There ain't no reason you can't message your buddies so long as you don't open a support ticket."

"Yeah, we don't need a support ticket," Carter said, quickly tapping the Horn awake and trying the trick with the logo image. "It worked!"

"'Course it worked. I didn't just fall off a turnip... truck. Hey, that's pretty funny, considering."

It really wasn't.

Carter glanced back at Buck. "But how will my friend know the messaging trick?"

Buck reached for the Horn and clicked a few buttons before handing it back. "There. That'll wake up his Horn and make it yodel. The message page will appear instead of the Turnip Blight newspaper."

Yodel. For fuck's sake.

I began barking orders. "Tell Hux I need translation for the cockpit controls of an Antonov An-2. I need help navigating, and I'll sure as shit need help landing in Socopó."

Carter climbed into the copilot's seat and belted himself in before reading Hux's response. He looked up at me with all the fear in his eyes again.

"He says we can't go to Socopó. The military is doing exercises there."

Carter tapped messages back and forth. "He can't be serious," he muttered under his breath.

"Why? What's he saying?"

Carter looked up at me again. "He says we need to fly into Colombia. Isn't that illegal?"

This situation was so ridiculous, I wanted to laugh. "More illegal than hijacking a drug lord's plane, drugging our pilot, and flying without a license?"

Carter bit his lip. "You don't have to be sarcastic—"

Before I could respond, the plane started to dive, and everyone, including me, started screaming.

16

CARTER

Riggs pulled back on the plane's steering wheel thing, and the plane leveled out just a little. We were still losing altitude, but less like a missile intent on screaming to our deaths in the Venezuelan jungle… and more like a ticking time bomb, hurtling toward possible death somewhere in Colombia.

"Good job," I told Riggs, patting his shoulder and hoping he couldn't tell how badly my hands were shaking. "*Excellent*. Really. That's a neat trick to have in your back pocket. Thank God for your military training, huh?"

Riggs shot me a raised eyebrow over his shoulder. "The Marines do not train us to fly planes, Duchess. This neat trick was a hundred percent thanks to Alan Riggs. My dad's favorite forced family-bonding activity was making us watch *Iron Eagle* and *Top Gun* and every other '80s military movie ever."

"Aw. That's adorable."

Riggs rolled his eyes. "Yeah, well, there were serious limitations. I have a basic idea of how to keep the plane going straight, that's all. And if I were flying a SuperHornet and needed to blow a MiG out of the sky while doing a barrel roll like a total douche, obviously I'd be all over that too."

A snort-giggle escaped me before I clapped a hand over my mouth to shut myself up. I still had gallons of adrenaline flooding my system, but somehow William Riggs could make me laugh under even the darkest circumstances. *That* was the real trick, and I was pretty sure it wasn't something he'd been taught; it was just an essential part of his personality.

Riggs's lips pulled up when he saw my smile before he shook his head and got serious. "I don't know where I'm going or how to orient myself when I can't read the dials. And as far as I recall, they never showed Maverick *landing*, which is why I need Hux to get me a copy of How to Land a 40-Year-Old Russian Plane For Dummies, baby. As in, *now*."

"Right! Shit. Right." I unbuckled my belt and scrambled on the floor for the Horn, which I'd fumbled when the plane had dropped.

Meanwhile, Riggs called Buck forward and pointed toward the handgun, which was lying on the floor under the bench.

"You know how to use that, right? And you understand that shooting guns on planes is not advisable unless our lives are in danger? Okay, then. Your job is to keep an eye on the prisoners back there. Pat them down for weapons and keep them quiet."

"You got it, Chief!" Buck assured him.

I found the Horn under my seat, buckled myself back in, and started frantically typing.

KevsCuz: *Hux??? This is Carter Rogers again. Did you find a manual?? A translation?? ANYTHING?? Riggs isn't sure how to navigate and I'm pretty sure we're still descending.*

HogMasterHux: *Motherfucker. I told that idiot to learn Russian, but nooooo. He had to learn PASHTO, even though we don't even take assignments in Afghanistan anymore!*

I had a pretty good idea why Riggs would want to know how to communicate with people in Afghanistan, but I bit my tongue.

HogMasterHux: *Believe it or not, this stuff is not widely available on the internet. Especially not in English. I'll do the best I can. Can you try to find the altimeter?*

A frisson of panic zinged up my spine. "Riggs, Hux says to find the altimeter."

"Which one's the altimeter?"

KevsCuz: *Which one's the altimeter?*

HogMasterHux: *The one that looks like it's measuring altitude.*

Gah.

I clutched the Horn tighter as I stared at the control panel, which looked like something out of a sci-fi movie. It wasn't like on a car where there were maybe four or five gauges. There were at least three or four *dozen*, with more switches and levers on the ceiling. I was confident some of them were duplicates for the pilot and copilot.

Maybe figuring out the altimeter by process of elimination would have been a fun logic puzzle to figure out while sitting with a glass of wine in front of the fire on a rainy afternoon, but trying to do it while hurtling through the sky was significantly less fun. I hated that I had so little control over this. I couldn't even google the answer for myself.

My Horn buzzed with a new message.

HogDocKev: *Hey! Hi. It's me. Kev. Aka, THE GUY YOU DON'T NEED, who also happens to be the guy who crafted the tricked-out HOG that's enabling you to have this convo. I'm gonna head back home to UNNECESSARYVILLE in a minute, but first would you like me to explain how to fly and land the Antonov?*

I blinked down at the display in shock.

KevsCuz: *No way!! You know how to fly an Antonov?? Yes!! Hell yes.*

HogDocKev: *You remember how I was way into flight simulators a couple years back, right? This process is very straightforward and the machine does all the work. Promise! Ready for step one?*

KevsCuz: *Oh, thank fuck. Yeah, we're beyond ready.*

HogMasterHux: *STOP RIGHT THERE. There's literally no way you know how to fly a 640 ton cargo plane after playing Flight Simulator, Orc Humper. You're gonna make them crash the plane. Go play and come back when the grownups are done, pal.*

"What's going on?" Riggs demanded. "What's Hux saying?"

I relayed the conversation to him, and Riggs frowned. "Hux is right. *Flight Simulator* is not the same."

"But Hux doesn't have a better idea!"

My Horn buzzed again.

HogDocKev: **snort* 640 tons?!?! OMG, you think they're in an Antonov 225? Pay attention, Tuber Tickler! Carter just said they're in an An-2!!!! HAHHAHHAA.*

HogDocKev: *THIS IS HILARIOUS!!!! You legit thought they were in the largest fucking cargo plane in the world? With a 6 person cockpit, capable of transporting SPACE SHUTTLES?*

HogDocKev: *Do you know that those things need a 3/4 mile runway to takeoff??? And you think some rando criminal uses that one for his stealthy criminal shit? But *I* am the one who's gonna make them crash? Lolz. Thanks for playing.*

I shook my head in frustration, really wishing there were a voice capability on the HOG device so I could scream my head off at them.

"What *now*?" Riggs asked.

When I read the convo out loud, he groaned and scrubbed a hand over his head.

KevsCuz: *Guys! Hello? We're in a plane here. You're supposed to be helping us, remember?*

HogMasterHux: *I made a simple mistake, loser. Now close your pumpkin hole and let me look for the correct specs.*

HogDocKev: *They don't need you to find them the specs, 'cause I already have the specs. And THIS isn't a simple mistake. A simple mistake is when a newbie player wandering far from his lands tryna hustle for a pip or two to feed his ice cow takes a SINGLE PIECE OF FRUIT from what appears to be an unclaimed tree to give him the health points he needs to survive the journey home!!!*

HogMasterHux: *Don't you play innocent noob with me, HogDoc. That tree was clearly on MY LAND… I just hadn't fenced it yet.*

KevsCuz: *Are you serious right now? OUR PLANE IS LOSING ALTITUDE!!*

HogDocKev: *If you don't fence the tree, it's not your tree! That's the meta of the game. EVERYONE KNOWS this.*

HogMasterHux: *What I know is, you passed a thousand fucking apples to eat the lone greenberry I needed to make the potion required to ascend to mage status. EVERYONE KNOWS the greenberry only ripens once a season! That was DELIBERATE, and it was HURTFUL.*

Holy shit. Were they kidding??

"Please tell me they're not still fighting," Riggs said.

"I could, but I'd be lying."

KevsCuz: *For fuck's sake, could you two stop bickering and help us?!?!*

HogDocKev: *You wanna talk HURTFUL?!?!?! You got a bunch of your buddies together and INVADED MY HOME-STEAD!! You stole my spelled claymore AND you killed my bronze goose, when poor Jaunty never hurt anyone. It's a wonder I survived the winter! Some mistakes are UNFORGIVABLE.*

HogMasterHux: *Jaunty was an unfortunate casualty of our* *war which YOU started. I wish things had gone differently. He was a good goose.*

Good. God. Really? *Really?*

KevsCuz: *Do you hear yourselves? If we don't DIE in a fiery CRASH, I am telling Champ AND Grandfather about this!!*

HogDocKev: *HA! You're only apologizing bc I'm the undisputed master of the game, and I've laid siege to the lands all around yours. Well, too fucking late.*

HogMasterHux: *Undisputed? Hahahahahahaasdjfajf. I dispute it. I DISPUTE IT. Come at me, Pyrite Warlock. See what happens!!!!*

HogDocKev: *Invasion is imminent, Hoax Master, and I will show you no mercy! JAUNTY WILL BE AVENGED.*

And that was when I lost my fucking mind.

KevsCuz: *SOMEONE NEEDS TO TELL US HOW TO FLY THIS GODDAMN PLANE, OR I WILL ASK THE GAME DEVELOPER TO BAN YOU FOR LIFE!!!!!!!!*

No messages appeared for maybe ten seconds, then…

HogMasterHux: *Wow. Dr. Rogers, I know you're a client and all, but there's no call for that kind of rudeness.*

HogDocKev: *Truth. I hate Hux's guts, but you don't just wish a BAN on someone. That's massively uncool.*

I sucked in a breath.

KevsCuz: *If we die in this plane, Kev, I will come back to haunt you and only appear when you're having sex, I swear. If you ever want to get off again, TELL ME HOW TO FLY THIS.*

KevsCuz: *Okay, okay, yeesh. STEP ONE, check your speed. Look for the second instrument readout on the left if you're sitting in the pilot's seat.*

"Uh. One forty," Riggs replied tersely when I read this aloud. "Maybe a little more. Is that good?"

I relayed the question.

HogDocKev: *Yeah, that's fine. Now, your altimeter should be right in the middle of the board. It's the display that looks like it has* *a picture of the horizon on it. You're gonna wanna make sure the arrow at the top center of the outer circle is lined up with the arrow on the dial. You'll see what I mean.*

I set a hand on Riggs's shoulder and leaned over him to look at the display.

KevsCuz: *They're lined up.*

HogDocKev: *Great!*

HogDocKev: *Now, gimme the number on the right side of that display.*

KevsCuz: *30765. Is that the altitude?*

HogDocKev: *Yep. There's nothing to worry about, but that number's a little low.*

HogMasterHux: *No it's not. You're fine where you are.*

KevsCuz: *Wait, which is it?*

HogDocKev: *You're low. You're heading to Colombia, which means you'll be flying over higher terrain.*

HogMasterHux: *Flying higher means it'll be harder to land.*

HogDocKev: *That's THE OPPOSITE OF TRUE. Carter, when you fly too low, you have no time to correct your approach. Trust me. Have Riggs pull up on the yoke again very gently and slowly until that number reads at 33-35k, then ease off. That's a better cruising altitude.*

"Riggs?" I squeezed his arm. "Kev says you need to gain altitude until we're at 35,000 feet."

Riggs hesitated. "*Kev* says? What's Hux saying?"

I licked my lips. "He says we're okay where we are. But he also hasn't found a manual."

"Fuck."

I read him the whole convo. "Kev wouldn't say he knew what he was talking about unless he did," I said staunchly. "We need to trust him."

"Your cousin who spends his entire day in your grandfather's basement playing with his Horn? You want to trust him with our lives?"

I thought this was very unfair, since it seemed like Hux played at least as much as Kev did, but unlike *some* people, I was capable of keeping a conversation on track.

"Yes," I said simply. "Trust me when I tell you we can trust him, Riggs. *Trust me.*"

Riggs's jaw worked before he nodded once. He pulled back on the yoke gently, and the nose of the plane tilted upward. We both watched tensely as it climbed to 35,000, then let out a deep breath as he slowly relaxed on the yoke.

"What's next?" he demanded.

KevsCuz: *We climbed.*

HogMasterHux: *Fuck.*

HogDocKev: *Good. Now I'm gonna contact air traffic control for you in Colombia. Looks like there's a little airport west of Mara-caibo in a town called Santa Irma that would work.*

HogMasterHux: *Seriously? Now you speak Spanish? JFC, this gets weirder and weirder. Dr. Rogers, please listen to me. I'm working to find you a manual. Just hold tight.*

HogDocKev: *Everyone knows English is the language of aviation. Duh. Now, hold on while I get you the radio frequency to plug into the Instrument Landing System, then they'll guide you through how and when to deploy the landing gear, okay? The autopilot will do most of the work. You're gonna be fine.*

KevsCuz: *Hux, is that a place you can get to easily so you can meet us?*

HogMasterHux: *Yeah. Santa Irma is the airport I was gonna direct you to. Our ETA is about forty-five minutes.*

I let out a breath and relayed all of this to Riggs, who set his jaw and nodded, his eyes scanning the instrument panels.

A few minutes later, a call came over the radio. "H765D, this is Santa Irma, Colombia."

"Santa Irma, this is H765D. We had a slight problem with our pilot..." Riggs explained the entire story—well, a heavily edited version that involved the pilot passing out from too much drink and us being forced to take over—and the air traffic control person explained in heavily accented English how to engage the autopilot system and input the coordinates for the airport so the plane could guide us there.

When they disconnected for a minute, Riggs looked at me, and his face broke out into a relieved smile.

"Does this mean we're safe?" I asked hopefully.

"As long as they can get us on the ground, we'll be home free." A little thread of excitement hummed beneath his words.

"So… we did it? Go Team Riggs and Carter?"

Riggs shook his head, though his smile didn't budge. "Not quite done yet." He lifted a hand to cup my cheek, running his thumb over my cheekbone. "But yeah. Go Team Riggs and Carter."

My heart thumped excitedly in a way that was part fear, part anticipation. And I figured if there were ever a time to take a risk, maybe it was right then.

"So, when we get back to Tennessee," I began, "Maybe you and I could—?"

The radio crackled again. "H765D, begin approach to Santa Irma."

Riggs winked at me. "Let's table that, okay?"

"Oh." I nodded aggressively. "Yeah, no. Totally. It can wait."

Riggs engaged the radio, and the air traffic controller guided him in for a landing. My vision sort of tunneled when she explained that the airplane had an updated computer that would do everything except engage the landing gear and the brakes—that did *not* sound safe—but Riggs grabbed my hand and squeezed it before letting it go so he could keep both hands on the controls. "Deep breath," he said.

I'd flown a thousand times before, but I'd never paid much attention to how quickly the plane lost altitude when it was time to land. The houses on the ground that started out as tiny specks grew larger and larger as we approached the airport and as our altitude dropped, my mouth flooded with the metallic taste of fear.

Believing in Riggs was one thing, but trusting the supposedly-updated mechanics of this ancient plane was a whole other thing. I knew I was never going to take this process of take-off and landing for granted again.

A calm voice on the radio instructed Riggs to pull back the lever to deploy the landing gear and he shot me a look that spoke volumes. This was it. The moment of truth.

The plane let out a horrible squeal of grinding parts, ending in a loud *thunk* that reverberated through the cabin. I clung to Riggs's arm, my heart pounding too hard for me to even try to play it cool. Had something gone wrong? After everything that happened in Columbia, would *this* be the end?

But then a voice came over the radio saying, "We have visual confirmation, your landing gear has deployed. Well-done!" and I released the breath I'd been holding in a shuddering sigh.

The moment our wheels hit the runway in Santa Irma was almost anti-climactic. The plane touched down with a bouncing jerk that rattled my teeth, and we thumped down the runway for a second, but then Riggs engaged the brakes with the competence of a guy who'd done scary shit a thousand times before, and suddenly people were rushing out of the terminal to put blocks under the wheels and deplane us. Then all the adrenaline that had flooded my system had nowhere to go.

"Duchess?" Riggs said with a quizzical smile when only the two of us were left on board. "You coming?"

"Yeah." I cleared my throat. "I feel more nervous now than I did an hour ago. Adrenaline crash or something."

Riggs stepped into my personal space, the way he always did, and rubbed his big hands up and down my biceps comfortingly. "You're usually good when the crisis is happening, you know that? When we're hijacking a plane. When we're in the kitchen and Buck's bleeding. When you've got a kid with malaria or a heart patient that needs tending. You don't let yourself feel the fear until you're alone or with me. It's normal."

I nodded jerkily, his words soothing something inside me. "I'm having all sorts of interesting revelations about myself on this trip, huh? Turns out I'm only okay in a crisis when I feel like I can control it—when I have the resources I need—otherwise, I get stressed. And yeah, I guess I compartmentalize things too. Don't let myself feel scared until I'm in a safer place." I bit my lip as I realized I was equating Riggs with safety and *admitting it*, but it was true, so I wasn't going to take it back. "I guess that's the one good thing that's come out of the whole kidnapping/hostage/being marked for death thing, huh? The silver lining, I guess."

Riggs's grin warmed, and the expression in his dark eyes turned teasing as he wrapped his arms around my waist. "Is that the *only* silver lining, Dr. Rogers?"

I laughed as I looped my arms around his neck. "Mmmm, maybe not the *only* one." I leaned into him, tilting my head back so I could smile up at him.

Riggs brushed his mouth over mine once, then twice, before parting my lips with his own and crushing me against him—a little maneuver that was uniquely *Riggs* and which I fucking loved. His tongue tangled with mine, exploring me with lazy thoroughness.

God, it was good between us. And I'd swear his kisses got better and more potent all the damn time.

It was funny how quickly a person could get used to a thing. To the singular way Riggs kissed, to the woodsy scent of him that lingered even when he hadn't had access to cologne in days, to the way I felt buoyant but also secure when he held me.

"Like I was saying before," I whispered hoarsely when he finally pulled back for air. "When we get home to Tennessee, do you think — ?"

"Fuckin' A, Riggsy!" a voice called excitedly from outside. Heavy boots hit the plane's stairs, making the metal groan. "The way you landed this bird was an instant classic. I got iPhone footage for the office Christmas par — oh." A man with a head full of wavy blond hair and a chin sharp enough to cut glass stopped short at the sight of me and immediately cleared his throat. His eyes ping-ponged between me and Riggs. "Hey there, Dr. Rogers. Nice to meet you. I'm Jasper Huxley, the guy you were texting with earlier. Sorry about that." He hooked a thumb over his shoulder toward the stairway. "I figured Riggsy — er, Mr. Riggs — would have secured *the client* in the airport first thing when he landed." He widened his eyes significantly. "Champ headed to the terminal first since he assumed that's where Dr. Rogers would be."

"Uh. *Shit*." Riggs took a giant step back, which was really awkward since my hands were still around his neck. "This isn't what it looks like."

It wasn't? What did it look like?

Thrown off-balance in more ways than one, I stumbled hard against Riggs's broad chest with an "Oof."

"Dr. Rogers is feeling weak and shaky. See? " Riggs

grabbed me by the shoulders to simultaneously haul me upright and push me away from him. "I was going to carry him in."

Carry me in? I shot him a look. *Dr. Rogers?* I mean, I didn't expect him to kiss me in front of his teammates, obviously, but were we not even supposed to be friends?

"Ohhhh," Hux said, his face breaking into a relieved grin. "Shit, man, I thought for a minute this was you and the Grindr hookup all over again."

Riggs stiffened and glared at Hux. "Huxley," he said in a warning tone.

Grindr hookup? What Grindr hookup? I frowned at Riggs, but he didn't look at me.

Hux didn't seem to notice the laser beams pointed in his direction. He set his hands on his hips, and his eyes danced around the plane, taking in the fixtures. His expression soured when he looked at the control panel, like it had done him a personal injustice. "Just sayin', hooking up with a dude while on your last mission was what got you into this mess! If you'd hooked up with yet another guy, Champ would castrate you," he said cheerfully. "And then the entire population of cute-but-helpless twinks in eastern Tennessee would go into mourning and—"

"*Huxley!*" Riggs gritted out at the same moment I said, "Excuse me?"

Neither of them noticed that I was directing my comment to Riggs.

Hux straightened his posture and swallowed convulsively. "Ah, crap. Sorry *again*, Dr. Rogers. I'm not usually so unprofessional. They don't let me out of my computer lab much."

"It's fine." I summoned a small, insincere smile and moved my arms over my chest, hugging myself. "Don't worry about it."

"I mean, you're clearly not the kind of guy Riggs would hook up with," Hux went on, trying to make things better and instead making them infinitely worse. "You're not a twink, for one thing. And he likes 'em pretty and a little stupid, anyway." His eyes widened at his own words. "Uh. I mean. I mean, not that you're not pretty. You're gorgeous! Just that you're, ah, clearly not stupid?" He sighed and rubbed a hand over his face. "God."

"And now we see why you don't get out of the lab much," Riggs said in a hard voice.

I forced a chuckle, because what else could I do? I was realizing I had the capacity to be a whole lot stupider than Huxley gave me credit for.

Here I was, giant cartoon hearts pulsing in my eyes as I imagined a sparkly unicorn future where Riggs and I… what? Settled down in the Thicket? One blue-blooded cardiologist and one former military brat turned professional badass, with a white picket fence, and a spot in the Thicket Holiday Parade of Homes, and a standing Tuesday date at the Tavern?

There was zero chance Riggs would want that future. Heck, I wasn't sure *I* did.

Thank *God* I hadn't said anything about making this permanent. Thank sweet tiny baby Jesus that we'd been repeatedly interrupted before I could make myself any more of a fool than I already was.

Hux clapped his hands together once. "So. Shall we?" He made a sweeping gesture toward the door of the plane like a game show hostess. "I promise, Champ's plane has way better accommodations than this, Dr. Rogers." He leaned toward me and whispered confidingly, "There are couches. And snacks. Plenty of room for all of us, plus you and Mr. Nutter."

"Mr. Nutter?"

"Er, yes?" Hux frowned. "Buck Nutter? The software developer you rescued."

I closed my eyes as understanding crashed down. And I'd thought I felt foolish before? Good gravy. Now that the adrenaline was fading, the puzzle pieces were assembling themselves before my very eyes, and the picture they formed was more mortifying with every second that passed.

"The magic seed man," I said, purposely not looking at Riggs. "Who was also being held prisoner by the cartel. The man whose leg I stitched up. He's Buck Nutter, Amos's great-nephew."

All of which Riggs had known. None of which Riggs had shared with me, even when I asked him point-blank.

Because I was not his friend, let alone his lover. I was his *principal*.

His job.

Just another guy he'd hooked up with while on a mission. A way to pass the time while he was away from all the twinks in Licking Thicket.

"Uh." Hux looked from me to Riggs and back, unsure what he was missing. "Yes?"

"Got it. Thanks for explaining that, *Hux*. Well, let's climb aboard, then. I could use a snack." I smiled mechanically. "And a couch."

"You go first, Hux." Riggs's voice sounded more like a croak. "I'll follow with C—Dr. Rogers."

"M'kay." He shrugged.

"Actually, no. Thank you anyway, Riggs, but I'm feeling much steadier, and I can't stand to spend another minute in this plane."

I smiled at Hux again as I slipped past him and made my way down the stairs into the hazy sunshine that beat down on the tarmac.

Hold it together, Carter. Just a few more hours to

Tennessee, and then… Shit. I had no fucking clue what would happen then.

My pocket vibrated, and I took out my Horn.

HogDocKev: *You good?*

KevsCuz: *We landed safely.*

I wouldn't say I was good.

KevsCuz: *Champion security has a plane here and we're heading back to Tennessee. I'm not sure what airport. Maybe you could tell Grandfather?*

HogDocKev: *Yeah about that… He already knows. All of it. The head of the security company told him a few minutes ago. We'll be there to meet you when you land.*

KevsCuz: *Both of you?*

HogDocKev: *Hells yes. You're my favorite cousin and I love you. Remember?*

I clutched the Horn tighter, my fingernails digging into the rubber casing.

KevsCuz: *I remember. And I love you, too.*

And *that* was what I needed to focus on. Family. Friends. That was my real life. The rest of this was nothing but a fantasy.

HogDocKev: *Glad you said that, cause Grandfather maybe also called Dr. Wright and explained the situation, and he said he "activated the Beautification Corps." I'm not sure what that's code for.*

I groaned.

KevsCuz: *It's code for him calling Ava Siegel, who'll throw a welcome home party AND mobilize a casserole posse. I won't have to cook for a month. They'll probably decorate my front porch, too. And someone will stop by every single day.*

HogDocKev: *Sounds amazing.*

KevsCuz: *It is. And it's not.*

HogDocKev: *You have so many friends. You're so settled in the Thicket. It's cool that you've found where you belong, Carter.*

I blinked in surprise. Kev had only been to the Thicket for the gala, and he'd spent most of it hiding behind a tree. How would he know?

Before I could ask any follow-up questions about this, a barrel-chested blond man with a wide, white smile jogged out of the terminal. "Dr. Carter! I'm Champ. Great to meet you finally."

I nodded politely. "Same. I wish the circumstances were better." This was the man who'd been trapped with Riggs in Afghanistan. The man who'd threatened to castrate him if he fucked another guy while on a mission. *Oh, God, do not think about that.*

"You took the words out of my mouth." His wide smile got impossibly wider. "I'd love to debrief you in a little while. Maybe we could step into the airport, you, me, Riggs, and the local authorities? We could talk about what happened, get a statement for the authorities—"

Wait. Champ, me, and *Riggs*? Sitting around talking about this whole experience, while Riggs pretended we'd never discussed anything more serious than the weather and I'd never taken his cock down my throat?

Fuck no. I couldn't even imagine it. That would be like pouring salt on an open wound.

I threw my shoulders back and lifted one eyebrow just a tiny bit—a trick of my grandfather's that made it seem like you were looking down on someone, even if they were taller than you. Then I summoned my iciest, most imperious tone as I interrupted, "Actually, Mr. Champion, I'd much rather you returned me home immediately. This has been a very difficult time, as I'm sure you can imagine. I'd be happy to make a statement, of course, but later. After I've seen my family again. After I've rested and recovered."

Champ blinked but said smoothly, "Of course, Dr.

Rogers. I was thinking maybe you'd like a minute to rest *here* before you—"

"No," I assured him. "I'm eager to get underway."

"Alright. Let me get you settled, and we can make plans to depart momentarily."

I nodded once, regally. "Excellent. Thank you."

Champ directed me to a brown leather couch at the back of the plane, where I sat and pretended to be engrossed in *Horn of Glory* as the team prepared the plane for departure. One by one, the rest of Champ's men—the ones he'd brought, anyway—filed into the plane. A guy with golden eyes, golden-brown skin, and honey-brown Jesus hair. A slightly shorter redhead. Riggs. Champ, who led Buck Nutter to the couch across from mine. Huxley. And an incredibly gorgeous Black man with close-cropped hair, who locked the door to the plane, then turned to the crew and said, "Locked and loaded, Champ. We ready?" before heading for the pilot's seat the second Champ gave him a nod.

From the corner of my eye, I saw Riggs stare at me as he walked toward the group of chairs where his buddies sat at the front of the plane, like he was trying to lift my gaze to his with the power of his mind. I would not look at him, though. What good would it do? I didn't want to see him look apologetic or regretful or, *God forbid*, ashamed.

It wasn't until the plane lurched forward for takeoff that I realized Champ might've had a good reason for wanting me to rest and decompress before flying again. My stomach heaved with the motion as the plane became airborne, and I clapped a hand over my mouth. The second it felt like we'd leveled off, I unbuckled my belt and rushed for the lavatory at the front of the plane.

Fortunately, the urge to vomit passed by the time I got there, but I stared at my reflection in the tiny mirror as I splashed water on my face. The yellow light made me look paler than I'd ever been. My face was puffy, and my eyes were ringed in shadow.

Not remotely twinkish. Not remotely cute-but-helpless.

Not at all Riggs's type. Which was *good*, because he wasn't mine. We didn't have a single thing in common.

My stomach burbled unhappily.

"You do not need him," I told myself in a low voice, blotting my cheeks with a paper towel. "You do not need his stupid strong arms around you right now. You do not need his kisses. You do not need his reassuring lies. You deserve something *real*."

I made my way out of the bathroom slowly, pausing in the doorway to take a deep, silent breath and psych myself up before I emerged into the hall…

Which was how I was in the perfect place to hear Champ say, "Proud of you, Riggsy! I admit, I was pissed when I gave you this assignment. I wanted to make you think twice and get your priorities in order. But I had no idea how tough this one was gonna be. Getting a difficult principal through kidnapping and a hostage situation, *and* finding HOG's missing programmer? You redeemed yourself."

A *difficult principal*? I almost gasped and gave myself away. I hadn't been difficult! Had I?

"Nah, it wasn't bad," Riggs said uncomfortably. "Dr. Rogers is a good guy. And I mean, at least the place had running water and AC. Not like that time in Niamey, huh?"

Someone hooted. "Oh, God. That was the *worst*. You remember—"

"Shut it, Elvo," Champ interrupted. "I'm not done. I've been hard on you about your inability to keep your shit contained, Riggs, and I'm sure I'll be hard on you again in the future. But credit where credit is due, man. You managed to keep the doctor safe, and that couldn't have been easy. You don't always keep your temper with the principals who give you an attitude, but clearly you figured out a way this time. You put the job first, as you should. Which is why..." He paused dramatically. "I've decided to reinstate you to the auricle implant training."

"No! Wait, really?" Riggs was clearly shocked. "You serious?"

"Would I lie? You proved yourself on this assignment. Whatever you did, keep doing it. Your dedication is fucking impressive."

I couldn't help the bubble of slightly hysterical laughter that escaped at that. *Oh, God.* The job. Always the damn job. If only they knew just *how* dedicated he'd been. He'd gone to great lengths to *handle* me.

The voices died as Champ's crew realized I was there. I pasted on a polite smile as I stepped away from the lavatory doorway, and Champ nodded at me, cool and professional.

"Doing okay there, Dr. Rogers?"

"Me? Oh, fine. Never better," I assured him airily, like I hadn't just rushed past them moments before with a hand clamped over my mouth. "People have remarked on my ability to compartmentalize."

From the corner of my eye, I saw Riggs shift in his seat and waited for him to speak up. To defend me and say I hadn't been a difficult principal. To put his arm around my shoulders and guide me to the back of the plane because he could see that I needed it. To at least speak directly to me like I was a human being and more than just an... an assignment.

But he didn't. Because I wasn't.

And a tiny piece of my heart that I hadn't fully acknowledged I'd written Riggs's name on withered and died right there and then.

I inclined my chin. "Thanks very much for the speedy rescue, Mr. Champion. I'm sure my grandfather will reward you handsomely for going above and beyond. Sorry for the inconvenience it's caused."

Champ nodded, but he frowned at the same time, narrowing his eyes like he was trying to read my mind.

I made my way back to the couches before he could.

"How's the leg, Buck?" I asked because I was a person who cared about other people and how they were feeling, unlike certain emotionless assholes named Riggs.

Buck looked up from his contemplation of the clouds out the window. "Oh, it's just dandy. It's my heart that's giving me trouble, Doc." He thumped his chest despondently.

"Your heart?" I frowned. "Want me to check your vitals?"

"Nah," he sighed, waving a hand. "I don't mean my physical heart. I mean my mental heart."

I snorted. "Your mental heart." I knew exactly what he meant, though I'd never heard it called that. I kinda liked it. In fact, I was pretty sure I was having a mental heart attack right at that very moment. Hurt like hell.

"You know, Doc," Buck mused, "sometimes all a man wants is a little validation."

I set my back teeth and glanced toward the front of the plane. "No kidding."

"Like me with this whole misunderstanding kerfuffle with Santiago. It all started 'cause Jacob Horn's a big jerkbag. D'you know, the game was originally supposed to be called *Nut of Glory*?"

"Was it?" I asked glumly. From the front of the plane, I could hear the rise and fall of Riggs's voice, sharp with tension. No doubt telling Champ and the boys all about how he'd rescued fearful, *difficult* Dr. Rogers time and again.

"It sure was! And the magic seed?" Buck went on. "It was meant to be a magic *nut*." His voice turned bitter. "Until *Jacob* came along, dangling all kinda promises in fronta me. 'You and me, Buck, we're a *team*! We're gonna change the face of gameplay!' *Pfft*," he scoffed. "Nothin' worse than a man who tells you you're a *team* when he really means he already *has* a team, and he just wants to steal away a little part of your soul and pretend he's never met you before. You can't trust a man after something like that."

"Never a truer word, Buck Nutter." Bitter fury, cold as the west wind, blew through me, and I darted a look at the front of the plane again. I hoped Riggs and *his team* and his *job* were very happy together.

"Now everyone's all 'grab your Horn and have some fun.'" Buck removed a Horn from his pocket—one he'd wrapped in a piece of velvet that looked like it had once been the bed hangings at Gustavo's crime palace—and stared down at it in disgust. He sniffled a little. "When I think that all this time, people shoulda been grabbin' their Nuts…" He broke off with a shake of his head. "It ain't wrong to expect a little respect from people when you've given 'em a little piece of your soul, is it?"

No. No, it wasn't.

"But I suppose if this whole life and death business taught me anything, it's that sometimes you have to let go and move on," he sighed, swiping a finger beneath his eyes. "Plottin' revenge only got me kidnapped. Bein' sad only made me sadder. Time to give it up and get on with my next brilliant idea, I think."

Tears pricked behind my eyes too, but I took a deep breath and ignored them. I was just tired. And suffering from an adrenaline crash. That was why I felt jittery and irritable. It was a hundred percent hormonal. Entirely phys-iological and explainable.

In fact, the whole affair with Riggs had been the result of stress exposure influencing my basic neural circuits, making me crave stability... even if that stability was William Bossy Motherfucker Riggs. Simple as that.

I threw my head back and sniffed away the last of my tears. "You know, you're right, Buck."

"Am I?"

"And you're brilliant."

He blinked. "More people oughta realize that, you know?"

"I think moving on sounds great. The best decision *ever*. In fact... maybe it's time for me to leave the Thicket." I didn't realize my thoughts were leaning that way until I spoke them aloud.

"Leave Licking Thicket?" Buck's blue eyes widened in shock. "Not permanently?"

"Probably not." My heart cracked at the idea. I hadn't realized how attached I was to the place, but Kev was right. I *had* gotten comfortable over the past half year, and the thought of leaving all the Johnsons and Nutters and Wrights and Churches was way more painful than I'd imag-ined it would be. But the alternative...

Ugh.

I darted a look in Riggs's direction *yet a-fucking-gain*. I couldn't make out their words, but someone was jeering at someone else, and everyone was laughing, and I was pretty sure that whenever Riggs was in my vicinity for the rest of my life, my eyes and attention would wander in his direc-tion... unless I stopped this right now.

I could take another Doctors Across Continents assign-ment. They owed me after this last one, honesty.

Or I could take over the Rogers Family Foundation and be boots-on-the-ground in some remote part of the world.

Or I could go back to Nashville. I had plenty of contacts there, and any contacts *I* didn't have, my grandfather did.

Or…

"No! Shut up. That's not how it happened!" Riggs protested about whatever they were discussing, but he was laughing too, clearly not worried about me at all now that the fucking job was over.

"Yeah, for a few months," I told Buck. "Just until things settle down."

Until I stopped turning my head every time I heard Riggs laugh.

Until I stopped wondering where he was or what he was doing.

Until I stopped looking back fondly on our time in fucking *captivity*, because at least then we'd been together.

"You know, Doc, that ain't a bad idea," Buck said thoughtfully. "I think you might have a little brilliance in ya too."

I snorted. Brilliant? No, I was a fool. A clichéd fool who'd fallen for the guy who was supposed to be guarding my body… and ended up letting him hijack my heart.

17

———————

RIGGS

Being pulled away from Carter during the aftermath of the crazy plane flight had been like losing my anchor in a storm. Suddenly, I felt oddly adrift and unsure of which way to go. I hated feeling out of control at least as much as Carter, so I did what I did best.

I focused on the job.

"Are you even listening to me right now?" Champ barked. I jumped in my seat at the conference table. Now that we were back at the office the day after the long flight home, things should have begun to feel normal again.

They didn't. I wasn't even sure what "normal" was anymore.

I met his eyes. "Yes. Christ. Can you give me a minute? I'm working on little to no sleep here."

I took a sip of the coffee in front of me as if to prove my point, but the hot liquid tasted like ash and hit my stomach like bricks. I shuddered and set the cup down.

"Riggs," Elvo said, leaning forward across the conference table. "He said you're back in the auricle implant program. You need to start prep tomorrow since the confer ence starts in a little over a week. The other attendees have probably been preparing for a while now."

This should have been amazing news, and it was. But thinking about jumping right into work again before I'd talked to Carter was a blow. No matter how busy I was going to be, I'd have to find time to see Carter and find out… maybe find out if there was the possibility of pursuing something beyond our crazy time in Venezuela.

Not to mention, I owed him some explanations about Buck and why I'd held back some information.

He'd acted strange on the plane, and by the time we'd landed in the States, he'd been downright distant. With Champ and the rest of my team watching my every move, it had been impossible to pull him aside and check in. I'd tried calling and texting since then, but he hadn't responded. Not knowing how he was feeling about everything had my gut in knots. I needed to talk to him and soon.

"Yeah, great." I met Champ's eyes. "Thanks, boss. I mean it. You know how important the AIP training is to me."

He nodded. "I do. And their selection of Champion as the only private company to consult on the program is an honor we need to live up to. They have high expectations for this program, and I assured them you were the best person to provide feedback in the field."

His words made me proud. They called to the part of me that always wanted to prove myself, to be considered worthy by my peers and the man I respected as a mentor and leader. But for some reason, there was still a part of me that felt unsettled.

"I won't let you down," I assured him.

"Again," he added with some kind of glint in his eyes.

I blinked at him before his words hit home. Hard. I gritted my teeth. "I won't let you down, again, *sir*."

He grinned at me, and I realized I'd misunderstood him. He was teasing. "I'm giving you hell, Marine. I'm proud of you. You went on an executive babysitting job and managed to secure the…"

He glanced at Elvo, who bit the side of his cheek before saying, "The Magic Seed?"

Champ's nostrils flared. "No."

"Buck Nutter," I suggested, also trying not to laugh.

"Jesus fucking Christ," Champ muttered, glancing up at the ceiling. "This job, I swear to fucking God."

"Nutter's seed," Hux added helpfully, tapping away on his laptop.

Champ rubbed his temples. "I should have let Santiago have the lot of you."

"I saved Buck Nutter, kept the cartel from hiding their money in the HOG, and brought home my principal unharmed." I sat up straighter and dusted my hands together. "All in a day's work."

Elvo snickered, and Hux closed his eyes and shook his head. He knew what was coming.

Champ pinned me with his glare. "Are you trying to get yanked off AIP again? Huh? Or are you just a dumb fuck intent on pissing me off?"

Elvo coughed. "Second one." Hux snorted and buried his face in his hands.

"Neither, sir," I shot back. "I'm just saying, this is the best possible outcome. Or the best we can get, anyway, since we know the Venezuelan government will protect both Santiago brothers from prosecution for kidnapping."

Champ ignored him. "Well, at least this time your dick didn't get you in trouble."

Hux stopped laughing and shot me a knowing glance. *Shit.* Between what I'd told him in our HOG convo and what he'd seen the day before on the tarmac, he knew way too much about what had really gone down with me and Carter.

I scrambled to cover up the sudden awkward silence in the room. "What did HOG say? Did they rehire us for their corporate security?"

I knew the chances were high they would. Champion Security was the best in the business, as well as the only security company worth a damn in the Thicket. Besides, the CEO, Jacob Horn, seemed to have a hard-on for Champ himself. I'd been surprised my mistake had cost us the account.

"Yes, but only on a probationary basis. And only if you aren't anywhere near the account." He eyed me with suspicion. "Are you capable of keeping your nose out of HOG's business after all this?"

Was he kidding? "I don't want anything to do with that shitshow after this," I said, telling the absolute truth. "And if I never see Buck Nutter again as long as I live, it'll be too soon."

Okay, I was exaggerating. Buck was a nice enough guy, but I wasn't a gamer. And I'd never really understood his explanation of how kumquats and passion fruits represented coke and meth. Thankfully, he hadn't completed the final upload of the Magic Seed infiltration for Gustavo Santiago, so he hadn't actually committed a crime, and HOG Corporate said they wouldn't press charges, mostly to keep the story out of the media.

"Well," Champ said, leaning back and running a large hand through his hair. "That won't be a problem. He's already in the wind. The minute HOG Corporate finished debriefing him about the magic seed last night, he told his girlfriend and his family that he was going far away where no one could find him. His plan was to lay low for a while and stay away from HOG and the cartel."

Elvo glanced at me with a smirk. "I believe his exact words were, 'I'm fixin' ta get Myrtle Beach drunk, but you know… not at Myrtle Beach or nothin'.' So he's most likely at Myrtle Beach."

He was probably right. "Hope he stays off Santiago's radar," I said. "Gustavo will be on the lookout for him when he finds out Buck didn't actually get the job done."

Hux clicked the keyboard of his laptop, and the screen lit up on the far wall. "Yeah, about that. We have a slight problem."

Champ glanced up at the screen. "What kind of problem?"

"He told us the guards took him back to the computer room the night before you left, and he killed the upload of the cartel's financial data, right?"

I nodded. "And Gianluigi was panicked enough not to double-check before ordering him onto the plane."

"Right. But…" Hux clicked another few keys and showed a surveillance video from the Champion jet. "Doesn't that look like a Horn Buck's showing Carter?"

My eyes froze on Carter's face. He was so damned beautiful, even as tired as he'd been on the flight. He'd looked wrecked—so exhausted, he almost seemed *sad*. I'd wanted to talk to him, to hold him, to make him promise we'd see each other again, but I'd wanted him to be well even more. I'd left him alone to catch a nap at the back of the plane well away from my noisy and nosy teammates, but it looked like Buck had yammered at him instead of letting him sleep.

I forced myself to pay attention to what Hux was saying.

"Yeah, so?" I asked, even though I was surprised Buck managed to get out of there with anything at all on his person besides his clothes and the bandage on his leg.

Hux shrugged. "He didn't have it when we debriefed him. And I somehow doubt Santiago would have let Buck bring his own Horn when the cartel kidnapped him, anyway. So, I'm wondering whose Horn it is, where he got it, and what happened to it between when he landed and when he came in here for questioning."

I thought back to the little reunion scene at the private jetport. Carter's grandfather and cousin had been there, and Buck's entire extended family too. Supposedly, his great-uncle Amos Nutter had wanted to celebrate Buck's home-coming with painted cows, but there hadn't been enough time. When I'd heard him say it, I'd looked over at Carter to share a laugh, but he'd kept his eyes on the ground.

My stomach twisted. Carter hadn't returned any of the texts I'd sent him since we landed. Elvo had assured me we had a security team in place to cover Carter and his family, but hearing clear status updates wasn't quite the same as seeing and hearing he was okay with my own eyes.

And hands.

And lips.

"Dude, where the fuck are you?" Elvo muttered, nudging me hard in the ribs with his elbow. "You trying to fuck this up for yourself again?"

I glanced at Champ, but he was busy considering Hux's news.

I cleared my throat. "Could he have handed it off to someone?" Hux and Elvo exchanged a glance. "What?" I asked.

"He could have handed it off to Carter. It might explain why he was showing it to him in the first place," Elvo suggested.

"So? What do we care if he gave someone his Horn?"

Hux and Elvo snickered.

Champ muttered something about working with

preteens. "Because there's no reason for him to hand it off to anyone. Nobody's accusing anyone of anything, Riggsy. It's just an open loop to be closed, that's all. Unless you're implying something more than that?" he asked Hux.

Hux shook his head. "Not at all. It's probably nothing, and I wouldn't have thought much about it, except he made a point of showing it to Carter, and now it's missing. And since Buck isn't around anymore to ask…" He glanced at me.

"*You* should ask him," I snapped. "You found the loop, you should close it your own damn self."

Hux's eyes widened, and Elvo made a barely perceptible cat-hissing noise at me behind Champ's back. I shot him the finger.

Champ turned back to me. I wasn't stupid; he'd seen everything. "Riggs will close the loop. He's the one with the client relationship, so he can sweet-talk the doctor for us. Go home and get some sleep. Tomorrow I want you to find out what Carter Rogers knows about that Horn. Got it?"

My heart picked up speed. "Got it."

It was official now. I needed to go see Carter.

My job depended on it, which meant I could stop wondering whether or not my heart did too.

I tried calling him on my way out of the office, but there was no answer. Showing up unannounced while he was trying to sleep off the misadventures of our trip wasn't a good idea. I could be patient. I texted him to let me know when I could come by, but he didn't answer the texts either.

For another twenty-four hours, Carter Rogers ghosted me. By the time I got up the nerve to ask Champ the next day where I could find Carter, I was shaking with a combination of nerves and anger. Did I mean so little to him that he couldn't even answer and let me know how he was?

Champ told me he was at the same estate where the gala

had been held. My plan was to simply show up and hope to hell he'd talk to me. I needed to convince him to give me a chance. I wanted more time with him. I wanted to get to know him better away from the craziness of our time in Venezuela.

By the time I showered, shaved, dressed in a decent pair of slacks and button-up shirt, and headed to my favorite wine store, I was nervous enough to make my car keys jingle in my hand as I stared down at the bottles on display.

I wanted something unique. Something that showed how much Carter meant to me but that wasn't flashy since I knew he didn't care about that stuff. Something as special as he was... which was a fucking tall order for a bottle of squashed grapes.

But as I scanned the wine descriptions, one label jumped out at me, and I laughed out loud in the middle of the store at the utter rightness of it. I hadn't known it would be possible to find something that perfect...

Which was kinda how I felt about Carter.

My nerves returned with a vengeance, though, when I arrived at the mansion. Somehow, it seemed even larger than it had the night of the gala.

It had turrets. And a servants' entrance.

And a Rolls-Royce parked in the drive next to a flashy BMW, two Mercedes, and a sleek convertible sports car that looked like something out of a magazine.

"Get it the fuck together, shithead," I mumbled under my breath. "This is Carter. *Your* Carter. You've been inside his body. He's not a strange —"

The heavy wooden door opened, and an honest-to-God butler appeared. "May I help you, sir?" he asked with a sniff.

"Yeah, uh... um..." I swallowed and started again. "I'm here to see Dr. Carter Rogers?"

Why had I formed it as a question? They had to have known who I was since I'd checked in with the Champion Security team stationed at the gate.

I repeated my words, this time more firmly. "I'm here to see Carter Rogers."

The older man lifted an eyebrow. "And you are…?"

Annoyed? Impressed? Peeved? About to shit myself?

"William Riggs," I said through tight teeth, standing a little straighter and barely resisting the urge to state my rank as well. I didn't like being a fish out of water. My clothes suddenly itched, and I was half a second from bolting. I'd forgotten what kind of world Carter came from, and it was obvious I'd been fooling myself into thinking a man like him could see a future with a guy like me.

"Wait right here," the man said, gesturing me into the foyer before turning and walking away.

I blew out a breath and looked around. The house looked like something that had been plucked from a rolling estate in New England and set down on the outskirts of Licking Thicket without regard to how out of place it would be in rural Tennessee. I wondered who'd built it originally if Dr. Rogers, Sr., had only owned it a short time.

The cool marble floor was tempered by the warm honey-brown paneling on the walls. A familiar portrait of the famous duchess ancestor adorned one wall over a fancy chest of drawers, and a grandfather clock that looked ancient stood tall against another wall. Its rhythmic *ticktick-tick* filled the quiet space around me until I realized there was a faint sound of muffled conversations coming from deeper in the house.

Finally, the butler returned and murmured instructions for me to follow him. When he led me into a large living room, I was surprised to see some kind of cocktail party in full swing.

Several people looked up in surprise when the butler announced me. I recognized the younger man curled in the corner of a sofa playing on a Horn as Carter's cousin Kevin. He was the only one in a T-shirt and jeans, and he even wore noise-canceling headphones to make it super obvious he wasn't interested in engaging in social small talk with anyone at the party.

Carter's grandfather was sitting in a high-backed armchair by the fireplace, holding a cut-crystal glass with amber liquor in it, and the couple who'd been dancing at the gala was standing with Carter nearby. I wondered which one was Tucker and which was Dunn.

Jealousy and confusion tumbled in my gut. Carter was having a party. I'd assumed the unanswered calls and texts earlier today had been due to him passing out and sleeping off his misadventures, but no. He was happily hobnobbing with friends and family as if nothing had happened. As if I hadn't been worried about how he was doing.

"Carter?" I asked, sounding way less sure than I remembered feeling in years. I cleared my throat and set the wine bottle down on a nearby table. "Can I talk to you for a minute?"

His face held absolutely no trace of warmth at my arrival. There was something in his eyes for a brief second, and then it was gone. "Mr. Riggs. What can I help you with?"

He made no move to approach me. I might as well have been a catering server coming in with an update from the kitchen.

I took a step backward, heat filling my face. Why had I come here? What had I been hoping to accomplish? It was clear from every ounce of his bearing that we were nothing to each other. Whatever bonding I'd thought had happened between us in Venezuela had either been temporary or a horribly wonderful figment of my imagination.

Instead of turning and walking out, I remembered there'd been another reason for my visit in addition to my desire to see him, hold him, beg him to spend the night with me.

I steeled myself and pushed forward. "I need to talk to you about an issue regarding the case."

I didn't imagine the flare of disappointment in his face, but I wasn't quite sure if it was disappointment that my visit was for business reasons only or because I was daring to bother him while he was socializing.

Focus on the job, Marine.

I turned and stepped out into the hallway, hoping like hell he'd follow. After a few beats, I heard his soft footsteps behind me. As soon as I saw him up close, I felt a sharp pain in my chest.

To my horror, I opened my mouth and begged. "Come home with me tonight."

"What?" His eyes widened before shuttering. "No. That's not a good idea."

"It is. It's a great idea. You know it, and I know it. I'm leaving next week for a three-week training program and—"

He held up a hand to stop me. "Yet another reason why it's not a good idea."

"Remind me, then. What's the first reason?"

Carter's nostrils flared in annoyance. "The fact that you're a liar and a hypocrite."

His words were a kick in the gut. He wasn't wrong—I'd known that he'd be upset when he found out I'd been keeping secrets—but he wasn't entirely right either. I bit my tongue against snapping back at him defensively and explaining how any lie I told him was for his own safety and because I was doing my job.

Carter folded his arms in front of his chest. The navy cashmere sweater looked soft enough to caress. My fingers twitched with the need to touch him, but I balled them into fists at my side. "Honestly is critical on a mission, Riggs. Or was that a lie, too?"

"It wasn't a lie. But it was my job to keep you safe."

He tilted his head. "Ah, right. I was your job. So then I guess I wasn't a team member then. Which is weird since I literally helped *hijack a plane* to escape. But then again, I'm just your *difficult* principal, right? I guess I got my *advanced medical degree* out of a gumball machine. I guess when they handed out awards for the *Distinguished Fellow in Cardiology* at Vanderbilt, they were just throwing darts at the damned employee directory. Because what the hell could I possibly know about anything, right?"

His voice had risen in strength and volume until his grandfather came to ask if he was okay. "Is this gentleman bothering you, Carter?"

Carter's grandfather eyed me with suspicion, so different from the trust he'd displayed the night of the gala. I felt like dirt enough as it was, but having Dr. Rogers, Sr., shoot me a condescending glare was the icing on the cake.

"No, sir," Carter said, calming down immediately and resuming the emotionless expression he'd shown me when I'd first walked in. "The bodyguard was just leaving."

The bodyguard. That was all I was to him. I stared at him, trying desperately not to feel like I was bleeding out straight from my chest. Apparently, I'd seen feelings where there hadn't been any.

I firmed my chin. "I just need to ask Dr. Rogers a few questions about the case, and then I'll be on my way."

Carter's grandfather looked between us before asking Carter if he wanted company for the interview.

"No, sir. But thank you. I'll be fine, and this won't take but a minute."

Dr. Rogers, Sr., nodded and returned to the party, leaving us alone again.

Carter turned to me. "What questions?"

My face felt numb. Reducing our relationship to debriefing about the case was my worst nightmare, but I had to do it. Champ had made it clear he expected me to come through for him on this part of the job, and apparently the job was all I fucking had anymore.

"Buck showed you his Horn on the plane," I began.

Carter's forehead crinkled with confusion. "Yes. He did."

"But when we questioned him back at headquarters, he didn't have it anymore."

"Okay…?"

I shifted from one foot to the other. "Do you have any idea what he did with it between showing it to you and arriving at our offices?"

He looked off to the side like he was thinking. "He… well, I know he had a lot of family there waiting for him at the airport. His girlfriend Kellie, his sister Kandi, his great-uncle Amos and Amos's wife… I think there were some siblings there too? I guess he could have given it to one of them to hang on to for him."

"But he didn't give it to you?" I asked.

"No. Why would he have given it to me?"

I shrugged. "I don't know, but I had to ask. Are you sure you only returned with one device?"

He ground his teeth together. "Yes, Mr. Riggs. I arrived at your company's offices with pockets full of many, many things. All the random medical supplies you shoved into my pants pockets as well as my own Horn, which you know is distinctive since it's *sparkly purple*. I was searched by one of your colleagues. I specifically remember calling out for you when some random stranger began trying to take your knife off me without my permission, but I guess you were too busy sharing fun stories with your dude bro friends to hear me or give a shit about what was happening. But feel free to ask your real fucking *teammates* because they took inventory of everything I had on me when I arrived at Champion Security. Now, if you're quite finished interrogating me, please get the fuck out of my grandfather's house."

I stared at him in shock and the beginning stages of rage. "Someone touched you without your consent? Someone at Champion? Who? What did he look like?"

Carter blew out a breath. "Calm down. It wasn't like that. He patted me down, and when he found the weapon, he freaked out… until your boss told him to calm down. I'm not telling you who it was since you're clearly looking for someone to take your anger out on. All I know is I asked for you, and you didn't come. That part I remember quite clearly." He cleared his throat. "Speaking of the knife, I'll have it packaged up by someone on my grandfather's staff. They'll bring it to you at the Champion office."

I felt stinging behind my eyes at the knowledge I'd let him down. "Keep it."

Carter shook his head once. "There's no need. We both know I never would have used it. I'm a principal, not a bodyguard." He smiled tightly. "As you keep reminding me."

Was this what heartbreak felt like? How sad was it that the first guy I'd given my heart to would be the first guy to break it?

"Keep it," I said again. "Even if you never use it, sometimes it just helps to know it's there." It would help *me* to know he had it.

Carter looked surprised for a second. Vulnerable. So I swallowed hard and tried one last time. "I… I tried calling you. I've been trying to get in touch with you since we landed. I wanted to explain everything. I texted…"

"Please leave," he said, finally looking and sounding as exhausted as I felt. "There's no point in discussing this anymore. You were right when you warned me in Venezuela this was a bad idea. We don't fit. You're going on your next mission, and I have a medical practice to run. Listen, it was fun while it lasted, and I really appreciate you saving my life. You did a great job landing that plane and getting us out of there. I'll always be grateful."

"You're the one who said it was a bad idea, Duchess," I said. My voice sounded rough, like I'd already spent hours begging him out loud instead of just in my mind.

"Did I?" He shrugged. "Well, then. I was right. And it's Dr. Rogers to you. Goodbye, Mr. Riggs." He turned to make his way back to the party, but I could have sworn I heard him murmur something under his breath that sounded like, "Be safe."

I stared after him until the butler coughed discreetly behind me and gestured toward the front door. It wasn't until I was halfway back to the shitty rental house I shared with Hux that I finally screamed my fucking head off and slammed my hand on the steering wheel enough to bruise my damned palm.

How could I have gotten things so wrong?

And how the hell was I going to make it right?

18

CARTER

After nearly a week without seeing Riggs, I was happy to report that I was doing fine.

Just fine.

Terribly, *terribly* fine.

I was firmly in control of my life—or, okay, that was a total lie, but I was in control of the important bits, at least—and that was exactly what I wanted.

Autumn leaves glistened wetly on the pavement as I pulled up the driveway of—sweet Jesus, it hurt my brain to even think the words—my new twenty-acre, eighteen-thousand square-foot home located halfway between Licking Thicket and Great Nuthatch.

Weirdly enough, the redbrick colonial with its massive white columns, second-floor balconies, and black shutters had started to feel like home in the week since I'd returned from Venezuela.

Of course, the fact that my grandfather had packed up all my belongings and given notice to my landlord while I was away—*"so you wouldn't be bothered with it, son, and no need to thank me"*—probably had a lot to do with that.

So did the fact that my grandfather and Kev were in residence for at least a few more weeks, since Grandfather claimed he'd joined several Licking Thicket social clubs while I was gone that required his attendance, and Kev was overseeing the conversion of the second floor of the northeast wing into the geek cave of his dreams, complete with "dedicated fiber-optic lines" and "multiple redundancies." Whatever that meant.

It also didn't hurt that the manse was located just far enough out of town, and contained just enough rooms, that it was difficult for my grandfather or Kev or various, incredibly persistent residents of Licking Thicket to come and harass me as part of Project Cheer Carter Up.

I loved them all. I did. Including Tucker and… yes, okay, Dunn. But a man could only eat so many casseroles, and I didn't want to talk about Venezuela or William Riggs. I didn't want to be cheered up. I wanted to go back in time and stop myself from giving my heart to a guy who didn't respect me, and barring that, I wanted to throw myself on the couch in the library to wallow in self-pity and full-sugar Coke.

The week since I'd seen Riggs felt like a year. And in my moments of wallowing, I vacillated between resolving to shove him out of my mind forever and obsessing about the frustrating man nonstop. How long would it take for me to put our unfortunate fling behind me and move on?

That seemed to be one thing I could *not* control, no matter how hard I tried.

I parked my Audi on the circular driveway out front and waved to my new security guard, John—a polite, balding, happily married, fifty-something guy Grandfather had insisted on hiring, just in case—to let him know I'd be home until it was time to go in for my next overnight shift. I dragged myself up the front steps through the early morning drizzle and let myself in. The place was so quiet, I could hear the big clock in the hall ticking, which meant Grandfather and Kev were still asleep.

Perfect.

I let myself into the library, closed and locked the door behind me, and immediately flopped down on the oversized couch, rubbing my tired eyes.

"Aragorn, play my Sad Songs of the Eighties playlist," I instructed the house computer. Kev was fanatical about privacy and hated the idea of other companies listening in on our private conversations, so he'd created his own.

You know, as one does.

"Aragorn, stop!" Kev's voice called out from one of the leather club chairs in the corner before Roxette managed to belt out the first note.

"Hey!" I protested, lifting my head. "What are you doing here?"

Kev was right. It was awful when people intruded on your privacy.

"I live here, remember? At least for now." He stood up and walked over to my flopping couch, lifted my feet, and sat his ass back down on the end.

"Hmph." It was a sad day when a man's own flopping couch was taken over.

"You haven't touched your Horn in a whole week," he accused. "Marisol's been playing every day on the Horn you asked me to send her, and she asked me why *el doctor guapo* hasn't been around."

Mostly because I'd stuffed my Horn in the back of my pajama drawer the second I got back here that first night, and I hadn't touched it since. Just the sparkly purple sight of it made me think of Riggs and get all maudlin.

By which I meant even more maudlin.

"Yeah, so? Was it Mulberry Harvest Day? Did I miss the Hug An Orc Jubilee?" I asked sullenly.

"First of all, don't even joke about hugging orcs. That's a one-way ticket to the great respawning room in the sky, my friend, and you would *never* find your way back to our homestead. Second… wow. Tucker was right." He pushed his glasses up the bridge of his nose and gave me a wondering look. "He told me you needed an intervention, but I didn't believe it at first. I didn't think you were capable of it. But you're *moping*."

I scowled. "What? Intervention? *Pfft.* Moping? *Pfffffffffft.* Ridiculous. And since when do you talk to my ex-boyfriend? And since when does my ex-boyfriend know anything about my mental state?"

"*I* knew Carter was capable of moping." Grandfather stood up and clomped out from behind the other club chair.

I thunked my head back onto the cushion with a groan. I'd been so careful to lock the door. I'd had no idea I was locking the meddlers in the room with me. "Et tu, Grandfather?"

"Jordan Kilpatrick," Grandfather told Kev. "Ninth grade."

"Jordan Kil—? Dear God, why?" I asked the ceiling. "Why me? Why now?"

"Who's Jordan Kilpatrick?" Kev demanded. "Why have I never heard this story?"

"Because there's no story. I haven't thought of the man in decades," I scoffed.

"He was your cousin's *very first* crush," Grandfather told Kev, pursing his lips meaningfully. "Led our Carter down the primrose path."

"No, he didn't." Though I'd wanted him to. Badly. "Jordan wasn't into me at all. I was way too nerdy for the likes of him. He was more into sports and fast cars, as I recall." Varsity basketball, even as a freshman. Led the team to three state championships. Drove a white Mustang. Had a single dimple in his left cheek. "Though who remembers details, really?"

"Carter tutored Jordan in chemistry—"

"Biology," I corrected, only realizing I'd fallen neatly into Grandfather's trap when he smiled at me triumphantly. "What? I mean, I remember *that* part," I grumbled.

"Made Carter feel special for a time, then hurt his feelings pretty badly when he moved on to some little jade named Thomas." Grandfather's eyes narrowed spitefully.

"Tommy MacDal is not a jade." I rolled my eyes. "I honestly don't even know what that means, but the man graduated from divinity school, and I doubt you can be a *jade* and also a reverend."

"Nevertheless," Grandfather said. "Jordan treated you poorly. And do you remember the advice I gave you, Carter?"

"To eat my vegetables?"

"Always a good idea, if not terribly pertinent to this situation." He raised one bushy white eyebrow. "I meant the other advice."

I sighed deeply. "That my heart is a precious thing and I should be cautious with it. I should save my love for someone who loves me back."

"Exactly." He perched himself on the hassock that served as a coffee table with a smug little smile. "So I think it's plain what you need to do here."

"See if the housekeeper will make me a veggie omelet? I concur." I nodded and moved to stand. "Good talk—"

"Nope." Kev held me down with surprising strength. "Intervention's just getting started. If you're saving your heart for someone who loves you back, why aren't you with your bodyguard? And I don't mean John. His wife wouldn't appreciate that."

"Because Riggs isn't my bodyguard anymore. He's not my anything." The gut punch of that hit me yet again. "I was his client. His *principal.* Now that we're home, our relationship is… is dissolved. Simple as that. So I absolutely don't require an intervention." I faked a smile like I wasn't close to tears. "You know, I should probably run upstairs, get changed, and then take a drive into town. Check in with Tuck and Dunn, since I haven't seen them for a bit."

Or go upstairs, sack out on my bed, and forget to leave. Either way.

"Mmm. And why haven't you seen them?" Grandfather demanded.

I gave him my orphan puppy-dog eyes. "Because I've been spending my days and evenings here, in the bosom of my beloved family."

Grandfather gave me the eyebrow lift again, and I collapsed with a sigh.

"Okay, fine. Because I didn't want to talk to the Bundt-Cake Brigade," I mumbled. "And I swear they have Spidey senses that tingle when I cross into Licking Thicket."

"We prefer to be called the Thicket Beautification Corps." Tucker scowled as he stalked in from a second door —a door I'd honestly thought led to a closet—with his arms crossed over his chest. "Our Spidey senses have no limitations. And we're more about community activism and empowerment than baked goods, FYI."

"Though we do enjoy a good bundt cake!" His husband followed at a stroll, both hands thrust into his back pockets and a good-natured smile on his face.

I threw both hands in the air. "Are you kidding?" I demanded of Kev. "How many more people are hiding around here?" I lifted the throw pillow on the sofa and peered under the end table. "Anyone else come to kick a man when he's down?"

"Funny you should ask, but Ava really wanted to come," Dunn said as he and Tucker seated themselves on the couch opposite me. "She said to give you her love and tell you she's there if you need a listening ear."

Hmph. Way to take the wind out of a man's sails. How could I be outraged at the nosiness of people when they went and said sweet things?

"And no one came to kick you," Tucker said reasonably. "We came because we love you and we're concerned that you're hiding out here—"

"I am *not*—"

"During the rare moments when you're not working overnights, *then* seeing patients for appointments, all while trying to fast-track a new portable cath lab program for the Rogers Family Foundation," Grandfather added.

"We're short-staffed since Cordelia—"

"And that by refusing to talk to anyone, you're missing the truth of the situation, which is plain as day," Kev interjected.

"I'm missing nothing! I simply choose not to talk about my personal—"

"'Cause some of us are just a *leeeettle* bit more foolish than others and need some extra prompting to see what's right before our eyes." Dunn winked, clearly remembering last spring when he'd been an absolute dumbass over Tucker and I'd set him right.

I deflated. "Look, I appreciate your concern. I do. But I promise you, this isn't like the situation with you two." I waved a hand between Dunn and Tucker. "You loved each other forever, and you just needed help seeing it. Riggs and I, we... *Ugh.* We had a thing. A brief, temporary thing."

"An affair," Tucker surmised.

"A liaison," Grandfather corrected.

"A fling." Kev nodded knowingly.

"He slayed your dragon." Dunn wiggled his eyebrows. "He made your wild ox moan. He was shakin' your bacon. He plowed your fallow field until—"

"Yes!" Tucker laid a hand on Dunn's knee. "Yes, baby. It's... it's crystal clear now. Thank you."

"The point is, I caught feels for the man. Okay? Fine. I admit it. I stupidly, ridiculously, improbably but very really caught feels for my bodyguard. I'm like... Whitney Houston but less pretty." I leaned my head back on the sofa as tears threatened. "He's just so... *good*, I couldn't help it. He's, like, genuine hero material. And I don't mean his muscles or his gun. I mean... I mean, he was selfless and competent and kind." Everything I never knew I wanted in a man. "When there was danger, he stepped in front of me. When he knew I was scared, he gave me his knife—our only weapon—just because he *knew* I'd feel better carrying it, even if I never planned to use it." I sucked in a breath, remembering him saying those exact words when he'd come to ask me about the case, and my chest constricted. How had he gotten to know me so well? "When I needed to be talked down 'cause I was freaking out—"

"*You* were freaking out?" Kev asked skeptically. "For reals?"

"For very reals," I said with a watery chuckle. "I couldn't control anything that was happening after we were taken hostage, and I lost my mind a little bit. More than once. But Riggs talked me through it. He told me stupid stories. He teased me. He made me believe things would be okay." I cleared my throat. "So my brain was like, 'Oh, he cares about me. I'm special.' But that's like... like a patient giving you heart-eyes because you save their life, you know? It wasn't romantic to him. It was a job. He was paid to keep me calm. And the feelings—I mean, the romantic feelings—were all coming from me. Which is pretty ironic since Tuck once told me I'm not the settling-down type."

Tucker tilted his head to the side and peered at me curiously. "I never said that, Carter. I said I didn't think you were the type to settle down *in a place like Licking Thicket*, which was where I knew I wanted to end up, since you were all about going out in the world and saving lives on a global scale." He shrugged. "But clearly I was wrong, since you're the most beloved doctor in Great Nuthatch, and that's almost the same as the Thicket."

"You've changed and matured," Grandfather said. "I told you so the night of the gala. I can't tell you the number of people who came up to me and told me how profoundly grateful they were to have you living here. You've made a difference in the lives of a lot of people, Carter." He sniffed just a little and cleared his throat. "Your parents would be so proud."

Oh. I rubbed at the ache in my solar plexus. "Well, I don't think that's really—" I began, shaking my head.

"Well, *I* don't think you're very good at looking at things objectively," Kev interrupted in a quelling sort of way. "For one thing, I don't believe your feelings were one-sided." He lifted his chin defiantly.

"It's true," I assured him. "I overheard Huxley mentioning how Riggs got in trouble for screwing around while he was on the job once before. And his boss said guarding me was his *punishment*. And when his boss joked that I was probably a difficult person to guard? Riggs hardly defended me at all. Plus, I *begged* him to be honest with me the whole time we were in the jungle, and he *promised* he would… but then he *wasn't* because he didn't tell me who the, uh, other hostage being held with us was, even though he knew." I kept Buck's name out of it, since that didn't seem relevant.

All four of them stared at me, stunned speechless by Riggs's treachery.

"I know, right?" I sighed. "It's a lot. So now I just have to get over the disappointment. I thought it would be easier than this, though." I forced a little smile. "I mean, objectively speaking, we spent hardly any time together."

Grandfather shook his head and sighed. "I blame myself for this."

"You shouldn't, Grandfather! God, no! Just imagine how bad the situation could have been if Riggs hadn't been there."

"No, Carter, I don't blame myself for hiring Riggs! I blame myself for giving you that ill-conceived advice when you were a teenager."

"What?" I blinked. "It wasn't! It was smart."

"What I should have said was, trust how the person makes you feel, son. Does he make you feel good? Strong? Happy even when life is at its worst? Do you trust him? Then you're a lucky man, and you should hold on tight."

"Wait." I scowled. "Wait, no—"

"Carter, that evidence you just presented..." Tucker shook his head and trailed off.

"It's so thin you can see through it," Dunn concluded cheerfully. "You can hardly hold things the man's *boss* said against him. That ain't fair."

"Or things that happened on a previous job," Tucker added, wrinkling his nose. "You can't blame a person for the people he dated before you."

"Can't you?" Dunn asked, his tongue poking the inside of his cheek. "Does that mean we can talk about my ex, Jenn—"

"Not. In. This. Lifetime," Tucker said firmly.

Dunn nodded, a little smile on his lips as he placed a proprietary hand on the back of his husband's neck. "Right. Thought not."

"Okay, fine," I agreed. "But even if you discounted those things…"

"Then you'd have a bodyguard acting like a bodyguard," Grandfather said.

"Precisely," I agreed. "That's the problem. I don't want to be his principal." I wanted to be his lover. His… love.

Kev frowned. "But isn't that a little like saying Grandfather was treating you like a patient when he told you to eat vegetables? I mean, sure, he's a doctor, and doctors tell patients to eat vegetables. But he told *you* because you're his grandson and he loves you and wants you to be healthy. He can't separate his doctor-ness from his grandfather-ness. Riggs can't stop protecting you just because he has feels. In fact, he'd protect you even harder because he does."

I blinked. "But… no. You're missing the point."

"Or you are," Tucker said.

They made it sound so simple, but it wasn't. It couldn't be…

Could it? Could I really have fucked this up so thoroughly?

"You're trying to control things. You're protecting your heart by pushing him away before he can push you away," Grandfather pronounced.

"Even though he wasn't *gonna* push you away." Kev moved to hand me his Horn, which displayed the group chat between my Horn, his, and Huxley's. "Read."

I took a deep breath, suddenly afraid, and clenched my hands into fists. "I don't need to read. I was there when he was chatting with you guys, remember? And I had the Horn while we were on the plane…"

"I don't think you read this section." He gestured again. "Go on."

I licked my lips, took the Horn, and started scrolling through the conversation Riggs and Huxley had the night before the plane. With every word Riggs wrote about me, I felt my stomach and cheeks grow warmer, like all the parts of me that had iced over that day on the plane were thawing finally.

Carter's a good man. Generous and kind. Funny as hell. Smart as fuck. And when he smiles… he makes people feel like they can do anything. I like him, Hux.

"Wow," I whispered. "Wow."

It wasn't a declaration of love. It wasn't hearts and flowers and poetry.

It was so much more than any of that. It was real and genuine talk from a Marine who didn't mince words and had no ulterior motive for typing what he'd typed.

I looked up at Kev, bewildered, and swallowed hard. "But if he really cared, why didn't he tell me? When he came the other night, he was asking questions about Venezuela, about a missing Horn…"

"He didn't say *anything* to you about your personal relationship?" Grandfather asked skeptically. "Because things seemed fairly tense between you."

"He maybe suggested he wanted to see me," I admitted, "but not in a loving kind of way." My breath caught remembering the sound of Riggs's voice. *Come home with me tonight.* "At least, I didn't think it was," I whispered.

"Probably because you kept asking him to leave," Grandfather suggested. "Even the most stalwart of young lovers might quake in his boots if the object of his affections told him to leave the premises."

I winced. I *had* done that. And told him I'd give back his knife.

"I know it's tempting to think it's not love because it happened so fast," Tucker admitted softly.

"Just like it was tempting to think it wasn't love for us because it happened so slow." Dunn pulled Tucker against his side. "But your heart knows, Carter. I mean, you fine folks can logic the crap out of it all the day long, but at the end of the day, you're the heart doctor, man. What's your instinct telling you?"

"It's telling me… maybe you guys are right," I admitted in a small voice. "I really want you to be."

"Hells to the yeah!" Dunn jumped up with a fist in the air. Then he cleared his throat and sat back down. "Sorry. Got a little excited there. It's my first successful intervention since Tuck had us join the Beautification Corps. Ava didn't think I could handle it. But I did."

"You did." Tucker patted Dunn's knee, his grin wide. "I think we need to celebrate that. And also devise a plan for how Carter's gonna grovel. Ava would say we need prosecco."

"No prosecco, but we have some wine left from the other night." Kev jumped up. "Pretty sure it's the bottle Riggs brought, which is kinda fitting, huh?" He disappeared into the living room and came back with an armful of glasses, a corkscrew, and a green bottle.

"Seriously? It's only nine thirty in the morning," I pointed out. "Besides which, Riggs is leaving later today for his training. Maybe I could just go—"

"All the more reason to be prepared so you don't waste a minute," Tuck reasoned.

Dunn snorted.

I sighed impatiently. I missed Riggs. As I scrolled through the Horn's chat, rereading the conversations, I wished he was with me. Wished I could touch him. *Smell* him. Kiss him the way I'd wanted to the night he'd come looking for me...

But maybe they were right. I'd screwed things up badly on my own, and I wasn't quite sure how to fix it.

Kev set his armload down. "We need to get Carter a whole groveling *schematic*. Shock and awe. Riggs won't know what hit him."

"Flowers," Grandfather suggested as Kev opened the wine. "Maybe a new knife to replace the one he gave you."

"Always turns Tucker up sweet when I offer to sit by him and pretend to help him do crosswords," Dunn offered. "But I don't know if Riggs is much of a crossword guy."

"How does Tucker make it up to you when he screws up?" I was genuinely curious.

"Ah." Dunn leaned back in the sofa, a huge grin splitting his face. "That's a little move we like to call —"

"Dunn Johnson, don't you dare —"

"—the apolojizz." Dunn wiggled his eyebrows and gave a happy sigh, pulling Tucker down against him. "Tuck can't screw up often enough, as far as I'm concerned."

Tucker gave a pained groan and covered his face with his hands. "Just to be clear, there will be *many* crossword puzzles in your future," he informed his husband.

Dunn didn't seem particularly perturbed.

Grandfather frowned. "The apolo—? Oh! *Ohhhh.* Yes, I see." Grandfather's eyes twinkled as he took a sip from the glass Kev handed him. "I was quite a fan of that in my day too."

"Ew." Kev shuddered as he passed a glass to Tucker after Dunn declined any wine. "I did *not* need to know that."

I heartily agreed.

"Uh... speaking of things we didn't need to know about our relatives... Kev Rogers, what's this convo down here about?" I demanded. I'd scrolled past the whole convo from the plane and gotten to some kind of insult-lobbing between Kev and Hux. "When Hux says he wants you to suck his greenberries, does he mean—"

Kev snatched the device with his free hand and stuffed it in his pocket. "That's... it's... just a couple of gamers being gamers," he stammered. "Trash talking. You know how it is. Rude, vile things. I'm, ah... I'm sorry you had to witness that, Carter. I hadn't realized it was on the group chat."

Hmm. I'd assumed it was just trash talking, and I'd mostly been trying to give Kev shit, but the way he blushed and stammered—the way he suggested that he and Hux had a *private* chat—made me wonder.

Kev gestured with the wine bottle in my direction. "You want? Or you wanna do this planning without alcohol?"

I shrugged. "I guess I might as w— Wait!" My stomach swooped as I noticed the bottle's white-and-blue label, and I stood up and grabbed the bottle from his hand immediately. "*This* is the wine Riggs brought? You're sure this is the bottle?"

He frowned. "Yeah, positive. I mean, *Capybara* isn't a brand of wine Grandfather usually orders, so— Carter? Where are you going? Get back here so we can make you a plan!"

"I don't need a plan!" I called over my shoulder.

I didn't need to control anything. I didn't need to protect myself.

All I needed was Riggs. A man I *trusted* with my whole damn heart. And I knew exactly where to find him.

19

RIGGS

I was fucking everything up. Had Champ put me into the AIP prep coursework a few weeks ago, before Venezuela, I would have been all in. My ability to focus on things like this was well-known. I was all about the job, and impressing Champ and my team with my dedication had always been a top priority.

But something was wrong this time, and I was well aware of what it was. Or *who* it was.

Carter Rogers was like the worst kind of earworm. He was a song I couldn't get out of my mind, the kind I found myself humming to in the shower and on my way to work. Even when I wasn't actively thinking about him, he was there, affecting the rhythm of my day.

The interaction between us at his grandfather's house a week ago had been brutal. If I hadn't spent all that time in close quarters with him, I would have believed him to be the snotty doctor I'd first assumed him to be at the gala. But I knew better. I knew Carter was vulnerable deep down inside, and he withdrew inside his aristocratic shell when he didn't want to be seen.

I saw him, though. I saw the real Carter Rogers, the man who'd looked hurt for a split second when I'd asked him about the case. The man who'd admitted his fears to me in the dark of night and who'd lost his parents at a young age. The man who carried a video game console in his suit pocket so he could maintain a relationship with his cousin.

The man I was beginning to recognize as an essential part of my own well-being.

"You're moping," Elvo said, shooting a crumpled-up piece of paper at my face. Thankfully, my reflexes were honed enough to bat it away before it hit me.

"Cut that shit out," I mumbled, not bothering to lift my head up from where my chin rested on my hand. "I'm trying to concentrate on this comms training prep. I fly out in a few hours."

"Bullshit." Elvo came closer and leaned over the reception desk to see what was on my computer screen. "Why are you researching hospitals in Tennessee? Is that part of the auricle stuff? I figured you were out here sulking about someone else protecting your hottie principal."

I quickly clicked out of it before he recognized the professional headshot of said "hottie principal." The Distinguished Fellow Award page had the best professional shot of him, but I still preferred the candid shot I'd snuck of him in Gelada when he'd just taken a bite of a pastry one of his patients had brought him. He'd closed his eyes and groaned in pleasure. His cheeks were pink from the heat, and his hair was messy from the industrial fan in the clinic. *That* was the Carter I knew. Not the stuffy cocktail party man I'd seen the other night.

Elvo's words caught up to me. "Wait, what? What do you mean someone else is looking after him? Is Carter in danger? Why does he still have close protection? Gustavo doesn't even know about him. Does he? Did something change?"

Elvo shrugged and flicked at a cup of Champion Security pens on the reception desk. "His grandfather insisted on protection for a little while just in case. I'm sure he's fine. That intruder the other night turned out to be an ex-boyfriend. Nothing to worry about."

I shoved the chair back and stood, propping my hands on the desk and leaning forward. "*Intruder*? What? Why wasn't I told about this? He has an ex who's stalking him?"

Elvo tapped his chin like he was deep in thought. "Not stalking exactly. I think it was more like… hmm… I'm having trouble remembering the details now. Baby Byrd was the one who checked the guy out. I'm sure it's fine. The perp didn't have much of a record."

I grabbed the front of Elvo's shirt and pulled him toward me, gritting my teeth. "Tell me what the fuck you're talking about right fucking now."

Once we were almost nose-to-nose, I saw the flicker of amusement in Elvo's eyes. "I guess Dr. Johnson just wanted to drop off a casserole. No harm, no foul."

Dr. Johnson. As in, Tucker Johnson, the man madly in love with his dairy farmer husband. The buttoned-up physician in the Thicket, who was more likely to ride buck naked and bareback on a local bull than forsake his beloved Dunn for another man, even someone as perfect and irresistible as Carter Rogers.

I tossed Elvo away from me with a grunt. "Fucking asshole."

"You got it bad, Riggsy," he warned with an annoying grin. "What're you gonna do about it?"

"Nothing," I muttered, sitting back down and dropping my face in my hands again. "I already tried talking to him and was politely shown the door. After more unanswered calls and texts, I finally had to admit the truth. It's over."

"Pfft. Man up, Marine. Since when do you let some hoity-toity richie-rich show you the door? Go in there and throw him over your shoulder. Tell him who's boss. Make him understand. Stake your claim."

"Stop talking," I grumbled. "You sound ridiculous. And how do you know about this anyway?"

He began ticking off on his fingers. "One, you're all mopey-eyed. Two, you get this weird jaw thing going on whenever Dr. Rogers' name comes up. The only other time I've seen that happen was when Broadwell put the moves on your sister that one time. And three, Hux told me."

"Goddamn it," I said. "Can't anyone keep his fucking mouth shut around here?"

"Um… no? And this isn't news, by the way. You're the one who told me about Jace knocking up that chick from the—"

"*Zzzt!*" I hissed, catching sight of our boss on the front walk. "Incoming."

"What the fuck are you doing out here?" Champ asked, walking through the front doors. "Where's Cole?"

"Who's Cole?" I asked.

"Fuck, I don't remember his name. The new receptionist. Cade? Colin? Chris?"

Elvo stood up straight and grinned. "Pretty sure it was Brenda, boss."

I wanted to tell Champ he was starting to remind me of Gianluigi Santiago, but I wasn't sure he'd see the humor in the comparison.

"Whatever. Where is she? You're supposed to be doing training prep sessions online."

I sighed and stretched. "And I am. I'm just doing them

up here in case anyone comes in or calls. So far it's been pretty quiet."

Elvo's eyes continued to dance. "Except for the whimpering of poor Riggsy's broken heart."

I shot him a look. "Shut the fuck up. Right now."

Champ looked confused. "Why are we talking about Riggs's heart? I thought he didn't have one? Now his dick, that I can imagine talking about."

I nodded. "That's what he meant. He meant my poor lonely dick. That's all. Maybe there'll be some nice ass in the AIP program." Before Champ could blow a gasket, I held up a hand. "Kidding. I'm kidding. Trust me when I say I'm not in the market for a hookup right now."

"That's not what I heard," Elvo singsonged just as the doors opened and Huxley came in carrying armfuls of takeout bags.

"You owe me one," he griped. "Lurleen Jackson 'accidentally' brushed against my ass the entire time I was waiting for my order. I almost called the cops for harassment. This town is nuts."

"It's a nice ass," Elvo offered with a wink.

Champ helped Hux set the bags down on the table and chairs in the waiting area of the lobby. It wasn't the first time we'd used it as an impromptu dining table, and it wouldn't be the last.

"No cops," Champ said, grabbing a french fry out of one of the bags. "They're still pissed at us for calling them out two nights ago for the false alarm at Dr. Rogers' house."

My head snapped up, and Hux made a *simmer down* gesture with his hand. "What false alarm?" I asked.

"I already told you about it, man," Elvo said. "Dr. Johnson showed up and let himself into your Dr. Rogers' house."

"He let himself in? As in, he has a *key*?"

"Maybe he's the one who watered Carter's plants while he was gone," Hux suggested in a gentle voice.

"Carter doesn't have plants," I said. "He told me he kills everything he tries to keep alive." Not to mention, the man had a butler now.

Elvo muttered, "Not a good look for a cardiologist. Just sayin'."

"Not true," Hux said. "The man's a master at farming. He had the highest-rated purple artichoke crop of the whole growing season! Kev said…" He caught himself and snapped his jaw closed. "Never mind."

"The point is," I said angrily, "the man doesn't have a key for watering the plants. If he broke into Carter's house—"

Champ pointed a fry at me. "He didn't. He had a key. And what the hell do you care? You're not on the case anymore."

I opened my mouth to suggest a deeper dive into Carter's security just in case, but Champ was right. It wasn't my job anymore. *He* wasn't my job anymore. Still…

"Did someone say Tucker had a record?" I asked.

Elvo chuckled. "No, that would be his husband, Dunn. Apparently Dunn's been caught in his birthday suit a time or two. The man swears naked fishing is a sport."

All of us took a minute to imagine the hazards of naked fishing. Champ shuddered, and Hux made a whimpering sound in his throat.

"Anyway," Elvo continued, "the man is a hoot. Do you know he has a pet pig named Bernie? And he lets him sleep in his bedroom."

"She," I muttered before taking a reluctant bite of my burger.

"Come again?" Hux asked.

"The pig is female. Bernie is short for Bernadette," I

said. "Carter told me about her. Dunn's really sweet with her. I guess it made Tucker all ooey-gooey, which made Carter gag, but really I could tell it was nice, you know? Like maybe Carter envied their relationship a little."

The silence around the table suddenly got weird. Well, it was weird that there was silence in the first place since I worked with a team of Marines who never shut the fuck up.

"Riggs," Champ began. He was using his kind voice, the one that grated on me and made me want to punch things.

"No, thanks," I said. "Whatever you're going to say, I don't need to hear it. *Sir.*"

I took another bite of my burger, bigger this time in case someone asked me a question.

Champ's eyes darkened. "Oh, well, far be it from me to say something you don't need to hear."

Oh shit.

"I mean, Jesus. I certainly didn't mean to interfere with your relationship with a *client* of ours."

Fuck.

"Besides," he continued, gathering a nice head of steam, "I'm sure relationship advice coming from someone who's married to a gun-toting drag queen may not seem like much to you, but—"

Hux leaned over to Elvo. "When, um... when did Champ marry a gun-toting drag queen because I'm gonna need photos of that."

Elvo shushed him and ate his fries like popcorn, watching Champ and me like we were the main tennis match on center court.

Champ continued. "But I actually know a thing or two about relationships and how to royally fuck them up. And I'm beginning to get the feeling you're in the thick of something just like that right now."

I clenched my teeth. "No, sir. I'm not."

"Don't fucking lie to my face, Marine."

I set the burger down and scrubbed my fingers with a napkin. "I'm not in the thick of something like that because there's no relationship to fuck up. There's no relationship at all."

Champ tilted his head at me as if assessing the situation and creating strategies. "You and the doctor."

"Mpfh." I shoved a fry in my mouth.

Hux tried taking one for the team. "He didn't mean to. It just sort of happened."

Champ sat back in his chair and crossed his arms in front of his chest. "So, what's the problem, then?"

I glanced up at him in surprise. "Uh, he was my principal? He was kind of a client? I wasn't supposed to think with my dick on assignment?"

"Again," Champ added.

"Again," I said through gritted teeth. "And I tried not to. Sort of. But, fuck. He's… he's… God, he's just a really good man. The best. The best kind of man."

"This is the real deal," Champ said, his face cracking into a smug grin. "You're having feels."

Elvo chuckled softly and got up to clean up some of the trash from lunch.

"I don't appreciate the smug face," I told Champ. "And before you kick me off the AIP again, just know I'm fine with that. I need to stay here anyway and make this right. I can't fly out while he thinks I don't care about him. While he still thinks he was nothing but my principal or a hookup."

Champ's jaw dropped. "You're fine giving up your spot in the AIP for this guy?"

I nodded and looked down at the remains of my lunch, wondering if I should just wrap it up and give it to Elvo to throw out while he was busy cleaning stuff up behind me. "I care about him. A lot. I need to make this right. He... he doesn't deserve the way I treated him on the plane. The way I acted toward him in front of all of you."

Champ's eyes flicked over my shoulder and back to me. "Why did you act like he wasn't important to you?"

"You told me not to fuck around on the job. You told me not to share personal info with a hookup."

"But he wasn't a hookup, was he?"

I shouldn't have been so surprised Champ was being supportive. He may have been pissed at me fucking around with a client, but he'd never stand in the way of me developing real feelings for someone. We'd all spent plenty of late nights talking about our hopes of finding a partner one day, and I knew Champ respected the difference between a casual fuck and a meaningful relationship.

I scrubbed my face with my hands. "No. Not for one minute. Even when I first saw him at the gala, I felt like I'd been kicked in the gut. This guy... he's like... he's everything. He's hot and sweet. He's smart as fuck, but he's naive in some ways because he just wants to think the best of people. He wants to help people. Make them better, make them happier. If he felt like he could get away with it, he'd sleep in a shitty third-world shack every night just for the chance to bring medicine to people who need it. And he's devoted to his family. He plays that damned game even when he's exhausted and on the verge of falling asleep because it's important to his cousin. And he let us protect him even though he didn't want to because he knew it was important to his grandfather." I closed my eyes and wondered how I was going to convince Carter to give me another chance. "I'm fucking in love with him, and I don't know how to tell him how I feel."

There was silence for a beat before a beloved, familiar voice broke it. "I think you just did a pretty good job of it."

I opened my eyes as heat flooded my face. Carter stood in front of me in a pair of wrinkled blue scrubs and rubber-soled shoes. His eyes looked incredibly tired, but his smile… fuck. It was a knockout punch. He was the most beautiful sight in the world.

"Duchess," I breathed, wondering if my strong emotions had conjured an illusion.

He walked over and pushed my chair away from the table before straddling my lap. My hands moved around his back to hold him there.

"But feel free to try out different ways of convincing me," he suggested before leaning his forehead against mine. "I'm open to hearing various attempts, and I'll be happy to rank them in order of effectiveness."

"I fucked up," I said.

"Yeah. You did."

"I'm so sorry. I was an ass."

Carter pulled back and ran his hands up my chest before cupping my cheeks. "No, *I'm* sorry. I wish you'd told me what was going on, but I should have given you a chance to explain. I should have trusted you." He pressed a brief kiss to my lips. "And you're an ass who brought me Capybara chardonnay. Because I'm the only person in the world you'd save from a rampaging capybara."

"You are." It had started out as a joke, but it wasn't anymore and hadn't been for a while. I'd walk through fire for Carter Rogers. He was heartbreakingly beautiful sitting so close to me and looking at me like I was someone important, like I was everything to him the way I'd realized he was everything to me.

"I love you," I said in a voice so low it was barely audible. Fear was a real thing, and it gripped me tightly around the throat. "Please forgive me. Please give me a chance to do better."

Carter's face was soft with affection that made my heart thunk double time in my chest. "Do you promise to stop calling me Duchess?"

I furrowed my brow. "No."

His face cracked into a wide grin. "Good. Then yes, I think I'll forgive you, if only for the close protection benefits. John is great, but there's only one man I want close to my body."

I grabbed the back of his head and kissed him hard, not giving either of us a chance to take a breath first. Wolf whistles split the air around us, reminding me my team had been there all along. I didn't care. Carter Rogers was in my arms, and he was willing to give me another chance.

I pulled back and caressed his cheek with my thumb. "I was going to come find you," I admitted. "I couldn't leave town without trying again to tell you how I felt."

Carter wound his arms around my neck and shifted in my lap. The press of his body against mine was making me lose focus. "Well, now you can go enjoy your program with a clear conscience."

I shook my head. "I'm not going. I don't want to leave you, not after we just—"

He cut me off with a quick kiss and met my eyes. "You're going. When you love someone, you support their dreams, right?"

I nodded, even though I knew how hard it would be to watch him go off to another dangerous Doctors Across Continents assignment in the future. Hopefully Champ would assign me to his detail again. "Yeah. Why? Are you leaving again too?"

"No, babe. You are. And I am supporting you." He leaned in close and pressed a soft kiss to my cheek before brushing his lips across my ear. "Because I love you too."

Warmth filled my chest, and my muscles seemed to

loosen as his words soaked in. It was too good to be true, but I wasn't one to look a gift horse in the mouth.

"Yeah?" I breathed, inhaling the familiar grapefruit scent of his bodywash and remembering the shower in Gelada.

"Mm, yeah. Definitely. And when you get back from your program, I'm going to be waiting for you. Naked and ready."

I was hard as steel. After glancing around, I realized we were alone now. The lobby was suddenly still and quiet. "Come back to my office with me," I begged, pressing my dick up into his.

He blushed and laughed. Gorgeous. "I can't. I have patients waiting. Besides, you need to get ready for your trip. But… you can call me later? Maybe a video call?"

His eyes were liquid heat.

"You bet your ass, Duchess. I'm going to video call the shit out of you."

After three weeks of video calls and late-night text chats, I was exhausted but beyond ready to finally put my hands on Dr. Rogers.

"Hey, Riggsy!" Hux called from the reception desk as I raced into the office to drop off the auricle implant assets before heading straight to Carter's house. "Celebration beer at the Tavern tonight."

"No can do," I said. "I have a hot date, and we will not have a moment to spare for a beer with the likes of you assholes."

"Tomorrow, then!" he called after me. I waved a hand in acknowledgment even though my brain couldn't possibly conceive of anything after my time with Carter tonight.

"Here's the stuff," I said, barging into Champ's office and sliding the hard-sided case onto his desk. "Secure it for me, please? I'll start the training tomorrow or whatever. Just not today, obviously."

I turned to bolt out of there, but Champ's deep voice stopped me in my tracks. "Go enjoy yourself, Riggs. You did good. I heard from the head of the program, and he was singing your praises. You can tell us all about it tomorrow."

I blew out a sigh of relief and nodded. "Thanks. Tomorrow. See ya."

When I pulled up to the mansion, I couldn't help but snort. It was so different from the small cinder-block clinic in Gelada where I'd first gotten to know Carter. I'd originally assumed Carter was like this estate: expensive, pretentious, buttoned-up tight with strict security. But my first impression of him had been so wrong. He was warm and kind. Generous and giving.

I'd discovered the estate was actually Carter's now, which was pretty damned funny. I wondered what he planned to do with the extra twenty thousand square feet he couldn't possibly need.

I parked my truck and hopped out, heading straight for the door and reminding myself to use my manners with the butler rather than flinging him to the side and barking out Carter's name in desperation like I wanted to.

But instead of the stuffy butler, Carter was the one who opened the door. His face lit up when he saw me, and it stripped away any hesitation I'd been carrying. I stepped into the large foyer and took him in my arms, spinning him around and holding him tight. "Fuck," I whispered against his face. "I missed you so fucking much."

His body was trembling. "Me too. I was afraid—"

Before he could say the words, my mouth was on his,

tasting him, drinking him in. "No fear. Not anymore," I murmured against his lips. "Just you and me."

He moaned into my mouth and let me push him against the smooth wooden paneling of the foyer and sink to my knees on the cold marble floor.

Carter's eyes widened, but they also went a little hazy, so I assumed he was on board with getting right to the best kind of hello.

"Been dreaming about this," I murmured, running my cheek and chin over the bulge in his wash-worn jeans. "Sucking you, fucking you, kissing you, touching you."

A noise from somewhere in the house startled me, and I glanced up at Carter. "Fuck. I forgot about the butler."

He laughed. "I dismissed the butler, the housekeeper is at a family thing, Grandfather is in Nashville, and Kev never leaves the basement."

"Want me to take you upstairs? Do this right?"

Carter looked down at me with a heated gaze. "Hell no."

I kept my eyes on him while I unfastened his jeans and reached inside his boxer briefs for his hard cock. He smelled so good. Every part of him turned me on. I ran a hand up under his shirt and across his warm skin. "I missed you," I said again before licking the head of his cock.

He made a gurgling sound and threw his head back against the wall. "Fuck. That's... oh God. That's amazing. Please."

His fingers grasped my hair as I tweaked one of his nipples and drew his cock into my mouth with my tongue. It was dirty and quick, but just being alone with him, being able to touch him and taste him, felt like the most decadent intimacy ever.

I wanted to get him off fast and hard to take the edge off but then spend my time driving him crazy in bed. I'd spent hours in a lonely hotel room in Arizona imagining mapping Carter's naked body with my lips and tongue and fingertips.

His balls were heavy in my hand as I rolled them gently. I sucked and licked and slurped, ratcheting up the intensity as he began making broken noises of debauched pleasure. "Come in my mouth, on my face, wherever you want," I urged. "Fuck me."

As soon as I swallowed him down again, he shouted and held my head to his body as he came in warm spurts down my throat. I scrambled for the buttons to my own pants and barely got them open in time to jack myself off onto the cold marble between my knees.

"Fuck, fuck," I panted, laying my forehead against his thigh. His grip on my hair turned to gentle caresses. I closed my eyes and focused on his touch, the smooth, soft fingers moving gently along my face.

Footsteps approached behind me, and I froze for a beat before yanking up my pants and turning around and trying to hide Carter's own nudity. I heard the quick hiss of his zipper and let out a breath.

Kev wandered past with his attention focused on the Horn in his hands.

"Hey, Riggs. Y'all want some snacks? Hey, do we still have any of that guac left from last night?"

Without waiting for a response or looking up from his game, he continued through the foyer toward what I assumed was the kitchen.

I turned back to Carter with a raised brow. "I thought you said—"

"I should have said he only comes upstairs for food," he said with a blush. "He's pretty oblivious when he's playing the game, though, and his village was just overcome with a gang of feral moon kittens. He's going to be spraying enchanted catnip serum for hours."

I chuckled and moved one of my hands down the side of his leg until I found something bulky underneath. I rucked up his jeans to reveal my knife strapped to his calf.

I glanced up at him. "Expecting trouble?"

He blushed and looked away. "No. But you once told me sometimes just knowing it's there was all you needed." He met my eye. "I like knowing it's there. It reminds me of you."

I pulled his pant leg back down over the knife and patted it in place before standing up and brushing off my knees. I made sure both of us were buttoned and zipped properly, and used my shirt to wipe the evidence of our activities off the floor. "Is this when I admit to carrying around the tin of antibiotic salve you gave me that night in Gelada?"

Carter blinked in surprise. "You're kidding."

"Heck, no. Antibiotic salve is dead useful, I'll have you know." I reached into my pocket and pulled out the little circular tin. It had acquired more than a few dents and scratches over the past few weeks. "Besides, you put this in my hand the first time you told me you trusted me."

Carter swallowed. "Because I did, even then. And I do now. With everything, with all of me." He curled my fingers around the tin. "You're not at all the man I imagined wanting," he said.

I glanced up at him in surprise and maybe a little concern, but Carter laughed. "That's not what I meant. I mean you're so different than the man I always thought I'd end up with, but that's a very good thing."

"Why a good thing?"

He pulled me close. "You're unexpected in the best way. On paper, we have nothing in common, but you fill up a part of me I didn't know was empty until we met. You challenge me. You're adventurous and wild, but you're also sweet and thoughtful." His cheeks turned even pinker than they'd been before. "Thank you for the naked mole rat, by the way. Kevin was so impressed, he begged me to marry you before someone else snatched you away from me."

I couldn't help but laugh. "Well, Hux told me it would be the quickest way to get your hill moved before the ice cow infiltration."

"It was. And the anteater helped too."

"I didn't send you an anteater," I said, distracted by the sight of his plush lips. I snuck a quick kiss and grabbed his hand to lead him toward the stairs and a bed.

"No, but Tucker did. He said once the naked mole rat starts moving dirt, it can trigger an ant colony explosion."

We were halfway up the stairs when I stopped and looked over at him. "You're accepting unsolicited gifts from other men?"

He opened his mouth, but nothing came out. I continued. "I gave you a fucking naked mole rat, and that wasn't good enough for you?"

When Carter realized I was joking, his face turned pensive. "Well, it wasn't a *real* mole rat. If you'd given me a real one…"

After a quick walk to the end of the corridor on the second floor, Carter led me into a bright, airy bedroom with windows on two sides. One side looked out on a large pristine lawn bordered by flower gardens, and the other looked out onto a thick forest. "It's gorgeous, isn't it?" he asked, walking toward one set of windows. "I didn't think I'd like it at first, but it's growing on me."

I watched his body move in that graceful way of his. "Yes. Gorgeous."

He turned back to me. "The estate, I mean."

"Mm. Come here, beautiful." I reached out my arms for him, and he walked right into them.

We kissed languidly for a long time, simply enjoying the touch and feel of being together again. By the time we were ready for more, both of us were naked on the bed, and Carter lay sprawled half on top of me.

"Want you inside me," I said in a rough voice. "Please."

Carter's hair was a complete mess from my greedy fingers, and his face was red with beard burn. Just the sight of him made me hard.

"Really?" he asked. "You do?"

"That okay?"

He closed his eyes and nodded reverently. "More than okay. I dreamed about being inside you."

It took a while, too long if you asked me, but Carter was diligent about prepping me. He prepped me into a manic, panting mess. "Now," I said for the millionth time. "Ready. Ready now."

"Mpfh," he grunted, stroking over my gland just hard enough to light me up without pushing me over the edge.

"Duchess. Fuck. *Please.*"

"Love to hear you beg," he said with an evil grin. I grabbed his face and kissed him hard before grabbing his covered dick and trying to bring it to my body. "Okay," he said with a laugh, batting my hand away.

When he finally pressed inside me, I felt like I could finally let go, could finally relax and know he was here with me.

"Love you," I hissed on a particularly good stroke. "Missed you."

Carter's arms tightened around me as he slid into me again. "Love you too. Not letting you leave again for a while, okay?"

"Same." I ended the word on a groan. Carter reached for my dick and stroked me until I couldn't remember my own name, much less his. I came with an embarrassingly loud choking, grunting sound and barely noticed Carter's own release as he pushed hard into me one last time.

Afterward, we lay there in a sweaty heap, tangled together and sated, at least for the time being.

It didn't take long before we were at it again, grasping at each other's bodies and lighting each other up with licks and kisses, greedy hands and thrusting cocks. I couldn't get enough of him, but this time there was complete joy in knowing I didn't have to. I had a lifetime of this, of *him*, ahead of me.

We continued on like that most of the night, only stopping long enough to sneak down to the kitchen for some of the snacks Kev had left behind. Finally, we fell into a deep contented sleep, curled around each other in Carter's big bed.

I was finally, for maybe the first time in my life, at peace.

The next morning, I woke up to an empty bed. After a quick shower in Carter's palatial bathroom, I found some pajama pants and a T-shirt in Carter's dresser that fit me well enough to venture downstairs where I heard Carter and Kev talking.

"He gave you a naked mole rat, Carter. That's like..." He sighed. "That's like pledging lifetime fealty to the king of the muckrakers, you know?"

"Not really," Carter said. I could hear the teasing smile in his voice. "But didn't Hux send a case of ghost-forged glass hammers to the tribes on your outlying islands? How was that not a declaration of... fealty?"

I clapped my hand over my mouth to keep from laughing out loud. Kev sputtered.

"It's... it's not! He *had* to send me those weapons! It was the least he could do after sneak-harvesting my striped skunk yarrow."

"Yes, but then he sold the yarrow at market for the highest price of the season. Had he not harvested it while you were sleeping, you would have only gotten thirty cents on the doll—uh, pip."

I chose that moment to enter the kitchen. Carter's hair was damp from his own shower, and he wore loose sweats with an oversized hoodie. I wanted to eat him up.

"Morning, sunshine," I said, moving straight to him and pulling him in for a morning kiss. The kiss lasted way longer than I'd intended, and it didn't end until Kev's voice punctured my haze.

"Hey, Riggs! I didn't know you were back."

I turned to him in confusion. "I saw you last night in the foyer."

"Oh. Really? Huh. Well, it's good to have you back. My cousin hasn't been himself lately."

"How so?" I asked, shooting a smirk at Carter.

Kev rolled his eyes. "He's all, *'Riggs says,'* and, *'If Riggs was here,'* and, *'I want Riggs to fuck me over the kitchen count—'*"

Carter cut him off. "What? No, I didn't!"

Kev dissolved into a fit of laughter and pointed at Carter. "You should see your face right now."

Carter reached over and flicked Kev on the shoulder with his finger. "Ass."

"That sounds surprisingly like what you called out for in your dreams last week," Kev teased, dodging Carter's attempt at another flick.

They reminded me of my brothers, and I realized how nice it was to have family nearby. I was happy Carter had this, had someone who obviously loved him and enjoyed his company.

I helped myself to some coffee while Carter turned back to the stove. A carton of eggs and various other omelet supplies littered the counter nearby.

"I told the guys I'd meet them for a beer tonight. Will you come with me?" I wanted Carter to get to know my friends, to be a part of my life completely.

His face brightened in a grin. "Really? I'd love to. You sure you won't be embarrassed by your rich boyfriend?"

"You're *rich*?" I asked, feigning shock with a palm to my heart and a gasp.

Carter looked around at the giant, commercial gas stove, the huge glass-front pair of fridges, the two high-end dishwashers, the intricately carved wooden frame around the built-in china cupboard, and the french doors looking out over a slate patio leading to a large infinity pool. "I mean… it's not much, but it's home," he said.

"I've always wanted a sugar daddy," I teased.

"Call me daddy one time and see how that goes for you," he warned with the hint of a smile.

"Yes, Daddy," I said breathlessly. "Whatever you say, Daddy."

"Why did I ever think you were attractive?" he groaned.

"Buy me a pony, Daddy?"

Kev muttered something about ensorcelled ponies being on sale right now in the Cloudlance territory of Bork. I ignored him and stared at the man who'd just called himself my *boyfriend*. I liked the sound of that.

"You hungry?" Carter asked me, suddenly blushing under my hot stare.

"Starving," Kev said, focusing on his game again. "Feel like I haven't eaten in years. Mrs. Clayborn makes the best pancakes. You shouldn't have sent her away."

Carter sighed and went back to the green pepper he was chopping on a cutting board. "I sent her to her daughter's wedding in Gatlinburg. She'll be back on Tuesday."

"Oh. Well, she could have at least precooked us some pancakes before she left…"

Carter glanced over at me a little guiltily. "The house-keeper. I had to keep her on because this house has at least ten thousand bedrooms, and I don't even know how to work half of these appliances."

"You're going to keep the house?"

Kev chimed in. "He has to. It's our superhero lair. I'm auditioning names right now, but so far I'm thinking Vagabond Base or Dusksword Retreat. Maybe Trinity Burrow... hm."

"Why trinity?" I asked, distracted by the tight curve of Carter's ass in those sweats as he turned back to his chopping.

Kev looked up from his game. "Uh, because there are three of us here now?"

"Your grandfather is moving here permanently?" I asked.

Kev shook his head. "No, you, me, and Carter. Duh." He went back to the game.

I met Carter's eyes while the warmth of Kev's acceptance washed over me. "And how do you feel about that?"

Carter's ears turned pink. "Well... I mean... it's a huge house. It wouldn't make sense for you to pay rent somewhere when I have all this and it's paid for..."

He busied himself with the food prep. I set my coffee cup down and moved behind him, careful to reach for the hand holding the knife before wrapping my other hand around his front.

I brushed my lips against the back of his neck. "Are you asking me to move in with you, Duchess?"

"Uh..." He sucked in a breath when my lips moved to the sensitive spot behind his ear and my hand moved lower on his abdomen. "I mean... uh... *ahh*..."

"When are the pancakes going to be ready?" Kev asked.

"Next Tuesday, damn it!" Carter barked, almost making

me jump in surprise. I laughed and began to step back, but Carter grabbed my arm and held it tightly to his front. "Stay."

I didn't know whether he meant here against his body or here in the crazy Rogers family bat cave, but it didn't matter. The answer was the same.

"Always."

EPILOGUE
CHAMP

"Cheers." Hux clinked the neck of his beer against mine and ran a hand through his messy blond hair. "Here's to us landing another whale contract for Champion Security. I can't believe HOG not only permanently hired us back for facilities security, they want us to collaborate with their motherfucking *cybersecurity team*. Do you know how big a coup this is, you guys? Do you?"

I drained half my beer in one swig and met Riggsy's laughing eyes across the Tavern's wooden table. "If we didn't know when I signed the contracts, Hux, I think we got it after the third time you asked *do you know* when we were still back at the office."

Hux's cheeks went pink. "It's just cool to have a client that's in my wheelhouse, that's all."

"Don't give Hux too much shit," Riggs said. "This is the equivalent of me being asked to protect Zac Efron. Or you being asked to protect... I dunno, Ronald Reagan? Whoever was considered hot when you were young, Champ."

I lifted an eyebrow at him. "I'm thirty-seven, dipshit. As in, only one year older than your... your *boyfriend*."

Yeah, it was gonna take me several minutes to get used to saying *Riggs* and *boyfriend* in the same sentence. I was happy for him—I was. I just couldn't imagine finding someone I'd be as eager to tie myself to as Riggs was with Carter. Not again, anyway.

I'd been there, done that, and all I had to show for it was a fixer-upper Victorian I had no desire to fix up and a highly anxious poodle named Hercules.

"Age isn't just about the number, though," Riggs teased. "You've got that whole older-man grumpy vibe happening—"

"Fuck off." I wadded up a cocktail napkin and threw it at him.

"No, seriously," he laughed. "It's a *good* vibe. Guys dig that vibe. Or they would if you'd learn to live a little and not scowl like you're gonna tell 'em all to get off your lawn."

I held his gaze and shook my head. "Huxley, remind me to fire Riggs tomorrow. For gross insubordination."

"Hmm? Oh." Hux looked up from the red plastic Horn in his hands. He shut the device off and returned it to his pocket when he saw my face. "Uh, sorry, boss. The Purple Shag Shepherds of the Northland are revolting, and I've been trying to subdue them, but you know there's only one way to subdue a Shag Shepherd—"

"No," I said emphatically. "I've made it a point not to know."

HOG Corporate might be my largest client, and it might be my business to learn all about their employees, facility, and now cybersecurity, but I refused to be involved in their game.

"You have to wrestle 'em," Riggs said knowingly, and Hux nodded.

I shot Riggs a look of betrayal, and he held his hands up in defense. "I know I said I'd never get into it, but the game's fucking addictive once you start playing it. Especially when your boyfriend plays it too." His sappy grin made me wanna smile too, but I rolled my eyes instead.

"Yet another reason I will *not* start playing it." I crossed my arms over my chest.

"Nothing wrong with having hobbies," Hux countered. "Or boyfriends. In theory."

I shook my head. "Champion Security *is* my hobby, and that keeps me plenty busy. I don't have time to waste on silly shit. Especially not on relationships."

Riggs snorted. "Spoken like a guy who's about to be hit over the head with a two-by-four of love. Just sayin'."

I smiled smugly. If Riggs knew a thing about my love life, he'd know that I had a better chance of wrestling a purple... whatever the fuck it was... than falling in love. But unlike these yahoos I considered my best friends, I knew how to keep my shit contained. I would *never* be caught spreading my relationship drama around.

"Speaking of two-by-fours..." Huxley smirked. "Don't look now, but there's a guy at your five o'clock, Champ, and he seems to find your intimidating glower attractive— Hey! I said don't look!"

But it was too late. My head had already swung in that direction, and my gaze slammed directly into a frank, curious, blue-green one.

I sucked in a breath. The guy was good-looking—okay, *gorgeous* —with artfully floppy dark hair, puffy lips, and a sharp jaw, but he was tiny—like, five six if I was being generous—when I usually liked guys built more like me. Also, the man wore some kind of complicated getup—a high-buttoned shirt, plaid pants, and a waist pack slung diagonally across his chest—that looked high fashion and probably cost more than my house. The direct-stare, quirked-eyebrow, mysterious-smile thing he was giving off was attractive as all hell, but he looked like the kind of guy who expected breakfast the morning after a one-night stand, sooo...

I turned back to face forward. "Pass. Too expensive for my taste," I said.

Riggs shook his head sadly. "Too bad. He's hot."

"Who's hot?" Carter teasingly demanded, draping himself over Riggs's shoulder from behind. "You looking at Dunn Johnson's ass again?"

"Baby! I thought you wouldn't be here for another hour." The honest delight on Riggs's face when he looked up at Dr. Rogers left no room for Carter to be remotely jealous, and it was clear Carter knew it.

The way they'd gotten together was utterly ridiculous, but the connection between them was as strong as anything I'd ever seen—way stronger than anything I'd personally experienced—and even my cynical ass knew it was real and permanent.

"I know, but everything went shockingly smoothly for once, and the board meeting ended early." Carter bit his lip against an excited smile. "The first mobile cath lab sponsored by the Rogers Family Foundation is set to roll into Gelada tomorrow, which is record timing, and Luz is going to be their first patient. Marisol is over the moon." He gazed at me across the table. "Thank you, Champ. I know you pulled strings to help get us the security we needed."

"Nah." I waved a hand. "I made a phone call to someone I trust. You're the one footing the bill."

"Still," Carter began, and then his gaze caught on someone over my shoulder. "Oh, hey! Tucker and Dunn are leaving. I'm gonna go tell Tuck the good news before he goes."

"I'll come." Riggs slid his chair back and jumped up, ready to follow Carter anywhere—to the other side of the room, on another medical aid mission, probably even down the aisle one of these days, since Riggsy didn't do things half-assed and he was clearly all in with his cute doctor.

It was adorable. If you were into that kind of thing.

"Think I might be ready to call it a night," Hux said a minute later, draining the last of his beer. "Gotta get home and do… you know… stuff."

"Once again, Huxley, I make it a point not to know what *stuff* you might be getting up to of an evening, especially since your former roommate is now shacking up at Carter's place." I grinned. "But whatever it is, enjoy it. Tomorrow afternoon we meet with HOG Corporate to go over the specs."

He returned my grin with one of his own. "Can't wait."

Neither could I.

I looked around for Alana, our server, so I could pay the tab, but before I spotted her, my phone rang. Unknown caller, but a local number, so I answered just in case it was someone from HOG.

"Champion."

"Percival," a familiar cultured voice said. "Guess you haven't changed your number. I wondered if you might after all these years."

My shoulders instantly went tight, my chest burned, and my stomach churned.

"Vince," I managed to say smoothly. "How's my least favorite DEA agent? Do the other agents not trust you to use the phone number lookup function, even after all these years? Don't worry, buddy—I'm sure you'll graduate to big-boy jobs soon."

"I go by Vincent now," Satan's hand puppet corrected. "As you know."

I snorted. "How would I know? I do not make a point to keep up with your life. *Vince.*"

"But your mother sends me a lovely card each year on my birthday," he sniffed, "and I return the favor."

The burn in my chest flared hotter. Vince was the sort of son Isobel "Bunny" Champion always wanted. Figured she'd kept him, even after we'd broken up.

"Was there a reason for your call?" I demanded. "Has hell frozen over already? Did you want to make sure I fed Hercules? Because I have. Every day for the last five years. Every day since you —"

"I'm calling as a professional courtesy," he interrupted. "It's come to my attention that your little band of rent-a-soldiers may have been involved in an incident down in Venezuela last month."

I seethed. I wanted to believe Vince had been a decent human at some point and that I hadn't wasted my time trying to make things work with someone so self-centered... but I honestly wasn't sure.

"You'll have to be more specific," I hedged. "Champion Security deals with any number of incidents every single day."

"This would be a memorable one, given that it involved infiltrating a villa reportedly owned by Cartel de la Luna and operated by Gustavo Santiago."

Ugh. I'd been afraid he was going to say that. The very last thing I needed was to have fucking *Vince* investigating something that could have potential blowback on HOG... and by extension, Champion Security.

"I'm holding a signed report you provided to the authorities," he continued, "in case that jogs your memory."

I scowled. "If you have my report, then I can't imagine what more you'd like me to say."

This was not entirely true.

The report I'd filed with the authorities made our involvement sound like a simple hostage rescue situation—one kidnapped American tourist, one simple extraction from one drug lord's compound. We'd kept the HOG security breach and the real reason for Buck's abduction out of the reports. We'd also kept any mention of Carter and Riggs out of the report so Gustavo wouldn't learn of their presence at his compound. We hadn't mentioned Gianluigi's involvement either, since he'd freed our guys in the end and had done a hell of a good deed in making sure Buck got on the plane too, especially knowing how angry Gustavo must've gotten.

So, in essence, that report had more holes than a slice of swiss cheese and concealed more facts than it actually "reported." Still, it was my story, and I was sticking to it.

"It's come to our attention that sensitive cartel data was stolen out from under Santiago's nose, most likely in the form of a thumb drive. It's made Santiago extremely unpopular with the big cartel bosses in Caracas. We've heard there may even be a power grab coming, which would be..." Vince hesitated. "Dangerous. And inadvisable."

"Inadvisable for who? Is America getting involved in drug cartel politics now?"

"Of course not. But better the devil you know, as they say."

I grimaced, even though he couldn't see me. That saying characterized a lot about my last few months with Vince, with me hanging on and hoping our relationship could get back to what I'd thought it was, and him... not.

"Let's just say it would be inconvenient for everyone should that data end up in the wrong hands and further destabilize things in the region," Vince went on. "My colleagues and I would react *very* unfavorably."

Right. I knew a threat when I heard one. And if Vince

had known me half as well as I'd once believed he did, he would have known I never backed down from a threat. "I'm not sure what you think that has to do with me. I'm no thief, nor is anyone on my team. We were there to rescue a tourist from Gustavo Santiago—"

"See, that's funny, because airport surveillance saw Gustavo Santiago—the *real* Gustavo Santiago—arriving in the United States a full ten days prior to this incident. So I imagine the man your associates dealt with wasn't actually Gustavo, but one of his men impersonating him."

"Not my problem. We got the tourist back, so—"

"Funny thing about that tourist. Buckshot 'Buck' Nutter of Frogpole Lane, Licking Thicket, happens to have been the lead developer of *Horn of Glory*, and I do believe HOG Corporate is one of Champion's clients. That's a heck of a coincidence."

Mother. Fucker.

"That… is indeed a coincidental coincidence," I said breezily, though my palms were starting to sweat.

"And yet you're *sure* that he just happened to be kidnapped on a snorkeling trip for no reason whatsoever? And you don't think it's possible that Mr. Nutter isn't an innocent victim but the man who stole that sensitive information from Gustavo Santiago?"

I thought of the surveillance footage from the plane that Hux had shown us a few weeks before—footage that showed Buck Nutter unwrapping a *Horn of Glory* Horn which he'd somehow gotten rid of by the time we brought him back to the Champion offices for a debrief—and an idea formed in my mind. A wackadoo, one-way-ticket-to-bad-choices idea that was so ridiculous I was almost positive it was true.

Had the whole world lost its damn mind?

What would possess a man like Gustavo Santiago to

take cartel data and put it on a $10 hunk of plastic that yodeled when the battery ran low?

What in all the hells would make Buck Nutter, a man who'd already been kidnapped, held prisoner, and threatened by Gustavo Santiago, steal a Horn full of sensitive data that was bound to get him killed?

Vince's call had officially gone from being the worst part of my day to being the worst part of my *year*.

But was I going to tell him that the DEA should be looking for a stolen Horn and not a flash drive, and that Buck was probably exactly the culprit they were looking for?

Oh, fuck to the no.

Especially not when Champion Security had, in effect, been driving the getaway plane. And especially-especially not when the theft involved HOG Corporate, Champion's biggest client.

"Nope!" I said shortly, crossing my fingers under the table. "As far as I can see, there's no connection."

"Hmm. Well, according to his sister Kandi, no one has seen 'hide nor hair' of Mr. Nutter since he left town the day after you got back from Venezuela," the Bearer of Bad News continued relentlessly. "He ended his relationship with his girlfriend, a Ms. Kellie Tuffy, also of Licking Thicket, just over a week ago via phone call, which was a, quote, 'rat-bastard thing to do to a woman who's wasted her prime husband-hunting years on a man.' End quote."

Shit, damn, sod it all.

After Riggs had asked Carter about the Horn that Buck had shown him, I'd had Hux try to contact Buck directly, but he'd been unreachable, so I'd let it go. I'd told myself not every open loop had to be closed when I'd known better. I *knew* better.

And now Buck was in the wind.

"I can say for certain that I haven't seen him since the day we brought him back." And then I added, "Too bad your guys were so slow in putting all these facts together, huh?"

Vince made an impatient noise. "If you see Mr. Nutter, you should impress upon him that he's in very grave danger as long as that data remains unsecured."

"Yep. Sure will. If I happen to see him." I would find Buck myself and *literally* impress that on his forehead if his skinny ass didn't cough up the Horn.

"And you might tell him that if he sells, gives away, or loses the information, not only will the cartel want to find him… so will we. And we won't be quiet about it."

I grimaced. *Awesome.* I envisioned a nightmare scenario where Champion Security made front-page news for aiding and abetting a thief with a name like Nutter. The puns—and Jesus Christ, I hated puns—would write themselves unto infinity, and the company I'd thrown my heart, soul, sweat, and tears into would never recover.

"Always great talking to you, Vince," I said in a bored tone. "We'll have to catch up in another five years. Or ten. Or never."

"Tell Bunny I say hello," the smug bastard said.

There was literally no way. "And give Igor my best."

"His name is Ivan, Percy. Don't be petty."

Petty? I'd give the cheating bastard *petty*. I was going to find the fucking Horn, and I was going to take it directly to Vince's supervisor.

I jabbed the End button before I said anything that would get me sent to Guantanamo or trigger an IRS audit.

Before I could send a group text warning my team about an early morning all-hands meeting to tackle this issue, Alana stopped by my table. "You ready to cash out, Champ?"

I drummed my fingers on the table, pondering this. The urge to get seriously drunk—drunk enough to lose myself for a few hours, to maybe forget how Vince's nails-on-a-chalkboard voice sounded when he said the word *Percy*—was hard to resist.

"I know a drink called a Howling Turtle that'll cure whatever ails you," a sweet voice said as the dark-haired man from earlier slid into the empty seat beside me. The look in his eyes was dialed up from attractive to blatant-eye-fuckingly-irresistible, and he smiled blindingly as he held out a hand for me to shake. "Quinn," he purred.

"Quinn," I said softly, tasting the weight of his name on my tongue and leaning into his space. He smelled like salt water and herbs, something way subtler than I would have expected based on his outfit. "If you think a single drink can cure me, baby, then you don't know what ails me."

His smile softened, deepened, *heated*. "Then maybe what you need isn't a drink at all."

"Maybe it isn't."

He bit his lip and laid one small, soft hand on my thigh, just high enough for me to imagine it even higher. "Maybe we start with a drink and see what comes next?"

I took a deep breath and thought about throwing myself into a mindless night of stress-relieving sex with this beautiful stranger. Tomorrow I could focus on solving the problem of the missing data. Tonight I could focus on getting a little drunk and a lotta laid.

I held up my hand for the server. "Two Howling Turtles please."

∽

Want to know what happens with Quinn and Champ and the

Howling Turtles? Turn the page for a sneak peek of Hitched or grab your copy here → http://readerlinks.com/l/1938654

Want more Licking Thicket romance? Check out more hilarious reads set in the punniest small-town in America…
Fakers (Brooks and Mal
Liars (Diesel and Parrish)
Fools (Dunn and Tucker)
Turkeys (Charlton and Hunter)

SNEAK PEEK OF HITCHED

QUINN

I was *not* a morning person.

I hadn't been one back when I was a kid spending summers in Licking Thicket, even though my Aunt Cherry had bribed me with baked goods, blasted '80s pop songs loud enough to make the windows of her old Victorian rattle, and reminded me crisply that, "Spending your time dreaming is as useless as pining for a man, Quinn. Reality never lives up to expectations."

And at age thirty, despite founding *two* successful event-planning businesses, accumulating a roster of incredibly demanding clients, and having enough failed relationships under my belt to recognize that Cherry had been spot-on when it came to men, I'd accepted that I was never *going* to be a morning person either.

Dreams were just more compelling than reality, period-period.

So when I sensed morning light filtering through my curtains one January morning, was it any surprise that my first impulse was *not* to jump out of bed or even to roll over and check my phone for the onslaught of messages from the half-dozen nervous brides on Taffet Events' current client list?

Heck no.

In fact, I pulled my pillow over my head to block out the light, yanked my quilt up to my chin, and slid right back into a dreamy, sensuous slow dance with the handsomest, most charming man I'd ever met—a man whose tan skin set off his sun-kissed hair and blue eyes, who was witty and intelligent, whose biceps were as big as my thighs, whose lips tasted like amaretto and secrets, and who said my name all hot and slow, like…

"Quinn? Hey, Quinn!"

Um, *no*. My personal Prince Charming wasn't supposed to say my name in that curt, impatient tone. He was supposed to *rumble* my name from the depths of his chest, the way he had the first time he kissed me. Or to *shout* my name, hoarse and helpless, like he did when I made him mindless with wanting. Or even to *whisper* my name sleepily, like he sometimes did when he wrapped his arms around me in the dark of night. He was definitely not supposed to say—

"*Quinn!*" A big, callused hand shook my calf, knocking me out of my dream entirely. "Fuck's sake, man. I've seen dead bodies that were easier to rouse. Did you see where my T-shirt ended up? I have a meeting at work this morning, and I'm running late."

I heaved a sigh, shoved the pillow off my head so hard that it tumbled to the hardwood floor, wiped the drool off my face, and sat up to confront reality—all six feet and several blond-haired, blue-eyed, grouchy-as-fuck inches of him.

Staring directly at the magnificence that was Percy Champion was a little like staring at the sun. He wasn't actually a dream man, I reminded myself. Just a regular old guy.

With a run-of-the-mill gorgeous face and garden-variety broad shoulders, trailing down to a plain-as-dirt narrow waist and dime-a-dozen eight-pack abs that glistened with tiny water droplets from his morning shower like a benevolent god had encrusted them with diamonds.

And while he might bear a slight resemblance to the Prince Charming of my dreams, there were many critical differences. For example, my Prince Charming smiled a lot, and not just when we were drunk on Howling Turtles and flirting at the Thicket Tavern, like the night we met.

Prince Charming wouldn't avoid even the most harmless personal questions as if the answers might incriminate him.

He'd also never say something egotistical (and patently false) the morning after our first night together, like "I can tell you're a relationship kind of guy, Quinn, and I need to tell you, I'm not into relationships," which really should have been my first red flag where Champ was concerned, because if he'd simply *asked*, I'd have told him I was *soooo* not into them either.

Prince Charming would be as sweet and funny when the sun came up as he was when he came by the shop at night to "check on you, because I saw your light was still on."

He would not have a weird split personality that enabled him to talk sweetly to me for hours about everything from our favorite movies, to funny stories about Champ's time in the military, to the ups and downs of owning a business, *then* sex me up until I was cum-drunk, *then* spend the night in my bed... only to freak the fuck out the next morning like he thought I might tattoo his name on my forehead as a symbol of my undying love if he acted the slightest bit friendly.

And Prince Charming—

The bedroom door opened so fast it hit the wall with a *bang*, and a tiny fluffball predator attacked my discarded pillow with glee.

Oh, yeah. Prince Charming wouldn't be the most irresponsible dog owner in the entire freakin' universe.

It was a good thing Aunt Cherry had decided to spend her retirement traveling around the country with one of her Bunco friends, because she would legit disown me if she knew I'd spent not one, not two, but *twenty-six* nights with someone like Percy Champion. Hell, I was ready to disown myself.

"How the heck should I know where your shirt is?" I demanded. My voice sounded rough and wrecked, which was partly because I was still half-asleep and partly because of, you know… other things.

Things like blowing Percy Champion's monster cock the night before.

Twice.

Despite solemnly vowing on Sunday morning that I would break the cycle of booty calls and morning-after regrets by absolutely, positively never going anywhere near said cock again, and that this time, I meant it.

Damn it. I flopped back onto the mattress and squeezed my eyes shut. For real, Aunt Cherry could never know about this.

"It was my favorite vintage Harley T-shirt," he grumbled.

"Oooh. Bummer."

"It was faded to the perfect softness."

"You should probably have taken better care of it, then, hmm?"

"And this is the third time one of my shirts has gone missing over here," Mr. So-Not-Charming barked, like he was back in the Marines and expected me to give him a jaunty salute. "So could you sit up and help me look?"

Seriously, why did the universe make the hot ones so damn annoying?

"M'kay." I rolled to a sitting position for the second time and gave the man a piece of my mind. "I'm gonna do the world a great service right now and clue you in on a little secret. That deep, commanding voice thing? It only works on me if one of us is about to get our dick sucked. Otherwise, if you want me to do you a favor, there'd better be a bag of fresh, honey-glazed donuts from Annie's in your meaty paw and a big ol' smile on that pretty face, *baby*."

He stared at me for a second, and then his gaze heated. I couldn't tell if he was turned on by my attitude or just imagining getting his dick sucked—again—but my stupid, traitorous body didn't know how to *not* respond to that look. I was *this close* to sliding out of bed and getting rid of his bad mood the old-fashioned way...

And then he went and ruined it.

"Don't call me baby. I hate pet names. And I am not bringing you donuts in bed, Quinn. Ever. That's not... that's not what we *do*. You know that, right?"

Ugh. Seriously? I flopped back down, pulled the blanket over me, and muttered, "I am aware that we are not in a relationship. Just because they're ring-shaped does not make them a symbol of commitment, Champion."

He shook my leg again. "I'm being serious. We need to discuss this—"

"I assure you, we do not." But I was probably running late for work, so I sat up once more—*three sit-ups counted as an ab workout, right?*—and threw off the covers.

Champ made a kind of strangled noise and rubbed a hand over his mouth like he was fighting a smile.

I narrowed my eyes. "What's funny?"

He shook his head. "Nothing? It's just that you're..." His eyes strayed up toward my hair. "Cute."

Cute? Oh. Oh, *fucking fucksticks*. I glanced in the antique oval mirror over the dresser and confirmed my worst nightmare. While Champ looked like a freshly laundered Captain America with his perfectly coiffed blond locks and ogle-worthy pecs, I'd gone to bed with my hair wet and product-free after a postcoital shower, and it was at that moment doing a spectacular impression of a chestnut-colored cotton ball.

The morning got worse and worse.

I slid out of bed in just my boxer briefs, shouldered past him, and padded down the hall to the kitchen, where the coffee was already brewed and waiting, which I guessed was the silver lining of Champ's visits...

Okay, that and the truly phenomenal sex. And the laughter. And the witty conversations.

But these mornings after were killing my mojo.

I poured myself a cup and called over my shoulder, "I don't think we need to discuss anything. We covered all of your concerns during your freak-out on Sunday morning. And Friday. And Thursday. And last Monday. You don't want a relationship. *Terrific.* Neither do I. Don't blame *me* because you find me irresistibly attractive, okay? If you're ready to put an end to this, then stop coming around."

And I would be fine with that, I told myself, despite the pang in my stomach that called me a liar.

A huff of laughter from the doorway was the only thing that alerted me I'd been followed down the hall. The man was too damn sneaky by far.

"Obviously, I find you attractive. Very attractive. Too

damn attractive. I'm just concerned you're making this into something it's not, Quinn. I don't want you to get hurt."

Sincerity rang in every syllable he uttered. The man truly, truly believed what he was saying.

It was very sweet.

It was also utterly maddening.

Which was pretty much on-brand for my interactions with Percy Champion.

"Sweet Jesus." I sipped my caffeine juice. "Let me make sure I understand. You're being a jerk to *save* my feelings, you assume I'm a 'relationship guy' even though I've given you no reason to believe this, and you're confident that any man who *did* want a relationship would want one with you. Have I got that right?"

Champ spread his hands. "You're a wedding planner," he said softly, like that explained everything.

"No shit," I shot back, because it kind of did explain everything, just not the way Champ thought.

I loved my job—loved the challenge, and the romance, and the pageantry of it—but there was something about planning a bride's third wedding in eight years that took the bloom off the rose when it came to "forever." Most wedding planners I knew felt the same.

Plus, I'd been partly raised by my Aunt Cherry, who liked to remind me, "Lovers are like baby tigers, Quinny— adorable at first, but more dangerous the longer you keep 'em around."

And if all that weren't enough, the last time I'd decided to play the odds and risk a commitment, I hadn't just gotten burned, I'd been *charred*, thus proving once again that Cherry was always right.

"I keep telling you, but you keep not hearing me, so this time, please pay attention: I do not want a relationship. Not ever again," I said bluntly. I set my empty cup in the sink and dusted my hands. "And I'm tired of waking up to your assumptions and regrets and… and… weird, totally unfounded accusations of clothing theft."

"They're not unfounded. Shirts don't just disappear—"

"When you're ready to apologize," I interrupted, "I *might* consider listening. But until then, maybe spend your evenings at your own house—the house you *claim* to have, despite never inviting me over—"

"I told you, it's under renovation. And you're missing the point—"

I lifted my chin. "Are you going to apologize for yanking me out of my dream and killing my morning vibe?"

Champ set his jaw.

"Just as I thought. Then this discussion is over. See yourself out." I strolled down the hall toward the bathroom, stripping my boxers into the hall hamper along the way.

I heard his breath catch as I sashayed my naked ass through the bathroom door and shut it with a click, and I congratulated myself on making the best flounce in the history of flounces.

I wouldn't waste another second of my day thinking about Champ.

Quincy Taffet: 1, Percy Champion: 0.

But when I emerged from the bathroom a few minutes later, I realized my point-scoring had been a little premature.

"The man is either fucking diabolical or criminally negligent," I fumed. "How the hell am I supposed to aggressively not think about him now?"

The golden-brown fluffball in the middle of my hall runner cocked his head as if he were unsure also.

"Champ?" I yelled, though I could tell instinctively that I was the only human in the house.

Damn it. This was the second time this week Champ had left Hercules behind when he ran out the door in the morning.

The poodle jumped to his feet and spun around, barking happily the second his owner's name was called.

"Poor Herc. He's trying his best not to be in a relationship with you either, huh?" I knelt down to pat his soft, curly head. "Why do we put up with him? Is it that mischievous smile? Or the good neck rubs? Or that thing he does with his tongue that… er, never mind. You don't need to know about that. I'll get us some breakfast, and then you can be my assistant until your owner remembers you exist, okay?"

Hercules barked happily.

But on my way to the kitchen, I grabbed my phone and typed out an angry text.

Me: *Missing anything, Champion????*

For a man who was concerned about the symbolism of bringing me a fresh donut, he sure as hell left his pet behind all willy-nilly.

"Ah, crap. The Drakes-Dunwoody wedding party needs to move their initial consult up to ten o'clock," I told the dog as soon as I opened my laptop. Hercules didn't seem nearly as perturbed by this turn of events as I was. He barely looked up from where he sat at my feet, chowing down a bowl of the organic dog food I'd bought him the *last* time Champ left him here. "That's in just forty minutes."

I scrolled through Marissa's long, apologetic email, down to her email signature. Beneath her title — Marketing Coordinator for Drakes Automotive — was a promotional picture of her father, Tommy Drakes, dressed in a red Speedo and carrying a rescue buoy like a Baywatch-era

David Hasselhoff, captioned "I'm here to save you! Save you… thousands off the sticker price on your new car or truck!"

I winced, and Herc paused his eating to tilt his head up at me.

"Hey. I'm not judging," I informed him. "Those ads are paying my exorbitant fee, and some of us have to source our own kibble, buddy. Besides, Tommy Drakes does other stuff too. Manufacturing. And real estate. And… horse things."

Actually, based on my client research, the horse stuff seemed less about bringing in revenue and more about supporting his only daughter, Marissa, my potential client. She was an accomplished equestrian, and Tommy was a proud papa.

Carlotta Drakes, on the other hand, seemed the type to care more about the horse's pedigree or whether her daughter was wearing couture while riding, but I was trying to reserve judgment on her too.

My phone buzzed, and I glanced down quickly, then just as quickly rolled my eyes.

Delusional McBossypants Champion: *Uh, yeah. Already told you I'm missing THREE shirts.*

I rolled my eyes.

That's what *he* thought. He was actually missing at least four, by my count. Though maybe he'd been too drunk that first night at the Tavern to remember that he'd been wearing a Captain America T-shirt under his button-down and that I'd teased him about it until he'd pushed me down on my bed and we'd…

"*Nope,*" I said aloud. I needed to delete those memories from my brain, not revel in them.

Delete, delete, delete.

I probably also needed to delete the collection of

recently liberated T-shirts from the back of my linen closet before Champ got a warrant to search the place, like the badass security company owner he was.

I grumbled, and when Hercules looked up in confusion, I snapped his picture and sent it to Champ.

Me: *Never mind the shirts. I meant YOUR DOG. You left him again. I'm going to hold him for ransom.*

I clicked off my phone and scrambled to my feet. "Come on. Let's take a walk, and then you can charm my prospective clients, okay?"

I grabbed the dog's leash off the coatrack by the door — where Champ had left it last night specifically so he wouldn't leave Hercules behind again — and led him to the tiny strip of grass between my building and the street so he could do his business while I made some phone calls.

Talking to my clients and focusing on business centered me, as it always did.

I spoke to Marco Perlman about offsetting the carbon footprint of his spring wedding with locally sourced organic food options.

I talked Aurelia Evers down from her dress panic by assuring her that there was plenty of lace on her bodice — in fact, too much lace if you asked me, but brides rarely did. I was there to make *their* dreams come true, after all, so I made it my policy to never offer advice or opinions unless asked… and even then, I was cautious.

I was just pulling up Posy Martinez's phone number to respond to her "bouquet emergency" when a toddler's high-pitched cry pierced the air.

My head swiveled toward the noise, and I saw Parrish and Diesel Partridge leaving the doctor's office down the street with their little girl. I hadn't met any of them, but it was impossible to live in the Thicket without knowing who they were, even for an outsider like me.

Parrish, who was shorter than his heavily tattooed husband by at least a foot, was the one carrying the baby. He also had his arm braced around Diesel's waist.

"Vaccines are never fun, baby," Parrish said soothingly as they approached. "But you were so brave. I think you deserve a cookie from Annie's."

Okay, so I might not be down for relationships, but there was something about a guy saying such sweet things to his little girl—

"Thanks, Parrish," Diesel said in his gruff voice. "I don't mean to get upset. It's just so hard to see Marigold cry, you know?"

"I know. 'Cause you're a great dad."

Oh. Oh, damn. That was even cuter.

Parrish wouldn't balk at buying *Diesel* a donut or accuse him of wanting a relationship when he didn't, that was for sure.

Hercules yapped excitedly, and Diesel lifted a hand in greeting. "Hey there, Quinn."

Despite me knowing most people in town by name, it was still odd to think they knew who *I* was. I hadn't joined the Thicket social scene since I didn't plan to live in town long—just long enough to build up my business while living and working rent-free in the building that used to house Aunt Cherry's dressmaking shop—but Diesel and Parrish seemed really nice.

"Morning!" I returned.

"This your dog? Mind if I pet him? He's adorable." Diesel bent down to pet Herc after I nodded.

"Not mine, I'm afraid. I'm dog sitting." Against my will. "Hercules is great for business, though. Clients enjoy him."

"Of course." Diesel balanced his daughter on his knee, and she smiled as she watched Herc jump around.

"Diesel's an animal lover," Parrish said, looking down

at his husband fondly. Then he glanced back at me, and his gaze narrowed. "Speaking of clients, how *is* your business going? Is your calendar… booked up, would you say?"

"Oh, um. Going well. I'm busy. On the road to Nashville a lot."

"Ah, that's rough. Long drive, especially in winter," Parrish said.

I shrugged. "Not unexpected, though. Not much need of my services around here." I chuckled at the idea of there being a big-budget event in the Thicket—and then remembered hearing that Parrish Partridge was the heir to the Nashville-based Partridge Pit BBQ restaurant chain. I cleared my throat. "Never too busy to squeeze in a hometown client, though! Were you… looking to plan a wedding?" I glanced down at his hand, which already sported a scuffed-up ring.

"Us?" Parrish laughed lightly. "Oh, no. We're not the wedding type."

"Nah. We're the marrying type," Diesel agreed.

"Oh-kay?" I gave him a wan smile, though I had no idea what he meant.

"We have a different kind of event in mind that you'd be perfect for, though!" Parrish said happily. "We'll be in touch soon, okay?"

Later, I'd remember that this almost sounded like a warning, but I was too busy preparing for my client meeting and *not* thinking of Champ to worry about it.

Fortunately, the bright, airy showroom was already pristine, just the way I'd left it the night before. I lit some candles, tweaked the flower arrangements, and plumped the cushions on the vintage green sofa that Aunt Cherry had reupholstered shortly before she'd retired and left me her shop. Then I headed to my office/storage room in the back of the shop to brew some coffee and put together the planning binder I'd started for Marissa Drakes.

I knew there were a lot of people—for example, my ex-boyfriend Scott—who thought I was crazy for moving all the way to Licking Thicket and taking over Cherry's shop, but it wasn't so bad. The space was perfect, really. I just wished it was located somewhere a little less... *nowhere.*

Besides, it was thanks to Scott—and his brand-new twenty-three-year-old soul mate, Onyx, and his "teeny cash flow situation" preventing him from buying out my share of the event business we'd started together—that I'd had to relocate in the first place, so who cared what he thought?

"All in all," I told the dog firmly as I leaned over to pull a client questionnaire from the bottom drawer of my filing cabinet, "I am *over* men and their ridiculous opinions."

"Not all men, I hope."

I whirled and jumped, hand over my heart. "Mr. Dunwoody! You startled me."

"Trey," the man said softly. He was dressed in head-to-toe Ralph Lauren and seemed equal parts nervous and determined. "M-my name's Trey. You said on the phone the other day that we should call you Quinn, so you should call me *Trey.*"

"Right." I blinked. "Yes. Whatever sets you and Marissa at ease, *Trey.*" I forced a smile and extended my hand for him to shake. "Nice to meet you in person. Can I get you a cup of—?"

"I like your office. It's real nice."

"Oh." I looked around the organized chaos of the storage area. "Thanks?"

Trey swallowed nervously and ran a hand over his hair, then took a step toward me.

Hercules barked, and the sound made Trey flinch.

"Hush, Herc. Well!" I said brightly. "Why don't we go wait in the showroom for your lovely fiancée and her—"

"I saw you online," Trey blurted. "On your website, I mean. Your picture was there. With the pictures of the weddings. *Gorgeous.*"

My eyes widened. He meant the *weddings* were gorgeous, right? He must. I chose to believe he did.

"And you looked so understanding," he went on. "I said to Marissa, 'That's him. That's just the man we need.' And she called you."

"Wow. That's… thank you. I work hard to make all of my events spectacular," I said firmly, "just like I will for you and Marissa. And even though six months isn't a very long time to plan, and I know you're probably nervous about all the work involved, I want you to know that I'm a professional and you're in good hands. You can count on me to take care of everything, and it'll all work out. Okay?"

"Yes." Trey exhaled a relieved breath and bit his lip. "I just knew I could count on you." He shuffled his feet. "You see, when I asked Marissa to marry me at Christmas, I-I wasn't sure if I was doing the right thing. She's so beautiful. So bright and kind. And I love her so much. I didn't want to lose her." His eyes were shiny. "But I have so many questions."

"Well, of course you do!" I relaxed enough to smile. "Mr. Dunwoody—*Trey*—large-scale weddings like these are complex. Otherwise, I wouldn't have a job. But all you need to do is love your bride and plan a wonderful honeymoon! Leave all the details to me."

"But my question is… do I love Marissa enough to marry her? H-how can I tell?" His words came out in a rush.

My jaw dropped. "I… I have no idea," I admitted. "Maybe you need a counselor? Or to talk to a friend?"

"Maybe…" He took a step toward me while Herc barked his head off. "It's just…" He tripped over a box of votive candles on the floor next to my desk and lurched toward me. I grabbed him to try and keep us both upright, but we tumbled to the floor in a heap, half-hidden behind my desk.

Trey lifted his head up and stared at me. The warm breath from his frantic panting hit my face, and I could have sworn there was a semi-hard dick between us that was definitely not mine.

I tried to push him off me, but he reached up to cup my face. "Quinn…" For some crazy reason, I got the feeling he was going to kiss me, so I pushed against him.

"Get off me," I said. "Marissa's going to be here any minute, and I'm not interested in anything other than that."

"No, wait. I just want to—"

"You have precisely three seconds to get the fuck off of him," a deep, familiar—and really, really *welcome*—voice growled from the doorway.

Trey jumped away, eyes wide and panicked like a deer in headlights. "What? No! I was just… we were talking! About the wedding." He jumped up and swallowed hard. "And we fell. But it was just an accident! I'm his client. Right, Quinn?"

I hesitated.

"Not anymore you're not." Champ folded his enormous arms over his chest and his no-nonsense tone made me shiver.

Under other circumstances, that protectiveness would have worked for me in a maaaajor way—okay, fine, even under *these* circumstances it was working, as the half-boner in my pants would attest—but I also really needed well-connected clients in order to build my business, and I couldn't afford to turn them away over a single embarrassing misunderstanding.

In truth, I had no idea what was going on with Trey Dunwoody. Was he questioning his sexuality? Was he having cold feet? He wasn't my friend, and it wasn't my place to sort his shit. My job was to get my clients through the nerve-racking process of wedding planning and to see them walk down the aisle.

"Trey is right," I said firmly. "He really did trip over a box of candles. As long as we all remember our roles from now on and act *professionally*, we shouldn't have a problem."

Trey nodded furiously, his cheeks pink. "That's… yes. Professionally. Of course. Thank you. I'm sorry. I'll just…" He coughed lightly. "I'll just go wait for Marissa in the front room." He made a move toward the door, and when Champ didn't budge, he sidestepped around him. But before he left, he hesitated. "Um. Are you… do you… work for Mr. Taffet?" he asked Champ.

Champ glared down at him, and then his gaze flicked to me for one quick second and his scowl morphed into a smile that was, frankly, way more menacing. "No, I'm not Quinn's employee. I'm his fiancé." He leaned toward Trey until their faces were inches apart. "And if you touch him again, *Trey*, losing your wedding planner is going to be the least of your worries."

Oh. My. God.

~

Grab *Hitched* here → http://readerlinks.com/l/1938654

LETTER FROM LUCY & MAY

Dear Reader,

Thank you so much for reading *Hijacked*! If this is your first book by one of us and you'd like to read more, we suggest you start with Lucy's *Borrowing Blue* and May's *The Date*.

We would love it if you would take a few minutes to review *Hijacked* on Amazon. Reader reviews really do make a difference and we appreciate every single one of them.

We've been friends and fans of each other's work for a couple of years, so working together on the first three Licking Thicket books was an amazing experience! And once we'd fallen in love with those characters—especially "heart doctor" Carter Rogers—we knew we had to tell his story.

Now we're excited to bring you the stories of the Champion Security crew, continuing with Champ's story *Hitched* and Hux's story *Hacked*, which are both available now!

Be sure to follow Lucy and May on Amazon to be notified of new releases, and look for us on Facebook for sneak peeks of upcoming stories.

Feel free to sign up for our newsletters, stop by www.Lucy-Lennox.com, www.MayArcher.com, or visit Lucy's Lair and Club May on Facebook to stay in touch.

To see fun inspiration photos for this book, check out the Pinterest board for Hijacked.

Happy reading!
Lucy & May

MORE FROM LUCY AND MAY

Licking Thicket

Flakes

Fakers

Liars

Fools

Turkeys

Peacocks

Champion Security

Hijacked

Hitched

Hacked

Honeybridge

Firecracker

Mr. Important

ABOUT LUCY LENNOX

Lucy Lennox is the USA Today bestselling author of over fifty gay romance titles including the GoodReads Hall of Fame winner Wilde Love. Born and raised in the southeast USA, she is finally putting good use to that English Lit degree she earned before the turn of the century.

Lucy enjoys naps, pizza, and procrastinating. She stays up way too late each night reading romance because it's simply the best.

For more information and to stay updated about future releases, sales and audio news and to grab some free and bonus reads, please sign up for Lucy's author <u>newsletter</u> on her website at <u>LucyLennox.com</u> or to stay in the know, join her exciting reader group, <u>Lucy's Lair</u> on Facebook.

facebook.com/lucylennoxmm

instagram.com/lucylennoxmm

amazon.com/Lucy-Lennox/e/B01N0IOYPT

bookbub.com/authors/lucy-lennox

patreon.com/lucylennox

pinterest.com/lucy_lennox

ALSO BY LUCY LENNOX

Find me online → https://linktr.ee/LucyLennox

Read my books:

Made Marian Series

Forever Wilde Series

Aster Valley Series

The Billionaire Brotherhood Series

After Oscar Series (with Molly Maddox)

Twist of Fate Series (with Sloane Kennedy)

Licking Thicket Series (with May Archer)

Champion Security Series (with May Archer)

Honeybridge Series (with May Archer)

Find a complete list of my stand alone romances and novellas at www.LucyLennox.com along with audio samples, freebies, suggested reading order, and more!

ABOUT MAY ARCHER

May is an M/M author who lives in Boston. She spends her days planning vacations, mainlining diet soda, avoiding the gym, reading M/M romance, and when all other forms of procrastination fail, writing it.

Visit her website at <u>mayarcher.com</u> to sign up for her <u>newsletter</u> to hear about sales and upcoming releases, freebies and behind the scenes info and more! Or join her Facebook group, <u>Club May</u>!

facebook.com/may.archer.author

instagram.com/mayarcherauthor

amazon.com/May-Archer/e/B075JQVGLX

patreon.com/MayArcherRomance

bookbub.com/authors/may-archer

ALSO BY MAY ARCHER

Find me online → https://linktr.ee/mayarcherauthor

Love in O'Leary Series

Whispering Key Series

The Sunday Brothers Series

Copper County Series

The Way Home Series

Licking Thicket Series

(cowritten with Lucy Lennox)

Champion Security Series

(cowritten with Lucy Lennox)

Honeybridge Series

(cowritten with Lucy Lennox)

For a comprehensive list of titles, audio samples, freebies, suggested reading order, and more, visit my website at www. MayArcher.com!